Cover designed by Miblart

Map by Inkarnate

eBook ISBN: 979-8-9881090-8-2

Hard Cover ISBN: 979-8-9881090-9-9

Trade ISBN: 979-8-9881090-7-5

For rights and permissions, please contact:

Bobalou Publishing c/o Robert Vielee

PO Box 127

Clarks Summit, PA 18411

r.c.vielee@outlook.com

For Louise, love always.

SALVATION BLEEDING

FORGE OF THE SOUL STONE

AWARD-WINNING AUTHOR

R.C. VIELEE

Content Advisory

Salvation Bleeding: Forge of the Soul Stone journeys through the fantasy worlds of Tartica, Evidar, and Black Haven. It explores dark themes that can be disturbing, such as fantasy violence, torture, blood, references to past childhood emotional and physical abuse, and sexual content that includes sexual violence. It is intended for mature readers.

THE UTOPIA FALLING SAGA RECAP

For those interested in a recap of *Utopia Falling: A Darkness Rises* and *Chaos Ascending: A Feast of Betrayal* before diving into *Salvation Bleeding: Forge of the Soul Stone,* please navigate to a hidden page on my website that I've set up just for you. The password is salvation.

rcvielee.com/recap-chaos-ascending

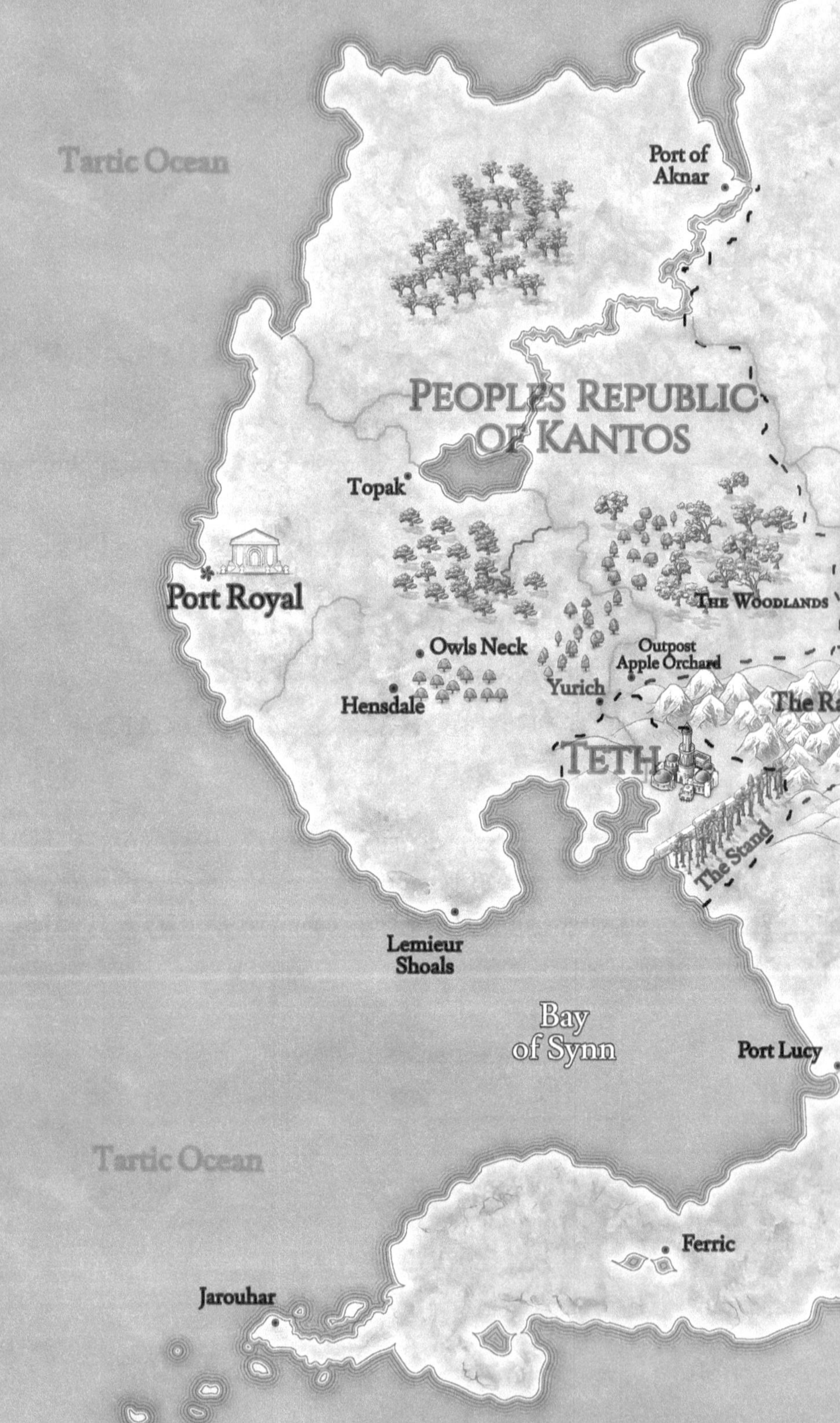

Tartic Ocean
Port of Aknar
PEOPLES REPUBLIC OF KANTOS
Topak
Port Royal
THE WOODLANDS
Owls Neck
Outpost Apple Orchard
Yurich
The Ra...
Hensdale
TETH
The Stand
Lemieur Shoals
Bay of Synn
Port Lucy
Tartic Ocean
Ferric
Jarouhar

Tartic Ocean
GREENLIN
Lake
Louise
New
Condordia
Dead Crow
Ciara Desert
Ishtar
Pfister
Bay
Hunters
Point
ehrlich
Tandure
KINGDOM
OF
ADELLE
TARTICA

That Ain't Mera and This Ain't Evidar

Black Haven

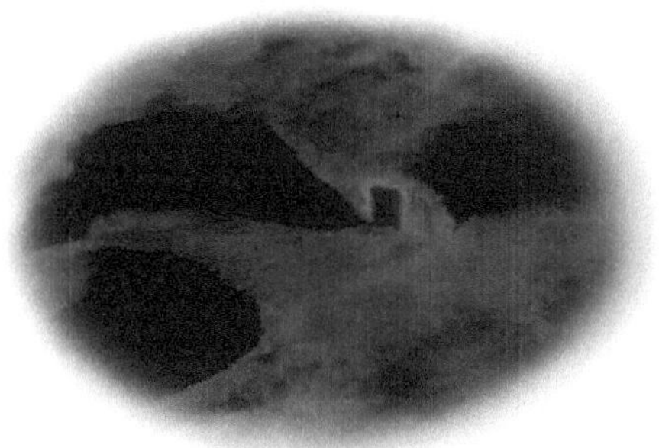

Reyne

Darkness consumed the office space at the bottom of the long underground staircase where Reyne Brenton stood a prisoner. As his detainer had sworn to do before fulfilling his promise to have Reyne summarily killed, the man Reyne thought to be the Devil's Blacksmith struck a match, revealing himself. Yellow light from the small flame danced across his face for an instant before the aphotic nature of Evidarian black-fire stole away all light-giving qualities.

It was long enough.

Reyne staggered at the revelation. One word, a whisper at best, floated on breath gutted from his lungs. "Mera?"

Confusion engulfed his mind.

Back on Tartica, Mera is dead. But here he stands?

It can't be.

This is a mistake.

Realization slammed into his brain like a sledgehammer crashing against his skull.

Fuck me! I rode the wrong Probability Wave out of the Void.

This ain't Evidar!

The conclusion stunned him. His knees threatened to give out. Panic seized him and squeezed his gut.

The man Reyne recognized as Mera called out, "Aderlee, come here."

Aderlee, he's supposed to be one of ours. That's on Evidar. Who's Aderlee in this world?

"Yes, Boss," came a voice from inside the darkened compound. "Be right there."

"You seem to know me, Mister Brenton. I don't recall meeting you."

With his mind reeling, Reyne struggled to understand the complexities of multiple Earths existing in interdimensional realms. He'd only had the Mera-from-Tartica's stories to go on. He'd already encountered a version of Neladith—the Evidar assassin who attempted to murder him and who killed his brother on Tartica—who now claimed ignorance of the deed.

A different Mera on each world?

Or maybe just one Mera. It doesn't make any sense. Gotta be two different Meras. A Mera in each dimension.

Shaking the cobwebs from his thoughts, Reyne declared, "I knew someone I called Mera. Looked just like you. Not with your fancy way of speaking, but the same voice. Same face. Same height. You're not him. He's dead."

"Yes, my name is Albert Meratoruc. I answer to Mera. Should I be surprised Tartica has someone who looks like me?"

"I don't know, should you be?"

"You're a funny man, Mister Brenton. No, I'm not surprised."

"Aren't you the smart one?"

"It's not all that rare. With multiple versions of the same Earth, the universe has revealed itself to us in the Many Worlds Interpretation put into practice. Reality exposes countless surprises, wouldn't you agree, Mister Brenton? This man you call Mera, his death affects me not and concerns me even less. His is simply the death of a stranger."

Reyne's thoughts frayed at the implications. He couldn't grasp how such a thing was possible. If a third version of Earth existed, and if this wasn't Evidar, he wondered, could there be hope of a living, breathing version of his dead brother Daedyn in the place? His heart yearned to know if there was another rendering of himself sharing a life with Daedyn.

"What of me? You seem to know who I am. Is there another Reyne Brenton?"

"Possible, although not probable. In what remains of Earth here on Black Haven, unlike on Tartica, humanity has carved out a small foothold since the Great Destruction. I've reached out to contacts who've searched for you in all these places, to no avail. My Damus tells me of your potential destructive impact... should you live. When you are gone, I'm sorry to say, there will be nothing left of you in either world."

"The man I knew as Mera on my version of Earth warned me about this Damus."

"Damus is simply a title I devised from a figure in Earth's history long ago for one skilled at divining future events. Although my Damus has replaced the practice of staring into a pot of water and herbs with precise mathematical computations... I digress. To you, it matters not. Your future is rather limited."

In the near-lightless cavern of a room, the hearth threw impotent black flames into the surroundings. The ravenesque gloom and the dissembled hope of a renewed existence with Daedyn sucked the life from Reyne's resistance. He surrendered himself to his fate. "Now what?"

The Mera Reyne didn't know replied softly, "Now... you die."

A wisp of air grazed Reyne as a body swept through the room. Unable to make out its details in the all-encompassing darkness, Reyne saw it as a murky shape in the form of a man and heard the voice he assumed to be that of Aderlee. "Here Boss. Whatcha need?"

"I have another for you to dispose of. This young man here needs to die. No reason to soil my office. Do it outside."

"Yes, Boss." Aderlee seized Reyne's arm tied in front of him at the wrists.

Reyne yanked it free. "Wait."

The Mera of Black Haven replied, "Please, Mister Brenton, you've impressed me to this point. Don't ruin it begging for your life."

"Ain't gonna beg. Do whatever you gotta do. The Goddess Teth knows I wouldn't want to do anything to hurt your opinion of me. Ha!... But I got one nagging question."

"That's the Reyne I'm going to remember. Laughing in the face of death. Go ahead, you've earned your question."

"Did you know there's another world just like this one? It's called Evidar."

"I doubt there is only one, Mister Brenton. The Many Worlds Interpretation posits infinite possibilities. Now you can go. Aderlee, do your job."

Aderlee again grabbed hold of Reyne. This time didn't let go. "Come on, you."

The Black Haven assistant pulled Reyne along. All the while Reyne resisted the effort. At the base of the stairs, Reyne turned his head to shout back, "Evidar wants to merge with Tartica."

Aderlee pushed Reyne up the steps.

Step by step, Reyne shouted back to Mera, "That can't be good. Evidar's plan to merge all of Earth's dimensions is gonna fuck up Black Haven. Doesn't matter if Evidar even knows about this place. Black Haven's gonna get caught in the crosshairs." Reyne hadn't a clue if it were true, but it sounded good.

"Nice try, Mister Brenton. I'm not buying what you are selling."

After forcing Reyne to the top of the stairs, Aderlee swung open the door and, with his foot against Reyne's backside, kicked him through the portal.

Back at Camp

Black Haven

Gina

The short, athletically built, dark-haired Gina was freed from her rope manacles, permitting the Tartican native open access to the tribe's encampment. Only days earlier she'd unintentionally hitched a ride through the Void via Reyne. Together they'd been deposited on the unfamiliar and brutal dark world thought to be Evidar. Seized not long after their arrival, she and Reyne evaded certain death while tied and staked to wooden posts only after Reyne relented in his stated desire to kill the woman … their captor. A woman who was the spitting image of the person who murdered Reyne's brother Daedyn back on Tartica: Neladith.

With a tentative understanding reached, she and Reyne had been freed. It came at a cost. Neladith demanded both Gina's and Reyne's cooperation in a deadly plot. According to the plan she, Reyne, and Neladith's doppelgänger agreed to, Reyne was about to be dangled as bait. If any part of the plan went wrong, Reyne was a dead man.

Gina stayed behind as Neladith and Reyne put the negotiated scheme into action. Gina sat stoically for what seemed like forever, awaiting this version of Neladith's return. It proved impossible for Gina to accurately estimate time's passage without the sun in the sky as a gauge. After a while, based on her internal clock—rendered unreliable by the ever-present darkness—she guessed enough time had passed for Reyne to be in the Devil's Lair by now… setting the trap.

Unable to discern the ebony morning sky from the ebony evening sky, Gina accepted the tribe's declaration that it was early in the day when someone announced, "Breakfast."

Whatever the mushroom concoction the tribe provided tasted good, and Gina attacked it with vigor. It settled better in her than Reyne. She figured he had good reason; his life depended on trusting a woman neither of them knew anything about. The woman looked a lot like Neladith, yet there were subtle differences. Making matters worse, the Neladith they had previously encountered on Tartica was anything but trustworthy. She had to ask herself if this person calling themselves Neladith could be trusted. Her life, Reyne's life depended on it. *This is some fucked up shit.*

Gina didn't have to wait much longer. The tall, wiry, buxom youth with reddish-orange hair calling herself Neladith sauntered into camp. She walked up to Gina. "Dropped off Reyne. Plan's in motion. Fingers crossed."

Without warning, the Neladith-look-alike's upper body jerked. Her words stopped short. She grabbed her stomach, bent over, and spewed out a stream of green vomit.

The Neladith-looking woman winced at what Gina could only assume to be the taste of bitter stomach acids mixed with chunks of masticated food bits that trailed against her tongue on its hasty exit. Puke splashed against the gloomy landscape's hard surface, bouncing in all directions, with a rancid gob landing on Gina's boot.

Gina sprang up, kicking the offended foot wildly about, eager to free it of the woman's morning meal. Emancipating her boot of the regurgitated remains required several attempts. "What the fuck?" Gina shouted.

"Ugh, that's disgusting," the reddish-orange-haired native complained as she wiped her sleeve across her mouth.

Gina asked, "Stomach bug, Red? Or something you ate?"

The woman smacked her lips dispelling the obvious, awful aftertaste of regurgitation. "I'm fine... Red?... That's what you're calling me now?"

"You're Neladith yet not exactly the Neladith I recall from my encounters on

Tartica. She has fiery red hair. Yours is red with an orange tinge. Got alarms goin' off in my brain, something not right. Givin' you a new name to keep things straight in my head. I'm goin' with your hair color."

"Ain't been to Tartica. The new name, I kinda like it. Red it is then. Maybe I should come up with a name for you."

Not surprised by Neladith's claim she'd never been to Tartica, Gina thought, *Ain't been to Tartica? Hum, is she lying? They all lie. Can't trust anything she says. Somethin's off here, I can sense it.* "No need. Gina's just fine."

With her sense of distrust on high alert, out of habit, Gina took it all in. Years of planning and completing assassination assignments taught her success rested not only on her extraordinary set of skills but also on accurate intel. Gathering information about an unfamiliar environment was endemic to her core. This world proved unlike Tartica in every way. Her survival, Reyne's survival—her ticket off this miserable world—depended on understanding her surroundings.

Red's village encampment was established along a tree line at the outer edge of a massively tall mushroom grotto. Fungi plants standing fifteen, maybe twenty feet tall, trunks a couple of feet in diameter with open canopy tops, formed the outline of a sparsely populated thicket. Twenty lean-to structures had been constructed under the mushroom caps, taking advantage of the tall toadstools' natural roofing. The way each housing structure encircled the oversized mushrooms reminded Gina of a yurt with mycelium popping out the top. Some shelters were larger, others smaller, yet each was wrapped in a durable covering with an oval opening for egress along the side. A dark-flamed fire pit ten feet across established the tribal focal point. Men, women, and children mulled about. Each looked Gina up and down as they passed.

She studied each of them in turn.

She took in every detail.

How many people in the tribe?—*Thirty-one.*

How many men—how many women?—*Twelve men. Fourteen women. Five kids.*

Do any look like fighters?—*All of them.*

She evaluated the layout of the camp, the landscape.—*Dismal.*

Calculated escape routes.—*My best bet, straight into the mushroom forest.*

Assessed how individuals moved, how they walked.—*Apprehensive, careful.*

She scanned for objects that she might use as weapons.—*Six in the open.*

Looked for the subtle signals of the social structure.—*Family cooperative.*

Searched for signs of the tribal hierarchy.—*Red, top dog.*

Gina's assassin-trained mind observed and learned. In the absence of sunlight and unable to see more than thirty feet from where she stood, she gathered intel about the tribe as best she could.

With the new alliance between herself, Reyne, and Red, Gina hoped all the information she'd gathered wouldn't be needed, but she knew better. People couldn't be trusted, and that applied to people everywhere: Tartica and here, what she believed to be Evidar. In Gina's experience, humans were rotten to the core, no matter what world they were from. At the first hint of danger or the slightest of pressures, self-interest always won out. Red didn't engender any degree of trust in Gina's short-lived exposure to the woman. Eventually, Gina was going to have to kill some of those she studied mulling about. She just didn't have a reason to—yet.

Red, having finished giving back all she'd eaten, said, "Your boy is in the lair of the Devil's Hammer as we speak. I turned him over and watched him go through that fucking orange door. He could be dead already. The good news for Reyne is the Devil's Hammer doesn't like blood and guts all over his office."

Gina stared down Red. "For your sake, you better hope he pops back up from that hole in the ground."

"Big words from a small woman. Look around. There's only one of you and more than twenty adults. This ain't Tartica. These folks struggle every day to get by. They're not soft like those from your world. I'd take one of mine against ten of yours any day."

"There's only one of me and I like the odds." Confidence oozed from her every syllable. Gina had a full stomach, and that made her pleased. Fueled up, she was ready to rumble... if needed. Although she'd been cut off from her Third Eye since her passage through the Void, she was deadly enough moving at normal speeds.

Yet, she lamented the loss. Mera had shown her how to access her Third Eye; a gift he bestowed on her eighteenth birthday. She remembered him saying, "The Eye of Heaven, your Third Eye, it's buried in the human brain's frontal lobe and rarely ever used. For those who can, it opens the world to untold possibilities." What it opened for Gina was the ability to move faster than any person alive... on this world or any other, she assumed. Just not anymore.

"Please," Red replied to Gina's bravado, rolling her eyes. Pointing to a young girl no more than twelve, Red added. "That little girl, Sissy, is more than you can handle."

Gina thought, *It's better to be underestimated. They won't know what hit them.*

"If you say so, Red," Gina replied, indifferent to Red's boastful claims. Then asked, "Shouldn't we be setting up near the Devil's Lair?"

Red chuckled. "It ain't the Devil's Lair. Although, not a bad name. We refer to him as the Devil's Hammer... never to his face. A few have made that mistake. They're not with us anymore."

"Whatever you call him, we should be heading over there."

"The Devil's Hammer likes to talk a lot. Thinks he's profound. Reyne will be down there awhile, I suppose. But sure, why not? If it makes you happy, we can head over there and get set up."

Following Red walking away, presumedly towards the Devil's Lair, Gina asked, "Who's joining us?"

Without turning around, Red replied, "It's gonna be you and me." She laughed. "Didn't you just tell me you liked your odds?"

"Fuck you."

Red teased, "Now, is that anyway to talk to your new bestie?"

"We haven't even discussed a plan. What are we doing?"

"Reyne comes out, we save him. There, we have a plan."

Gina grabbed Red's arm and stopped. "Not good enough. We're goin' in blind. We don't know how many of them we're facing. How we goin' to do it? What's my role? What's yours? Is this how trained operatives from Evidar do things?"

"Evidar?" Red questioned with a face that reminded Gina of a confused puppy.

"Yeah, Evidar. This dismal shithole."

"Hey, that's my village you're talking about. Guess you can see why I want out. The Devil's Hammer has dealt with deserters before. A few who made it to your reality got a taste of Tartica and the soft cushy life. If I believe the reports, every one of them is now dead... on his orders. I hope to be the first who doesn't end up worm food."

Gina crossed her arms and planted her foot. "Call this place whatever you like. We need a plan, or we'll both be worm food."

Red hung her head and huffed. Picking it up with eyes wide open, Red's sympathetic face and words appeared aimed at easing Gina's worries. "Look. I've been inside his office a few times. I know the layout. The Devil's Hammer is a creature of habit. Most likely it'll be two people coming through that orange door. Reyne will be one of them. You and me can handle that. My people watched you fight... remember... before one of them cracked you in the head with that log. You can tussle. We can do this."

Gina demanded, "Give me a weapon."

"No." Red scanned Gina up and down. She smirked and slipped her arm under Gina's. "Come on. By the way, you ever been with a woman?"

Gina ignored the question and ripped her arm free. "Lead the way."

The two women walked in silence for a while. Then Gina thought, *why waste the opportunity to gather more intel?* "Tell me about your camp. Who were those people?"

"What, you think I'm stupid? If you want info, just ask."

"Alright. I want intel."

"Not that it will matter much; sure, why not? We mostly live in tribal structures. Twenty to seventy-five per. The one you were just at is mine."

"How many tribes are there?"

"Hard to say. Around here, we all keep to our territories. Who the fuck knows how many tribes are out there?"

"Then, from your travels, you must have encountered other tribes. Just in your neck of the woods, how many?"

Red looked up and away. It told Gina that Red was contemplating an answer. "Again, hard to say. The farther you spread out, the more tribes you run into. The more you run into, the less likely it is that you'll ever be seen again. Some ain't above eating those they capture. Not a lot of goodwill between people pitted against each other for survival. But you're gonna just keep asking, so I'm gonna say there're a dozen different tribes around here."

Gina tilted her head to the side as though processing what she heard. Then pressed on, "Any towns or villages?"

"Yep, they're in the domain of the Devil's Hammer. He cares for them. Protects them. But there's a tradeoff. You live by his rules. Break 'em and you pay."

Gina observed, "So it's a compromise. Free in the dangerous world outside or eat well under the Devil's thumb on the inside."

"It's the thumb of the Devil's Hammer."

Gina waved off the correction. "Yeah, yeah. Devil's Hammer. Big bad man. I got it."

Red continued, "Anyway, he plucked me from my tribe when I was just a kid. I split my time between here and a village called Concord City. That's where they trained me. Seven, maybe eight hundred people live there. Tribes don't go near Concord City. Well, those who have, let's just say they win in the short term, steal food and supplies. Long term... those tribes no longer exist. The Devil's Hammer wipes them out in retaliation. Wouldn't be surprised if he didn't chop them up for food. My tribe stays away from the villages even though they know I was forced to be part of one."

"Does this Devil guy know you're back with your tribe?"

"It's Devil's Hammer, not Devil Guy... you're having a tough time with his name. And no, he doesn't. If he did, I wouldn't be talking to you right now. All's the more reason we have to do this. As far as he knows, I just got back from scouting the area for Reyne. His people told him Reyne had made it here. The rest you know. We just delivered Reyne to him."

Gina dug deeper. "And after this, Red? What's next for you?"

"The Devil's Hammer has to die if I have any chance of leaving. He owns me.

He owns us all. That's where you and Reyne come in. I can't do it alone. After that I plan on retiring to some quiet outta-the-way place in your world." Red stopped suddenly, mid-sentence, bent over and puked again.

Gina watched and wondered. "You gonna be alright, Red?"

Between gags, Red complained. "Not much came up. Oh, this sucks."

"No, I mean, you gonna be able to do what we have to do if you're sick?"

Red snapped, no longer playfully entertaining Gina's quest for information. "Fuck off. I'll be fine. You just do what you have to, and I'll do the same." She spit out the acrid bile coating her palate. "We're just about there, so shut the fuck up."

Gina ignored the demand and the sudden change in attitude. She wondered aloud, "Red, how old are you?"

"I told you to shut it. And I got no idea." Anger flavored the tone that hit Gina's ears. "This ain't Tartica, and I never had a birthday like your people do. No one ever told me when I was born cause there ain't no calendars... like on Tartica."

"You claim you never been to Tartica. How do you know all about it?"

"You disappoint me. Already told you, been trained by the Devil's Hammer. Well, by his people anyway."

Gina relented, "Yeah, you did say that."

"This ain't Tartica. Here, ain't no winter, no summer. There's only one season... dark. Look around, every hour, every day looks exactly the same. Who knows what day it is? Who gives a shit? Now, like I said. Shut. The. Fuck. Up."

Gina heeded Red's advice while contemplating, *How sad it must be growing up on Evidar.*

Red turned from Gina and brushed away debris at the base of a large rock pile. "We'll hunker down here. It'll provide good cover."

The pair settled in.

The orange door in the distance was barely visible to Gina's Tartican eyes.

Gina whispered, "I'm worried about you, Red." Although she wasn't. She was fishing for more intel, this time attempting to piece together Red's stomach troubles.

"Don't. I'll worry about me. You worry about you. Would you just be quiet already?"

"You still haven't—"

"Do you ever stop talking?"

Red swept up a bow and a quiver full of arrows, concealed under an accumulation of dead palm frond foliage. One by one, she drove the arrowheads into the hard dirt—standing straight up for easy access.

Gina had the reputation of a more reserved, less talkative person, but she needed all the information possible if she expected to make it on Evidar, at least until Reyne got them both back to Tartica—once they figured out how. "You're full of surprises," Gina exclaimed, nodding towards the newly acquired weapon. "Guess this mission is better planned out than you've let on. Got one of those for me?"

"Just the one... sorry. And yeah, I might've left out a few details. Now, please, would... you... shut... up."

She opened her mouth to press Red for more. Before she said a word, Reyne burst through the orange door.

LET HIM DIE

BLACK HAVEN

Reyne

The sole of Aderlee's boot rested on Reyne's butt for only a second before shoving him forward. The orange door from the underground compound flung open just in time for Reyne to stagger through it. The ebony veil covering the dismal landscape proved only fractionally better than what the black-flamed hearth offered inside the complex. With his hands tied in front, Reyne stumbled, lost his balance, and hit the ground hard. His utter confusion suffocated the visceral response of the beast lurking in his soul.

He thought he was on Evidar. He wasn't.

He thought the man who'd sent him to die was the Devil's Blacksmith. He wasn't.

He thought that the man was Mera. He was... and he wasn't.

He thought the Mera-look-alike remained sequestered in the underground complex. He didn't.

The man who was Mera-but-wasn't appeared from out of nowhere and glared downward at Reyne.

Reyne looked up into the dark eyes of the Mera doppelgänger and knew he was about to die.

If fated for death in this miserable realm, Reyne wouldn't go down easy.

Reyne shot up.

Half bent over, he drove his shoulder into the man from Black Haven who looked just like Mera. Reyne's six-foot plus muscular frame delivered a powerful blow. The soles of the man's shoes slid backwards several inches before friction took hold. Black Haven's version of Mera stood his ground.

Both bodies came to a stop. Reyne straightened up in an instant. Yet with both hands tied, Black Haven's Mera easily grabbed onto Reyne's arm and, with an iron grip, secured Reyne from further eruptions.

"Reyne Brenton, I'd like you to answer a question for me. Maybe we can help each other after all. Perhaps your imminent death can be avoided."

"Can't be!" A woman's voice cut through the ever-present ebony veil of Black Haven.

Reyne's head spun toward the sound. The dim light penetrating the ashen-gray sky of a world forever in darkness offered little illumination. Yet, Reyne's Tartican-born eyes opened wide to see through the darkness. He spied Gina, peeking out over a pile of rocks not more than thirty feet away.

Gina jumped out from where she'd been hiding and shouted, "Mera!" faster than Reyne could react. Reyne watched helplessly as she raced to the man thought to have been killed on Tartica by an arrow from an Evidarian assassin meant for him. Tears dripped down her cheeks as she ran. Reyne wondered how Gina's cautious life in the shadows as a killer for hire could be tossed aside so carelessly.

As she sprinted, her face lit up. And Reyne heard the joy in her voice when she called out, "Mera, you're alive."

Before Gina could reach the man she claimed to be her mentor and the only genuine friend she ever had, Reyne shouted, "GINA, NO!"

His plea died on the wind as an arrow flew over Gina's shoulder. It missed her ear by inches. Her arms shot forward as though somehow reaching to snatch it out of the air.

Reyne knew before transfiguring to the realm thought to be Evidar, Gina would have focused her mind, opened her Third Eye—as Mera taught her to do—and called on her special ability to move faster than any human alive. She'd seize the arrow in flight before it delivered death. Not this time: Gina's Third Eye was blinded in the transition through the Void.

It all happened so fast.

And then... came the sound; a gentle *thwack* flittered on the air announcing the arrow found its target. Through soft delicate flesh, it bit deep into the man Gina believed to be Mera from Tartica. Black Haven's version of Mera remained upright for several seconds as she continued racing forward. As he dropped, Gina fell to her knees. "NO!"

Her soul-piercing screech drove deep into Reyne's heart.

For the second time in mere days, Gina couldn't save Mera.

Aderlee, the man whose boot sent Reyne through the orange door, immediately shouted a war cry. He fled past Reyne. He charged past Gina. He headed straight for the rock pile from where the shot originated.

Where Red stood her ground.

With bow in hand, Red swiped her free arm downward. In one fluid motion, she snatched an arrow from several she'd planted upright in the dirt and nocked it to the bowstring. Her movements were seamless. Practiced. Skilled.

She drew back the arrow... and let it fly.

It all happened in less than a heartbeat.

Aderlee stuttered forward a few steps. With the bolt half buried in his orbital cavity, he crumpled to the ground like a marionette whose strings had been cut.

Men and women from behind the mound of rocks framing the orange door, allies of the dying man, popped out from myriad hiding places. Reyne made out twelve pairs of retinas reflecting back what little light Black Haven offered. The eye-shine, like that of a cat in the night, was the telltale sign of people born to the darkness. Armed and angry, a dozen combatants fired arrows at Red's position. They flew straight with purpose, but she ducked behind a massive boulder as the barrage whizzed overhead.

Sprouting up from under leaves and dirt, archers from Red's tribe responded en masse. Reyne reeled. This wasn't the way it was supposed to go down. Dangled as bait, the plan called for only the two women to both save him and kill the Devil's Hammer. It was obvious to Reyne the operation was more extensive and better planned than he'd been told.

New-Neladith lied.

It tasted like betrayal.

Still, he blamed himself. He knew better than to trust new-Neladith; despite his reservations, he did. Yet, it was clear to him that neither he nor Gina were the target of either team.

Arrows whizzed overhead while Gina crawled on hands and knees to the body of the man she thought to be Mera. Tears filled her eyes. Reyne never thought Gina was capable of such feelings.

Screams of pain, shouts of anger, and threats of retaliation filled the air. Men and women were dying in the skirmish.

Gina wormed her way to Mera, sat up with her legs crossed, and cradled Mera's head in her lap. Ignoring the din of battle and the danger all around him, Reyne's heart went out to her. Gina's longing gaze into the dying man's face told Reyne she cared naught for any of it. She looked like a vulnerable little girl, not the stone-hearted assassin he knew; helpless, as Mera's life slipped away before her... for the second time.

With both hands still knotted together, Reyne grabbed Gina's arm. "That's not the Mera we know."

Her confused look replied where words could not.

Reyne squeezed her arm, "Let him die. That... ain't... our...Mera. And that ain't the Neladith who killed Daedyn."

A man burst through the orange door.

He dodged, dipped, and avoided everything Red's tribe fired at him. He skirted every effort to drop him. A heartbeat later, he was hovering over Gina with an arrow seated in a bowstring pulled tight. He pointed it directly at Gina from only feet away. Unable to invoke her ability to move beyond normal human speeds to disable, disarm, or even race from the scene, Reyne could only look on as she faced certain death.

He coiled, ready to throw himself at Gina's antagonist. A sudden knife to his throat from behind stilled his hand. He tensed. His muscles locked. Helpless, anger roiled in his core. The beast lurking in his soul fed off his rage. It laughed at his feeble response. *Let the monster out*, he thought. At that instant, before he could, everything stopped.

No one moved.

No one spoke.

No arrows zipped past.

No screams of anger.

Enemy combatants froze in place.

Gina looked up from the dying man in her arms.

In a slow motion, her head turned upward to meet the gaze of the would-be killer looming over her.

Reyne's gaze locked on the man standing over Gina. With his bow and arrow cocked and ready, the man took aim at Gina's face.

THE BATTLE FOR MERA

BLACK HAVEN

Gina | Reyne

Mera's head rested in Gina's lap. Why Reyne claimed it wasn't the Mera they knew, she didn't understand.

His hair, a bit different.

His skin, much paler.

Those were Mera's eyes.

That was Mera's face.

Gina found no reason to doubt herself. The darkness challenging her Tartican sight invaded her perception at every level and tainted everything—Mera included. He lay dying in her arms, and there wasn't a fuckin' thing she could about it.

Helplessness invaded her soul: unable to save her only friend.

Gina didn't understand why her ability to move faster than any human alive had been denied her from the moment she arrived in the miserable realm. For over a decade since Mera unlocked something in her Third Eye, she'd been able to access her gift without hesitation. With a cocked arrow pointed at her only inches from her head, her gift failed her.

With the skirmish paused for reasons Gina didn't understand, facing her own death, her only concern was the head in her lap. She looked away from the person she knew to be Mera to the stern determination written on the face of the arrow-wielding man.

"Miss, gently settle his head on the ground and step back," the man holding the weapon commanded. A nod to his compatriot—who'd secured Reyne with a dagger pressed against his throat—signaled him to release Reyne and cut the ropes binding his wrists.

Gina didn't move. Reyne, freed from the blade at his gullet, put up both hands and backed away.

The Mera look-alike's blood soaked into Gina's pants. She gave it little notice. Running her finger through his hair, she pleaded, "Speak to me, Mera. Please."

"I won't ask again," Arrow Man said in an unexpectedly polite tone. "Either move away from him, or you'll join him. Now move your ass."

Gina couldn't pull herself away. How he was alive, she couldn't fathom. She'd watched him die on Tartica only days before. Except, here he was, alive, and she couldn't let him die—not again. "No."

Arrow Man drew back the bolt even tighter. The sound of the bowstring straining to its limits announced its warning. Arrow Man lined up his aim sighted at Gina.

Reyne shouted, "Gina! Move away. It's not who you think it is, dammit!"

Gina, with pools gathering on her lower eyelids, looked up at Reyne, confused. The arrow pulled back another inch.

"Gina, I beg you. Trust me. It's not him."

Arrow Man began, "I don't want to kill you, but I will. Get up."

Unmoved by his plea, Gina stared hard at Reyne.

Reyne's look pleaded with her to believe him.

Arrow Man started the countdown to Gina's death. "Five... four... three..."

Trust in others came hard for Gina. Reyne had breached her defenses, if only in his promise not to abandon her on this miserable shithole of a planet. He sacrificed his return to Mithany until he found a way to transfigure them both back to Tartica... for her sake. Although her instincts told her it was Mera, Reyne seemed so certain it wasn't. While trust didn't come easy, Reyne earned hers... if only just a little. If he was wrong about Mera, she'd make him pay.

Gina threw up her hands. "Alright."

Arrow Man did not immediately release Gina from jeopardy. He nodded to his team without taking his gaze off her. Arrow Man shouted a command, "Take him."

Four associates of Arrow Man appeared from the edge of the darkness as though specters emerging through a wall of impenetrable black smoke. They picked up Mera's limp body, leaving her kneeling in his blood. Arrow Man kept his arrow aimed at her head. The four carried the body back into the ever-present black gloom surrounding the limits of her Tartican eyesight.

Her heart sank. If Reyne's adamant proclamation proved wrong, four men just carried away Mera's dead body. If Reyne was correct, whoever they called the Devil's Hammer, was just as dead. Of that, she was certain.

A call from beyond her visual perception—a sound hidden behind the black curtain of ever-present darkness—rang out. *Aw Caw. Aw Caw.*

One foot precisely placed behind the other, Arrow Man retreated. Step after step he inched backward, keeping his cocked arrow and his gaze pointed at Gina.

Slowly, Gina spun her head around. Red's team appeared tense and anxious, ready to strike at Red's command. Gina turned back to face Arrow Man, only to find him beyond her Tartican eye's ability to pierce the enveloping charcoal-colored expanse. Only the eye-shine of her would-be assailant reflected back at her. As the small silvery circles of reflecting pupils faded further and further away before disappearing from view, Gina understood their retreat ended the skirmish.

Reyne raced to Gina as he fiddled on the ropes dangling from his wrists. He wrapped his arms around her, happy she'd not been harmed. Her palms slammed into his chest, pushing him away.

"Get off me," she demanded.

Reyne scoffed, "There she is, the Gina I know. Not the sensitive, caring little girl cradling that familiar face. Worried for a man she thinks is the Mera she loves."

"Don't call me 'girl'. And fuck you. You're an asshole."

"You're not the first to make that observation. My brother Daedyn brought it up every now and then."

The flesh around her angry eyes pulled in tight. In a harsh tone, Gina demanded, "You said that's not Mera. Explain."

Red approached the two Tarticans. "You two can work all that out later. I think we just declared war. They got the body of the Devil's Hammer. You can be damn sure that ain't gonna be the end of it."

Reyne ignored Red. "Gina, this ain't Evidar. The woman who we made the deal with might look like the Neladith who killed Daedyn, but she isn't. And the man dying in your lap wasn't the Mera you know. How any of this is possible, I ain't got a clue. We're on a world called Black Haven. Before he died, back in his lair, the Mera from Black Haven called it the Many Worlds Interpretation. Multiple versions of Earth means multiple versions of the same people in each of these different Earths is possible... or some bullshit like that."

Gina stared at him for a few seconds, "Get the fuck outta here. That's not possible. This has to be Evidar. Look around. It's fuckin' miserable. You're tellin' me there's another shithole of a planet just like Evidar. Impossible."

Red stepped between them. "Whatever you two idiots are jabbering on about, save it for later; we gotta get outta here. Now." She scanned the surroundings. "Figure all your shit out later. Now move your asses."

Red turned and walked away. She waved her arms over her head. "Come on you two. Get moving."

Reyne turned from Gina and sidled up to Black Haven's Neladith. "Why did everyone stop fighting when the guy pointed his arrow at Gina? Thought you'd of let her die."

Red smirked, "You're not that bright, are you? They didn't kill her because she was leverage. My side stopped because you, me, and that Gina chick made a deal. If we kept fighting, she'd be dead along with you. They can have the body. I nailed him with a solid shot. I'm sure it killed him. I'm free now. You're free. We all got what we wanted."

Reyne nodded, "Thanks."

"Don't mention it."

The two walked together, and Gina caught up with them. "Red, what's Reyne talking about? He says this ain't Evidar?"

"You're both whacked. Never heard of Evidar."

Reyne beamed. "See, I told you."

"Shut up." Gina shoved him.

Reyne shuffled back a few steps. "Gina, look at me. If that were the same woman who murdered Daedyn, do you think I'd be walking alongside her chatting?"

Reyne slinked alongside the woman Gina called Red—Black Haven's version of Neladith. "You ever kill a guy on Tartica named Daedyn?"

Red shrugged. "Never heard of him."

Reyne pressed, "A couple of weeks past, were you on Tartica hunting me down with other trained assassins?"

"Nope. The guy I just killed might've wanted you dead. It's just that he didn't send me to Tartica to do it."

"When you first met with us when you had us tied to the stakes in the ground, you said you just got back from somewhere. Me and Gina here just assumed you returned from our world, Tartica."

"Explains why you acted so crazy when you saw me."

"But, did you?"

"Never been there. Others I work with have. They say it's real nice. Like I said, would like to raise my kid there. When it's born. If that's possible."

Gina stooped. "What? Is that why you been puking all over the place? You're pregnant?"

With a shove from behind, Red said, "Just keep walking."

Reyne turned to look over his shoulder at the trailing Gina. "See? What'd I tell you? That wasn't Mera, just a look-alike, and this ain't Evidar."

Gina's face soured. "Well, genius, two things. Like the real Mera says, they all lie. Second, if what you say is true, and we didn't make it to Evidar, we're fucked."

I Found It!

Evidar

Emosh

A black infestation of hopelessness within the Void had its grips on Evidar's Damus, the youthful, silver-haired, mathematical genius Synja Emosh. She'd begun to explore Probability Waves of futures that would likely come to fruition, as well as others that had little chance of ever being realized. She faced down one after another, hundreds heaped upon thousands. Her one desire: to find a path, a future, to give her world—Evidar, a planet forever in darkness—a chance to survive. If it meant the total annihilation of humanity across all of Tartica's reality... so what?

Her body lay motionless in an isolated sleep chamber set in the underground compound of the Devil's Blacksmith. Soundproof walls, secured door, and bedding befit the Damus's wants protected her body's self-induced catatonia from concerns of the physical realm. Her mind, disassociated from its corporeal housing, roamed freely, existing as pure thought through the Void's endless, aphotic ebony.

The Void, a hub through which the Probability Waves of every life force traversed, trillions upon trillions of possible futures flowing through it in an unending ocean of exponential derivatives of reality. What would come to pass was hidden somewhere in the Void, and the future leading to Evidar's salvation was merely one rare timeline of improbable events for Synja Emosh to find.

She bore witness to futures as real as the heart beating in her temporarily abandoned body. Most would never come to pass. She searched for those of more certainty. Without physical substance, absent eyes, or ears, existing only as conscious energy, Synja Emosh probed wave after wave in search of the one her sense of taste teased as the more likely to be realized. Flavors of bitter ash and acrid water touched her mind's palate with every Evidarian life force Emosh experienced. She swept one after another aside in milliseconds or over days; how long she searched held no meaning. In the Void, like photons of light absent inside its vastness, time did not exist.

Her consciousness, free of its earthly form, experienced the pain of a broken heart. Future after future delivered nothing except total darkness and desolation for every Evidarian life she tasted. All crumbled under the weight of a world forever in darkness—Evidar's gloom. Hopelessness heaped upon her soul, impaling grief into her essence until she could bear it no longer. With a voiceless scream, Synja released all her mental anguish into the emptiness of the Void without a sound. As her pain expelled into the inky-black emptiness, the Void responded by crashing Probability Waves carrying the sorrow of millions of helpless lives at her, tormenting her soul to its core.

Her consciousness railed against experiencing the futures of countless, desolate lives sweeping into her mind. It left Synja Emosh broken, beaten, wanting nothing more than to give up.

And then...

Like a single snowflake in all the heavens, set to drift along serendipity's whim, she grasped onto hope from the smallest of Probability Density Functions. She tasted the death of an untold number of Tarticans. An overwhelming, powerful flavor of decaying human flesh rising off the rotting corpses slammed into her consciousness. Synja had never tasted anything so utterly foul. Harsh. Caustic. Yet, the awful sting on her mind's palate was utterly delightful.

Death never tasted so good.

Quick to respond—not wanting to permit the ebullient moment or knowledge of the opportunity to escape—her non-physical awareness that existed as

Synja Emosh within the Void grabbed hold of and followed the Probability Wave. It teased her with hope, leading her to a possible future on a battlefield of two massive, opposing Tartican armies. Complex flavors from myriad life forces swirled within her thoughts as the raw palate of war where men and women, frantic, mindless, and terrified, killed each other. She savored their fear, their hatred, their terror, all of it carried on the thousands of Probability Waves slamming into her moment from moment.

She savored it as though enraptured in the arms of a lover. Joy pushed aside all the residual sorrow eating away at her soul.

Amongst all this carnage, the future turns on two lives ... no... I taste three.

One man, Reyne Brenton, must not survive.

A First Lord must rise to lead an army.

One specific soldier must die in battle... yet which one?

I sense the battle. I can taste so much death.

But only if...

Evidar's salvation rests atop Tartica's decaying biomass... YES!! That's it! Thousands die in the battle... wait... it's not over... it goes on... a second battle occurs. Only if that one soldier lives to see the second.. Which one? Which one!

Oh, it's so beautiful, two Earths.... Planet sized dimensional frequencies in sync. I can taste it!

I FOUND IT!

Still, it's slim. Only a one-tenth of one percent chance all these factors come together.

Two soldiers. One must die, one must live, for thousands more dead Tarticans... securing the convergence. Which one needs to die? And why is the other important?

Each must fall onto the timeline for it to play out. Brenton dead. A First Lord risen. War. Soldiers.

I need more...

The Void slammed every soldier's Probability Wave from that battlefield into her perception; millions of outcomes from thousands of lives in the form of Probability Wavefunctions. Wave after wave crashed into her consciousness, disrupting her hold on the two soldiers. Who they were, she had only names. *Jaynes? Loseff?* She scrambled to hold on to either, but their flavors blended into the melee like a rich cocktail that the tastebuds of consciousness experienced as a singular flavor, unable to separate into it component ingredients. The flavor of Jaynes's Probability Wavefunction was gone. The taste of Loseff was like a single grain of sugar in a gallon of molasses. She couldn't separate one from the others.

AGGGHHHH!!

Her time in the Void ended too soon. With her consciousness and body reunited, Synja Emosh's eyes sprang open. She jumped from the bed and took off through the sleeping chamber's door. She sped down the hallway. As she ran, her mind sorted through what she experienced in the Void. She converted each event into a number representing its likeliness of coming to pass. As she raced down the hall, she calculated the complex equations deriving mathematical outcomes.

Reyne Brenton had to be stopped. If not, she determined there was a ninety-eight percent chance he'd kill her, ending Evidar's chance for salvation. As Evidar's only Damus, she had to survive to advise the Devil's Blacksmith with last-minute adjustments as the future unfolded. She calculated there was only a seven percent chance the First Lord would lead Teth's army into battle. The desired outcome hinged on it. The futures she'd witnessed of Tartican soldiers named Loseff and Jaynes lacked specificity. Yet, both had to unfold just right. Still, she had to account for the uncertainty in her calculations. She crammed in a placeholder value.

She raced down a long hallway of the underground compound, giving little thought to the smooth hand-polished finish of the rock walls. She required neither pen nor paper to complete the complicated computations representing a singular permutation dependent on sequential outcomes. Turning one corner, then another, she sped toward her destination plugging numbers into an impossibly complex formula as she ran. And finally, she solved Evidar's probability equation that delivered salvation—a beautiful, mathematical truth.

Her calculation defined a clear path to dimensional convergence—a reunited Earth with Tartica and Evidar as one. She beamed with pride. She'd discovered the one timeline that would deliver salvation. Slim as it might be, a future *did* exist that freed her world from its perpetual darkness.

Excited, her heart pounded. Reviewing her calculations along the way, with one hand, she reached out to grab onto the corner of a wall, navigating the sharp change in direction, the momentum of her long silver strands whipping about behind as she completed the turn. Beaming, she burst into the Devil's Blacksmith's office.

Skidding to a stop, breathing heavily, she shouted, "I got it!"

The Devil's Blacksmith shot up from his high-back chair. His black, empty pupils glared anger at Synja for the interruption. A man seated across the desk twisted his neck to follow Synja's voice.

"Miss Emosh!' The Devil's Blacksmith's harsh tone boomed across the room. "What is the mean—"

With disregard for the punishable offense of cutting him off, Synja Emosh, Evidar's only Damus, swallowed, took in a deep breath, and proudly exclaimed, "Convergence! I found it! I saw it happen. It won't be long now.... But we have to thread a needle to get there."

At her proclamation of a solution, his anger fled him. A rare look of delight broke across his face. "Go on, Miss Emosh."

She bent over with both hands on her knees. Breathing hard, she lifted her head. "First, there must be war... Second, Reyne Brenton absolutely must die. Third, a First Lord, I couldn't make out who, leads an army into battle. And last, one specific soldier must survive the first battle to lead the second... and then thousands more die. Voila, a massive biomass reduction will nudge both dimensional frequencies into synchronicity... convergence will be ours."

A Plan Gone to Shit

Tartica: 12th Day of the Harvest Moon

Quith

Relegated to a life on Tartica—branded an Evidarian traitor for fucking up the Reyne Brenton assassination and turning on his own team shortly thereafter—the white-haired, middle-age, well-built Selundra Quith's plan seemed simple enough. Wait for the right opportunity. Kill Mera. Take the Soul Stone from him, and the rest would fall into place.

Ah, the Soul Stone. That'll keep me alive when I take on the Devil's Blacksmith and the minions he's sent after me.

Two nights past, Quith thought he'd burned Mera's dead body. *Except you didn't die on the funeral pyre with my old boss Dylla going up in the blaze. You rolled out of the flames. Unharmed. Gotta admit I was more than surprised. That's when I knew the Soul Stone wasn't just a fable. The Devil's Blacksmith is rumored to hold one of his own. I'd never seen it. Now I got proof it exists. It will be mine.*

Armed with its mythical life-extending and extraordinary healing abilities, Quith figured with a Soul Stone in hand, he'd be impervious to death. He had a score to settle with the Devil's Blacksmith and his emissaries. Evidarian agents Kebra and Harvin had been sent to Tartica to hunt him down and kill him. Quith's discovery of the Soul Stone's existence gave him hope. Without the Soul Stone, he didn't stand a chance.

On a frosty morning in the backwoods of Kantos, somewhere between Owls Neck and the southern border of Kantos, it all went to shit.

When Quith woke… Mera was gone. Their tentative truce, a lie. Quith had only himself to blame; too exhausted to watch over Mera when they'd settled in for the night, Quith couldn't stay awake. With Mera gone, the Soul Stone slipped through his fingers.

With a hand to his brow, Quith surveyed the forest thicket for any sign of movement. He stopped, stilled his heart, perked up his ears, and struggled to locate a single sound resembling the measure of a man. Through angry, flared nostrils, hot fumes like those escaping a charging bull spewed out into the cold air. Realizing the opportunity lost, Quith exploded, "F U C K!"

The eruption filtered through denuded branches hosting a murder of crows spread over the upper reaches of the otherwise empty treetops. A united flutter of wings and a few pronounced full-body stretches amounted to an otherwise unmoving response by the bird collective. Except for the occasional caw, the little bastards gave nothing away.

Turning his attention to the leaf-covered forest floor for signs of disturbance, Quith hoped at least to detect which direction Mera was headed. How Mera's footsteps crunching through the brown-dried and dead foliage failed to arouse Quith from sleep puzzled him.

Sneaky sonofabitch.

Mera one. Quith zero.

This game isn't over yet.

Quith cupped his hands to his mouth and poured heat from his lungs into his chilled fingers. The temporary warmth did little to relieve his anger aimed at himself for allowing sleep to cloak Mera's departure. He picked up a small rock and hurled it into the air, falling well short of the resting crows overhead. "Fuck you too! You could've said something." Unmoved by Quith's display or his effort to scare them off, the birds ignored him.

Looking down, he kicked a small stone and followed its path across the empty field. "You only have yourself to blame."

After starting a small fire, Quith planted his ass on the ground not far from the comforting heat. Hands held out, palms spread open, he pushed aside every bit of the chilly Tartica autumn, and a part of him longed for the constant heat of his home world.

"No. Can't think about that. I'm here for good unless Reyne Brenton somehow kills the Devil's Blacksmith." He laughed aloud. "Like that's ever going to happen. Face it, Quith, you're stuck here."

He wondered if Mera's Tartican friends knew he was still alive and whether that changed anything for him or his plans. Reflecting on the night he and Neladith came upon Mera's body—and that of their old boss, Dylla—Reyne, and an unknown companion had left behind a set of clothes at the spot where he found Mera's body. After he and Mera battled to a draw, Mera replaced his burned duds with one set of the clothing left behind. He figured finding two sets of apparel lying on the ground, Reyne must've had a cohort with him when he transfigured to Evidar. *Did they go off to Evidar believing Mera dead?* Quith resigned himself to it being one of those questions in life he'd never get answered.

He turned his attention back to the Soul Stone and slapped his hands together. "You're not a quitter. You're not a victim. Soul Stone's out of reach for now, not forever, just for now. Back to Plan A... clear the board. Dylla, Grafph, and Tylus are already dead. Neladith returned to Evidar. That leaves Kebra and Harvin on Tartica for me to deal with."

He stared deep into the flames. They danced and flickered, absent of any pattern, much like his life at the moment.

"What's my best play?" he asked aloud.

Quith ruminated over dozens of scenarios and concluded, *All roads lead to Teth. Sooner or later Kebra and Harvin are going to turn to Teth. They're going to get Dylla's contact in the Thuggery to help track me down. And if luck smiles on me, Mera's going to be there as well.*

Not sure he could trust anyone in Teth's loose confederation of thieves, cut-throats, drug dealers, and purveyors of every other illegal operation where money was to be had. Before she died, Dylla always said the Thuggery could be counted on... for the right price.

Quith kicked dirt atop the small fire making sure it wouldn't fight back. *No reason to leave any telltale signs I been here.* He scattered dead leaves over the entire site.

Teth it is, then.

Always liked me a good ambush.

RETURN TO EVIDAR

EVIDAR

Neladith

The version of Neladith Mithany and Arek had come to know on Tartica retreated to her home world of Evidar. Her transfiguration from Tartica back to Evidar commenced from a bed in Hensdale; in the home of two dead apple farmers and her Evidarian compatriot Grafph decomposing on the living room sofa.

She'd entered a deep sleep, leading her to a state of lucid dreaming where her mind freed itself from her body. Her consciousness navigated the astral plane and punched through the metaphysical barrier into the Void, while her physical form remained tied and bound on the bed where Arek left her and where he expected the Hensdale authorities to find her. She knew they never would. First into the Void, then on to Evidar. All they would find would be an empty set of clothes and ropes dangling from the headboard.

Of the very few capable, those who entered the Void experienced it in their own way. For Neladith, existence as thought-without-form inside the Void, sight, sound, feel, and taste all fled her in the inky blackness, save for her sense of smell. Total darkness engulfed her consciousness and set the tendrils of her non-corporeal nerves atwitter. With only one prior transfiguration under her belt, her non-physical awareness of scent locked onto a familiar location on Evidar. Like a person who could feel an amputated arm, she experienced phantom limb syndrome of her absent senses.

Her thoughts fed her with the smells from millions upon millions of distinct Probability Waves. Her mind reconstructed the scents into images of familiar places. Each held a unique olfactory marker, detectable to Neladith as she existed in the emptiness of the Void. She collected the odors, understood them, and her consciousness constructed perfect representations of the reality each offered.

The acrid aroma, the smell of the ashen air, and the musty familiar fragrance that lingered on a breeze, told her she'd found the exact Probability Wave, pulsing, rippling and ultimately, pointing the way home. A dozen others held similar promises. Even so, she wasn't fooled.

I hate this fuckin' Void.

A new Probability Wave drifted into her awareness. It carried a delicate, sweet, flowery fragrance mixed with hints of a pungent, animalistic, desire-inducing musk. Neladith knew it instantly.

Mithany!

But which?

No, don't get distracted.

The Void didn't listen. Wave after wave crashed against her sense of smell, exposing Neladith to envision multiple versions of an idyllic life with Mithany on Tartica. One offered a vision of the future where they grew old together, its appeal virtually impossible to deny. Neladith struggled to rip free of its hold. Her cold heart, born of Evidarian blackness, felt the slightest pang of loss and she longed to take it. However, rational thought pulled her back in the realization she'd burned all possible futures with Mithany to the ground. Only days earlier, she hoped to find a way to remain on Tartica, exploring a blossoming relationship with Mithany, the petite Hensdale woman. But when Arek, Mithany's brother, unexpectedly showed up—whom Neladith thought she'd killed—the option of a life with Mithany on Tartica evaporated; regardless of what the false Probability Waves offered.

She screamed at the Void without a physical voice. *Leave me alone. Empty promises!*

Then the odor of burning trees slammed into her. Hundreds and thousands of

Probability Waves threw themselves at her, offering Neladith a Tartican timeline in Hensdale as a member of a community rebuilding. One future imagined her on trial for setting the Brenton alphen orchard ablaze. Another with soldiers marauding through Hensdale. The small village in utter chaos provided her with a diversion to escape justice. And still another, with Mithany, naked, wrapped in her arms.

Get out of my thoughts!

With iron will, Neladith focused on the harsh, acidic scent of Evidar. Its tang bit at her awareness.

Yes! That's it. More, I want more.

And her non-corporeal self seized on the aroma. An oasis opened within the Void, not to her sight—to her olfactory senses. Inside the refuge, surrounded by ebony space, synesthesia—gifted to her in the Void—brought her mind to smell the yellow color of the door embedded in its familiar cairn. A dozen or more Probability Waves, nearly identical, radiated from the same location. Several with an orange door didn't fool her.

They poured through her. Frantic, Neladith drew in myriad odors infused in each wave crest, searching for the one true timeline to carry her home. A tiny scrap of body odor from the Devil's Blacksmith sent off alarms in her mind. Like sweaty testicles, revolting yet compelling, its musk reeked of testosterone fueled sensuality; animalistic and impossible to deny. Manly and dangerous, the aroma filled her senses. And it carried on it a delicate hint of juniper. *That's him, that's the one!*

Without allowing for doubt, she seized the wave crest resonating a hint of his smell. Her mind stretched impossibly thin over distances she could not comprehend. Over the distance of light-years or maybe only inches, Neladith felt her perception sucked through a ribbon, the diameter less than a strand of human hair. Beyond her experience of existence in the Void as pure thought energy, transfiguration had begun and pulled both Neladith's consciousness and her body through an immeasurably small tendril as she rode the amplitude frequency of the Probability Wave to the remote setting on Evidar at the foot of the familiar yellow door. With body and mind reunited, transfiguration complete, lying on the hard ground of Evidar, Neladith took comfort having successfully navigated the Void for the second time.

She opened her eyes to a world forever in darkness.

Ah, home.

With a deep breath pulled in through her nose, Neladith took in the familiar smells of the dark, gloomy setting of Evidar.

The dismal gray sky and foreboding landscape lifted her spirits.

Naked, like everyone else who traversed dimensions to exit the Void, Neladith welcomed the warmth of the hard surface, infusing her body with comfort. She sprang up, looked around, and detecting no one else in view, she brushed herself off.

Forced to abandon Tartica and return to Evidar, she'd nonetheless proudly account for her actions to the Devil's Blacksmith. She expected him to welcome her with open arms.

Fuck it. Let's get this over with.

Neladith figured the Devil's Blacksmith's reaction to what she had to report hung on what Quith conveyed when he should have returned to Evidar a day or two before her. At least that's what Quith told her he'd plan to do when they burned the dead bodies of Dylla and Mera. Neladith never trusted Selundra Quith, with good reason. One small double-cross in whatever details Quith reported to the Devil's Blacksmith and her life would be forfeit. Her other concern, how long had she been in the Void—where time did not exist—minutes, hours, days?

Disappointed at leaving Mithany and Tartica, Neladith made her way to the yellow door and knocked several times. She waited. Knocked again. A measured, professional voice called to her through the door, "Coming."

The assistant to the Devil's Blacksmith, a short, slight man, popped through and opened the door. His gaze rode her body up and down. "Miss Neladith Karlis, Agent Arrow, I see you have just returned to us from Tartica. Come with me."

At the bottom of the long narrow staircase, the pair entered the office space.

"Wait here, and I will determine if he can see you." The little man slipped off his suit jacket. "Here, please put this on. While I understand your situation, as a sign of respect to our leader, it's better than nothing." And he set out to his master's private office.

The sleeves barely covered half her forearms and the bottom hem reached down to hide her navel. The lapels hung open, covering nothing much. Neladith giggled to herself. "Like this is doing any good."

The wait ended quickly when the Devil's Blacksmith strode into the room. "Welcome back Miss Karlis."

"Thank you, sir. Just Neladith." She folded her hands in front, not out of embarrassment. She didn't know what else to do with them.

"You need not feel uncomfortable, Miss Neladith. I have met with many agents upon their immediate return. You need not be embarrassed."

"Thank you, sir. I'm not."

"Good. Then let us get to the point of your visit. Tell me of your report from Tartica."

"I guess I should ask what Selundra Quith reported. He returned a day or two ago."

The Devil's Blacksmith made his way to the bar. Pouring himself a drink he asked, "Can I offer you anything? Before you answer, please consider, I have asked you to report. What Mister Quith has or has not reported is immaterial."

Neladith rubbed her thumb over her eyebrow. "Sorry, sir. Didn't want to waste your time rehashing what you already knew. And, no drink for me... Thank you."

The leader stopped and set the bottle of spirits on the bar and turned to face Neladith. Anger flared across his face. His empty black pupils, as dark as the Void itself, stared harshly at her. His clenched jaw parted. Silence hung in the air. The tall, well-built, dark-haired man carried himself with a sense of entitlement. "Miss Neladith, you and I have spoken little in the past. Let me be clear. I will account for your inexperience only once. The way this works, I ask, and you provide a direct, truthful response. Now, please give me your report."

You're a grumpy bastard, aren't you?

"Whatever you say, sir. Sorry, didn't know. Okay, so I'll give you the big picture summary."

"That will be fine, Miss Neladith. Go on without the commentary."

She wanted to say, "Fuck you. How's that for commentary," but knew better.

Stories of him were widespread amongst Evidar's local inhabitants. A reputation for dealing with subordinates harshly and demanding perfection made him a hard man to please. However, for those who met his high expectations, he rewarded them well. Neladith should have been frightened, yet she wasn't.

"Grafph, Tylus, and Dylla are all dead. Reyne Brenton is still alive. And Quith thinks he's here in our version of Earth." It came out just about as smug as she intended and without the prerequisite *sir*. Then she thought the better of her approach. *What are you doing? You're only gonna piss him off.*

Pursed lips pulled in tight and wide eyes told Neladith either she surprised him or he was really angry. She jumped in to recover, taking a stab at him being surprised. "I'm sorry, sir, I thought Quith reported all this to you."

He erupted. "I told you—" yet just as quickly cut himself off.

Fuck me. Now I did it.

"Sir, I'm not good at this. I don't mean to cause you any problems. I came to you first thing 'cause I thought you needed to know this stuff. Maybe if you ask me specific questions, I can avoid saying things that will make you angry." She fidgeted with the jacket pulling tight at her shoulders. "Do I need permission to take this thing off? It isn't covering anything up and is very uncomfortable."

A rare laugh escaped the Devil's Blacksmith. "You are quite a unique young woman, Miss Neladith. I gather your disrespect unintentional. You just do not know how to behave."

Neladith shrugged. "Sorry, sir. I am what I am." She wiggled her shoulders against the restrictive garment. "Can I take off the jacket?"

"Yes." With his drink in hand, the Devil's Blacksmith moved to the sofa, leaving Neladith standing.

Slipping it off, she let it drop to the ground. "Ah, that's better."

"Now come and sit here with me." He patted the cushion.

Is he hitting on me? she wondered. "Thank you... sir." Neladith plopped herself at the far end away from the man she might need to kill one day if she ever rekindled her desire to live out her days on Tartica. She settled in and crossed one knee over the other.

The Devil's Blacksmith yelled out a command, "Assistant. A robe for our guest."

He returned his attention to Neladith. "I am very sorry to hear of Dylla's passing. I was fond of her. Tell me what you know of it." He rearranged himself to face Neladith.

"Again... sir, not sure how much you know or where to start the events to report. So, here goes. I came across her body in an area where Meratoruc, they call him Mera, and Reyne were. My best guess is that, oh yeah, forgot to tell you, Mera's dead too. Anyway..."

"What? Mera is dead?" He slapped his hand on the arm of the couch. "You saw this?"

"Me and Quith dumped his body, along with Dylla's, on a fire."

His head dropped. "Did you watch it burn to ashes?"

"Started to at first. Then Quith told me to get back to tracking down Reyne. I left him there with the two dead bodies on the fire. Quith didn't tell you all this?"

The Devil's Blacksmith leaned forward. "Mister Quith has not reported in. I have not heard of his return. Do you have any further details?"

"Sure," Neladith offered with girlish enthusiasm. "The way it looked, Dylla caught Mera in the process of getting Reyne into the Void. By the time I got there, only a pile of clothes remained of Reyne. There were two sets. Anyway, I figure Reyne made it through the Void. Quith said he was going to return home and go after him. First, he planned to report in to you."

"Miss Neladith, please continue."

"Well, like I said, Dylla probably got there too late to stop Reyne. On the plus side, she landed an arrow in Mera. He must've somehow got the better of her and slit her throat. After killing her, looks like he bled out."

"And what of agents Tylus and Grafph?"

"Quith thinks Mera got them both. I saw Grafph's body. He's dead for sure. Never saw Tylus's corpse. Just took Quith's word on it."

"And what of Reyne? If he lives, does it mean you failed to eliminate him? I sent you to Tartica as an expert archer. Did you miss the shot?"

"Not at all. Quith directed me to take the shot. I nailed it. Perfect. Turns out, Quith had me shoot the brother, not Reyne. I did what my unit leader told me to do. I did my job."

"I know. Dylla made her way back here before returning to Tartica, where you said she met her demise. She reported to me you did well. Although she did not report Mister Quith gave the false order." With hands cupped below his chin, the Devil's Blacksmith closed his eyes.

Wow, if I only had a knife. Perfect chance to kill this fucker.

A moment later, they sprang open. "Mister Quith needs to be located along with Reyne Brenton. You think they are both here?"

"I'm pretty sure Reyne is, but if Quith never reported in, makes me wonder about if he ever returned. Maybe he's lost in the Void."

The Devil's Blacksmith slid closer to Neladith. His raven-black eyes stared into hers. "I have not received reports of either man being here. Either or both could be. Mister Quith, though, worries me. He told you one thing but failed to follow through. Although, he too could be dead or lost, as you say."

"What makes you think that?"

"There is much you do not know of Mera. He has a knack for evading death. Mister Quith may have fallen at his hand. The alternative is that Mister Quith is avoiding us, knowing the order he gave you failed to terminate Reyne Brenton, and he has therefore put our objective in jeopardy."

"Huh. Didn't think of that. Gotta say, though, this Mera guy looked dead as dead gets."

"Mera has appeared as dead-as-dead-gets a few times. He is someone I will have to deal with personally. If you encounter him in the future, avoid him. You are a loyal and useful agent. Although, your behavior needs work. We will work on that together. In the meantime, I would not want to see you come to harm."

Is he hitting on me, she wondered again.

"Thank you, sir. I do my best for you and the cause."

"My assistant will return with a robe for you shortly."

"I'm fine. You mentioned loyalty. I know, you are aware of my entire life, short as it has been. I did prove my loyalty to you on this assignment.' She paused. "I saw her, you know. Not the Mithany I grew up with here on Evidar; Tartica's version of her...My Mithany's been dead a while. Imagine my surprise when I discovered her look-alike as the fiancée of the man you sent me there to kill. You knew I'd see her when you sent me. That was cruel. And yet... I still came back to serve you."

The Devil's Blacksmith rested both hands across his lap. "It is rare our two separate dimensions produced an outcome of identical individuals in both realities. What is also rare is an agent of your talent. I only account for the factors affecting an operation's success. Dylla left your lost love unspoken in your assignment brief in order to avoid any distraction from your mission objective."

Neladith took in a deep breath expanding her chest and let out a huff. "This was a test. Guess I passed. Tartica's Mithany wouldn't of worked out anyway... That's behind me. What's next?" Neladith did her best to push through it. She knew of the possibility of people existing in both realities. Other agents told of such encounters, and that only a handful were known to exist.

What are the odds my Mithany had to be one of them?

"Next, Miss Neladith, I have to replace Dylla and reassess many factors. You can assist me by locating Selundra Quith. If you are correct and Reyne Brenton is here, I have others to finish the job. Unfortunately, I have no one else available in my organization at this moment, save you, who is immediately available to transfigure to Tartica. If Reyne is not here, sending you after Quith on Tartica will serve two purposes. First, find and terminate Quith, or prove he is already dead. Two other agents, Miss Kebra and Mister Harvin, transfigured to Tartica several days past. Dylla was given orders to hunt down the person responsible for failing to kill Reyne Brenton, who you now say is Quith. If Dylla knew it was Quith, she had already set them on his trail. Join them if you can in finding Quith. Second, if you come across information Reyne Brenton has returned to Tartica,

I will need to know immediately. If so, return to me with haste. Now, go home to your ancestral tribesmen. Do not dally. Yes, I am aware of your visit to your clan upon occasion... against my orders. I expect you to leave within the day."

Neladith stomach clenched. She understood, returning to her tribe, even for a visit, was a punishable offense. Yet she didn't understand why he allowed it. With a head tilt, she asked, "You have a reputation that is much harsher than I can account for here today. Am I missing something? Is it 'cause I don't have any clothes on?" She stood and turned in a full circle for his inspection.

The Devil's Blacksmith snickered. "Please sit, Miss Neladith. No. I have seen thousands upon thousands of bodies sans clothing in my many years. The passion flesh once stirred has given way to inattentional blindness. The question you ask of harshness, know that I have followed your progression since you were recruited as a child. I see in you more potential than I have come across in quite some time. I am hopeful you can develop into something rare and exceptional. We shall see after the convergence. Be warned, my patience has its limits. This will be your last visit to your clan... one way or another."

The assistant entered the room. "Miss Neladith, may I ask that you stand?" As she did, he draped the robe over her shoulders, turned, and faded back into the darkness.

As she closed the robe's front panel and tied the waistband, pride surged in a way Neladith didn't expect. *This sonofabitch thinks I'm special. Isn't that nice? Maybe I don't have to kill him after all. And I am going back to Tartica, where I want to be. I can do that... with pleasure. Quith, oh Quith, where can you be? You lying sack of shit, I'm coming for you.*

"One last item, Miss Neladith. If your efforts take you to Teth, find a man named Jerithan Cree. He is the former First Lord of the Temple of Life. I have a means of communicating with him. Update him on your progress, and he may have information on Quith or further instructions from me."

Burned to the Ground

Hensdale: 12th Day of the Harvest Moon

Mithany

Mithany, her brother Arek, and the Brenton Family Orchard's General Manager, Santander, set out just after dawn to begin a thorough assessment of what remained of Reyne's beloved orchard. Acres of prolific alphen nut trees had been wiped out by the devastating fire. A conflagration that Arek believed had been set by Neladith.

Less than three acres of alphens escaped the blaze. Santander's quick thinking and the heroic efforts of Topak's refugees—whom Mithany brought to Hensdale offering food and shelter after their own city had been destroyed by escapees from the nearby birthing farm—saved what was left. Mithany lamented that her promise to the displaced homeless also went up in smoke because of Neladith.

A melange of steam and smoke rose off the remains of smoldering stumps and gnarled husks of blackened trees. It met up with the damp, water-soaked ground evaporating into the cooler autumn air creating an eerie, pungent fog enveloping the landscape.

Arek hobbled through the veil like a ghostly apparition of the man he once was. To Mithany's sight, her brother's limping silhouette embodied a future hidden behind a curtain of uncertainty brought about by an evil force. Arek, like the Brenton Family Orchard, had been delivered to the edge of ruination at the hands of one woman: an evil force named Neladith. Mithany wondered how she could have been so wrong about Neladith.

The full use of Arek's leg had yet to return. Mithany guessed it most likely never would. The cuts to his face left him with scars. A cane that replaced his broom-handled crutch sunk into the water-soaked ground with each step. Before Neladith tried to kill him, Arek would have held his head high, towering over her as well as the burly, gray-haired Santander. Now, with hunched shoulders and hangdog, downcast eyes, Arek's soul seemed drained of the happy-care-free-good-time persona he once exuded. Mithany's heart sank, reflecting on what he'd become.

Santander kicked aside the charcoal stalk of a once prolific alphen-producing branch. "You were both asleep last night when I got an update on Neladith's whereabouts. Judjurex Tetrip went out to the farmhouse late yesterday evening, where you, Arek, said you left her tied to a bed. She wasn't there. The ropes were still knotted, and her clothes were still there, just no Neladith. She's gone. Tetrip came across the dead body of some guy he'd never seen before inside the house. The corpse had been there a few days."

With his free hand, Arek reached for Mithany's. "I'm sorry, Sis. I went out there thinking I could do it. You know, make her pay for killing Daedyn. And it was her fault Doc Brenal died. I had the knife at her throat. Couldn't do it." He didn't, he couldn't, look up. "It's my fault she got away."

Mithany stepped in front of Arek. "Stop that this instant." As he leaned on the handle of his cane, she put her hand over his. "Look at me," she pleaded.

He didn't.

She dropped to one knee and looked up into his eyes. "Don't do that to yourself. She did all this. Look what she did to you. She's the one who we're angry with. You were brave confronting her. I'm proud of you for not killing another human being. Even her. That's not who we are. You're a better person for it. Just another reason I love you... because you couldn't." She rose and kissed him on the forehead.

"Sis, she got away."

"Come on Arek, that doesn't change a thing. You and me gotta help Santander put all this back together. Whenever that's done, I promise, if she isn't caught by then, I'll go with you. We'll track her down together. Cross my heart."

Mithany slipped her arm through his non-cane-wielding limb and said, "Forget about her. She'll get what's coming to her someday. So what if it's not today? I'm happy you're alive with all you've been through. That's what's important."

Santander interrupted, "What do either of you know about grafting trees?"

Arek shrugged. "Not a thing."

Mithany gave him a thumbs-up. "I've watched you and Reyne do it. Doesn't look that hard."

"It's not really. You just gotta do it right. Here's what we need to do. First, whatever remains of the crop, we gotta harvest right away. We need these Topakers to stick around to get it done... and there's a lot more to do after that."

"I can help you with that. I'll talk with them. Standard pay rates?" Mithany asked.

"Sure, why not? Should be some coin left in the coffers. After picking the alphens that didn't burn, we'll leave them in their shells this year. If any of the fire-damaged nuts are still salvageable, we'll strip them of their husks. If the meat inside survived, they'll be good to go."

Santander stopped and rested his boot on a charred stump. "Gonna need workers. Look at this one, a good two or three feet of nice-looking bark here. Cut everything above and we got ourselves a source to graft onto."

Mithany asked, "What about the ones too far gone?"

Santander patted his belly. "Root system still might be productive. If not, we gotta dig them out. That's hard work. Needs to get done before the ground freezes up. I'll want to get new saplings in those spots come planting season. That only gives us a few weeks. We'll graft onto whatever's left at the very end of winter just as spring is about to kick in. I'll mark the cuttings we'll take from the good trees. Lots of work to be done. Gonna need your help. Both of you. You up to it?"

Arek rested one hand on the other atop his cane. "Sis, we still have our shoppe to take care of. You and me will have to switch off between the shoppe and the orchard. The woman we have in there is young, and she's good. I just don't think she can run the place all by herself. Santander, if you're okay with that, I'm in."

Mithany added, "Me too. It'll mean a lot to Reyne after he gets back. That is"—she swept her arm one hundred eighty degrees—"after the shock of seeing all this wears off."

The Gift of Knowledge

Tandure: 12th Day of the Harvest Moon

Loseff

General Loseff Tomelai, the recently commissioned nineteen-year-old son of Chancellor Tomelai of the Kingdom of Adelle, bowed in jest, telling his childhood friend, Verek Jaynes, "My dear fellow, I give you the Tomelai Secret Library."

Jaynes's eyes lit up. "Look at all these books nobody has ever seen. At least nobodies like me. We could be here for days. The brown-haired young man with toffee-color eyes, standing several inches taller than Loseff, joked, "I'll check the upper shelves."

Loseff swept his arm across the scene. "This collection is a testament to patience, theft, and bribery. It represents my proud heritage as a Tomelai. My family's stolen book collection contains exact copies of every manuscript the Temple Secret Archives ever held, volumes of written words only a very few have ever... or will ever read. The Tomelai Family Secret Library has them all.

"Jaynes, keep an eye out for any titles remotely related to military strategy or waging war." Loseff's fingertips glided over rows of ancient book spines. "Since my father dumped out of the Covenant, Kantos, Greenlin, and Teth broke off relation with us. They're mustering an army as a unified front to force us back in line. War has its sights on Tartica. From the time of the Great Destruction, humanity resurrected in the aftermath never had cause to know military conflict. Although it's taken fifteen centuries, people being what they are, war was inevitable. Peace had a pretty good run."

Loseff Tomelai's features resembled his mother's side of the family. Thick black hair cut along the nape, lavender-colored eyes, and topping out at five-foot-eight, his slender features leaned more feminine than the rugged looks of his father or sister. Yet, the nineteen-year-old held as much promise as any other general in Adelle's newly formed military, given the utter lack of any living soul with battle experience. War titillated Loseff for the excitement of battle and the thrill of power. Growing up as the spare to the throne of Adelle, behind his older sister Tane, his life lacked purpose until now.

The role of general suits me. It'll do... for the time being, he thought.

"Remember what I told you, the Temple's Secret Archive and the Tomelai's copy of it are both well-guarded secrets. You're not supposed to be here. Speak of this to no one."

Waving off Loseff's concerns, Jaynes whipped his hand and added, "It goes without saying."

Loseff tilted his head sideways, scanning book title after book title. "Ah, Captain Druin Derr, the infamous leader of my father's secret police, says they built this place special. Hundreds of years ago. Down deep below the mansion. Constant temp. Low humidity and all that shit needed to keep their precious books safe. The Temple Secret Archive section had to be copied in some clandestine nonsense and smuggled out of the Temple Palace. It took over a hundred years through the reigns of several Chancellors, page by page, to get copies of all the Secret Archives into Tomelai hands."

Jaynes slapped both palms atop his head. "Before today, never heard of The Temple of Life's Secret Archives."

"Few have. Just learned about all this not too long ago myself. Guess Mother and Father finally had to tell me since they want me to see what I could find in here to help prepare for the coming war. That's their mistake."

Both laughed.

"The Temple Library housed the written memories of the seventeen hundred eighty-two signers of the Covenant depicting life before the Great Destruction.

Since nothing survived the Great Destruction, they recreated it all from memory. Books outlining Earth's history, its achievements, its horrors, its wars, and as many novels, manuals, philosophies, treatises, and everything about humanity as best the survivors could recall, was put to pen. The thousands of books they fabricated from memory took decades to create. Years later, the books the first Temple lords didn't want anyone to see were hidden away. Well, that's the story Mother shared." Loseff shrugged.

Loseff slipped a book off a shelf. *Teachings of Buddha*. With reverence, he ran his palm over the hard brown leather cover. Inside, he read the title page. "Listen to this, Jaynes: *Teachings of Buddha*, penned in the second year of the Third Age. Copied in 322 of the Third Age, and twice more; in 789 and again in 1262. This is the 1262 version. I guess those older copies are dust by now."

Jaynes continued searching the upper shelves, never turning away, said, "Never heard of Buddha. What did he teach?"

After scanning a few pages, the young general noted, "Looks like lifestyle stuff." Loseff closed the book and shoved it back on the shelf. "Not what we're looking for."

"We've visited quite a few Celebratoria of Knowledge. Maybe not the ones in Teth, but the ones in Adelle. Each and every one of them a sacred temple to the Gift of Knowledge. None of them are anything like this... this is the home of forbidden knowledge."

Loseff offered a polite bow. "While that is certainly true, somehow I don't think the Goddess Teth intended the Gift of Knowledge to have a secret reference section. Chalk it up to hypocrisy... by way of the Temple of Life."

Jaynes laughed. "How did you get permission to see these cloak-and-dagger books?"

"Never knew this place existed. As a kid I thought I'd found every secret hiding place in this mansion, and there are a lot of them. Guess I was wrong. What a shame. We could have been reading this stuff all along."

"Instead, it'll be a crash course in the art of warfare."

Loseff confessed, "My father suggested I read a book by some guy named Sun

Tzu. I haven't found that one yet. The name is spelled funny. With a *T* and it has a *Z*. How that spells Sue, I'll never know."

"That memory of yours should help. Never seen anything like it," Jaynes reflected.

"Just lucky, I guess. I remember everything I read—word for word. And if it's interesting, it drills down deep into my brain."

"So, have you read anything interesting so far, General Tomelai?"

"I'm foregoing the Tomelai. It's too confusing. The troops and other officers will make the connection to my father. Using his name will reinforce the idea of me as an undeserving elitist. Every salute, every mention of the Tomelai name will cement that notion. I can't have that."

Jaynes asked, "I don't get it. Don't you want that association? You're the Chancellor's kid. They have to listen to you."

"If that were the case, they might as well call me Junior instead of General. No. That's just it. I want to be respected on my own terms. For my own accomplishments. I'm going to be better than the lot of them. One day, I'm going to take control of Adelle's entire military apparatus based on my talents. Not dependent on the Tomelai name. Next time we're at a staff meeting, address me as General Loseff for the others to hear."

"Sure thing, General Loseff," Jaynes offered, followed by a proper salute. Loseff and his close friend sauntered through the maze of books. The expanse stretched fifty yards deep and ten yards in width. Dark-stained wood shelves housed thousands of books, artifacts, and displays lined up row after row. Lume crystals hung from the low ceiling and others sat in decorative sconces set in the end caps. The natural crystal's soft, gentle green glow added a sense of ephemeral fantasy to the experience. Laid out in a grid, ten sets of shelving across and forty wooden structures deep, over four hundred artisan-crafted bookcases made up the Tomelai Library.

Jaynes observed as they strolled through one aisle after another, "Kinda nice down here. Not too hot. Not too cool. Just right."

"Listen, you're going to have to leave. I wanted you to see this place. I've got to see the head librarian and you can't be seen in here with me. Remember, you're not supposed to be here. We don't need to get them all riled up. You take off. I'll talk with you tomorrow." With a head twitch and in mocked disdain, Loseff concluded, "Now get lost."

With Jaynes's exit, Loseff headed off to locate the Chief Librarian.

Loseff drew in a deep breath. *Smells like "old" in this place.*

His hand rode over hundreds of leather spines while wandering through aisle after aisle of bound treatises on religions, Second Age history, electrics, art, political theory, science, unthinkable technologies. It was more than Loseff could have ever imagined.

How much humanity might have progressed had books like these not been stored away in the Temple of Life's musty basement? My family gets part of that blame. Well, at least Father is finally pushing for electrics. Got to give him that.

Loseff recalled his mother's words, "Dear, you will not find a single book dedicated to weaponry. These have been denied us in the aftermath of the Great Destruction." He wondered if the Second Age was truly an idyllic civilization or if they fucked it up so badly they withheld passing their sins on to the next incarnation of humanity.

Loseff poked his head into the librarian's chambers. "Excuse me."

A grumpy-faced older man put down his pen and, just as slowly, turned away from his work to look up at Loseff. Four other men and women in the room continued copying older volumes and gave no heed to Loseff's interruption. The Chief Librarian managed a staff of seven well-paid and highly trusted Tomelai loyalists. The bookkeeper's physique was rounded by age and advanced in years. The uncombed gray hairs on his head matched in color the smattering of strands poking out his ears. Slim, rectangular-shaped spectacles rested across the bridge of his nose. The librarian cleared his throat and asked, "How may I be of service to the Young Master?" He folded his wrinkled, ink-stained hands on his desk.

Loseff played along, like a child teasing a helpless fly. "Chief Librarian, thank you for making the accommodation to assist me. I only hope I'm not interrupting anything important."

"*Hurmph,*" the Chief Librarian offered before answering. "Young Master, what we do every day is of great importance. We methodically copy the older volumes before age steals their wisdom from us. With thousands of books and being unable to stop time, it is a never-ending quest."

"Your work is very important and my family thanks you for your loyal service. I hope you can help me. I am having a hard time locating a few books in particular."

"Your mother has requested that I assist you in any way I can. First Lady Kaythlin is a wonderful woman, and I am happy to do anything she asks of me. So, let's have it, Young Master, what books do you seek?"

"I suppose you know what's going on. The other nations of Tartica will be sending their armies into Adelle. They aim to invade us."

One of the copy-scribes looked up from her work. Loseff couldn't tell if she was trying to flirt with him or had offered some sort of librarian-silent-protest to his prediction of war.

"Yes. Terrible. *Humph.*" Adelle's Chief Librarian sat back and crossed his arms. The chair appeared as old as the man and a loud wooden creak reacted to the strain.

With one hand above his head resting on the doorjamb lintel, Loseff leaned in and asked, "Well, I've been through a lot of titles. I haven't found much that might help me prepare to fight them off. You understand, I'm looking for subject on weapons, strategy, military tactics that will help me save the people of Adelle."

"*Humph...* You won't find anything with those subjects in the title. I know every book in this library."

Loseff buried his amusement at the old man's pride knowing it held the key to getting his cooperation, and Loseff couldn't afford to offend him. "How then can I save our people? Please, help me prepare for this awful burden that's been asked of me. You, Adelle's honored Chief Librarian, may be the Kingdom's only hope."

Four faces turned up from their desks and beamed at their Chief Librarian.

"*Humph.* Last hope, you say?" The man appeared to be as ancient as the books he guarded. Scratching his chin, he appeared deep in thought. "I suppose there may be a few tomes to help our cause. You must know what you're looking for."

Loseff figured flattery changed the old man's mind and stayed the course when he replied, "Oh, what do you mean?"

With a puffed-out blubberous chest, sporting sizeable man-boobs, the pride in his knowledge and in his pending contribution to the war effort were written on his face. "You'll need to look in the biography section. You will not find works on warfare in this or any library. However, there are nuggets of wisdom on battle strategies hidden within these walls. Let me introduce you to several famous generals of the Second Age."

Loseff shot out his arm. "May I shake your hand, sir? You have done your country a great service. I failed to find these gems, although I admit to searching only book titles or authors with a military reference. I came away empty."

Adelle's Chief Librarian stood, extended his hand, and proudly accepted Loseff's adulation. Loseff noted, *No humph this time.*

"You see, Young Master, these biographies offer only names sans rank in the titles. One needs to know what to look for. May I suggest you search out biographies on Caesar, Napoléon, Grant, Westmorland, and Alexander. By the time you've read those, I will have prepared a list of others for your review."

Loseff gratefully accepted the Chief Librarian's advice, shaking the old curmudgeon's hand with vigor. *That display of appreciation should buy me some goodwill.*

With an effort, the Chief Librarian plopped back into his wooden chair worn to a shine from decades of silk robes rubbing against its surface. "I'm impressed with you, young lad." He leaned in and spoke softly, "You are much more polite and respectful than your reputation."

"Thank you, sir. That is so very kind of you to say." His words betrayed his thoughts as he reflected, *If you only knew. Mother taught me well... how to manage staff. Show them sincerity, real or imagined, mix in a little gratitude, and they're yours.*

The Chief Librarian gave Loseff a nod of appreciation and added, "Row fifteen, bookcase thirty-two, bottom shelf. Start there with the names I gave you."

"Thank you, sir," and off Loseff went in search of knowledge.

At row fifteen Loseff located the bookcase in question. He crouched down and pulled out three volumes for review: biographies on Alexander, Caesar, and Grant. From the dust accumulations, none had been touched in years. Loseff's hand bumped the shelf while reaching for a fourth biography. A thin, leather-bound book dropped from above.

It puzzled Loseff. The book must have been secured on the underside of the shelving above, hidden. The book was ancient, and the binding showed signs of cracking. Curiosity forced him to open the cover. The paper on the title page showed signs of extensive yellowing. The ink had faded to a barely visible light brown. He ran his eyes over it. Most surprising of all was the creation date: *Penned in the fourth year of the Third Age.*

He noted secondary copy dates were absent. *An original? This could be interesting.*

If it's an original, how did it get here? Every book in this place is a copy from the Temple Secret Archives. A mystery for another time.

He tried to turn the page, but the corner of the brittle paper broke off and crumbled in his fingers.

Loseff closed the book, looked down at the cover, and pondered the title.

Dawn of the Third Age by Albert "Mera" Meratoruc.

War Council

Tandure: 13th Day of the Harvest Moon

Derr

The sandy-haired, steel-blue-eyed Captain Druin Derr of the Kingdom's Chancellor's Guard sat along the wall apart from Adelle's military's senior command staff. They all donned their recently minted azure-blue dress uniforms, including braided epaulets and rank insignias. Derr's rank of captain, and outfitted in his usual KCG garb, suggested his position was inferior to that of the generals. In the big picture of Chancellor Tomelai's governmental hierarchy of senior staff, Derr outranked them all. His superior standing in the de facto pecking order was a cudgel to be used only when Derr believed it necessary. Not part of the official armed services, Derr otherwise withheld public involvement in the minutiae of Adelle's military operations. Unknown to them all, Chancellor Tomelai's secret police, the KCG under Derr's direction, monitored every officer in the room, General Loseff Tomelai included.

Derr was always watching.

Joining Derr in the backbench arena and seated to his right was First Lady Kaythlin Tomelai—the violet-eyed, brilliant, yet charming wife to Adelle's Chancellor. A host of aides-de-camp weighed down with piles of notes, books, and various reference documents each general might need at their fingertips sat quietly along the wall, ready to jump into action if called upon. Military matters and the planning for war required knowledge of battle conditions, troop deployments, strategy, tactics, and so much more. Experience nobody in the room possessed.

Experience nobody on Tartica possessed.

Outside, a smattering of snowflakes drifted across the panes of glass of the hastily updated yet unfinished military headquarters building. Kaythlin settled her hand on Derr's. "Chamette's people did a fine job with this installation. He spared no expense."

"He spared no expense with *our* coin," Derr added. "But yes, it's a fine facility. We can only hope it serves your husband's purpose well."

Kaythlin's graceful elegance was out of place for a gathering of military personnel, as was her God-given glamorous looks. Armed militias were mustered to kill people and break things. She represented just the opposite as the finest of Mother Earth's creations. In her familiar genteel yet confident voice, laced with a mixture of charm and education, she said, "Have faith, my dear Druin."

Others were easily taken in by her charms, while Derr understood Kaythlin all too well. Hidden behind the façade of her stunning beauty was a mind as sharp as any and a will stronger than steel. It's what Derr liked most about her.

Chancellor Tomelai stood at the head of the enormous conference table. Artfully carved into the surface was a map of Tartica, its geography, cities, waterways, primary roads, mountains, forests, and infrastructures of note—bridges and the like.

Derr spoke from the side of his mouth, "Kaythlin, you ask me to have faith in these people? You're teasing. I'm not a man who relies on others to do what they're supposed to do. So often they don't. That's why you and I are here."

Kaythlin replied with her trademark tenderness and a quiet laugh, then patted his hand. "Let's see how they do today. Now hush, I want to hear my husband."

Tomelai gave Kaythlin a wink just before the first words rolled off his tongue. "Generals, and all gathered here, today is the first time in our illustrious history we must say, the Kingdom of Adelle's armed forces are preparing to defend our country. It is a sad day that we are called to do so, yet it is my duty to secure a safe and prosperous life for our citizens. And with all of you at my side, we will deliver on that promise to our people."

In unison, the eight generals repeatedly slapped their right palms on the newly minted table in a chorus of support. Derr's eyes darted from general to general, noting the voracity of each hand's acclimation. Eight hands pounded away at Tomelai's words.

Derr observed Loseff's enthusiasm and found it wanting.

Tomelai interrupted the applause. "I am pleased to announce that Commander General Kiple will oversee Adelle's military as my voice in defending our nation." The Chancellor's appointment of Kiple as Commander General was made official that morning, despite Derr's input to the contrary. Tomelai selected Kiple given his long tenure running Adelle's national civil police: the closest thing to a military unit otherwise prohibited by the Covenant.

Tomelai took his seat. The elderly, tall, and lanky Kiple stood. "Thank you, Chancellor. I will make you proud, as I will everyone in this room and all across our nation. We will prevail. I've the utmost confidence in the men and women here today, and I congratulate all of you. Yet, we've much to achieve before we can truly say we're in a state of preparedness."

Kaythlin leaned in. "You see, Druin, Kiple speaks with confidence and commands their attention. Besides, who else is there to fill the role? You are needed in other endeavors."

Derr craned his neck to face Kaythlin with a single raised eyebrow.

Adelle's chief military officer leaned on the table. "You all have been assigned specific duties. Although not a glamorous role, one of the most important functions falls to you, General Kevine. Logistics."

Derr angled his head to the side for Kaythlin's ears only and, speaking softly, said, "Kevine was the best choice given her background running the ports and moving tons of goods every day. Still, she appears hesitant. I know we all agreed to her appointment, yet now I'm thinking you may need to work with her. There are a lot of overbearing personalities at this table."

"You have nothing to fear, Druin. I have spoken with her many times. My husband's presence unnerves her, and she has confided in me you do as well." Kaythlin squeezed his hand and grinned. "If she only knew you like I do. As for the others, she will eat them alive."

Thirty-seven years old and inching towards portly, General Kevine rose from her seat. "Sir, I will not let you down." She looked at her fellow officers—Derr noted she bypassed his gaze—then continued. "While I know nothing of battle, I *do* know how to move product. An infantry, a navy, and cavalry have shared, as well as specific, requirements. You can be assured of being adequately supplied before you even know what you need." She nodded and sat.

Kiple appeared to offer General Kevine an approving headbob. "Three of you have been assigned army units as Brigadier Generals, two assigned naval fleets as Admiral Generals, and one lone Master-of-The-Horse as Master General commanding our calvary. It is my objective to increase our calvary capacity within the month as well as meet our ongoing troop enlistment targets. As of this moment, you are equal in rank and will take your orders directly from me."

General Loseff stood. "Commander General, may I ask a question?"

"General Tomelai, speak freely."

"Thank you, sir. Although, if not an imposition, I prefer General Loseff to avoid any confusion."

"Fine. General Loseff, what's your question?"

"Will there be anyone at the general rank serving as master-at-arms?"

"Not at this time. A lower-ranking master-at-arms will be filled within each of your units and will work closely with General Kevine and yourselves. General Kevine will see that your troops are provided the required weapons while each unit each will manage its own distribution and maintenance. Thank you, General Loseff. You can sit down."

Loseff remained on his feet. Kaythlin gripped Derr's hand. Derr shot a look to Chancellor Tomelai who shook his head as if to say, "I have no idea what he's up to."

Derr patted Kaythlin's hand, "Your husband wanted a man who questioned authority when he appointed Loseff. Now you got one."

"Commander General," Loseff asserted in a firm tone.

Kiple cut him short. "General Loseff, I gave you an order. Now sit. You may follow up after accepting and acknowledging your compliance."

The room went silent.

Derr, Tomelai, and Kaythlin anxiously waited for Loseff's next move. Kiple glared at Loseff, who slowly moved his hands to the arms of his chair behind him, and even slower, lowered himself into his seat.

Chancellor Tomelai rose. "Thank you, Commander General Kiple, and all of you here today."

Derr understood his friend and Chancellor well. *That could've gone off the rails. The young pup needs to learn his place.*

"Winter is soon upon us," Tomelai continued addressing his senior officers. "We will use this time to prepare. We expect an attack from the United Front in early spring when the weather allows. We will be ready. I am counting on each of you. General Kiple expects you to report on your unit's current state of readiness in four days. You are the defenders of Adelle. Our mission is clear: to secure our borders and to repel any attempt to invade our nation. In the course of this war to come, if the security of our nation demands an offensive action, then and only then will we be the aggressor. I will not be the first to draw blood."

Derr knew it for the lie it was.

THE BIG GAMBLE

THE WOODLANDS: 13TH DAY OF THE HARVEST MOON

Mera

Deep into night on the twelfth day of the Harvest Moon, Mera snuck away as Quith slept, leaving the Evidar agent to his stated purpose of hunting down a pair of fellow Evidarian operatives. One, an intelligent behemoth of a man named Harvin and the other, a petite woman, as lethal as she was cunning, named Kebra. According to Quith, the duo had been tasked with eliminating both Reyne and Quith by the Devil's Blacksmith. Quith pledged to Mera he'd impede their mission, and for selfish reasons—his own survival—he'd kill them both before they could do the same to him.

The proclamation by Quith that he no longer sought to kill Reyne seemed plausible given all the available evidence; most notably, Quith hadn't set off for Evidar in pursuit of Reyne. As best Mera figured, the facts on the ground skewed in Quith's favor. And yet, Quith's history as a deadly, deceitful agent of Evidar kept rattling around in his thoughts.

The tradeoff for Mera in not killing Quith in his sleep had the advantage of removing two additional deadly players from the board, Kebra and Harvin. Mera would otherwise have to pursue the pair to protect Reyne, delaying him even further. If not pressed by events speeding out of control, Mera would have preferred to dispose of Quith, Harvin, and Kebra himself. Conflicted about trusting Quith, he didn't like his options, yet he didn't have much choice. He needed Quith.

Trekking through the dense forest of The Woodlands, he wondered if his decision to leave Quith alive would come back to bite him in the ass. A deadly mistake if believing Quith proved wrong. Yet, in Mera's assessment, the bigger mistake would have been to stay with Quith, who'd certainly try to kill him to get his hands on the Soul Stone.

Mera understood the risk when he left Quith to his own devices, although it worried him that Quith could still pose a danger to Reyne's mission. Mera didn't trust Quith, and he trusted him even less out of sight.

Running his palm over the top of his head then down along the back of his neck as though coaxing comfort from the tactile stimulation of nerves so close to his brain, he paused. *Decision made! Move on*, he told himself. Yet, navigating the thickly wooded forest on his way to meet a familiar ally, doubt kept leaking in.

Chaotic and destructive events Mera witnessed firsthand in Teth and later in Topak threatened to snowball across Tartica as the seeds of rebellion against the Covenant were spreading fast. He was determined to stop its momentum before irreparable damage to fifteen hundred years of utopian peace set in. While preparing Reyne for a mission to Evidar, Mera'd been out of the loop for days. Days Tartica didn't have. Mera's plan to stop what was coming required Reyne to achieve success on Evidar while he attended to Tartica's salvation.

Throughout the extended life afforded him by possession of the Soul Stone, Mera engaged a multitude of personas under assumed names when exigent circumstances arose now and again in Tartica's long history, each time threatening the utopia he helped shape. Over those many years, Mera tinkered amongst the powerful more than a few times to sustain Tartica's survival, although he'd not done so in many decades. In his assessment, the current trajectory of events proved more precarious than all the other crises he'd helped to avert in Tartica's storied past. Tartica needed him once again in the halls of power.

My first stop's got to be the Temple Palace in Teth.

Yet, second-guessing his trust in Quith refused to subside. If Quith double-crossed him, Reyne's mission on Evidar would be at risk.

Reyne's failure meant Tartica's demise. Ruination would be the price all would pay if Mera was wrong about Quith.

Fallen leaves crunched underfoot. Mera paid them no mind, deep in contemplation, searching a solution to his conundrum when he considered, *There are fragments of Quith's former boss, Dylla. The dead do tell tales... sometimes. And I know exactly where to find you. Your charred remains, anyway.*

Her bones were all he needed to conjure the past from what was left of the deceased Evidar leader. Dead Dylla held the promise of answering the question of Quith's true intentions. He smirked thinking of Dylla's unwilling betrayal of Evidar's cause.

He stopped, rested one hand on a nearby tree, angled his head back, closed his eyes, and drew in the crisp, fragrant mélange of autumn's decaying flora. Opening his eyes, he told himself, *It could be done. It'll be difficult. No guarantees. I've extracted small bits of memories from burnt bone before.*

Mera pushed aside all thoughts of the many times he'd failed to coax the past out of fire-damaged bone, achieving the impossible only once.

A minor delay. At best, a few hours out of my way.

It's worth a gamble.

THE UNUNITED FRONT

TETH: 13TH DAY OF THE HARVEST MOON

Hermens

Minkin Hermens lamented the anemic response to the request for volunteers that had gone out two days past, following the failure of the Peace Conference to resolve Adelle's withdrawal from the Covenant of Absolute Universal Obligations. "I've requested this inaugural meeting of our newly treatied United Front to address the looming debacle of troop enlistments." Hermens, the recently elected Prime Minister from the People's Republic of Kantos, glared at the other two leaders comprising the UF's ruling Triumvirate, First Lord Garragent Serco of Teth and President F'Saad Dimenk of Greenlin. "Our plans for the UF to quickly amass an army of thirty thousand to face off against the Kingdom of Adelle with a stated purpose of forcing Adelle back into Covenant compliance is off to a pathetic start."

The outwardly confident thirty-five-year-old Dimenk, who carried her extra pounds well, cut in. "Thank you both for accepting my condition for this Triumvirate to meet without advisors or support personnel. While always ready with insights and information to support our respective positions, they would also bear witness to mistakes, slights, positional abdications, and all-around behaviors that might otherwise impede us from speaking freely to each other. Being the first face-to-face meeting of the UF heads-of-state, it is a sign of trust between us that we've all agreed to bring only our wits. We are going to need trust and cooperation between our nations to defeat Tomelai."

Like Hermens, First Lord Serco was new to a leadership position, having dethroned Jerithan Cree mere weeks ago. "Prime Minister, Madam President, let me thank you both for agreeing to meet here in Teth. The Temple Palace is the symbol of national unity across all of Tartica. What better place to kick off the inaugural gathering of this important compact amongst our like-minded nations?"

Hermens studied the pudgy First Lord as he spoke. *He doesn't look like a leader.* His thin lips and narrow-set, small eyes engendered suspicion in her assessment of him. Maybe there was more to him than he appeared. However, Hermens didn't think so. She had her measure of the man and turned her attention back to his words as he continued speaking.

"...and yes, Teth's call-to-arms went mostly unanswered with less than five hundred total enlistments; much like Greelin and Kantos, with similarly disappointing results."

Attentive to Dimenk, Hermens studied her in turn as the Greenlin leader spoke, "The problem," Dimenk told her counterparts, "is that we are asking those who adamantly believe in the Covenant to ignore the principles it stands for, in order to force others to live the very rules we are requesting our people to violate. Do you see the problem? We are asking of them to enlist in a cause antithetical to their core beliefs. We must put our people to the task of penetrating this inherent contradiction with the right messaging."

President Dimenk, a woman robustly built with soft rounded curves, exuded confidence in every syllable. Hermens knew of the President's reputation and admired her from afar. That didn't mean Hermens would acquiesce out of respect. Hermens considered herself as good as, if not better, than those with whom she shared UF leadership.

The forty-year-old Hermens was considered brilliant by the politicos of Kantos. The tall, green-eyed blond exuded confidence of her own and rarely backed down from a position she'd staked out. "The UF, with a combined citizenry approaching one million, amounts to the entire continent of Tartica absent the single nation of Adelle. On paper, the UF's combined resources, labor force, and territorial boundaries encircling Adelle give us an overwhelming advantage. However, given the UF has yet to muster an adequate military, in reality we are nothing more than a paper tiger. We are here to remedy this situation."

Hermens paused to look over the facial reactions of her compatriots before concluding, "Propaganda and messaging are only a starting point if we are going to meet the terms of Article 1 and assemble a force to stand up to whatever Chancellor Tomelai brings to bear. The question isn't if Adelle will launch a strike. The question is when."

At the heart of the treaty—prepared and signature-ready, prior to the Peace Conference in anticipation of Adelle's reticence to rejoin the Covenant—was Article 5, which bound each nation to the mutual defense of the others. An attack against one was an attack against all. Article 1 called for the creation of a standing UF army, whereas Articles 2 through 4 set forth cost sharing, resource acquisitions, military oversight, and the guidelines of power sharing; principally, majority rule within the Triumvirate—the UF ruling body made up of its three heads-of-state.

The stout, narrow-eyed Serco slapped his palm on the table. "We haven't even taken back our cities and you talk of engaging Adelle in battle. My dear Prime Minister, it's your priorities that are all wrong. Look outside the gates of this Palace. Hundreds, maybe a thousand or more, gather every day. That's the immediate danger we face. The UF will be defeated from within before Tomelai is even remotely prepared to strike us."

"First Lord Serco," Hermens offered, sweet in tone, "we don't know each other very well. If you are going to behave emotionally and continue with your condescending wordplay, my dear, Teth may find it has more problems than just the people at your gate or from Adelle. I strongly suggest you reconsider your approach."

President Dimenk jumped in, "Please. Enough." The senior stateswoman's actions clearly aimed to take control of the UF Triumvirate. Her forceful intercedence threw down the gauntlet and set the stage for two powerful women, each practiced at getting their way, as to who would wrest control of UF leadership.

Unbeknownst to First Lord Serco, Hermens didn't even consider him in contention.

Hermens gave Dimenk a harsh stare in reply. Serco gulped, crossed his arms in a pout, and sat back.

Dimenk said, "Yes. Both points are valid, yet, First Lord Serco, consider this, our cities and our countries will be overrun by Tomelai's forces unless we field a sizeable militia before he can strike any of us... or all of us. For all the time, effort, and manpower we dedicate to our own internal issues, we give Tomelai the opportunity to sweep in and grab whatever he wants while we dote about. Until we enlist sufficient forces to attend to both problems, we must set priorities."

The husky-appearing, confident-sounding Dimenk leaned forward and glowered at First Lord Serco, who she made clear was well short of her equal. Based on Hermens's reading of Dimenk's behavior, the jury was still out on how the senior stateswoman measured her.

Hermens offered, "And that's not all. We have ourselves a Samer problem to deal with. While our Covenant affords same-sex relations once individual progeny quotas to rebuild our population have been met, it's no secret that the Samer community has always harbored an undercurrent of resentment at those restrictions. And who can blame them? Tomelai, in denying the Covenant, has not only created a sanctuary for licensed and non-licensed Samers, it is a beacon to their cause."

Dimenk added her support. "They are fleeing each of our countries in droves and in greater numbers than any of us could have foreseen. Tomelai will, no doubt, gather a sizable force of our Samer expatriates willing to fight for an unincumbered life the Kingdom of Adelle now offers them."

The passion in Dimenk's delivery gave Hermen's pause. Hermens picked up an undercurrent of sympathy in Dimenk's words. A clear nod to Greenlin's president's well-guarded, secretive appetite for the affections of other women outside accepted behavior permitted within Covenant strictures—the very Covenant the UF Triumvirate intended to force Adelle back into compliance with. Although kept from the average Greenlinder, most inside Tartican circles of power, Hermens included, knew of Dimenk's proclivities. Not that same-sex couplings were excluded from Covenant stricture; one only needed to be licensed, and Dimenk wasn't. Dimenk's unlicensed assignations with other women weren't a problem for Hermens: those in power played by different rules.

Serco shrugged. "Now we have two problems."

Dimenk, the more tenured yet younger of the two women, shook her head. "First Lord, if you think we have only two problems, the UF is worse off than I had hoped."

In Dimenk's rebuke of Serco, Hermen read it as an attempt for Dimenk to set herself above Serco and, in so doing, to place herself at the head of the UF. Hermens let it be known she would have none of it and planted her own flag right there in Dimenk's face. "Madam President, if you cannot see the irony in your own words, I must agree with your assessment of the UF's prospects."

President Dimenk leaned back in her chair in a dismissive gesture to Hermens's challenge. "Article 4 establishes this Triumvirate yet is silent on its operating procedures other than to say, blah, blah, blah... majority rules. Might I propose we choose one of us to speak for all three so that everyone outside this room hears only one voice that represents the thinking of the UF?"

In unison, Hermens and Serco replied, "No."

"The UF has a Press Secretary who will handle that function," Hermens replied, "and I can read between the lines to gather your intentions."

Dimenk maintained her composure, although a red face gave away her frustrations. "Then I think the first order of business, even more threatening to the UF than Tomelai, is to figure out how we are going to work together."

Prime Minister Hermens stated matter-of-factly, "We'll work together just fine as long as none of us thinks themselves superior. Procedurally, we'll discuss, debate, vote, and appoint others to carry out the agreed-upon strategies. In private, you want to shout... go ahead. You want to sulk... go ahead. In the end, two of us have to agree before the UF does anything."

The First Lord nodded in agreement.

Dimenk lowered her head. When she looked up, facing Hermens's harsh glare, she said, "Alright then, let's discuss Article 1."

Serco threw out an idea. "We can't get them to enlist voluntarily, so let's consider conscription. I say we look at the forced enlistment of one able body from each family. Let's say between the ages of eighteen and thirty to start."

Dimenk said, "Prime Minister Hermens, what do you think of that idea?"

"I don't need your permission to say my piece. You want to use my voice to tell him why that won't work? Do it yourself." Hermens' words came out soft in tone but as sharp as a pointed sword in their meaning.

"As you wish. First Lord, I fear the internal revolt we'd each face in our separate countries would open us to war on two fronts. Those who oppose the Covenant already amass considerable support, and conscripting a beloved son, daughter, husband, or wife would be the impetus for those who currently support our cause to abandon us as quickly as the Samers have. The protesters outside this palace compound will seem like small potatoes in comparison."

Before Serco could respond, Hermens took a dominant swipe at Dimenk as though affirming her approval of the explanation. "That was well said, Madam President."

Dimenk's sour visage offered Hermens her reply.

"That's not—" Serco began.

Hermens cut him off. "First Lord, I believe we just voted two-to-one against forced enlistment. Move on."

He angrily spat out, "I will not be so easily dismissed."

In a genteel, practiced diplomat persona, Dimenk offered Serco advice. "First Lord, as we move forward together, each of us will have our ideas rejected. We are all leaders and are accustomed to others acquiescing to our intentions. This Triumvirate is going to challenge each of us. No disrespect has been proffered. We've simply decided for the UF. With your permission, I would like to move on and ask about the secret Temple Archives. We all know of the books. Your Order has wisely withheld from public consumption the more sensitive tomes. What books are there on weapons? It could be of considerable advantage to the UF if we could gain access to such writings."

Serco, controlling something the others did not, grinned. "What are you talking about?"

Hermens tilted her head to the side, opened her eyes wide in feigned disbelief, and said, "Come now, First Lord. While I may be new to my post as Prime Minister, I didn't get the job by being gullible. The secret Temple Archives haven't been a topic in my daily briefing. You must recognize all our governments know of the Secret Archives."

Dimenk said, "I bring them up now to consider if they hold anything that might aid our cause."

"Agreed," Hermens added. "Of particular note would be anything written on weaponry or strategic war theory from the Second Age. Knowledge the Temple of Life has denied the people of the Third Age."

Serco declared, "There are no such books."

Dimenk asked, "Is your answer, no Secret Archives, or no books on weapons?"

"That is correct."

Hermens pounded her fist, rattling the table's contents. "By the Goddess Teth, you are a frustrating man. Either we share freely between us, or we will each surely suffer alone when Tomelai comes calling. Out with it, First Lord. Books. Weapons."

Serco, First Lord of the Temple of Life and keeper of the Secret Archives, folded his arms over his chest. "There are no writings on weaponry in all the volumes housed by the Temple. Our scholars have concluded since no known original books exist from the Second Age, the people who survived the Great Destruction penned just about everything they could recall before the information faded into history. By intentionally withholding what they knew of weapons, it appears they wanted a better future for the world they were rebuilding. In simple terms, they didn't trust the generations that would follow with such knowledge. That's our best guess."

Dimenk smirked. "That leaves us swords, pikes, bows and arrows, and the commoner favorites, cudgels, pitchforks, and knives."

Hermens threw in, "At least Adelle's no better off than we are."

"What do you two suggest?" Serco asked, then added, "You've voted down my suggestion at conscription. You've given up on taking back our cities. You're looking for some secret weapon to save our cause. Frankly, you both disappoint me."

The trio faced off in silence.

Hermens turned from Serco and offered Dimenk frown lines coupled with raised eyebrows. In response, Dimenk nodded towards the First Lord while rolling her eyes towards him. With an almost imperceptible nod, Hermens offered her agreement. The unspoken consensus: Serco's limited thinking spoke loudly in his protestations. A man capable of leading the pious—maybe. A strategic thinker in a time of war—absolutely not.

President Dimenk spoke for both women. "First Lord, you may not like what I am about to say, so please keep an open mind. I ask only for the good of our cause. The success of the UF is at stake. There is a man who is cunning, sneaky, duplicitous, deceitful, and yet strategic. Many of these qualities make him a loathsome human being: nonetheless, those same deplorable characteristics are advantageous at a time like this. He could be a helpful advisor to this council."

Serco replied without hesitation, "No."

Hermens squinted through furled eyebrows. "Please think about it."

Serco again stated firmly, "No. No way. I didn't rip the First Lordship from his grips when the Council of Prudents voted revocation to allow him access to any semblance of power once again. I can't trust him. You shouldn't either. I have him where I want him... and there he will stay."

Dimenk continued to press. "He's a sly bastard and I don't care for the man. I know what he means to you, yet he is devious, and he can help us."

Serco slammed his hand on the table. Spittle flew from his maw. "I said no, dammit!"

With a knowing grin, Hermens nodded to Dimenk.

"Wipe that smirk off your face, Hermens," First Lord Serco demanded. "He's been confined, and that's where he's going to live out his days."

Her smirk didn't evaporate as Serco commanded. Hermens replied, "That's fine with me, First Lord. My interactions with the man were never pleasant. When first we met, he had a hard time lifting his eyes from my chest. Nevertheless, if President Dimenk is right in her assessment—"

Serco roared. "NO! I will hear no more about it."

Hermens turned to President Dimenk. "I suppose the former First Lord Jerithan Cree can always consult through the walls of his cell."

As the two women made their way from the UF's inaugural Triumvirate meeting, leaving Serco behind to sulk, Hermens stated, "Serco's going to be a problem."

Dimenk nodded. "Neither you nor I have risen to positions of leadership by allowing the ignorant to stand in our way. I believe the UF will benefit from a Samer roundup before any more flee to Adelle. I've already set it in motion in Greenlin; you should follow suit in Kantos."

"Agreed. Except do it quietly... and quickly."

Sit Tight

Black Haven

Reyne

Reyne, Gina, and Red arrived at the tribe's encampment quite some time after the attack at the underground compound. Reyne couldn't be certain how long it had been, given his inability to distinguish night from day. Along with the seven others who assisted with the assault on the Devil's Hammer, all had survived, albeit not without injury.

"Reyne," Gina asked, "do any of these faces look familiar? I think that woman over there is one of the six who attacked us the other day when they tied us to the stakes."

"Wish I could tell you. Wasn't myself at the time. Remember, I was doing my wild-man impression."

"Can you believe that bitch Red? She never told me anything about her plan. People popping up from hiding spots to attack the Mera look-alike. She arranged it all. Red didn't trust me or you to give us a heads-up."

"You've said so about a dozen times already. Gina... let it go. We agreed goin' in, I'd be the bait to get that guy out of his compound. When he stuck his head out, Red killed him. That's the plan we agreed to, and that's what happened."

Red sidled up to Gina. "You two should talk softer. And yeah, she's the same woman Reyne rammed into the day we captured you two. He broke a few of her ribs. She'll be okay. She's tough."

Gina poked an aggressive finger into Red's chest. "You couldn't tell me? Why? Who would I have said anything to? You couldn't share the plan about your people lying in wait? What, you think I'm some sorta spy?" As she spoke, Gina's foot shot out, stamping hard against Black Haven's surface as though demanding of an explanation.

"Do what your buddy told you. Let it go."

"I can't."

"Look, you two. I don't know shit about either of you. You show up, claim to be from Tartica, and immediately attack people from my tribe. I'm supposed to trust you? You could've been setting me up."

Gina waved her arms wildly about. "Attacked your people! They attacked us. We just wanted help."

Red shrugged. "Not how they tell it. You charged at them."

Reyne jumped in, "They're liars."

A smirk took root across Red's face. "What? I should believe you? Never met either of you before. Going with the story from folks I know."

Crossing her arms, Gina huffed. "Fine."

Red slipped her arm under Gina's. "What's it matter anyway? We rescued your boy Reyne, and I killed the guy I needed to kill. We all got what we wanted." Taller than Gina, Red nuzzled in close, resting one cheek atop Gina's head.

Gina brushed her off and yanked her arm free. "Not gonna happen, Red."

With a grin that went from ear to ear, Red said, "We'll see."

The sense of betrayal Reyne experienced during the attack gave way to acceptance. He and Gina had survived, and they left Devil's Hammer dead or dying as he was carried away. Despite misgivings with how it went down, what choice did he have? He and Gina still needed Neladith's help to get back to Tartica. With a burning desire to return to Mithany, he pushed aside all other concerns. "You two done flirting?" Reyne blurted out. "We have bigger things to worry about than who's getting laid."

Red lifted Gina's chin and stared into her eyes. "Maybe you do."

Gina drew her eyelids down and tipped her head back. She sucked in a deep breath. "Red, can you keep it in your pants and just tell me how to get off this rock? Reyne and I need to get back home."

"Could be a way." With one finger, Red ran it gently down the nape of Gina's neck. "I know someone who just might help."

Gina's face soured, and her body shivered.

Reyne couldn't figure out if her reaction was born of disgust or excitement. "Our problem is that Gina can't transfigure on her own. When we arrived here, she had somehow hitched a ride. You ever hear of such a thing?"

Pulling her fingers away, Red looked down at her hand. "Don't really know. Like I said, I know a guy. But it depends," she said, leering at Gina. "How bad do you want to go home?"

Gina's head dropped. "Not this again."

"Yeah, this again."

Gina half-relented. "How about we just say that if you come through, I'll consider it?"

"Good enough for now."

"Great," Reyne threw in. "When do we see this guy you know?"

"Couple of days," Red replied, walking away. She waved her hand over her head with her back to the pair. "Gotta check on a few things. You two talk. Come find me later."

Gina shouted, "Couple of days! Not good enough, Red."

Red's outline faded into the engrossing blackness. "Gonna have to do."

Gina yanked Reyne's arm. "Can you believe this chick? First, she lies to us. Then she tries to get into my pants. And now we got to sit around here for days. This sucks."

"What can we do? I don't like it either. I want to see Mithany. Still, we ain't goin' anywhere without Red's help."

Gina looked around, then said, "Now that Red's gone, there's something I got to tell you."

"Last time you said that, it wasn't good."

"Neither is this," she said, shaking her head. "Back at the skirmish, I tried to call on my gift... again. The moving fast thing I do. Again... nothing happened. I tried it a few more times on the walk back. Nothing. I keep trying... it simply ain't workin'."

With both hands atop his head, Reyne frowned. "I don't understand."

"I know. My Third Eye isn't responding. I don't feel it," she said, tapping the side of her temple. "It's like it's gone."

With his hands still on his head, he opened his palms, looking like antlers atop a confused buck. "What's gone? Your ability to move fast, or is it some feeling you get?"

"I try to reach into my mind to touch the spot Mera taught me: The Eye of Heaven, the Third Eye. Like you had to when you used it to open the Void. It's like it's not there anymore."

"How's that possible?"

"That's what I'm telling you. I don't know."

"Wish Mera was here. He'd know what to do."

"Well, he ain't," Gina shot back in an angry tone. "He's dead. And we're stuck on Black Haven. We're not even on Evidar, where we should be. The only good news is that this version of Neladith isn't the one who killed Daedyn."

Reyne's stomach clenched at the thought of his brother's murder. "We're alone. Go ahead, try it again."

Gina closed her eyes and almost instantly popped them open. "Nope. Nothing there."

"This just keeps getting better and better."

She slapped him on the back. "Look at the bright side. At least she didn't puke on either of us this time."

"How far along is she? You know, the baby she's carryin'."

With an eye roll, Gina spat, "Are you an idiot? How do I know? You think just because I'm a woman, I know everything about being pregnant?"

"Just askin'. No need to get all pissy."

With her eyes bugged out and her neck projected forward, Gina said, "I don't give a shit. How's that for an answer?"

"Just figuring since Red told us she wants to raise the child she's carryin' on Tartica. How much time does she have before she needs off Black Haven?"

"That's not bad, farm boy," she said, clapping her hands. "Red can't be too far along. She's not even showing. We could be here a while."

ALL OR NOTHING

TETH: 13TH DAY OF THE HARVEST MOON

Jerithan

The Second Obligation of the Covenant insisted upon humanity to *Do No Harm*. Given its status as the Covenant's religious holy ground, the Temple of Life's palatial enclave lacked adequate facilities to be properly called a prison for the dethroned Jerithan Cree to suffer in the manner befitting the degradation First Lord Serco promised Jerithan upon his internment. The room Serco selected to serve as Jerithan's cell had every amenity removed save one chair, a straw mattress, and a rarely emptied chamber pot.

Jerithan paced back and forth across his small, makeshift cell high in the northern tower of the Temple Palace. He looked up at the narrow sliver of a window that lacked the benefit of shutters or glass to keep out the advancing cooler weather. Familiar with every inch of the Palace, Jerithan knew it faced the rear gardens. Though the window proved too high up to afford him access to the outside world.

The Voice, Jerithan's intermittent nameless companion, spoke into his thoughts, *No doubt Serco teases you with access to view the palace grounds, knowing it is beyond your reach.*

At one time, Jerithan imagined the Voice to be that of God's. After the Voice abandoned him for a time, followed by humiliation at Derr's orders, forced to live in the gutter, shackled, and turned over to Serco, Jerithan disavowed any notion the Voice was that of a deity. Although the Voice had returned, Jerithan knew better now. Despite the Voice's demotion from god-status in Jerithan's perception of it, alone, confined to live out his days in the small room, Jerithan welcomed the Voice's presence.

Jerithan offered the Voice his thoughts. *If I'm ever to get out of here, I will see to it Serco pays for his offense.*

The Voice offered him comfort in reply. *"You will see freedom one day, and while the path has not revealed itself to us, together, we will find a way."*

Roiled at the thought of his demise and the degradation he endured, set in motion by Serco's hand, Jerithan squeezed his fists tight. *I'm isolated, cold, and alone, aside from the posted guard who refuses to answer or speak. I wish I had your optimism. I don't see it getting better anytime soon.*

Klunk.

The sound of the metal door handle bounced off the walls of the near-empty space and sent Jerithan's heart pounding. His head snapped toward the noise and his eyes locked on the latch, wanting desperately for any sign of its movement.

The door swung open. The guard stood in the opening and announced, "Prime Minister Minkin Hermens of the People Republic of Kantos to see you, Mister Cree."

"I'm still a Prudent, and you will address me as such," Jerithan demanded.

"Do not take your anger out on the guard. It is a slight most likely ordered by Serco," the Voice advised.

She'd been announced, yet it came as a surprise to Jerithan when Hermens stepped through the chamber door.

She extended her hand. "Good afternoon, Prudent."

Jerithan brushed himself off. Clothed in a commoner's outfit, Jerithan had been stripped of every symbol of authority at Serco's insistence. A bit eager, having seen no one for days, Jerithan announced, "Miss Hermens, I recall meeting you."

"Yes. That's correct." She bowed her head slightly. "We've met before."

"Yes, Miss Hermens, I remember you."

"This one is pretty," the Voice spoke within Jerithan's thoughts.

Not now, Jerithan replied to his thought companion.

With a smug grin and a nod, she added, "It's now Prime Minister Hermens."

"Then congratulations are in order. We two, here in this room, are on separate paths. Your star is rising, and as of late, mine seems to have fallen." He offered a graceful bow of his own.

"Nice touch with the bow. You show her respect. I do not think it will remove her memory of you leering at her chest during your first meet. All the same, it shows you are trying."

I doubt she remembers.

"I'm so sorry to see how Serco is treating you."

"She obviously wants something. Notice she avoided calling him First Lord. She is offering you a measure of respect."

"Thank you for your concern. May I ask what bring you to my chambers?" Jerithan finished sweeping his arm one hundred eighty degrees of the small, one-room prison.

Both stood in the middle of the mostly empty room. Hermens asked, "Do you recall the night we met? I, a mere district representative, not even in our PM's cabinet. What a gala that night was, and I got the impression you admired my strapless forest-green gown."

"Ah, she remembers. And yet she brings it up with intention. What is to come next? A titillation for your consideration in exchange for the favor she seeks. I wonder."

If it gets me out of this room, what choice do I have? First, I need to hear her offer.

Jerithan looked at her through narrow eyes, half leering, and replied, "How could I not remember one such as yourself? You stole my attention, yet I cannot say I recall much else of that evening."

Although her girlish laugh came off forced to Jerithan's ears, words held truth within them. "That is such a guy thing to say. I swear, women dress more for other women's approval than for the attention of men who only care about what's underneath."

"Lest we not forget the licensed Samer women with the Gift of Flesh in their thoughts as well. They might be the most skilled at appreciating another woman's dress, her complete presentation, the effort it took to pull together, as well as for the gift beneath that it teases."

"Speaking of those we hold in esteem, though we had only met once, I followed your career from afar. I've always admired your quick wit and thoughtful mind."

That did not take long. I suspect she rehearsed much of this.

What else do I have to do? I am happy to drag out our conversation as long as she is willing to have me. There's no need to rush her along. Besides, she is pleasant to look at. I miss women.

"Madam Prime Minister, please excuse my manners. I don't have much, save a single chair to offer. Please accept my humble appreciation for your visit. Sit."

"Thank you, Jerithan." She moved to sit, and Jerithan, more symbolically than required, took control of the back, sliding it under Hermens as she settled in.

"Have they treated you well?" she asked.

"That is a complicated question with an answer that exposes all my frailties to such a lovely woman. I'm simply pleased with having a visitor."

"Well said. She is buttering you up, you realize."

Whatever she wants, let her butter away. If it gets me free of this room, I'll most likely say yes.

"Do not be too hasty. Promise me the opportunity to think it through between us."

I promise nothing, especially to you.

"Come now, Jerithan, no need to be like that. I am here to help you."

"I've come to visit you despite Serco's objections. As Prime Minister, I get certain perks others have been denied. To the purpose of my visit, war is coming, and I believe you have a place in it. I may have a way for you to strike back at those who have not been kind to you."

Jerithan, resting against the wall, folded his arms over his chest. He reacted more in show than expressive of his true feelings at her implied opportunity. "Your words are well intended and reach wanting ears. Although forgiveness is central to a faith-based life—and even more so, I fear locked away in this room—I cannot attend to this coming war that concerns you."

"We are negotiating. See how much she needs you and is willing to give away for it."

Be quiet unless you can help me through this.

Hermens stood and, with her knee bent backward, kicked away the chair behind her. "There's the man I've heard so much about. You think me a schoolgirl. I understood everything you meant. And yes, we are negotiating. We can play word games all afternoon or we can get down to it."

"The mask is off, Jerithan. I like her better this way."

"You impress me, Miss Hermens."

"It's Prime Minister Hermens."

"As you say, Prime Minister. I see a different woman before me than entered this room."

"Same woman. Foreplay's over. Time to get what I want."

"That was quick. And what is it you want?"

"You, I want you... I want access to your strategic mind."

"Serco beat me. Why would you want a defeated man?"

"Captain Derr beat you. Serco just happened to be standing nearby to pick up the pieces."

"He still won. He's your man."

"You and I both know Serco is not her man or she would not be here. Yet I like the way you keep pushing her away. Either she will grow frustrated with you or, like the foreplay example she noted, you are drawing out the buildup."

"Serco's a simpleton. He doesn't see what I see in you. Let me be honest and direct. You have a reputation for being clever, creative, and, excuse me for saying, duplicitous. What better qualities are there for our side to present against an enemy?"

Jerithan bent his leg back and rested his foot against the wall. "What are you offering for my help?"

"The opportunity to strike at the Kingdom of Adelle. To strike at Tomelai. At Derr."

"You can get more. That is a pitiful offer."

I know. I am sure she does as well. Negotiations take time. Today is the opening round.

"Prime Minister, thank you for your generous ante. Sequestered in this small room, I've been afforded much time to think. It occurs to me that Kantos, Greenlin, and Teth will come together to face off against Tomelai's Adelleian forces at some point. Save for your minor problem of mustering forces. Between the probable Samer exodus and the reluctant faithful to betray their core beliefs, it is not too difficult to conclude you face a recruitment issue. I've a few ideas to solve that."

Clapping her hands together, "Yes. Jerithan, this is exactly what I'm talking about." She waited. "Please, Jerithan, go on. What exactly are your thoughts?"

Jerithan pushed off from the wall projecting his body forward. He opened his arms as though beginning communal services to the faithful. "Perhaps you and I can continue this discussion elsewhere."

"You understand you are not leaving this room. Serco will not allow it."

Yes, I know. She does too. More importantly, she now knows my price.

"Clever, Jerithan. I do so wish for your freedom. Sadly, it's outside my purview to grant. Albeit a few helpful suggestions from you may be enough for Serco to see your true value. To that end, I ask again, what exactly are your thoughts on this nagging enlistment issue?"

"And to that end, I must decline. There is a path to build a military to face off against Tomelai. However, trapped in this room, it calls to me from beyond. You, Madam Prime Minister, need only set me free that I might get it for you."

"Jerithan, you and I have not found a solution to Teth's military recruitment problem."

You and I know that. Hermens doesn't. If she gets us out of here, we'll come up with something.

"I'd hate so much to leave here today in a stalemate." She bowed in a sign of respect. Her heavy chest on display... as she intended Jerithan suspected.

"She definitely remembers you."

"Prime Minister, you are now perhaps being too subtle." He bowed in return.

"It *is* a point of interest that I hold dear and a rather enticing offer. And while I do appreciate putting more on the table than just revenge, it can be no secret that my dream is to be released from this room, along with the return of what has been lost to me."

She smirked. "To dream is good... but, to plan is better."

"And you have such a plan?"

"Please understand, Jerithan, some plans take a long time to come to fruition. Yet a man of your appetites might die for want of relief, alone in this room, until you either realize your dream or the curtain drops one final time. Think of what you could be enjoying while you and I cooperate to secure your freedom. Taste victory in small bites."

"We will need to consider her short-term offer measured against your long-term isolation."

Even if she does have great tits, it's not enough. I don't trust her. If she wants my help, it's my freedom now, not at some time in the future she can't guarantee.

DAWN OF THE THIRD AGE

TANDURE: 14TH DAY OF THE HARVEST MOON

Loseff

Loseff consumed the biographies of Grant and Alexander within hours of emerging from his first War Council. His immediate reaction was that Adelle's living generals failed to measure up to the two long-since-dead military leaders of Earth's Second Age. That is, if any of what he'd read could be believed.

Each of the General's biographies remained silent on the details of weaponry. However, of equal importance, strategy filled many pages. A healthy dose of skepticism accompanied Loseff's exploration of the Grant and Alexander tomes, given every volume contained a qualified introduction that read: "As compiled from the recollections of..." followed by a list of Great Destruction survivors who'd contributed to each book's creation. Loseff understood the biographies weren't originals from The Second Age; all were merely compilations of the collected memories of those who'd survived the Great Destruction. Specifically, the pages reflected what was known of the man, the facts the authors could recall, and the judgement of history carried through the ages. While all such books were accepted by Tartican society as historical retellings, how accurate any of it was, no one, including Loseff in the year of 1543 of the Third Age, had a clue.

On the plus side, Loseff was certain the UF's military leadership fared no better. He delighted in the opportunity the coming war presented, imagining himself the only one positioned to seize this rarest of openings. All his life, he'd been nothing more than a spare to the Chancellorship. Being a general gave him purpose.

From his reading of Grant's recreated biography, he came to understand the importance of selecting the battlefield to match his army's strengths, where factors such as topography, time of day, food supplies, morale, and how so many of the *little things* combined to affect a battle's outcome. Through Grant, Loseff also grasped the significance of relentless pursuit in giving no quarter or rest to an enemy.

After putting aside the hardcovers of the long-dead war heroes, Loseff contemplated the ancient manuscript, *Dawn of the Third Age*. A nagging want to explore its full measure wouldn't release him. With curiosity needling his every thought, he knew he wasn't going to get anything done until he took a deeper dive into the book's contents.

Hoping to avoid further damage to the centuries-old brittle pages, Loseff slid the long edge of his knife between the cover and the opening page. The length and broadside of the blade supported the fragile paper, and he gently turned to the first delicate leaf of the manuscript without causing damage to the ancient text.

The ink had faded. Many of the letters were but ghosts of the author's hand. Fortunately, the book had been shut out from the light during its many untold years in hiding. Enough remained legible for him to make out what had been laid down over fifteen hundred years ago.

He salivated in anticipation and gulped down the pooling saliva as his eyes attacked the first page. Absent was any notation of who contributed to the book's creation aside from its singular author. Unlike all the other books recreated from the memories of Great Destruction survivors, this one appeared to be an original, penned by one man. This wasn't a recreation of the lost Second Age, a time in history that held little meaning to Loseff. This book was unique. Its title promised a look inside the events that gave birth to the world he knew, the Third Age, and it teased his interest in whether the truth behind the Great Destruction would be revealed in its pages. His eyes rolled over each word as he absorbed them into his mind:

Dawn of the Third Age

By Albert "Mera" Meratoruc
2089, Earth Before the Great Destruction
Prologue: Seeds of Teth

Loseff turned the page and read on:

And so it began… On March 20, 2089, a mere three days after it was first detected, NASA announced that a sixteen-mile-wide object would strike Earth on April 19, 2089.

With the proclamation of worldwide, imminent destruction, unseen since the last days of the dinosaurs, humanity had been assigned an expiration date.

The discovery of the previously undetected M-Type asteroid screaming through the solar system at fifty thousand miles per hour threw civilization into a frenetic panic. Even before the massive asteroid struck Earth, governments fell, laws were abandoned, and the entirety of civilization utterly collapsed.

Humankind was afforded less than a month to put its affairs in order. Exactly who would remain to benefit from any such planning was uncertain, and judging by the calamitous global reaction, any organized effort to prepare for post-apocalyptic survival wasn't going to happen anyway. Every living thing on the planet was fucked, plain and simple.

In spite of last-minute heroics to throw nukes at the beast, a reprieve wasn't in the cards. After that last gasp of heroics failed, NASA was never heard from again.

How the cosmic rock had gone unnoticed, experts and conspiracy nuts had their theories, yet in the final days with no miracle in sight, it didn't matter. Assigning blame in the face of unstoppable death satisfied only the bitter.

All that mattered was stopping the damn thing, and that was outside the purview of all earthly knowledge. Prayers from the billions of religious brethren of every faith joined the multitude of newly gained converts to plead their collective case to God for salvation… from whom a response never came.

Reports by faceless ham radio operators worldwide kept those who cared to listen informed. Money, gold, and every measure of wealth had been stripped of purpose, as were titles, status, race, religion, and the notion that any one individual was better off than the next.

Many tried to live out their days in peace and enjoy the time that remained. However, that proved impossible due to the vast majority of everyone else who made every effort to take whatever they wanted from anyone they wanted to take it from. Without police or armies to stop them, the strong swept through the meek unchallenged, taking food, supplies, sexual liberties, and whatever else they deemed desirable. Although untold millions died in the chaos, it drew little concern as Asteroid TQ-680 promised to take the rest.

Elizabeth Green, who everyone just called Beth—whose story this is as the unwitting founder of the Third Age—along with two thousand five hundred

eighty-six others from the nineteen scientific
delegations stationed amongst the various research
outposts on Antarctica, prayed for themselves, their
loved ones, friends, family, and for the people of
Earth. Last, they prayed for the remotest of possibilities, that they, living on the least populated
land mass on Earth amidst the harsh, uninhabitable
climate of Antarctica, just might be humanity's only
hope to survive its inevitable doom.

You Don't Say Much

Neladith

While still on Evidar, Neladith prepared herself to enter the Void on her journey of transfiguration back to Tartica.

The Devil's Blacksmith of Evidar tasked her with hunting down Selundra Quith. Quith had never returned to Evidar as he promised he would on the night they burned Dylla's body. Unless he was dead, Quith had turned traitor, and that required he be eliminated. Quith had to be on Tartica, so that's where the Devil's Blacksmith sent her. She had her orders: track down Quith and end him, with extreme prejudice.

Under the watchful gaze of her fellow Evidarian tribesman, under the veil of the ever-present fusain sky, Neladith lowered herself to the ground. She didn't plan to be in that position long. Lying flat, she didn't bother with clothing, knowing whatever she wore wouldn't join her on Tartica. She spread her open palms and drilled her fingers into the soil, connecting with the warmth of Evidar as she prepared to transfigure, body and mind. Her assignment to track down Quith and kill him seemed clear enough. Maybe Mera had already finished him off, for all she knew. Despite the possibility, she hoped for the chance to do it herself.

I'm gonna find you... you white-haired prick.

A prodigious lucid dreamer, sleep quickly welcomed Neladith. Soon after her consciousness separated from her body, she entered the astral plane as only pure thought. From there, she forced her mind through the metaphysical barrier between realities, and the Void opened to her.

Transfiguring from Evidar to Tartica challenged even the strongest willed person to maintain a focus on one's desired point of destination. Neladith was no exception. Within the Void, every future carried on the untold number of Probability Waves appeared real. Probability Wavefunctions filled with the promises of futures that had infinitesimal chances of coalescing into existence teased her mind with myriad versions of reality.

It all crashed into Neladith's thoughts at once; thousands of Probability Wavefunctions dangled alternative futures of untold lives, haunting her. The Void demanded every scintilla of her attention as it tossed her non-corporeal metaphysical existence about like a cloud of fumes struggling to maintain adhesion inside the funnel of an unstoppable tornado.

Her third experience in the Void proved no less daunting, uncertain, or exhilarating than her previous two trips through the mind-bending black emptiness. In her mind's eye, she'd secured the landscape near the mosaic patterned, lichen-ridden surface of the isolated boulder in the open glade of Tartica's Woodlands several miles outside of Hensdale.

The Void offered her dozens of Probability Waves to access it. Unlike previous encounters in the Void, where she merely tasted existence on her non-corporeal pallet, this time sounds and images opened to her. Instinctively, she knew the right one. Her mind grabbed hold of it and prepared to ride the Probability Wave crest to Tartica.

Like a wisp of smoke flittering off a burning cigar, her mind and body transfigured, stretched into a tiny thread over a vast distance, or perhaps only inches separated the dimensions. Coalescing exactly where she wanted to be, her target a location on Tartica twenty feet north of the large boulder in a glade somewhere between Hensdale and Topak. The familiar spot embedded in her memory from which to anchor a transition between realities. Although exactly where it showed up on a map, Neladith could only generalize.

For the few capable of transfiguration, the Void was a big, dark, scary place with no guarantee of making it through alive. Nevertheless, while Neladith hated it as much as anyone who entered, she thrilled at the danger it exposed to her; cognizant and proud, she'd conquered it once again.

Her body instantly grasped awareness of the cold attacking her exposed skin. Unlike Evidar, a world persistently warm, Tartica's Harvest Moon brought chilly weather to the remote corner of Kantos. Lying in an open field, the frigid ground softened by the wild grasses clinging to life in Tartica's autumn sucked heat from her body.

On her back, Neladith gazed up at the stars. A nonexistent sight in the ash-laden atmosphere of Evidar, the twinkling lights in the heavens above told her she'd made it. The sight of twinkling lights against the black sky delighted the Evidarian native.

She laughed.

Honey, I'm home!

As with her previous ventures, grasping even a hint of how much time she'd spent in the Void proved both pointless and impossible. How long the journey took to complete hid inside the mystery of the Void. For all she knew, it happened in only a few heartbeats, or, just as likely, it had taken years. The world could have ended during her time in the Void, yet her eyes told her the scene had changed little from her last visit. Relief washed over her. She recognized the large boulder conspicuously out of place in the center of an open glade surrounded by trees hanging on to the last of their leaves.

"Motherfucker... it's freezing," Neladith whispered, careful not to give herself away should anyone be nearby. A forest tree line encircled the outcropping of boulders from sixty yards away in every direction. Lifting her head, she scanned the open space. Finding nothing moving and given the open field's proximity to nothing of note, her concern for being discovered melted away. She sprang up.

A vapor cloud of the exhaled words appeared from her hot breath. She slapped her upper arms, trying to generate whatever heat friction offered. Her hands vigorously rode her thighs up and down as though willing warmth into them.

Shit, this place is cold.

Hopping from foot to foot, determined not to surrender the fading remnants of Evidar's warmth, her eyes swept over the area. Finding herself alone eased her mind.

"I didn't pick this place for nothing," Neladith said aloud. "I know you transported to Evidar from this very spot, Reyne Brenton. Now, where are your clothes?" Neladith remembered stuffing two sets of clothes from view into the space between the slab and the ground during her initial visit to the site—the day she discovered a dead Dylla and a seemingly dead Mera. Several quick hops put her near the expected hiding place.

The abandoned farmhouse where her compatriot Grafph sat decomposing on the living room sofa would have been a better choice. Her own clothes were most likely still there on the bed from which she initiated her return to Evidar. However-er, the prospect of Arek returning with Tetrip—as he promised—to apprehend her tied to a bed made a return there impossible. In all likelihood the farmhouse was empty save for Grafph. Still, she couldn't take the chance.

Down on her haunches, Neladith reached under a crook at the base of the boulder.

There were two outfits here, if I recall.

She searched without success.

Where is it? I put it right here.

With one hand, she searched further into the crevice as far as her arm's length allowed. Her fingers touched smooth leather, and she savored the feel. Yet, her hand came back with only a pair of boots.

"No!" Neladith hated Quith more than ever.

"Quith, you sonofabitch, what did you do with Reyne's civies?" Neladith kept on talking to herself as she donned the footwear. "Hum, small feet."

"Fuck me." She stood as the cold leached into her muscles. Anxiously, her eyes searched the area for anything out of place, to no avail.

"Quith, you bastard. Did you burn Reyne's clothes after I left? For that alone, I should kill you. I'm freezing my tits off out here." She rubbed her hands rapidly back and forth over her breasts. "You're gonna pay for this, Quith."

She circled the huge rock until she reached the other side.

She stopped.

Her eyes opened wide.

Out near the ash pile, where Dylla and Mera burned, she spied a brown lump.

"Ah, there you are."

She sped off for the garments.

After swiping the shirt off the top of the pile, she held it up for inspection. Then the pants. *Gonna be a bit tight. I know I jammed two sets of clothes into that crook. Huh? The Devil's Blacksmith said Mera could still be alive. This Mera guy might've taken the other set.*

It became clear to Neladith that the clothing she found was not Reyne's. It had to be from the other person Neladith figured joined Reyne on his trip to Evidar. Who once fit into the female outfit Neladith recovered, she didn't know, but was grateful for them. Whoever the woman was, she was smaller than Neladith.

Neladith pulled, squeezed, tucked, and shimmied her way into the leather pants. The leather stretched over her body tighter than her own skin. The hem of each leg stopped just below her calves and the inseam bit into her crotch, leaving a telltale outline. The leather drawstring holding together the opposing vest panels strained to keep her breasts from overwhelming the thin leather straps or the knot holes they laced through.

It'll have to do. The fit's tight. At any rate, better than romping around without them in this cold.

After gathering a small pile of sticks, she started a fire to warm herself near the smaller of the boulders, having set aside concerns for anyone else out in the middle of nowhere in the dark of the night. Unlike Evidar, Tarticans mostly kept to the daylight. As the flames grew, her shadow danced against the lichen mosaic backdrop Nature painted on the rock surface. She held out open palms to the fire, warming every inch of her chilled fingers.

While on Evidar, she had gotten little rest. *I'll set up here for the night. Start my hunt for Quith in the morning.*

She rubbed her hands together and stretched out her legs with her feet only a yard from the burning pile. Soaking in its warmth, concern for the frosty evening air drifted from her thoughts.

Now then, she slapped her palms together. *First things first. The Devil's Blacksmith had misgivings about Mera actually dying. Said something about not being sure fire would do the trick. Let's just see if we can find what remains of Mera in that pile of ashes.*

She made her way to the nearby remains of the funerary pyre—now a mound of cold ash—that she and Quith previously constructed and set ablaze to consume the cadavers of Dylla and Mera, lying in a mound of cold ash. Neladith's dark-sight, born of Evidar's gloom, easily read the details by starlight written in the long dead coals.

Neladith swept her borrowed boot through the cinder heap. Speaking aloud, she said, "Looks like only one body burned here. Gotta hand it to the Devil's Blacksmith. Mera ain't here. He called this one." A few charred sticks survived, as did one intact femur. The other bones splintered in the heat of the blaze. There were assorted charred skeletal remains. She could make out pieces of ribs, fingers, longer remnants that could have once been arms, along with other various-sized unidentified bone fragments.

Only enough here for one dead. All this has gotta be Dylla.

With a foot, she continued sifting through the pit until she found her prize, a skull. Just one. Part of the lower jaw was missing, though the cranium remained fully intact. Remorse for the dead Evidarian black-ops leader never entered her thoughts.

"Hi Dylla," Neladith called out in a friendly voice looking down at the skull's empty eye sockets. "Is that you? You look different from the last time I saw you."

She bent down and picked it up, palming it by its crown. Holding Dylla's skull-face close to her own, she said, "Got a lot to tell you... and I have questions, too. First of all, your buddy Quith turned out to be a traitor." Neladith tilted her head at Dylla and asked, "Did you already know?"

One hand let go of the skull, and it fell into her other hand, waiting below. "Can you tell me where Quith went and why Mera's bones aren't here amongst these dead embers?"

Neladith returned to the fire she'd started earlier only a dozen yards away, threw on a few sizeable branches, sat, and nestled Dylla's skull in the crease of her outstretched legs. Her hands rode over the top and down the sides as though brushing Dylla's missing hair. After several passes, Neladith asked Dylla, "If you were Quith, where would you go? Would you hide or go after Harvin and Kebra? Oh, yeah, the Devil's Blacksmith told me all about them. They're here looking for Reyne, unless you gave them different orders."

Neladith rubbed her chin and looked into Dylla's black orbital cavities. "How did you die? I thought Mera killed you. Then again, maybe Quith did the deed." Neladith poked one finger into an empty eye socket. "What did you see?"

Neladith waited for a reply she knew would never come, then continued questioning the remains of her deceased leader. "Tell me, Dylla, what should I do?"

After another long pause, she said, "I never told you I've grown to like Tartica. Was gonna try to stay here or, at the very least, get posted here." She offered Dylla a look of surprise. "You didn't see that coming, did you?"

With steepled hands in front of her face, Neladith said, "My assignment is to hunt down Quith and kill him. I expect it could take a while. Now that I'm back on Tartica, too bad that little tight ass of Mithany's is off the table." She brought a finger to her lips. "You knew about her looking like my Mithany born on Evidar, just like you and me. You should've told me about her in our mission briefing. You might not think I got feelings. They're in here somewhere. I didn't know you long. Kinda figured you for a cunt. Well, now, you're a dead cunt."

Neladith picked up Dylla's skull and rested it in her palm. She brought it close to her face and ran her other hand from front to back over the fire-darkened cranium. "You know what I think, Dylla? Quith ain't one to run away. Thinks too much of himself to do that."

Neladith tossed Dylla from one hand to the other like a child playing with a ball. "He's going after Kebra and Harvin. That's what a trained killer would do."

She moved Dylla's bony head with its missing jawbone to her ear. "What's that you say? Speak up. Oh, you agree."

With her legs stretched out, Neladith rolled the head along the crease of her lap until it came to a stop at her knees. She twisted it around to face her. "In my briefing for the Reyne Brenton hit, there was intel on your contacts within the Thuggery in Teth. I think Quith is going to reach out to them sooner or later. Seems like as good a place as any for me to start."

Neladith picked it up and leaned in close to where Dylla's ear had been before her flesh burned away from her skull. "Just between us girls, did you know Quith wanted to fuck me? Ugh, as if."

Her knuckles rapped the top of Dylla's cranium. "Does that surprise you? You had to know he's a horn-dog. I wonder if you two ever boned?"

She stood and stared at Dylla as if waiting for a reply. "You don't say much."

In one hand, Neladith tossed Dylla's fleshless head up and down several times. Then stopped. With the skull resting in her palm, she looked into Dylla's vacant eye holes. "Would you like to come with me? Keep me company on my adventure?"

"You got nothing to say?" Neladith stuck out her arm over the fire and let what remained of Dylla roll off her fingers. "If you got nothing to say, then back to where you came from."

Dylla's empty braincase fell onto the burning logs with a hollow *thunk*. Flames crackled, and embers shot up from under her missing mouth, rising into the air as though giving voice to Dylla's lifeless screams.

"Tomorrow I'm off to Teth." She sneered, gazing into Dylla's skeletal face staring back at her. Fire poured out from where the dead black-ops leader's eyes had once been.

Neladith answered a question Dylla's flickering fire-tongue never asked. "Sorry, you can't come with me."

Neladith threw more wood on the fire, enough to keep her warm through the cool autumn night. She took off her vest, balled it into a pillow, and laid down.

She turned her head to face Dylla's skull. Death always aroused her.

After loosening the top of her pants, she slipped them down just enough. The frigid air tingled her delicate flesh, increasing the titillation of what was to come.

Slowly, she slid a long, thin, anxious middle finger into her mouth. After rolling her tongue over it for several long passes, her hand began its journey, gliding over her navel.

She delicately brushed the exposed flesh above her waist with her nails, teasing herself in anticipation of that single moistened finger. It gently eased between waiting lips. She quivered at her own touch.

She began slowly, making delicate circles at first. She took joy in imagining Dylla watching and listening from the firepit as the soft moans of pleasure surged to a crescendo the faster and faster her hand moved. The skin along her throat stretched as her head tipped back and her eyes rolled into her head. The first wave of sensuous pleasure washed over her. Her entire body shuddered. With the specter of Dylla as an audience of one, her performance was far from over. The intensity grew with each climax Neladith drove herself to, knowing Dylla was dead and forced to watch. Once satiated at the nexus of carnal release and the shadow of death, Neladith pulled up her pants, left them unbuttoned, and drifted off into a carefree, peaceful sleep.

She dreamt of fucking Mithany.

She dreamt of killing Quith.

Nocturnal Symphony

Hensdale: 14th Day of the Harvest Moon

Mithany

While seated in Reyne's favorite rocker on his front porch, with Arek in Daedyn's old chair next to her, Mithany counted the number of cricket chirps over a fourteen-second window. "Three chirps," she told Arek as the siblings looked out over the orchard's remains. Hours earlier, the sun had dipped below the horizon and cool evening claimed the night.

Again, she counted, "One..."

"... Two..."

"... Three..."

"Yep, three chirps. That means it's forty-three degrees. Sun's gone; it'll be getting even colder."

"Sis, how can you make out just three? There's hundreds of them little buggers sounding off, and the frogs haven't shut up either. I'm amazed there's that many critters left after the fire."

"I focus on the loudest cricket. It's probably under the deck just below us. Reyne and I love to sit here enjoying the nocturnal symphony, just the two of us. I miss him so much, Arek."

Arek reached for her hand, "I know, Sis. We all miss him... Daedyn and Doc Brenal, too."

Her chest rose and fell as a pang of sorrow drifted out in her words. "Don't ever leave me."

"Cheer up, Sis. I'd never do that. I'll always be at your side."

With a gentle squeeze of her hand on his, in a soft tone, she asked, "Stay with me tonight, please. I don't want to be alone."

Arek turned to look into her eyes, and with a familiar tenderness in his voice, he offered comfort. "Of course, Sis. Can never say 'no' to you."

"How did it all fall apart so fast, Arek? Me and Reyne were only days from gettin' married. Then, Mera showed up, and it all went to shit."

"I don't know, Sis. It's more like Neladith showed up and it all went to shit. She's the one who killed Daedyn, not Mera. He tried to warn us. We didn't listen. And Neladith tried to kill me, too. She almost did. The Doc died savin' me. If it wasn't for her leavin' me this way, that wonderful old man would still be alive. I miss him. Doc was a good friend."

A single tear dripped down her cheek as she grabbed Arek's arm. "I still have you."

"You'll always have me, Sis."

"I know at some point, you're goin' after Neladith. Don't go lettin' her finish the job once you find her," she pleaded with a jab at his bicep.

"I *will* find her, that I can promise you. But nothin's gonna happen to me, Sis."

"How did you or me ever let her get that close to us?"

"With me, it's easy to figure out. You know what I like." He sat back with both arms open wide. "She made it simple."

"Yeah, I know what you like all too well... brother," she laughed.

"Sis, don't feel bad that you and Neladith slept together. I know you just as well as you know me. You were hurtin' and needed Reyne. I see the guilt in your eyes, but don't do that to yourself. What Mother did to us, nobody could ever understand the consequences. You needed comfort and for better or worse, Neladith was the one you turned to before you knew what an evil bitch she is."

Rising from the rocker, Mithany moved to Arek's lap. She pulled her short legs off the floorboards, bent them at her knees, nestled them across his, and wrapped her arms around him.

In kind, Arek draped his arms around her petite frame and pulled her in tight. "Sis, I miss you sometimes."

With her head nestled in his chest, Mithany whispered, "I know. But I'm with Reyne now."

Arek confessed, "I'm just sorry I couldn't end Neladith's hold on us when I had that knife to her throat."

"I'm glad you couldn't take a life... even hers. That's just one of the many reasons why I love you."

Arek kissed the top of her head. "I love you too, Sis. Always will."

In comfort and silence, the siblings didn't move or speak for several minutes. They didn't need to.

A question crossed her mind interrupting the cuddle they shared; lifting her head from his chest, Mithany started to ask, "Arek, why did you—"

In a soft tone, he cut her off, "I didn't want to." Several heartbeats later, he continued. "She had me tied to a chair and stripped naked. Didn't have many options. Had to give you time to get out of Hensdale, where Neladith couldn't find you. Every minute I kept her in that basement, I did for you. Protecting my little sister is more important to me than lettin' that woman have her way with me, as much as I hated her at that moment."

With her head once again on his chest, Mithany took comfort in listening to Arek's heartbeat.

As they sat quietly entangled, like when they were children huddled together, hiding from the wrath of their mother, Mithany felt she owed Arek an explanation. "In Reyne's bed with me... I knew it was Neladith. It's just that when we were doin' it, every second her body and mine were intertwined, when her lips touched my lips, when her hand caressed my breasts, I imagined Reyne's lips, Reyne's hands, and that he was the one there with me. I know it sounds stupid, and it's no excuse."

"You don't have to explain yourself to me. We're both broken... Thanks, Mom."

"One thing does worry me, though. Spetzer walked in on me and Neladith rolling around in the bed. Neladith threatened to kill him if he said anything. She's gone, and I'm glad she is, except I don't trust him to keep quiet about it."

Arek pulled Mithany's compact frame in tight and rested his head on hers. "Sis, I'll always protect you. Leave that annoying prick Spetzer to me."

In silence, the siblings returned to their shared contemplations as the nocturnal symphony played on into the night.

Delays, Delays, Delays

The Woodlands: 14th Day of the Harvest Moon

Mera

Night settled in as Mera trekked through The Woodlands to meet up with Dylla's remains.

Never seen, only heard, Mera guessed hell hounds were tracking him based on the faint intermittent sounds moving in unison with him, always coming from off in the distance. Deer, elk, and other cervine were certainly large enough to make similar noises brushing against the forest clutter or crunching twigs and leaves underfoot. Though all were clumsy in their passage through the woodland and never took intentional steps to hide their approach. Wolves and bears also fit the bill, yet none had been seen in The Woodlands for decades. And then there was Quith to consider as the progenitor of the acoustic warning signs.

How Quith knew of the Soul Stone, Mera could only guess. Nonetheless, Quith had knowledge of it and that created an enormous problem for Mera. An extra modicum of caution came into play with every decision and every action Mera considered, forcing him to always be on the lookout for Quith lurking somewhere in the shadows, ready to strike. A part of Mera hoped it was Quith. A pack of hellhounds presented a much greater danger.

As skilled as Quith proved to be over the years, in the light of day, Mera would have spotted him making his way through the forest thicket. Mera pushed hard from the moment he woke, intent on making up time for the short delays Dylla's bones would cost him.

Just keeping up with the pace Mera set would have exposed Quith or anyone else.

After much consideration, discounting Quith as the source, Mera concluded it had to be hellhounds. The vicious four-legged beasts, twice the size of the largest dog, usually hunted in packs of three or more. And if these were hellhounds on his scent, this pack was skilled at stealth beyond any he'd previously encountered. Villages like those of Owls Neck and Hensdale vigilantly kept tabs on the carnivores' whereabouts, killing any that ventured too close to town. Of all the critters large and small in the wilds, hellhounds feared only one creature other than man: the Great Yetgnal. And it was debatable just how much hellhounds feared men.

Hellhounds had the reputation for being cunning, fast, smart, and deadly... yet so was Mera. Although confident he could handle the one-off predator, any more than that, he was in trouble. The Soul Stone would be useless if he was torn limb from limb. The occasional rustling that reached Mera's ears put him on guard to expect an attack.

I don't have time for this.

Topak's fallen.

Teth's fallen.

Events are moving too fast.

Mera feared these delays brought Tartica that much closer to ruination.

The frequent stops he made throughout the day each time he heard something caused him to fall further and further behind. A familiar outcropping he planned to reach before dusk was still two miles away, and night had already settled in. Hellhounds proved formidable in the light of day. They were deadly and unstoppable in the dark.

Crunch.

Mera froze. *That's too close.*

Mera rarely knew fear. The prospect of hellhounds thirty feet away quickly reacquainted him with it.

Slowly, he turned his head.

"Who the fuck are you?"

Lost Opportunity Costs

Derr

Druin Derr sat in Chamette's office with his hands folded in his lap. "Chamette, I've had guildins in large denominations delivered to your main bank this morning. Twenty million in total."

Ja'Rou Chamette, the de facto leader of the loose confederation of Adelle's wealthy elites known as the Hidden Hand, replied, "Yes. I've been informed by my staff. Thank you."

With the infusion of coin delivered into Chamette's hands, Derr hoped to further his plan to convert the Hidden Hand's previous opposition to the Covenant's demise to that of a partner of Tomelai in seeing it purged from Adelle's societal precept.

"Five million to cover your initial expenses, getting electrics moving forward, and eight million for construction of the barracks, the armories, the uniforms, weapons, and all the rest. I'm told production is moving ahead, and you are on target to deliver a large cache of uniforms and weapons soon."

Chamette quipped, "Very generous of Tomelai, or was it all your doing?"

"As far as you're concerned, we're one and the same. Tomelai's Exchequer tells me your total costs amount to no more than thirteen million. That's twenty million in payment for what cost you thirteen."

Chamette nodded. "Like I said, very generous."

"Keep four for yourself and that leaves three million for you to divvy out to the rest of the piranha. Not everyone of the Hidden Hand is in line yet. I read the Tandure Messenger this morning and didn't care for the news coverage. Tomelai would like to keep the façade of a free press. We both know reporting the news has become weaponized of late. Right now, it's a weapon in the wrong hands and pointed at the wrong target. I could intervene directly, although my preference is to have the people involved believe it's of their own doing... or yours. Folks seem to accept corruption from within more so than from official government sources."

"Settle down, Captain. With the coin you deposited, I'll have it pumping out anti-Covenant drivel starting tomorrow."

"Ja'Rou, you disappoint me. I expected you to handle it before you gained access to my coin."

"I understand what you're saying. Please consider all I've had to lay out for building and material costs you just reimbursed me for. You had my finances stretched thin."

"Come now Ja'Rou, we both know that isn't true. You own several banks in the wealthiest city across all Tartica, for fuck's sake. And what I don't understand is why you're spending so much coin in Teth. Hear this. I don't give a fuck about Teth. You're a smart man. You know the game and you know the consequence of failure. Stay focused on Adelle and I'll see to it you'll receive more than enough coin to cover your lost opportunity costs in Teth."

The uber-wealthy sixty-five-year-old Chamette added, "One more thing. There's do-gooders on the paper's staff who adamantly support the Covenant and what it stands for."

Derr asked, "So what? Get them in line or have your contacts stick them on the local beats. Is this something I have to tell you? Do I have the wrong man for the job?"

"No. You're right. My apologies. I've been juggling a lot, but that's no excuse."

Derr moved his hands to the arms of the chair, pushed off, and stood. "Good. Don't make me come to you again. Anticipate and handle it. Oh, and there's thirty-two daily or weekly newspapers published in Adelle. Tomelai's staff gets every one of them. Get them all in line. I'll also expect an update from your people on electrics next week. Have the plan outlined for Tomelai staff to approve by then."

After leaving Chamette Mansion, autumn nipped at Derr's hands as he made his way to visit with Loseff Tomelai to review the status of recruitment efforts and developments in military training of those already enlisted. Rain threatened overhead and Derr considered, *Good. Military drills in the wet mud should help them prepare for one more obstacle. Better they face it now than for the first time in battle.*

Derr's coach rolled up on an open field where dozens of units, twenty soldiers in each, engaged in exercises under the leadership of their respective drill instructors. General Loseff Tomelai stood atop a platform from which to review the collective efforts of his Division. His adjutant, Lieutenant Verek Jaynes, a long-time friend of the newly minted general, stood at Loseff's side as Derr approached.

Raindrops, gentle at first, touched Derr's face as he walked up the stairs of the platform. By the time he reached the last step, the sky opened and unleashed a torrent. Derr paid it no mind as though it did not differ from a bright, sunny day. One foot breached the stage and Lieutenant Jaynes snapped to attention. His hand swung upward from his side. Before he could complete the military acknowledgement, Derr cut him off.

"Put your arm down, Jaynes. I'm not a soldier."

Jaynes, in quick, halted military speak, stated, "Captain Derr. Sir. Yes, sir." Jaynes was shaking.

Derr knew it wasn't from the cold, wet downpour. "Again, not needed, Jaynes."

Jaynes's lips parted. Derr expected another annoying reply. Before any words left Jaynes's mouth, Derr raised a finger to his own lips. "Shhh."

Rain pelted the trio, and water washed over the entire camp. The sound of drops pounding every surface drowned out all other sounds trying to reach up from below.

General Loseff laughed at his friend's awkward response to Derr. In a loud voice, he half-yelled, "Jaynes, can you run down and ask the Sergeant to push his troops through the obstacle course? Let's get them down in the mud. Make them taste it. When he's done, get the other sergeants to send their units through."

Jaynes snapped a salute and shouted back, "Sir, roger that!" Eager to impress, the young lieutenant sped off. Derr suspected Jaynes's reply was for his benefit more than Loseff's.

With the heavy rain continuing to batter the review stand and the two men who remained perched atop it, Loseff, now soaked to the bone, said, "What can I do for you, Derr?" He, like Derr, appeared to ignore Nature's outpouring.

Cold air and wet clothes would have made the average Tandure citizen run for the warmth of the indoors. Not Derr. He wondered if Loseff was putting on a show for him, stoic against the wind, the cold, the rain, or if the young man had more to him than these past nineteen years of pampering delivered. For Loseff's father's sake, for Adelle's sake, Derr hoped so.

Raising his voice over the chorus of falling water, Derr said, "Nothing. I want nothing from you other than for you to exceed your father's expectations. Just meeting them won't do."

Loseff smirked through the deluge as though it affected him little, yelling in reply, "Not to worry, Derr. My plans take me well beyond what Mother and Father think me capable of."

Derr watched. He was always watching. Dark sky, cascading rain, and Loseff's evil grin set off his mental early warning bells. "Care to elaborate, young Loseff?" Derr left 'general' out of his reply to probe just how full of himself Loseff Tomelai had become. Loseff's lip curled at one end, and water ran down over his smirk.

Derr caught the amusement on his face. *You figured that out pretty quick. Smarter than he lets on. Good.*

Bellowing in return through the din of pounding rain, Loseff replied, "Right now, I'm just one general on my father's senior staff. Before this is all over, he's going to put me in charge of the entire war effort. I'm going to not only show Father what I am capable of, I will prove to him I am worthy of his respect as his top military officer. Is that what you want to hear, Derr?"

Derr bypassed Loseff's query. "If it's true." Derr believed Loseff desired to ascend above the others, yet remained unresolved whether Loseff's words matched his intentions. "How're your studies going?"

"How did you three keep that library from me all these years? I'm impressed. I've been digging through some of the books you and Father recommended. Some of the great generals have been fascinating reading: Grant, Napoleon, and I love Alexander the Great's story. Still haven't found the one by Sun Tzu. Came across one book that's quite interesting. We can discuss it another time."

Derr asked, "And what have you taken away from your studies?"

"Logistics, terrain, supply chains, and so many little things add up to victory beyond battle strategy. It's not just slugging it out with the enemy."

Derr probed deeper, wanting to understand Loseff's level of comprehension. "Is that all?"

"No. More than anything, the great ones have a connection with their soldiers. And, as complicated as war might seem, at the heart of it, it can be simple yet brutal in its execution. I have a long way to go. Even so, I'm years ahead of the other mopes Father appointed as my fellow generals. You may want to get copies made of books on strategy for my fellow commanders and their staff personnel to read."

The downpour continued its relentless attack. It failed to hold sway over either man. Derr replied, "It's already in the works. Although I appreciate the suggestion. Changing subjects. How long before they're ready?" Derr nodded to the field below.

"Couple of months for my division. The others are on a similar schedule. However... Father has underestimated how many we'll need. Some of these soldiers are going to die. And, we are going to be spread out too thin when they do. Tartica's a big continent. I've told him that already. Maybe he'll listen to you. Tell him to double the recruiting target to twenty thousand."

"Twenty thousand? Based on what?"

"What do any of us have to go on? The last war? There's never been one. Best guess."

Derr was pleased with Loseff's change in attitude and respected the boy's command of the material he'd been asked to read. General Loseff Tomelai exhibited signs of leadership as Derr assessed it and planned to report back to the Chancellor the positive developments. However, his earlier performance during the meeting at command headquarters left Derr unsure of the young man's true intentions. Derr replied to Loseff, "I'll talk with him."

"Good. Now, if you don't have anything else and this evaluation is over, I've got soldiers to train."

Derr took no offense at Loseff's dismissive words, just the opposite. It pleased him to see Tomelai's son coming into his own. "Might I offer a suggestion, General?" Through the windswept rain splattering across his face, Derr nodded towards the field below. "You want them to connect, to respect you, get down there with them."

"I was just thinking the same thing." Loseff moved off towards the stairs. "Give my Father an excellent report." He laughed and sped down the stairway.

Derr remained on the reviewing stand for several minutes. Long enough to watch General Loseff Tomelai attack the obstacle course with the same vigor he expected of his soldiers. Impervious to the pounding rain, Derr watched and wondered, *Too good to be true? What's going on in that head of yours, young Loseff?*

Never to be Spoken Again

Black Haven

Reyne

Reyne stood transfixed by the ebony fire flickering in the pit. Eerie in its deep purple, almost black flames, it threw off little light, yet it bathed Reyne in a familiar warmth. The men and women of Red's tribe, along with Reyne and Gina, all came together in a circle around the firepit at Red's request.

War was coming to Black Haven—at least their little slice of it.

While Red scanned everyone's faces, within the limits of Reyne's Tartican sight afforded him, he kept attuned for any sudden movements. The people of Red's tribe saved his life. That didn't mean he trusted any of them. One woman in particular, whose ribs he'd broken when six of Red's tribesmen attacked him and Gina days earlier, brandished harsh eyes at him from the moment he joined the circle. Gina had her own stalker, if Reyne read the man's evil glare correctly.

An elbow jolt from Gina into Reyne's side pulled his thoughts back to the present. She whispered, "That guy's eyeballin' me. I think he's the one who tried to rape me. If only I could access my Third Eye, he'd be dead where he stands."

"Enough already," Red ordered. "Everyone here's gotta put it behind them." With both arms held out in front she motioned up and down for everyone to sit.

Reyne lowered his butt, yet wasn't sure who Red aimed her comments at: him, Gina, Miss Broken-Ribs, or Mister Would-Be-Rapist. While Reyne silently mulled it over, Gina couldn't hold back. "Easy for you to say, Red. That motherfucker right there"—she pointed at Would-Be-Rapist—"I'm gonna kill him."

The accused man's non-verbal reply appeared to taunt Gina with his wide grin and juddering eyebrows.

Gina shot up from her mushroom stump of a seat. Reyne grabbed hold of her wrist in an iron grip.

Red snapped, "Sit down!"

Acquiescence wasn't in Gina's nature. She remained standing and demanded, "That asshole tried to stick his dick in me. You serve up justice in Black Haven… huh, Red?"

"Yeah, we do, but he also saved your life back there at the compound. And what, you think you're the only one? Every woman in this circle, and a few of the men, have either lost that same battle to some scumbag from one tribe or another. Myself included. Or, like you, got lucky and fought them off. It's wrong. It's always wrong. Here, or on Tartica. But here, there ain't no one to stop it. Let it go."

Gina didn't follow Red's suggestion. "Doesn't make it right. Something's gotta be done."

Red hung her head and huffed. After picking it back up, she offered Gina a sympathetic reply. "Listen to me. You're far away from Tartican justice. Life's a struggle every day here. In a perfect world, I'd cut his balls off for what he tried to do to you. Truth is, we need him. Those people back at the compound will be coming for us. Saving your boyfriend put my tribe in the crosshairs of some mean motherfuckers. So, I'm sorry. My man keeps his balls."

Reyne protested. "She ain't my girlfriend and you weren't just savin' me. You sent me in there as bait. You did it for yourself. Said you needed to get him out of the way so you could be free of him. Let's be clear."

Gina, ignoring Reyne, glared at Red and demanded, "Empty words. Tell me something, Red, what did you do? You just live with it?"

"Nope. I tracked him down. Cut his dick and balls into a hundred little chunks over the course of two days. Did it slow. Took my time. Piece by piece. Them two wrinkly flesh bags bleed more than you'd think. I kept him alive in agony as long as I could. He screamed a lot. I *made* him suffer."

"What's good for you ain't for me?" Gina protested.

"I can't give you that same justice as much as I'd like to. I need everyone in my tribe to keep all of us alive with the shit storm that's coming. I wish it were different. It ain't. So, stop your pansy-ass whining and shut the fuck up about it."

Gina opened her mouth to continue pushing. Red erupted, "Enough! Say another word about it and I'll have you both tied to the stake again. Now shut the fuck up."

Reyne reached across with a consoling hand on Gina's. She slapped it away.

Leaning in for only Gina to hear, Reyne whispered, "Red ain't goin' for it. You and me can take care of him in our own time."

The two Tarticans locked eyes. Anger poured out of Gina's. As seconds passed, hatred gave way, and she nodded in agreement. Red was saying something. Reyne wasn't listening. Friendship required his full attention on Gina. Her needs far exceeded Red's ramblings about tribal business.

A grin from Reyne, as if to say, "Okay, we have a plan then," offered Gina an unspoken pact between them: Mister Would-Be-Rapist will pay for what he did... just not today.

Reyne turned his attention back to Red, who was finishing her thoughts to the gathered, and he heard her say, "... and what, make a run for it?"

The native Black Haveners all said their peace. Names were used, but Reyne cared nothing for remembering any. An older guy stated, "These are our ancestral lands. Gonna be awful hard to find another place like this that some other tribe ain't claimed."

Still another replied, "Ain't worth shit if we're all dead."

Broken-Ribs added her thoughts. "We been in scrapes before and pulled through. Thinkin' we can again. Besides, if we run, gotta cut through other tribal lands. That never goes well."

Gina cupped her hand to Reyne's ear. "I'm gonna kill that bastard. Red can't save him forever."

Reyne whispered in return. "Yeah, but look at who they're all speakin' to. Every word's directed at Red. She runs this shit show."

"You two," Red interrupted. "This involves you as well, so listen up."

Thwack.

Every head snapped towards the sound. An arrow buried itself into the woman Reyne knew as Broken-Ribs. She slumped forward and died without making a peep.

Red shouted a blood-curdling command. "AW! AW! AW!"

Her clan sprang into action.

Thwack.

Another tribesman hit. He fell back. Dead.

Arrows flew all around. Reyne dove behind the protection of a mushroom log doubling as amphitheater seating. H reached up and pulled Gina down with him. He lost sight of the attackers from behind his former seat. With their heads only inches apart, Reyne demanded, "Gina, try it again. Do your fastest-human-alive thing."

A second later, "Nothing. I got nothing. It's gone."

Fwop. Fwop.

Arrows flew overhead.

Reyne spotted Red reach for her bow. Then she bolted for cover. Red crouched. Zigging left. Zagging right. She took up behind a giant mushroom stalk.

The man identified as Mister Would-be-Rapist rolled, swept up a macahuitl, and rushed at a woman reaching into her quiver. His wooden club embedded with razor-sharp obsidian crystals came down hard. The blow ripped into her shoulder. Blood spattered. The woman screamed. Her arm hung barely connected to her body. Blood slapped her face and flooded down her torso.

Reyne whipped his head around back to Gina. She was gone.

I got no weapon. Can't see shit in the dark. Can't tell anyone apart. Fuck! What do I do?

Then he saw Red.

She dropped two opponents before he blinked.

Arrow after arrow flew from Red's position.

She nocked and released. Nocked and released. One after another.

Red appeared as a rapid-fire arrow machine.

Hitting attackers to her left.

Attackers to her right.

Then back to her left.

Each shot deadly.

Arrows flew from her like nothing Reyne had ever witnessed.

Rapid footsteps drew close. Reyne turned. Looked up. A man jumped over the stump protecting Reyne. In flight, the attacker turned mid-jump. Pulled back his bow. Floating overhead, in mid-air he pointed it at Reyne's chest. Reyne called out. He covered his head and shouted, "No!"

Would-Be-Rapist slammed into the man above Reyne. The attacker's arrow released wildly into the air. Would-Be-Rapist rolled. Jumped to his feet. Then whipped his macahuitl into the guy's neck. Blood gushed out.

Thwack. Would-Be yelled out, "Fuck! I'm hit!"

Reyne looked up to see an arrow sticking out of Would-Be's thigh.

Coming from behind a yurt, Gina exploded through the darkness. She sprinted straight for Would-Be with a knife in her hand. From behind Gina's running form, Reyne caught sight of Red. She followed Gina with her eyes.

Red raised her bow.

Aimed it at Gina.

Reyne sprang up.

He raced toward Gina.

He drove his shoulder into her side.

The two tumbled forward.

Their bodies rolled. Arms entwined. Legs entangled.

Their bodies slammed into a stump. Reyne's massive size pinned Gina under him. She shoved frantically to free herself. Wildly, she punched at Reyne, screaming, "Get off me!"

Reyne picked his head up. Lifted his eyes to Red. She nodded approval and quickly turned away. In one smooth motion, Red aimed and released an arrow at still another attacker.

Thwack. It landed. The attacker kept coming. *Thwack,* another. The attacker stumbled forward and still kept coming. *Thwack. Thwack. Thwack.* Red's skills were deadly. The attacker dropped. He never had a chance.

Three short blasts, *Fweet, fweet, fweet* rang out. The attackers responded. The camp emptied quickly of enemy combatants. Except for the scattered dead bodies left behind.

Red gave out another call, "Macaw. Macaw."

Would-Be snapped off the bolt sticking out his thigh and threw it to the side. Limping, he sped into the darkness. A small girl, no more than ten, came racing out of the gray veil from the edge of the camp. The child bore an evil grin beyond her years, held a hunting blade at her side, and was covered in blood. She scampered up to Red, who patted the girl on the head. "Well done, Sissy."

"Macaw. Macaw," Red yelled out.

They waited.

"Whoop. Whoop," came the reply.

Silence filled the pause.

"Whoop. Whoop." In another voice.

And then a third, "Whoop. Whoop."

"Alright," Red shouted. "All's clear."

Red's fellow tribe's folk flittered in one-by-one back around the black-flame firepit.

Along with the last of the stragglers, Would-Be hobbled in.

Bent over while brushing herself off, Gina lifted her head and glared at him. Upon standing, she slammed both open palms into Reyne's chest, knocking him over. He hit the ground. A second later, she thumped her boot onto his chest. "Why'd you stop me, asshole?"

Reyne saw hatred in her eyes. He grabbed her calf and shoved her foot away. "Don't be a jerk. Red had you lined up and would have killed you before you reached him."

She stuck out her hand to pull him up. "Fine."

"How about, thank you?"

Gina said nothing.

Reyne brushed himself off.

With a quick nod, a wink, and wide grin from Red, he'd not only saved Gina's life, he'd gained a small measure of trust from Red.

Red turned from side to side, assessing the damage, and asked, "How many?"

They looked around at each other. An older woman spoke up. "Looks like we got seven of them. They got two of ours and four others got injured. I'll get them patched up."

Red addressed her people. "Don't gotta say who. The dead ain't here at this gathering. Their names are never to be spoken again. We'll send them off proper... later." She paused. "Listen to me. All of you. This was an in-and-out operation. They aimed to pick off a few of us and get out quick. We got more of them than they expected. I've done this same thing for the Devil's Hammer. I know what they're up to. We can't stay here. They'll keep coming. They'll kill us two and three at a time until none of us are left. No more discussion. Everyone, pack up. We're leaving."

The tribe dispersed. Reyne leaned close to Red. "Is all this worth it? How many people gotta die so you can go live on Tartica?"

"Fuck off."

A Foundation of Lies

Tandure: 15th Day of the Harvest Moon

Loseff

Loseff sat back in a chair near the window of his bedroom. *Dawn of the Third Age*, the book supposedly written over fifteen centuries ago by Albert "Mera" Meratoruc, rested in his lap. To Loseff, the author had been lost to history.

The manuscript's physical condition gave rise to support its alleged date of origin. Loseff decided he'd accept its claim on antiquity for now. Believing in its contents, however, would require deeper introspection. It gnawed at him to think the foundation of Tartican civilization was built on a lie. The truth it revealed fed into his lifelong resentment at being the spare to his sister's birthright claim on Adelle's chancellorship. Bitter at his second-class station, Loseff saw the world through resentment-colored glasses. Yet, his recent elevation to General not only gave him purpose beyond that of an understudy, it also offered him a reason to believe he mattered. And now, *Dawn of the Third Age* threatened to rip even that from him.

With fascination and anger rolling around in his head, Loseff was eager to read on hoping to find answers. Although references to radios and television were foreign to him, from the context Loseff gathered their purpose, along with an appreciation for how much more advanced the Second Age was compared to the common understanding of it the Third Age presumed. He opened the book to the next chapter... and started to read:

Dawn of the Third Age
Chapter: McMurdo Station
March 28, 2089

The FoxCNN twenty-four-hour news channel played nonstop in the dormitories, administrative buildings, the Berg Field Center, and the Albert P. Crary Science Engineering Center from the moment word reached the Americans at McMurdo Station on Antarctica that a space rock threatened all life on Earth. McMurdo's residents monitored the news in the billion-to-one chance of hearing an announcement that the asteroid's path had been recalculated to miss Earth. That is… until every news organization, commercial radio, television station, internet streaming service, or satellite feed went silent within days of the proclamation of Earth's imminent doom. Whether destroyed by rioters, abandoned by staff, or cut off from the resources to broadcast, the electronic feeds that kept everyone across the globe connected failed.

Chaos had its grip on humanity.

The cause of the news blackout mattered little to the information-starved population of Antarctica's nineteen research outposts. Yet one source did survive. Shortwave radio signals bouncing off the Earth's ionosphere, called skywaves or skip propagation, kept the McMurdo Station inhabitants informed after all other communications ceased to function. Ham radio operators from the ranks of the doomsday-prepper-survivalist population hunkered down in below-ground bunkers and fed the world a stream of unreliable news. In normal times, it would have been judged worthless by fact-based sourcing standards. These weren't normal times. The few ham radios available to McMurdo's residents were monitored for the infrequent radio signal able to cut through Antarctica's brutal weather.

As daylight streamed across the largest research outpost on Antarctica, a familiar electronic squeal broke McMurdo Station Building 203A's solitude. It was late March and McMurdo's residents enjoyed eleven hours and forty-two minutes a day of sunlight. By April 11, 2089, only twenty days away, the sun would dip below the horizon and not rise again over Antarctica for another five months. Not that anyone expected to be alive to greet the Antarctic September dawn.

In the empty common area, sitting alone on a shelf, the radio spat out, *Crackle… crackle…* "This is Iceberg calling Snow Queen. Come in, Snow Queen. This is Iceberg. Snow Queen, come in. Over."

Thirty-three-year-old Beth Green showered and was dressing in her small dorm room when the shout-out to Snow Queen reached her ears. In the summer months, there were as many as four to a room. It was now March, and most of the staff had fled the promise of another harsh winter when temperatures could reach 90 degrees below zero. The others from Building 203A who'd stayed behind to brave the winter were off commiserating at the Coffee House, leaving Beth to monitor incoming news.

Antarctica offered two seasons: summer and winter. Summer limped in from October to February, and winter claimed the rest. So, when the dark-haired, blue-eyed Beth sped into the common area sporting only a bra and panties, there wasn't anyone to judge her. Not that it would have bothered her much if they had. Communal living through the many tours she'd spent at McMurdo Station stripped her of all polite societal rules or decorum when it came to covering up the human body, hers or anyone else's. Besides, she wasn't shy about her body, proud in fact of the results her daily workouts contributed to the gifts she had been born with—from her mother's side of the family.

Amongst McMurdo's residents, Beth was not alone in her nonconformist attitude. It was embedded in daily life. As a matter of policy, condoms were provided freely throughout the complex. Like candy dishes offering sweets to eager children, bowls of prophylactics were placed in bathrooms, on open counters, and every red-blooded enthusiast had one at the ready just in case his or her similarly minded red-blooded partner failed to carry one of their own. The precautionary distribution of birth control proved a necessity, given the lack of pregnancy-specific medical services available in the ice world environs of Antarctica.

Most at McMurdo were dedicated scientists, as were they young, adventurous, and horny. With a ratio of almost three men for every woman, it was a Sadie Hawkins wet dream. Even though every scientist was expected to work fifty-four hours, six days a week, that still left another one hundred fourteen hours every week, week after week, over the eight dreary, lightless months of winter with nothing much to do except sleep, read, and fornicate. And you can only read so much before your eyes get blurry.

In the Bohemian, carefree, hard-working, hard-playing, self-contained world where Beth met her husband several years earlier: a tall, dark-haired geoscientist from Sweden working on the American team at McMurdo. Janek, otherwise known by the call sign Iceberg.

The radio transceiver belched as she ran to grab the mic before the caller abandoned his efforts. "Snow Queen, are you there? Pick up. Over."

Beth attempted to slide into place as she raced to the radio, but her bare feet grabbed the surface of the flooring, and she tumbled forward.

The caller had given up on radio protocols. "Beth. Do you copy? Over."

With nothing injured except her pride, she popped up quickly. In a smooth sweeping motion, she snatched the mic from the hook and frantically squeezed the call button. "This is Snow Queen. Affirmative. Janek, is that you? Over."

"Affirmative. Oh, thank God. It is so nice to hear your voice. Over."

The front panel of the black box streaming Janek's voice could have as easily been his face, if measured by the love in Beth's powder blue eyes. She stared lovingly at it as he spoke. "Roger that. I'm here, my love. Miss you so much. Over."

Playfully, he asked, "Are you being good? Over."

An unidentified voice broke in, "Hey Snow Queen, what's your twenty? I'm being good. I miss you too. Over." Interrupting a private conversation was normally off-limits. Much like the rest of civilized norms, the world of ham radio had become a free-for-all.

Janek, call sign, Iceberg, broke in, "Hey pal, what's your call sign? And can you cut us some slack? Listen in if you like, but please give us the room. Over."

Silence.

Beth continued. "Janek, you've only been gone a few weeks. Besides, you're the one who had to go back. Over."

She heard the sadness come through the speaker. "I'm sorry, my dear. Seemed the right decision at the time. If this asteroid strike really happens, we might never see each other again. I can't accept that. Over."

Another anonymous operator added her own thoughts: "Hey, Snow Queen, you sound sexy. I would've never left you. Over."

Janek added, "Honey, ignore them all. It's just you and me. Over."

A third undesignated voice added, "Affirmative. And me. It's just the three of us. Wouldn't that be nice? Over."

Beth pleaded into the mic, "Is there any news? Has anything changed? Over."

Janek reported, "Radio operators are all over the dial, but nobody really knows anything. A few claim to be astronomers, but they're the most pessimistic about our chances. Over."

A fourth voice objected. "This is Jupiter Six and fuck you, Iceberg. I'm an astronomer and we're just calling it like it is. Asteroid TQ-680 is gonna hit. We're all fucked. Over."

Beth forced herself to change the subject. "Janek, it's a shame the video feeds no longer work. You'd like what I'm not wearing. Over." Nevertheless, her heart sank as she released the call button.

Janek asked, "Roger that. My favorite outfit? Over."

"Negative. I still have on a bra and panties. Over."

The original intruder returned to the mic. "Roger that big time. Bra and panties are good enough for me, Snow Queen. Over."

Janek ignored them all, telling Beth, "Be still my heart. That's it, I'm coming to you. Over."

An unfamiliar voice piled on. "Thor's Hammer here. Hey Snow Queen, I'm coming too. What's your twenty? Over."

Janek protested. "Negative, Thor's Hammer. What happened to decorum and protocols? Over."

A fifth voice stated, "Buddy, there ain't no rules no more. All of us have only weeks left to live. You want privacy, get a room. Oh, yeah, over."

Beth said, "Janek, my dear, there's nothing in the world I'd like more. It's just that you can't make it through the Drake Passage this time of year. I know you too well. That's why you called. You've already decided, haven't you? Over."

"Thor's Hammer here. The Drake Passage, fuck that. Bra and panties sound nice, just the same. Not worth dying a few weeks before everyone else. You're on your own, Iceberg. I hope Snow Queen is worth it. Over."

Janek proclaimed for everyone on the band, "Affirmative. She is. Beth, I just wanted to let you know, I'll try to reach you by radio once I set out, although I'm not counting on it. The asteroid is due to hit north of the Russian land mass. And it's a monster. If they're right, you're exposed sitting along the coast of Antarctica. If the continent has any chance, you should be at Amundsen-Scott Station right in the middle, at the south pole. Can you get there? Over."

The radio crackled and hummed, absent human interference for almost a full minute.

After Snow Queen failed to reply, Janek added, "Do you copy? Over."

Beth said, "Affirmative, just thinking of what you said. Over."

"Roger that. Hägglunds might make it. It's going to be dangerous."

Beth pleaded, "How can you get here in time?"

"I'll find a way. I'd rather die trying to get to you than face dying without you. If it's a million to one, if you have any chance at all, the pole looks to be the best choice. Even if I fail, you'll have a chance. You've got to get to Amundsen. Over."

"Janek, I worry sunset at the pole already hit last week. Won't come up again until late September. That's going to be one rough winter with limited supplies. I also worry it's just too far. Not sure I can get to it in time. What do you think about the other two inland stations, Vostok or Concordia? Over."

"You're right, honey. In the snow crawlers, Vostok and Amundsen might be too far. I'd say Concordia Station is your best bet. When TQ-680 hits, it's going to generate massive tidal waves in every ocean that'll cover the entire planet. Every Antarctic station on the coast will get wiped away. High elevation inland is your only chance. It has to be one of the three. And Concordia is the closest. Over."

"Agreed. Plus, with the station's rebuild in the seventies, the new seed vault they built just might survive the impact. Over."

"Beth, you're right. As always, Concordia Station sounds like the right place to be. It will still have daylight for a few hours a day for another week or two, and it's over ten thousand feet above sea level. Over."

"What about you? You can't get there by boat and flying's dangerous. Over."

"Don't worry about me. I'll find you. Over."

Beth asked, "What if you can't? I don't want to go on… on a dead planet with little hope of surviving in the coldest, most inhospitable place on Earth

```
without you. To what end? Over."
  Janek's words came through in soft tones. "I
promise I'll find you. If anything of humanity
remains after April 19th, there is no one better, in
all the world, to seed its future than you... Over."
```

After closing the book, Loseff stared out his bedroom window. He contemplated the purpose of the author to write about these people. *Who's Beth Green? Never heard of her. And who's this Janek character? Is he important or just a name in a story?* Loseff wondered of what importance either held to Tartica in the Third Age. The author claimed Beth to be the unwitting founder of the Third Age, yet Loseff had never heard of her.

Knock, knock.

Annoyed at the interruption, Loseff yelled, "Come in."

A uniformed messenger popped her head through the door. "Sir, your father has requested your presence. He's expecting you in the War Council meeting room."

With a wave of his hand, Loseff attempted to dismiss the woman. "Tell him I'll be along in a little while."

Standing her ground, she added, "Please excuse me, General. I was instructed to make certain you attend to the Chancellor's request immediately. There's news of the United Front."

CONCORD CITY

BLACK HAVEN

Reyne

Reyne counted on Red's promise to meet up with a guy who'd instruct him how to get Gina hitched to his wagon through the Void. Gina had yet to agree to Red's terms for a romantic dalliance as the price for setting up the meeting, and that put getting off Black Haven in jeopardy. Although Reyne was pretty sure Gina would have no choice except to acquiesce in the end.

With the city just ahead, Reyne's thoughts of returning to Mithany tugged at his heart. Weighing on his mind, he wondered: *Did information reach this place about the attack at the Devil's Hammer's compound and the death of their benefactor at Red's hand? If it did, we're all screwed.* It was a risk, yet a risk Reyne had no choice but to accept. A yearning to escape Black Haven's persistent despair had its teeth into Reyne, yet he committed to remaining until he'd found a way to take Gina back to Tartica with him.

The closer Reyne got, Black Haven's gossamer veil gave up its ghosts. Silhouettes of huge structures reduced to rubble revealed themselves in small measures with each step forward. Reyne added up all the visible wreckage and considered the immensity of the structures before the demise that took them.

Through the ever-present darkness, Reyne spotted an inscription on the corner of one building rising out of the earth like an iceberg with part of it below ground. Embedded in a massive chunk of cement rubble, rising ten feet out of the ground at a forty-five-degree angle, the broken plaque read *CONCORD*.

Reyne ran his fingers over the *O-R-D* letters of the plate. The relief barely rose above the ancient metal surface, having been worn over time by weather and an untold number of others doing exactly what he'd just done. Only half the brass tablet survived, split diagonally below the letter *D*. What had been written on the missing piece would remain a mystery. It mattered little, however. Although several other words were still visible, they were in a language incomprehensible to the Tartican nut farmer.

He looked away and his eyes caught sight of Gina scaling one of the medium-sized, concrete moss-covered ruins. She cupped one hand over her brow and scanned the horizon—or at least as far as she could see into the ubiquitous gloom. She shouted, "Where is everyone, Red? Thought this place would be hopping. You said eight hundred lived here."

Curiosity got the better of Reyne. "Hey, Red, you know what this plaque says?"

Gina ignored Reyne. "I don't see anyone, Red. What's going on?"

Reyne ignored Gina. "Red, can you read this language?"

"Do you two ever shut up? Is this what I can expect on Tartica?" Red turned away from them both and kept walking, joined by Sissy and the others of her tribe.

Gina gave Red the finger behind her back.

Strewn across the landscape, dozens of similar broken cement slabs with corners at every conceivable angle poking out of the ground lay scattered and covered in green moss. Like children's wooden blocks thrown haphazardly across a room, the man-made boulders varied in size from that of a small dwelling to knee-high slabs. Each piece had been driven into the earth. Reyne struggled to locate the edge of the rubble field as Black Haven's ever-present obsidian-colored sky held back its secrets from his limited Tartican sight.

Four ghostlike, massive beams hovering at the corners of his perception rose out of the ground and dissipated from his sight as each pillar reached into the ebony heavens above. He'd adjusted to the darkness, although that didn't give him the same abilities as those born to Black Haven or the ability to see just how far into the coal-colored sky above the four spires stretched.

Red held up a closed fist. Everyone came to a stop. She turned, threw two small sacks at Reyne and Gina and announced, "Get to it, both of you. You want to eat, better start scraping moss off them rocks."

Reyne grimaced. "Ugh, really?"

Gina shrugged. "We ain't in Tartica anymore, farm boy. You heard the saying, *When in Teth*. Besides, if they eat this stuff, so can we. Beats going hungry." She searched for a hand-sized rock, picked it up, and started scraping off chunks of moss for her next meal. As she did, she pressed Red, "I thought you said there's a village here. What gives?"

"Not far. Took a detour so we could load up on these meadow muffins. Never know where your next meal's coming from. I could ask you the same thing. What gives? You haven't given me your answer yet. You know, the price you pay for me introducing you to the guy who can help you two get out of this realm."

"I'm still thinking. Maybe there's another way."

"You want to meet my guy? There ain't no other way. If you want off this world, not much to think about. And you're running out of time."

Focused on the revolting prospect of eating moss, Reyne paid little attention to the two women. He grabbed a handful and nibbled at the corner. "Phew. Ugh, this shit tastes awful." He filled his mouth with water from a canteen Red provided, swished it around, and quickly spit it out.

"Maybe they boil it or something," Gina suggested, then shouted over to Red. "Hey, how do you cook this stuff?"

Red turned around with a green clump hanging from her mouth. "Hum," she mumbled.

"Never mind."

Reyne slapped the top of his head. "This just keeps gettin' better and better."

Gina continued gathering, stuffing her sack. "Hey, Red."

Without turning around, Black Haven's version of Neladith replied. "You have my answer?"

"Forget that. I don't understand why we're doing this. You said Concord City folks grow their own food."

Red shot back, clearly annoyed, "Keep scraping. Never said they'd share it with you. Maybe they will. If not, you want to take that chance?"

Reyne lost sight of the other Black Haven natives, having ventured beyond his eyesight's thirty-foot limit. "Gina, can you make out where the others went off to? I'm worried they're up to somethin'."

"I can't see them either. I can see Red. She's right over there and I'm pretty sure she wants to keep me safe. Keep foraging." Stuffing moss into her bag, she joked, "Sack up has a whole new meaning in this place."

"We gotta get off this world. You think she's being honest? She gonna introduce us to her guy?"

"That's what she says."

"You gonna do it? You know, with Red? I don't see any way around it if we're gonna meet this mystery contact."

"It's not as though I'd object to hooking up with her. She's got a great rack. Nice ass. Just can't abide by the thought of being blackmailed into it." Gina stopped harvesting. "I don't think I ever said this, but thanks for not leaving me stranded. I know you could probably get back to Tartica without me."

Reyne studied a handful of the green plant that somehow thrived in Black Haven's lightless environment and jammed it into his collection sack. "I think about Mithany constantly... even so, no way I'm leaving you here alone. Wouldn't be right... You're welcome."

In between scraping, Reyne heard a call off in the distance.

Mawee. Mawee.

It didn't strike Reyne as any animal he'd heard before. His familiarity with Black Haven's wildlife left him uncertain. "Red, is that one of your folks?"

"Yep, we got company heading our way. Stop what you're doing. Get over here with me... both of you. Don't say a word. I'll do the talking."

The trio stood silent for a few dozen heartbeats, waiting. Reyne opened his mouth to ask Red who she expected. She shut him down. "Shhh."

Moments later, three pairs of tiny whitish-gray dots hung several feet above the ground and glided through the darkness, growing larger as they bobbed and swayed closer. A pair of light-reflecting silvery eyes stepped forward. Three bodies poured out from Black Haven's persistent midnight veil like specters in a dream coming into focus the closer they came. A thin man, young, about Reyne's height, with long, dark hair, emerged into Reyne's vision.

The stranger's voice gave off an air of confidence. "Neladith, you've been gone so long. Welcome home."

The man sounded friendly enough. He wondered if the welcoming party had received word of the attack on the Devil's Hammer. The woman he and Gina called Red, who the stranger knew by her proper Black Haven name, Neladith, made it clear this village thrived under the Devil's Hammer's protection.

There weren't any weapons that he could see, yet there could be dozens more Concordians off in the distance beyond the limits of his visual awareness. Reyne squeezed his fists hanging at his side. Gina grabbed his arm. She leaned in and whispered, "Careful."

Red smirked. "Thanks, Mahtoney. How've you been? What's new since I left?"

Smart girl, Red. Find out what he knows.

From the side of her mouth, Gina aimed her words for only Reyne to hear. "He's a big fella."

"Nothing ever changes around here," the Concord City escort told Red. "The council will be excited to hear what you've been up to." He stepped forward, wrapping Red in a welcoming hug. After stepping back, he continued, "I see you brought along a couple of unfamiliar faces. That's not like you... saving strays."

Red pulled Reyne by his arm, thrusting him forward for Mahtoney's inspection. "They ain't strays."

"He doesn't look harmless, and his eyes don't shimmer. He's a big one. That's going to put everyone on guard. Going to need approval. Can't just let these two roam free inside. You know the rules."

Red slapped her palms together. "Let's get to it then. Is the council available? I need to introduce these two and I got news they need to hear right away."

Mahtoney turned to his two companions. "You go ahead. Let the council know she's back. They'll want to meet with her as soon as she enters the city. I'll be along right behind you. Now go."

The two sprinted away without a word.

Mahtoney then turned to Red. "Since you're bringing these two in, got to ask you to turn over your weapons."

"Mahtoney, come on. You know me. I'd never harm nobody from Concord City."

"Maybe so. No choice, you know the rules. Can't let you inside if you're carrying."

Reyne listened intently for any change in demeanor, but the conversation sounded cordial enough.

"You know me well, so you know I don't need weapons. Trust me."

"Can't do it. Council would have my head. While I trust you, they don't trust anybody. Keep what you got until we get to the gate. It's the best I can do for a friend."

Although Reyne hadn't taken his eyes off Mahtoney, he had an eerie sense of unseen eyes bearing down on him. He shifted his gaze and found nothing save the ever-present gloom. He shook it off, turning his attention back on Gina. She looked as though she readied herself to strike.

Red angled her head back in Gina's direction while continuing her discussion with Mahtoney. "You have nothing to concern yourself about. Look at her. Who's she going to hurt?"

Reyne noticed Gina smirk. He guessed she enjoyed being underestimated. And he also noticed Red's fingers moving ever so subtly, as though flashing signals to her people. None of the tribe who'd made the journey emerged from the shadows to meet the greeting party from Concord City. Reyne had no doubt they observed the entire encounter.

What are you up to, Red?

Mahtoney patted Red on the shoulder. "That'll be for the council to decide, my dear. Dangerous things come in small packages. Shall we go?" He bowed in jest and swept one arm across the field of rubble.

After an approving nod in response to Mahtoney, Red waved her hand for Reyne and Gina to follow them.

As the last words escaped her mouth, "Lead the way, old friend," Red doubled over, spewing green vomit.

No Escape

Neladith

Back on Tartica, Evidar's version of Neladith considered her mission to track down and kill the Evidarian traitor, Selundra Quith, a vote of confidence in her abilities by none other than the Devil's Blacksmith himself, and an exciting source of recreation. She intended to extract as much pleasure from her time on Tartica as circumstances allowed without sacrificing her objective—*terminating that prick.*

Neladith didn't discount Quith's skills—she expected him to present quite a challenge—yet her high opinion of herself outweighed any doubt of the outcome. With the transfiguration from Evidar to Tartica behind her, the hunt was on.

A diversion to stop in and visit Mithany was off limits inasmuch as she did try to murder the girl's brother, her once-but-no-more fuckbuddy, Arek. Neladith figured it caused too wide a chasm for any reconciliation with Mithany. However, it didn't stop Neladith from longing to bed the petite woman one more time.

After leaving Dylla's charred skull in the dying embers of her campfire, Neladith traveled through the day and into the night. She followed the familiar road between Topak and Hensdale, careful to stay out of sight of the few others she encountered. With Teth her desired destination, the tantalizing village of Hensdale lay not far off the intended route.

The night air nipped at her wherever flesh remained uncovered and, to a lesser extent, through the tight-fitting leather journeyman's outfit she'd acquired. The extremely figure-hugging pants bit into her crotch and she wondered, *Hum, a quick, clandestine visit to Mithany's leather goods shoppe in Hensdale's market square for a better fitting outfit would solve this problem. Just gotta avoid anyone who'll recognize me. Shouldn't be too hard.*

Skipping along the roadway, Neladith delighted in the idea of killing Quith, at skirting danger by visiting Hensdale, and enjoying the peace alone in the dark of night.

Just like home, only better. What a great day this is turning out to be.

She continued through the night, lit up only by the stars, arriving in Hensdale just after dawn. As she approached, Neladith noted Hensdale's village square appeared empty. Autumn had progressed, and the trees had given up all except for a few stubborn leaves. She peered out from a thinly-covered row of trees. The stark skeleton Nature left behind at autumn's end provided little in the way of a hiding spot. Sunlight, the color of a glowing ember in a Tartican firepit, much different from those born in the black flames of Evidarian fire, danced across the barren treetops.

Before her experience in the lighted environs of Tartica, dawn had been a foreign concept. Though her time on Tartica was short, she'd come to appreciate the explosion of color at the start of each day, so much different from the gray world she called home.

A briefing by Dylla weeks ago rattled around in her head. *A rural farm community gets going at first light. I could break in before anyone arrives and steal what I need.* The idea died as soon as it sparked. *No. What fun would that be?*

After a short wait lying under a gathered pile of leaves, Neladith observed one shoppe, then another open for business. The leather goods store was one of the last to get going when an average-looking woman, not much older than Neladith herself, unlocked the door and hung a sign outside, *Open For Business.*

A scan of the market square found several people making their way to the local bakery. Once the few stragglers departed the outdoor open space to enter the bakeshop, Neladith, shaking off her makeshift camouflage of rotting leaves, sprinted for Mithany's store. The chance of getting caught titillated her.

The attendant was still setting up and surprised when Neladith burst through the door with a jingle from the bell hanging above.

As giddy as a schoolgirl, Neladith declared, "Well, hello there." She slapped her hands together and continued, "I need some new clothes. As you can see, these are a wee bit too small on me. So, what do you got?"

The woman stopped what she was doing and walked to Neladith. She put one hand over her chest. "I'm Ilyn. I can help you."

Ilyn's eyes swept over Neladith, as would be expected from any clothier sizing up a customer. She locked on Neladith's chest, spilling out of the undersized blouse and vest. Neladith followed Ilyn's line of sight as it moved to where the tight-fitting pant legs joined, and the pronounced outline left nothing to the imagination.

Still staring, Ilyn snickered. "I can see what you're saying. How did you ever end up in them?"

Neladith shook her head and with a smirk, replied, "You wouldn't believe me if I told you."

With a shrug, Ilyn pried her gaze away to look up at Neladith. "If you say so. You're the customer. What did you have in mind?"

"Ilyn. Before we do that, I'm wondering, will Mithany or Arek be coming by today? I'd so like to see them. I'm a friend. I only met them recently and really got to know them both... intimately."

"So sorry to tell you, I don't expect either of them today."

"That's disappointing. Oh well, can you give them a message from me?"

"Of course."

Tilting her head and smiling, Neladith asked, "Can you tell them the lady with the red eyes from the apple farm dropped in to say hi? I'm in town visiting my mom's cousins."

Ilyn's eyes popped wide, "Are they the apple farmers who went missing? Everyone is so worried. Talk is, Judjurex Tetrip found some dead guy in the house. Nobody knows who he is."

Neladith dropped her head. "Yes, they are. It's awful. That's why I'm here. I'm going on a search to find them and need to get outfitted. I won't stop until I find him."

"Him?"

Neladith shot back, "Them," followed by a quick change of subject. "Judjurex? That's an awful first name to give someone."

"You're not from around here, are you? Judjurex isn't his name, silly. It's his title. The guy who handles civil enforcement around here."

"Oh, that's right. I remember now. I'm such a scatterbrain sometimes." She twirled a strand of her long red hair in one finger. "Anyway, how about I try on a few things?"

Ilyn scanned Neladith again, stopping at all the familiar places, and said, "I have a few things in your size. Brown? Tan? Do you have a preference?"

"An outfit like I'm wearing in any color is fine. Oh, I'll need a jacket. A waistcoat preferably. I don't like the cold much."

A bell hanging above the jam clanged and the shoppe door opened. A woman stuck her head inside. "Hi, Y'Vay," Ilyn called out.

The young woman with cinnamon-blond hair gave Ilyn a warm smirk and asked, "Can you close up for lunch around noon instead of the usual?"

Eyeing the intruder up and down, Neladith thought, *She's a cute one.*

Ilyn replied, "Sure, unless it gets busy. See you then."

The cute intruder winked, then closed the door behind her as she left.

Neladith put a finger to her chin, "That reminds me, if you see Spetzer, tell him that his buddy from the trip to Topak says hi."

Ilyn leaned forward, "You know that guy?"

"Yeah. Why do you ask?"

"I don't like to say anything bad about people. It's just that when he gets drunk, stay away from him. He gets handsy."

Neladith grinned and briefly debated whether to say what she was thinking. She leaned in. "Yeah, it's true. He can be a real douchebag, especially after a few drinks. I gotta say though, he's a great fuck." She leaned in even closer. "You should ride him sometime. He does not disappoint." She finished with a wink of her own and a big, shit-eatin' grin.

Surprise broke across Ilyn's face. Neladith pondered Ilyn's disbelief; was it Spetzer's talent as a cocksman or her brazen admission of fucking him?

This is fun! Just look at that face.

"I'm serious, Ilyn. Spetz might be a pest, but he puts that thing between his legs to good use. And that tongue of his... oufa!"

Neladith lamented she wouldn't be around to witness Ilyn's face when she'd next chance upon Spetzer. Laughing to herself, Neladith understood, having planted the seeds, Ilyn's thoughts of Spetzer performing his abilities were locked in for the next time they ran into each other.

I wonder if she'll heed my advice and take a ride on the Spetzer pocket-pintle.

Pleased with her decision to make the side trip into Hensdale, Neladith considered, *I'm having such a great time,* and slapped Ilyn on the back. "Now, show me what clothes you got for me to try on."

After pulling several garments off the racks, Ilyn handed them to Neladith. "There's a changing room just there," she said, pointing to the rear of the store. "The jacket is twelve guildins. The pants, ten. The vest and shirt are seven each."

"Can you also get me a pair of boots a size or two larger than these?" Neladith stuck out one foot. How she'd pay for it all without any coin didn't concern Neladith. She planned to walk out the door dressed in new clothes one way or another.

Dropping the requested boots on the clothes piled in Neladith's arms, Ilyn returned to attending to the never-ending duties of running the shoppe alone. She called out, walking away, "The boots are fifteen."

From inside the fitting room, Neladith pulled closed the privacy curtain. Quick to shed the ill-fitting pants, Neladith rubbed at her groin, scratching her fingernails through her netherhairs. *Ahhh, that feels good.* She threw her head back and blew out a deep breath. *Free at last. Won't miss those pants much... well, maybe just a little.*

She donned the new shirt, laced her vest, and slipped on the pants. Nothing spilled out on top. While down below, the mid-rise waist fit just right with an acceptable balance of a stylish feminine lines and with plenty of room in the groin for her body to breathe.

Oh, this is so much better.

She ran her hands down her legs, plopped on the bench that hugged the length of the wall, and slipped on a pair of socks, followed by her new boots. Standing, she strode the length of the small area back and forth, trying them out for size.

She inspected herself in the mirror. *Nice.*

One hand reached for the curtain, excited to show off her new look, just as the sound of the bell above the door jingled. She paused, just about to draw back the screen, and listened.

"Hello, Ilyn."

A man's voice. Not Arek.

"Good morning, Judjurex Tetrip. You're out and about early. How can I help you today?"

Shit.

Direct and matter of fact, Tetrip stated, "I'm stopping in to see if you need anything. Told Mithany I would. So, you need anything?"

The changing space was small, enclosed, and gave Neladith nothing in the way of escape.

"No. I'm doing okay. How is Mithany holding up?"

As though reading off a report and not offering friendly conversation, Tetrip replied, "She'll survive. Lots to do at the orchard. A few acres didn't burn down. Best to keep herself busy."

Neladith heard footsteps moving away, followed by sounds of the door opening.

Tetrip's leaving. Great, she thought with a sigh of relief.

"Before I go, have you had any customers today, Ilyn? I can tell Mithany I asked."

"Just the one. She's in the back getting changed. Says she knows Mithany and Arek. Called herself their red-eyed friend. She's not from around here. Says she's visiting the home of those two who went missing."

Fuck! Just the one door. No way out.

Neladith's head spun in all directions, scanning for an escape.

Think! She slapped her forehead.

Think!

Footsteps pounded the floorboards.

She looked at the screen. *Can't.*

She looked at the walls. *Too thick.*

She looked down at the bench. *Trapped.*

Five thundering heartbeats later, the curtain rings rattled. Four fingertips shot through and snatched the edge of the drape.

Neladith braced.

PALACE COUP

TETH: 15TH DAY OF THE HARVEST MOON

Serco | Jerithan

Atop a hill at the center of the holy city of Teth sat the Temple Palace. First Lord Serco paced anxiously inside the warmth of the enclave, while the crisp autumn air of dawn hung over a mob gathered outside.

The hungry, the homeless, the faithless, the true believers, and the devious assembled with a unified purpose: salvation from the suffering inflicted on the citizens of Teth in the aftermath of chaos. Each defined salvation on their own terms. Samers assembled, motivated by vengeance for years of repression. Shantytown's people amassed to strike at the ostentatious wealth the Temple lords horded behind its gates. Even the faithful assembled to demand action from their pious leaders in hiding, failing their faithful flock in desperate need. And mixing in unannounced, Thuggery scoundrels mingled in amongst them, intent on stirring up hatred and anger.

Serco's recent ascension to First Lord was not unfolding as he'd hoped.

Serco yelled, "Second Lord S'Leen! Where the hell is the Provost? I told you to summon him."

Second Lord S'Leen bowed, then rose with her hands clasped inside the cuffs of her vestments. "Yes, First Lord. I dispatched a dozen acolytes. All have reported in. The Provost is nowhere to be found."

Still shouting, Serco demanded, "Then send out another dozen to find him! I want him here. Now!"

"First Lord, we may need to consider that he's fled the Temple Palace."

Serco walked to one of the two-story-high ornately decorated windowpanes overlooking the Palace Square. "Look out there. There must be a thousand of them. They've got us surrounded. Either you get the Provost here immediately or I'm sending you out there to deal with this. Do we understand each other, Second Lord?"

"Yes."

"Then do your job." Serco turned away, ignoring the sound of the door closing with Second Lord S'Leen's exit.

With his heart pounding, looking out the window, his close-set eyes bugged out, watching a woman shimmy up the side of the iron fencing followed by another, then another. Over the span of a few seconds, dozens more followed suit, scaling every inch of the ten-foot-tall ornate wrought iron barrier of the southern gate. One panel of fencing gave out against the weight. It flopped to the ground with twenty or more demonstrators still clinging to its metal rails. A horde of angry protesters seized the opportunity and swarmed through the open space. They'd cover the seventy-five yards to the Palace in mere moments.

"Shit!" Serco screamed into the empty room. Racing mindlessly through the grand open space of the Temple Palace vestibule, shouting, "S'Leen! S'Leen!" Attending to his instructions to find the Provost, Second Lord S'Leen failed to appear.

Serco barreled through the halls shouting, "Guards! Where are the guards?!"

On the floor above, door after door popped open. Heads appeared, poking through as prudents and acolytes in various states of dress, having been woken early from sleep, reacted.

One Prudent rubbed his eyes, leaning over the balustrade. "First Lord, what's happening?"

"They're coming for us," Serco exclaimed.

An acolyte ran past Serco. He grabbed her by the shoulder. "Acolyte, wake everybody. We're under attack." Her eyes swelled either in surprise or horror. Giving her fears no concern, Serco dismissed her reaction. "Just do it." Fear in his voice crackled through his words, and sweat moistened his brow.

The Prudent raced down the sweeping staircase. He grabbed Serco and spun him around. "What! ... Who? ... Where?"

"Look out the fucking window." Serco screamed, yanking his arm free.

The Prudent demanded, "Surely you prepared for this."

Without answering, Serco sped away, racing towards the grand staircase. He bolted up, taking two steps at a time. With one hand on the railing, he stared down at the vestibule. His heart pounded. His head whipped from side to side, looking out through the two-story windows, taking in a broader view from the elevated vantage point.

All is lost. I've got to get to the exit.

He whirled and sprinted back down the stairs. At the bottom, suddenly... *Bang... Bang... Bang...*

Terror seized his motor functions. He froze. *The palace doors!*

Sound from the twenty-foot-tall double arched oak doors, each with iron bracing securing the rivetted wooden slats in place, resonated through the enormous atrium with each threatening, angry blow struck against it.

Bang...

Bang...

Louder and louder it grew as more fists from the other side hammered against it.

Anxiety paralysis nailed him in place. His arms, too heavy to move. His legs, fixed to the floor. His voice fled him. His thoughts scrambled in his head. His heart raced. His small eyes shot wildly from side to side.

Crash.

Frantic, his head spun to witness a large rock skid across the floor; broken glass scattered everywhere.

Crash.

Another window breached.

Crash.

Crash.

Crash.

Window after window shattered. Broken glass covered the floors.

Bodies came pouring through, one atop the other, clamoring to gain entry.

Bang...

Bang...

Unrelenting fists hammered at the door.

His chest pounded harder and harder. Yet, his feet still refused to move.

Inside the palace, people were rampaging about in every direction. Rioters... screaming. Prudents and acolytes... praying... as they fled.

With a thunderous squeal the hinges of the enormous doors gave out.

The giant wood panels slammed against the floor with a terrifying sound.

BOOOOM!

A powerful gust swept across the room.

Feces ran down Serco's leg.

The front of his vestments, now wet with his own urine, fluttered in the winds of the fallen doors.

Hordes flooded through the open arch as prudents, acolytes, and servants raced for the rear exits, but it was too late.

Screams filled the room. A cacophony of unintelligible utterings bounced off the marble walls.

Terror had its claws in Serco.

And so did a mob of enraged rioters.

From outside the door of Jerithan's makeshift cell high in the north tower of the Temple Palace, he heard S'Leen. "Guard. We are under attack. Go protect the palace. I have the prisoner."

"Second Lord, I've been ordered not to leave my post for any reason."

Jerithan pressed his ear to the door. He strained to hear S'Leen speak softly to the guard. "I understand you're following orders. Now I'm giving you one. The First Lord has been captured. I am in charge. Now do what I tell you."

"Yes, Ma'am."

Jerithan heard the guard's heavy footsteps fade away. He stepped back as the door to his imprisonment creaked open. "S'Leen. What's happening?"

Without answering, S'Leen grabbed Jerithan and wrapped her arms around him. "The Palace has been breached. I've got to get you out of here."

"Fucking Serco. How did this happen?"

"We must get away before the opportunity is lost." She took hold of his hand. "Come with me."

Stunned and confused, Jerithan let his friend, and Second Lord, lead the way. "Did Serco really get captured?"

"I don't know. I just said that. No more talk. We've got to get out of here. They find either of us... we're dead."

"Then, before we take another step, you need to get out of those vestments."

"Not as easy as you think. These robes are hot and I'm not wearing anything underneath." She blushed.

Jerithan quickly unbuttoned his shirt. "Get out of those. They see you in that, it's all over. Here,"—he tossed her his shirt—"take it. Do it now. I'll turn around."

Second Lord S'Leen slipped out of her religious garments and hastily donned Jerithan's shirt. "Thank you, Jerithan."

He turned and watched S'Leen with shaking hands fail to fasten it closed.

"Let me help," Jerithan offered, now bare-chested himself. Without waiting for her reply, he secured the garment. The shirttails hung halfway down her thighs as though a short nightshirt. "It will have to do. Lead the way."

Clomp... Clomp... resonated down the hall.

"Shit," Jerithan whispered. "Someone's coming."

"Quick. Back inside your room."

"We'll be trapped in there," Jerithan protested.

"There's no time. Follow my lead."

The pair made their way back inside. S'Leen demanded, "Get under the bed." Seconds later, the door flung open.

Sprawled out on top of the sheets, S'Leen stretched, yawned, rubbed her eyes, and asked, "Who are you? You're not the guard. He brings me breakfast."

The woman—her clothes tattered as though they were the only coverings she owned—looked surprised. "Who the fuck are ya?"

"I'm a prisoner. The Temple Lords caught me fucking women one too many times. I'm not licensed. They locked me away up here... Who are you?"

"Prisoner. Huh." Silence hung in the air for a few seconds. "That nightshirt ain't coverin' nothin'. Ya might want to pull that down if yer gonna join us. We're gonna fuck up all these assholes. Time for us to get some payback."

S'Leen looked down. She realized Jerithan's shirt must have ridden up when she jumped onto the bed.

"I'm lookin' for a guy they gots locked up. He's supposed to be here. They call him Jerithan Cree. You seen any other prisoners around here?"

S'Leen pulled the hem of her shirt down. "They keep me locked up. Sorry."

"That's all they gives ya to wear? Perverts. Well, screw 'em. We're takin' over. From now on, ya can fuck whoever ya likes. You ain't no prisoner no more." The woman turned and sped away back down the stairs to join the other swarming rabble.

Jerithan listened to the diminishing sounds of footsteps racing down the narrow flight of stairs. Once clear, he extricated himself out from under the bed, as S'Leen dangled her feet just above his head.

With her legs swinging back and forth, she said, "We can't stay here. The north tower has only one way in and one way out: a long, narrow, winding stairway. We will not remain safe much longer. People will keep coming. It won't be a swarm, although more rats are sure to follow."

Moments later, the pair stood at the top of the only means of escape—where they'd be trapped in the event of enemy pursuit. Getting out of the palace alive consumed Jerithan's every thought. Through bulging eyes, he peered around the corner with S'Leen at his back. With both hands on Jerithan's shoulders, S'Leen leaned in close, pressing herself against him. She whispered, "You see anyone? Is it safe?"

Before Jerithan could answer, the Voice broke through the terror invading his concentration. *"You must get a hold of yourself, my friend. Yes, there is danger ahead. You cannot let it control you."*

A reply to either the Voice or S'Leen failed to materialize. Dread at moving forward and the fear of being discovered joined forces to prevent Jerithan from moving an inch from where he stood.

"This is your moment. We must use this chaos to make your escape. If you cannot navigate your way to a safe passage, allow this woman to lead."

Jerithan's eyes darted wildly over the descending staircase. Its curvature hid from him whatever secrets it held. A coward at heart, he couldn't force himself to move.

"JERITHAN!"

The Voice shouted into the mind of the former First Lord.

"JERITHAN!"

"JERITHAN!"

The Voice's cries into his thoughts broke the spell cowardice had on him. A whimper gurgled in his throat. "S'Leen, you take the lead. Perhaps they won't attack a woman so readily... dressed like you are."

Focused on the descending passageway, Jerithan reached behind his back. He wiggled his hand for S'Leen to take hold. Her delicate fingers graced his palm. Her soft, warm, womanly touch invoked calmness within him. With a gentle tug, he guided her to stand in front. "I'll follow you."

"Ruffle your hair," the Voice demanded.

He rifled through what little tuft nature left him. "Wait, S'Leen," Jerithan said softly. How far down the staircase his words would carry, he hadn't a clue. From behind S'Leen, he rummaged through her long dark locks, transforming the stately Second Lord into a haggard-looking scrubwoman.

"One more thing. Turn to face me." When she did, he ripped the top left shirt panel over her breast. It flapped partially open. He reached for the right panel with the aims to do the same to the other side.

S'Leen shot her hand atop his. "That's enough, Jerithan. They'll get the point."

He looked down and gave a head bob in agreement.

"Here. Let me help you." She ran the nail of her index finger across his chest, drawing blood.

"Ouch." A thin line of red oozed out.

The Voice threw in, *"Tit for tat, so to speak."*

"Don't be a baby. It's only a scratch." She raised her hand for another swipe.

Jerithan gently grabbed her wrist. "They'll get the point."

S'Leen snickered. "One good turn deserves another."

Jerithan froze. "Shh. You hear that?" Alarm bells clamored in his head. The sound of footsteps bounced off the walls.

"Someone's coming," the Voice added.

Jerithan's eardrums pounded louder and louder.

The clattering feet drew near.

S'Leen snatched Jerithan's hand and pulled him along, racing into danger. As they descended, he tried to stop her. Much to his consternation, she kept pulling him along.

"No. We have to." She called back to him. "Trust me."

With S'Leen and Jerithan bolting downward and others running up the rounded staircase, without warning, the parties crashed into each other. A stranger slammed into S'Leen. Three others behind the man plowed into him from behind. Jerithan grabbed S'Leen to keep her from falling. Too late, momentum carried her into the stranger's arms.

She blurted to the unknown man she'd just slammed into, "Oh, I'm sorry. Are you okay?"

Jerithan looked down over S'Leen's shoulder. The hard, grizzled face of a man stared back at him. It was an older face. A decade or two past its prime. The man was taller than S'Leen and very angry.

Taking a step back and up one rung, S'Leen stood between the intruders below and Jerithan behind.

"Get outta my way," Grizzledface demanded. He shoved S'Leen to the side.

Jerithan swallowed hard. He screamed his thoughts at the Voice. *He knows who I am!*

Grizzledface pushed past S'Leen and stepped forward towards the former First Lord. S'Leen clutched the man's arm and spun him back around. "Hey, asshole. What, you think you're better than me? You got some balls, buddy." With open palms she slammed them into Grizzledface's chest, bouncing him off the wall.

Grizzleface came nose to nose with the Temple of Life's Second Lord.

Jerithan clenched his butt cheek with everything he had, trying to keep from shitting his pants.

Without breaking eye contact with S'Leen, Grizzleface made a quick head tip aimed at Jerithan, "Who's he? And why you got no pants?"

S'Leen dismissed his concern with a wave of her hand, "One of our own ripped my clothes off and tried to stick his dick in me. This one here stopped him and gave me his shirt."

With glaring eyes, Grizzledface squinted hard at S'Leen.

She stared right back at him. "Don't fuck with me!" she shouted. "I've had all the shit I'm gonna take from assholes like you."

"I always liked this one," the Voice told Jerithan.

Grizzledface's expression shifted to one of confusion. "Who the fuck are you?"

S'Leen shot back in a commanding, loud voice. "Who the fuck am I? I'm the bitch they sent up here to check the north tower. So, what the fuck are you doing here, dickhead?"

'Well, I just thought..."

"You thought?" S'Leen shoved a finger into his chest. "That's your problem. We got a lot of ground to cover and you're wasting everyone's time. Now get your ass back downstairs and go do something useful."

"Who put you in charge?"

"I'll have your head on a spike along with the douchebag who ripped off my clothes."

"I—I—I—was just gonna check if anyone was up here. Heard there might be some high-level muckety-muck."

S'Leen crossed her arms. "We already checked it out. It's empty. Not even a security guard."

Grizzledface scanned S'Leen from head to toe.

Anger poured out of her reply, "You eyeballing me? Who... the... fuck... are you to eyeball me? Do I look like some high-level Temple of Life prissy cunt? Now get your ass outta here."

As he turned to descend, S'Leen booted him in the back. "Don't let me see you again, asshole."

Without turning, Grizzledface yelled back, "Yes, ma'am."

The inside of Jerithan's skull pounded against his temples. His heart raced.

Grizzledface and his companions sped away.

Jerithan swallowed back his fear. "Holy shit, S'Leen. Miss prim-and-proper turned all badass. Never knew you had it in you."

The Voiced chided, *"She is my new favorite."*

Shut up.

S'Leen's puffed cheeks released a gush. "A girl's gotta do what a girl's gotta do." With Grizzledface gone, she started shaking. "I don't like using foul language or yelling at people. My heart was pounding the whole time." She held out a trembling hand.

"Do not use her name again. Someone could hear and identify you both."

Now you're being helpful.

Jerithan pulled in a deep, calming breath. "You did great, S'Leen. You saved us twice. Once as a damsel in distress and the other as a hard-ass boss lady. You're full of surprises."

"I just told you not to speak her name."

Told me? Do you think you are in charge of me? Just be quiet.

"Thank you, Jerithan," S'Leen said with a graceful bow.

"One thing. Until we get out of here, we can't use our names. Call me Keflin for now. What do I call you?"

"Keflin. That's good. Call me..." She paused. With one hand and the whirl of her neck, she flipped back her scraggly locks as though modeling a pose, "... Faylun. Call me Faylun."

"Well, Faylun, we haven't gone fifteen feet from where they imprisoned me, and we've run into trouble twice already. We have a long way to go if we are going to get out of this alive."

A Little Excitement

Neladith

Neladith never knew the face of Judjurex Tetrip. He existed in her thoughts as a silhouette she spotted from a distance while he walked with Arek the day she set Reyne's alphen orchard ablaze to make her escape. The same day her dream of a new life on Tartica crashed into reality when she discovered Arek wasn't dead.

She braced herself inside the small fitting room. She looked up and realized the fingertips grasping the backside of the curtain had to be Tetrip's. Yet, it mattered nothing whose fingers they were: their intent to reveal her threatened Neladith and her mission.

A Judjurex's purpose was civil enforcement, as Ilyn defined it for Neladith only moments ago. And those civil enforcer's footsteps had made a beeline straight for Neladith. It didn't take much for Neladith to piece together the likelihood Arek revealed her as Daedyn's murderess.

Trapped. Each pulse flooded her with adrenaline and excitement. Although danger thrilled her to the core, she was in a tight squeeze and knew this one just might be her undoing.

Tetrip yanked back the curtain.

They stood eye to eye.

His shot open wide.

Cocked and ready, she sized up Tetrip.

Her hand shot upward before he could react. The tough sinew between her thumb and fingers, stretched tight, slammed into Tetrip's Adam's apple.

He gasped for air.

With both hands, he clutched for his throat.

Neladith slammed the heel of her palms into the side of his temples.

Tetrip staggered.

He crashed into the wall, stumbling backwards.

Neladith drove her shoulder into his side and shoved him away.

He fell to the ground.

She raced through the store.

Ilyn stood motionless; her mouth hung open as Neladith sped past her. Neladith burst through the door into the market square.

Dawn danced overhead.

Chilled air lapped at her cheeks.

The marketplace accumulated a dozen villagers mulling about during her time inside. As much as Neladith wanted to ignore them all, she understood the anonymous onlookers would reveal her escape route. Tetrip would come after her once he recovered. The trained operative understood it gave her the opportunity to leave a trail of false breadcrumbs pointing north.

All things considered, that went well.

She put her head down and bolted north.

She planned to circle back, covering any sign of her true destination... south to Teth.

Where she'd wait for Quith—and kill him.

Smart Girl

Tandure: 15th Day of The Harvest Moon

Derr

Derr held no official role in the Kingdom of Adelle's newly minted military structure nor within the War Council. All were new appointments hand-picked by Tomelai, as were all without experience planning for war or having any background fighting one. Derr sat along the wall, set apart from War Council members gathered at the conference table. He considered the utter lack of experience Adelle's top generals brought to the endeavor yet comforted himself in the knowledge the United Front fared no better.

Intelligence acquired by the Agents of Derr—known across Tartica as the Grays—concerning UF developments proved important enough for Tomelai to assemble his team to share what they'd learned. Tomelai said nothing while waiting for his son, General Loseff, to join the meeting.

Idle chitchat filled the room and provided ample cover for Derr's watchful eye as he studied each of Adelle's military leaders. He listened not only to what each said; he tuned into how they said it. He analyzed their faces, their reactions, assessed their confidence, their uncertainties; nothing slipped past him. He was always watching.

The recently constructed headquarters carried the smell of fresh-cut oak, and when the door to the room swung open, the well-oiled hinges gave nothing away. Except for the sight of it moving and a guard stepping through the portal to announce General Loseff's arrival, the war council personnel might have continued their private conversations uninterrupted.

Tomelai, strategically seated at the head of the table and positioned to face the door, gave off a look of annoyance visible to more than just Derr. The Chancellor's son had kept the Chancellor waiting. Son or not, Loseff held the rank of General and no longer enjoyed the privileges of a resentful, insolent offspring of the ruling family. Derr understood the ire on Tomelai's telltale face.

The guard stood with the open-door handle in one hand and announced, "General Loseff Tomelai."

"Thank you, Corporal," Chancellor Tomelai uttered. With an abrupt wave of his hand, Tomelai added, "You can leave us."

Tomelai's harsh eyes stared up at Loseff, and Derr knew his friend Rotti, the Chancellor of Adelle, was pissed. "Loseff, have a seat. Let's begin."

With a knowing snort, Derr noted Tomelai's failure to address his son as General Loseff, an obvious and deliberate slight for keeping him waiting. However, what interested Derr even more, Loseff shrugged it off. *There's something going on between these two. Young Loseff is driving it. Why though?*

Tomelai rested both hands on the table, slid them forward and back, and stated, "There is new intel concerning the UF that Captain Derr's agents, along with the KCG have uncovered that is of great import. I have asked Captain Derr to brief you on this developing intel. Captain, take it from here."

With a finger, Derr commanded his senior Lieutenant standing near the door. The Lieutenant scooped up a pile of folders and handed copies of a report to each of the officers seated at the table.

From his chair, Derr launched into the analysis. "You have before you the KCG's analysis of intel gathered from my Grays. On pages three through eight, you'll note the UF's recruitment levels with details of each nation's contributions and an assessment of UF militia demographics. While the UF's drive to muster an army has only just commenced, they are off to a poor start. Not a single UF nation's recruitment effort exceeds five hundred troops. Teth trails Greenlin and Kantos with merely three hundred thirty-six enlisting."

"Chancellor"—Loseff looked up from his brief to face his father, "Adelle already has eight times the UF's forces, and we're adding new recruits daily. If you desire to strike before the UF gets off the ground, my divisions will be ready within a few weeks. We can break them now."

"Perhaps," Tomelai offered in a dismissive tone. "Captain Derr, please continue."

Rotti's still pissed at his son, that's obvious, Derr concluded before returning to the briefing. "There's a lot more in the report. For example, turn to page fourteen. President Dimenk has held back sharing all her military enlistments with the UF for her own purposes. She's amassed another three hundred as a specialized force to round up Samers. Samers, who've been abandoning every UF nation in droves. Our assessment concludes three things: First, Samer will continue fleeing these countries; second, the Kingdom of Adelle is their destination; and third, Dimenk fears many of her expatriates are motivated to fight for the complete overthrow of the Covenant across all of Tartica. She fears some are willing to join Adelle's war effort."

General Kevine raised her hand.

With a frown, Tomelai replied, "General Kevine, there is no need to request permission to speak. I expect everyone at this table to be honest and to share with all of us whatever is on your mind."

"Chancellor, you know I am a licensed Samer, as you all refer to us who prefer others of our same gender. It's not a term we embrace." She paused to roll up her sleeve, showing everyone in the room her official Samer registration license number tattooed on her arm. "This is the only thing that permits me to have sex with others of my gender."

Verifying her claim, she turned with her arm held high for all to see. "It is known as The Mark. I don't wear it proudly but accept its necessity. It affords me and others like me legal protection. Yet, it is resented. I don't say this with any disrespect towards you, Chancellor, or towards our Covenant's directive to achieve humanity's repopulation goals. I understand what had to be done. Nonetheless, The Mark is resented just the same. Others like me have no greater desire than to see an end to the practice of disfiguring people just because of who they choose to love. Chancellor, when you announced Adelle's break from the Covenant, my heart swelled with pride."

She looked into the eyes of everyone in the room as a single tear rolled down her cheek. After a brief pause, she turned to face Tomelai. "I will follow you anywhere, sir. I am so proud of the stance you took. You are so brave." She squeezed her quivering lips tight and, after recovering, added, "I say to all of you, there are tens of thousands like me from every nation." Kevine turned to Derr. "Yes, Captain, your assessment of Samers' desires to be free of the Covenant is correct. Yet, I believe it is even more powerful than you could ever imagine." With a bow of her head in a sign of respect to Derr, General Kevine returned to her seat.

Derr reflected on the night he, Kaythlin, and Rotti devised a secret plan intended to eliminate further attempts on the Chancellor's life following the failed assassination of Tomelai inside The Stand on the Feast of Teth. Creating chaos across Tartica by denouncing the Covenant turned everyone's attention from Tomelai's push for electrics.

Silencing the Chancellor of Adelle became unimportant once measured against their own struggles to hold on to power with the seeds of revolution Tomelai planted with his speech at the Council of Nations. Chancellor Tomelai cared little for the freedom his withdrawal from the Covenant offered General Kevine or other Samers. They didn't know that. And Tomelai wouldn't deny himself the accolades or benefits derived from the unintended consequences of Adelle's abandonment of Covenant strictures.

Before Derr could continue, Loseff jumped in. "Chancellor, several hundred with The Mark are enlisting by the week. I've given thought to building a special force made up of..."

"There is more," Derr said, interrupting Loseff. "Dimenk has a few tricks up her sleeve, no pun intended. Spies from Greenlin have been newly tattooed with Samer licenses. Let me be clear: they bear The Mark but are not Samers. She has sent them out to infiltrate our ranks. She plans to deny us a ghet. I am certain she made sure my spies learned of her False-Samers."

Commander General Kiple joined in. "Troop movements. Battle plans. Preparedness. All of it will be fed to the UF if these False-Samers aren't ferreted out. If that's even possible."

One of the other generals piped up, "We've got ourselves a conundrum. Dimenk's put us in a tight spot."

Tomelai huffed, "Dimenk, smart girl."

Nice Day for a Stroll

Evidar

The Devil's Blacksmith

The Devil's Blacksmith awaited news on the search efforts across Evidar's habitable lands for Reyne Brenton. Neladith's report to the Devil's Blacksmith suggested Reyne had transfigured to Evidar just days ago. All efforts to find him had proved fruitless so far.

Sitting behind his enormous desk, the Devil's Blacksmith discussed the status of his plans with Synja Emosh, Evidar's Damus, a genius capable of calculating the likelihood of future events from her reading of Probability Waves inside the Void.

Reyne Brenton weighed heavily on his thoughts. While the young Tartican remained free, he existed as an obstacle in the Devil's Blacksmith's blind spot.

"Miss Emosh," the Devil's Blacksmith addressed the young silver-haired woman, who was his one and only Damus. "Join me. Let us venture out above. I have an item of import to attend to. We can talk along the way."

A mathematical prodigy and a skilled interpreter of Void encounters, Emosh nodded. The two made their way up the long staircase, out the yellow door, and into the gloom of Evidar. Over a span of one hundred yards, the barren landscape posited several other entryways similar to the rock pile framing the yellow door.

As always, her words fired out rapidly. "Sir, in all the times I've been to your office, I've never seen anyone enter or exit any of those other structures."

He kept walking.

Synja Emosh hurried to catch up.

"Miss Emosh, it is refreshing to be in the open, such as it is. You are too young to remember, yet I can recall a time before the Great Destruction when the sun bathed this entire world in golden light each morning."

Synja Emosh gave him a quizzical look. "Sir, I know Earth's history. That's over fifteen hundred years ago. How's that possible?"

Her eyes collected what little light reached Evidar's surface, and two small silver dots in their centers reflected its harvest. The Devil's Blacksmith stood out from all other Evidarians in that his eyes didn't reflect anything. His pupils were like small black holes sucking in every photon of light, leaving none to escape in reflection. "Your history is correct, Miss Emosh. I have been around for a long time. I have my wife to thank for a gift she shared with me from long ago."

"Sir, you're married? I've heard so much about you from others. Never anything about marriage."

"I might be still, yet I consider it unlikely. However, Miss Emosh, I am more interested in hearing what others have told you about me."

The desolate, flat, open landscape, highlighted by exposed outcroppings of feldspar scattered about, held no sway over either of them. It was the world they knew.

"I can see you are nervous, Miss Emosh. You need not be. Speak freely. I have not asked you what you think of me. I have asked what you have heard from others. I am aware these are not your opinions. So, speak openly."

Synja Emosh puffed her cheeks and slowly released the accumulation. "Sir, before I do, can I ask you something?"

"Certainly."

"How is it possible? How can you be more than fifteen hundred years old? One person I know spoke of something called a Soul Stone. I'm not a stupid girl. I deal in numbers, facts, and equations. The human body just can't survive that long."

A small laugh escaped the Devil's Blacksmith, a laugh as rare as the Soul Stone itself. "Miss Emosh, you are surely not stupid. I find beauty in your mind. And so I must ask: for all your time in the Void with your consciousness existing outside your body, dealing with the nebulous, observing futures which will never be, deciphering them from those that are likely to come to pass, to create a mathematical equation predicting future events—tell me, what are the limits of reality? You, more than anyone, must understand there is so much more to existence than our human brains can fathom. Inside the Void, you have been witness to the impossible. Is it too much a tax on your concept of reality to accept my claim?"

Synja looked down, kicked a small rock, watched it bounce away, and raised her head up. "You're as good with words as I am with numbers." A frown broke across her face. "Still, is it the Soul Stone? I thought it was just a fairy tale. Does it really exist?"

"Miss Emosh. There are some things of which I cannot speak. Certain information can be hazardous to one's health; yours, not mine. There are people who would endanger you if they thought you had the knowledge they sought. As such, there are secrets I must keep. Please, continue. And I will need the name of this person who spoke to you of the Soul Stone."

Synja Emosh dropped her head and, just as quickly, it popped back up. "Alright, but these aren't my opinions."

"I understand."

"To start, there are many that praise you for providing the villages with food and clean water, and keeping the marauders at bay as best you can. Although they're not too pleased when you take one of their own to serve you. Some say you can be brutal and unforgiving."

"A necessary evil, Miss Emosh. This cold war with Tartica has cost us all. And besides, who do they suppose prepares all the provisions they receive or hunts the rogues before they strike? ... Go on."

"Sir. Look up ahead," Miss Emosh said, pointing forward. "Four people are heading our way. Do we need to take precautions? It isn't always safe."

"Miss Emosh, while you are with me, you are always safe. They are here to meet with me."

With an arm waving overhead, a woman's voice called out as she approached.

"Sir, it is so nice to see you out and about. However, I thought we were gonna meet in your office."

The group's leader, a woman who only recently reached adulthood, stepped forward. Her companions, two men and an older woman, stood close behind.

His voice lost the politeness of his conversation with Synja Emosh. Words rolled off his tongue as dark and cold as his eyes. "I am looking forward to hearing news of Reyne Brenton. You have been hunting for him. As I scan the area, it is unfortunate that I do not see the Tartican with you."

With tightly pursed lips and a shake of her head, the woman declared, "Sir, he's just not out—"

The Devil's Blacksmith's hand whipped to his side. He scooped up a knife secured out of view and, in blinding fast motion, swept it forward, burying it deep into the woman's chest.

Her mouth hung open. No words came out. The surprise written across her face spoke in the only way she could just before she crumpled to the ground.

The Devil's Blacksmith pointed at a stunned, tall man, staring down at his former leader's dead body.

The man didn't move.

In a deep, commanding, eloquent tone, the Devil's Blacksmith demanded, "Look at me."

Three heads snapped forward to face the Devil's Blacksmith. "You are now in charge of the search for Reyne Brenton. There are four other teams on the hunt." Looking down at the dead woman, he explained, "She had command over them all. Now you do. She failed me. I expect better results from you. You have two days to find him."

The Devil's Blacksmith didn't bother to gather up his blade, leaving it in the woman's chest. He turned to Synja Emosh. The shaking Damus stood fixed in place. The Devil's Blacksmith eyed her up and down. With pleasantry in his tone once again, he said, "Miss Emosh, let us return to my compound... As we walk, I would like to hear more."

Her palms rubbed at her watery eyes. Her voice broke and squeaked. "Sir, what about the woman... her body?"

The Devil's Blacksmith gave a dismissive wave of his hand. "What of it?" He angled himself in the direction from whence he came. "Now, Miss Emosh... And I will have the name I asked you for earlier."

THE ROAD AHEAD, RECLAMATION

TETH: 15TH DAY OF THE HARVEST MOON

Jerithan

Jerithan's eyes watered, staring at the conflagration rising into the night.

The Temple of Life Palace, humanity's symbol of faith and hope, was burning.

Dusk painted the sky in shades of yellow while the orange flames of the Palace inferno reached higher and higher, lighting up Teth against the coming darkness. It mirrored the embers of hatred for Serco burning in Jerithan's core. Serco ripped Jerithan's First Lord's title from him and now, because of Serco's incompetence, Jerithan's beloved palace was destroyed. Jerithan roiled at his own failure to stop Serco's betrayal.

He blamed himself: *If only I'd been able to defeat Serco...*

Less than a mile from the fire consuming more than wood, against the chill, S'Leen wrapped her arms around her chest. Breathing hard, she pleaded, "Jerithan, we can't stop here. Look back. The Palace burns. The rioters will be pouring out. We have to go."

Out of breath, Jerithan's age and pampered lifestyle left him physically unprepared to flee for his life. Bent over and sucking wind, sweat gathered to him the surrounding cold like the wick of an oil lamp drawing fuel from its well. It sapped from him what little strength remained. He'd need more if he would survive the night.

Between them, they shared a single pair of pants, which Jerithan donned, and the shirt S'Leen wore. The warmth from the fiery destruction did not touch them this far out. Neither Jerithan, bared chested, nor S'Leen, exposed below the tails of her borrowed shirt, were in any condition to escape the drop in temperature the coming darkness promised.

Jerithan's chest rose and fell; he otherwise didn't move. Anguish and exhaustion had him in their clutches, both in body and soul.

The Voice broke into his thoughts. *"It is my sense you are conflicted in seeing the symbol of your life's achievement in becoming First Lord destroyed. Yet pleased to see the rule of the man who conspired to remove you from the velvet throne also consumed by the flames. You loved what the Temple Palace represented, yet you take delight in Serco's ruination."*

The blazing annihilation of the Palace he once ruled over left him empty, and yet he had to admit to himself the Voice had the full measure of it.

S'Leen shouted to him, "Jerithan!" She grabbed his shoulder. "We have to go."

Thoughts from the Voice played in his head, adding to S'Leen's demands. *"Jerithan, you must go on. The path ahead leads to your reclamation."*

A clear vision of what lay ahead evaded Jerithan's imagination. Exhausted muscles and labored lungs held his attention. All he wanted was to lie down and sleep. *Let them take me. I have nothing left,* he told the Voice, also ignoring the hand on his shoulder or the woman who saved his life.

"Look at what you have endured. Derr's chamber of horrors. Living as a beggar in the slums. Nail's attempt to put you on trial. Serco's humiliation of you. Tane's betrayal of you at the failed peace conference. You have survived everything they have thrown at you. You are better than this. Do not give up now. You are a fighter. You will regain what has been lost. Only if you get up... and run."

Words from the Voice struck a chord in his heart. Another deep breath swept will into his aching body and determination into his soul. *You're right. I can do this, if only to see them all crushed under my heel.*

From hands on his knees, he rose. "Thank you, S'Leen. You're a good friend. I wouldn't have made it out alive without your help." With a hand on her arm, he said, "I'm with you. Now, let's get the fuck out of here."

S'Leen scanned the area, looking uncertain as she peered in every direction. "Where do we go? Where will we be safe?"

The Voice offered Jerithan a suggestion.

Jerithan replied to S'Leen, "I'm reminded of a place that will afford us refuge."

Go Away

Mithany

M ithany put on a good show in public for Arek's sake, doing her best to face each day. Secluded from prying eyes, free from expectations, she curled up in Reyne's bed, crying and inconsolable. She gripped his pillow tight to her chest. Tears flowed freely. Mithany rocked back and forth, struggling to make sense of Neladith's purpose in destroying her life, destroying the orchard, and destroying Arek.

Reyne's beloved alphen orchard, much like Mithany's riven mind, existed as though of two separate and irreconcilable realities. Her inner self, damaged and forged into two unconnected personas from a childhood mired in abuse, found independence from the destructive effects inflicted on her soul in the absence of love Reyne showered on her. His departure, only days from their wedding date, challenged her ability to maintain a grip over her maimed subconscious, demanding to be unleashed in the chaos.

Coupled with Daedyn's murder, Arek's near death, delivered at Neladith's hand, had recently enabled her damaged soul to emerge dominant, if only temporarily. Wresting back control—precariously riding the edge of a knife—Mithany's heart sank deeper into despair at the ruination of Reyne's orchard. Soul-crushing conditions ripe for acquiescence to the demands of her broken self.

So much destruction. All for what? So Neladith had time to get away.

With only a small section of the prolific nut-producing trees escaping devastation, like Mithany's psyche, both stood on the precipice, facing a breaking point from which there was no return. Both faced an uncertain future. One path led to devastation, ashen, black, and barren. The other, a trail of breadcrumbs teasing her with hope, like the promise of a salvaged harvest from the remains.

Knock, knock.

The sound barely registered with her thoughts turned inward.

Knock, knock.

She sniffled, pressed the heels of her palms to her puffy eyes, then ran a sleeve over the mucus dangling from her nose. Her voice, hoarse and soft, "What?" She had no desire to talk to anyone.

Santander, the nut farm's general manager, a burly, gray-haired, older man, said, "I'm sorry, dear, I don't mean to bother you... Can I come in?" Delivered more apologetically and softer than in the usual commanding way he spoke to everyone else.

Mithany loved the man. He treated her like a daughter in all the years she and Reyne had been together. That didn't mean she wanted to speak with him at the moment.

"Can it wait?"

"Again, I'm sorry, dear... it can't."

Mithany sat up, pulled the pillow to her chest, crossed her legs in front of her and said, "Alright."

Santander plopped himself alongside her on the bed but didn't say anything.

Mithany rested her head on his shoulder and started crying again. She felt his arm around her and welcomed the comforting gesture.

"I'm worried about you, dear."

She wiped her nose again. "If any of them heard you say you worried about anyone, they'd be shocked."

"It's our little secret. You've never told anyone so far." He chuckled. "You'd ruin my reputation."

"You don't have to worry about me. I'll be okay."

"Come now, dear, I know you better than that. Besides, Arek was hurt when you sent him away."

"I didn't mean to. I just needed to be alone."

"He said it was the first time in his life you ever turned him away."

Mithany lost control, blubbering through her words, "I..." She tried to breathe. "Oh, what..." She gulped for air. "... did I..." She buried her head in his chest. "... do?"

"It'll be alright. He's a big boy."

She pulled her head back and looked Santander in the eye. "You don't understand."

"What don't I understand, dear?"

Mithany opened her mouth. For a moment, nothing came out. She stared at him for a few seconds. "We're always there for each other. No matter what. My entire life, I've never denied him before. He's never denied me... and I sent him away. It's so selfish of me... I just wanted to be alone. What's wrong with me? How could I do that to him?"

"With all you've been through, dear, you haven't been yourself lately. Everyone can understand that. Most especially your brother."

"Whenever mother would beat me, he always found me, consoled me. He always protected me whenever he could from her. I shouldn't have sent him away."

"It's fine, dear. You'll go find him and make it better."

Mithany scooched back, trying to pull herself together. "What did you want to tell me?"

"News of Neladith. Judjurex Tetrip ran into her at your leather goods store. She attacked him and stole an outfit. She got away. She's gone again."

"Why didn't anyone come and tell me?"

"Arek tried, dear. You wouldn't open the door."

"Oh, by the grace of Teth. I have to find Arek... What have I done?!"

Sit Tight

The Woodlands: 16th Day of the Harvest Moon

Mera

Mera stewed over the ongoing delay. It'd been near a full day since three armed men had come upon him in The Woodlands and escorted him to their encampment. They treated him well, fed him, but the only words any of them spoke were, "Kess wants to see you. She'll be back soon. Sit tight." Explaining the repercussions of his detention to anyone who'd listen neither elicited concern from his hosts nor allowed him to leave camp without the promise of physical harm. Kess might've been a friend, yet that didn't give her license to restrict him from leaving.

Kess's current makeshift camp wasn't much different than the last one of hers that Mera encountered. A small area had been cleared of brush with a firepit at the center. Primitive bedding encircled the camp, and one modest stick-built hut set apart as though it held a place of significance. The impromptu base functioned as a temporary outpost that went up as quickly as it came down. Kess's small band of followers prided themselves on using whatever nature provided. They permitted Mera free access to their provisions and to roam about freely. Just not to leave.

Pairs of alternating associates assigned to Mera at all times made sure he stayed put.

He debated making a break for it, certain they wouldn't kill him. Although, he didn't expect to come away from the attempt free of harm. And that was his dilemma: either sit it out and wait for Kess or risk a serious injury making a break for it. He wondered how far Kess's people would go. Mera counted sixteen armed men and women. He faced greater odds in the past and survived. They definitely wouldn't kill him; these were supposedly friendlies. In the end, he settled on a third option.

With his ass plastered on a stump, Mera slapped his hands to his knees and pushed up. "I can't wait any longer. Tell Kess she'll have to catch up with me on the road. There's too much at stake."

A tall, muscularly built woman narrowed her eyes and twitched her head, saying, "Can't let you do that, Mera. Kess says to keep you here 'till she gets back. That's what I'm gonna do. Now, sit your ass back down."

Although her tone was respectful and polite, her words clearly meant business.

Mera ignored her warning and started to walk away.

In an obvious threat, she nocked an arrow aimed at the ground and drew back the bowstring. Her male partner followed suit.

Mera stopped. "What are you going to do, shoot me? Not sure your boss is going to be happy if you do. Me and Kess have been friends a long time."

She replied, "You just might be right about that. Although, I'm certain she'd like it even less if I disobey orders. Sorry, Mera, my hands are tied. I'll shoot you if I have to."

The woman's male partner grinned at Mera and added, "Maybe just in the leg. Keep you from walking away. Or at least we'll have a blood trail to follow. You won't get far."

A third person strolled by just then. He said, "Hey, Mera, good to see you," and kept walking.

The man looked familiar, although Mera didn't recall his name. Ignoring the man and his greeting, Mera considered the Soul Stone's restorative capacity. He'd survive a leg injury; however, the Soul Stone's healing properties might take a day or two to repair the damage to his flesh. "Delays. More delays. I would've been better off with the fucking hellhounds."

Mera imagined Tartican civilization inching ever closer to its ruination. He had to stop it from getting away from his ability to impact events. Sitting in the middle of the woods doing nothing, Mera felt like he'd been neutered. It couldn't have been planned any better than if the Devil's Blacksmith himself held him captive… and Kess was supposed to be a friend.

Mera opened his mouth to protest but was cut off.

With her arrow still primed and pointing down at the forest floor, the muscular woman told Mera, "Kess wants to see you. She'll be back soon. Sit tight."

LAST BEST HOPE

TANDURE: 15TH DAY OF THE HARVEST MOON

Loseff

"Jaynes, you've got to hear this." Loseff carefully lifted the ancient book off his dresser. "I've been reading about the Second Age and how Earth faced an imminent threat. All that we've been told about the Great Destruction is nonsense. The Second Age didn't end because of the overconsumption of natural resources. That's just a story they fabricated."

Jaynes rubbed his chin. "I'll bite. What really caused the Second Age to be wiped from history?"

"Let me read this chapter to you. It's fascinating. Tartica used to be just one continent named Antarctica, and it was a freezing hellhole. This entire landmass was one enormous ice sheet. I'm at the part where a gigantic meteor is on its way to wipe out all of humanity. Or at least from what I've read so far, the story seems to be heading in that direction."

Jaynes asked, "Wow, you think your father knows all this? He just never told you?"

"I don't know. If he does, and he didn't tell me, he's a fraud."

Loseff fanned his palm over the cover, then opened the book and read:

Dawn of the Third Age
Chapter: Last Best Hope
April 2, 2089

With seven hundred eighty-six researchers, scientists, and military personnel squeezed into thirty-six snow-worthy transport vehicles, more than three-quarters of McMurdo's winter residents joined Beth Green on the cross-continent trek to Concordia Station high on the southeastern Antarctica Plateau.

By way of the continent's shortwave radio network, the other eighteen research stations had all been notified of McMurdo's mass exodus in the expectancy the other outposts would all join up at Concordia. Beth made her case to each research facility, hoping to enjoin others in humanity's last best hope. Most considered the plan folly and informed McMurdo planners their respective personnel would not be traveling to Concordia, instead choosing to face the deadly Asteroid TQ-680 hunkered down in place.

Those who remained at McMurdo did so believing all was lost—accepting their fate—while others considered the six-hundred-twenty-mile escape route only marginally less deadly than TQ-680. A handful doubted the promise of world-ending devastation, believing instead the cries of wolf to be overblown. They too were scientists and had concluded, based on the available data, TQ-680's impact would be best met safely ensconced in McMurdo's amenities.

Snow-Cats, Sherps, Hägglunds and every snow-terrain-worthy available vehicle had been commandeered

for the high-risk journey. All manner of transporta-
tion during the reign of winter on Antarctica was
dangerous, including the simple act of walking from
one building to the next. Adjacent to McMurdo, the
United States Scott Air Force Base maintained a
small contingent of military personnel through the
winter months. Its commander, Colonel Jase Breslin,
having arrived at the same risk assessment as Beth
and Janek—that staying put along Antarctica's coast
meant certain death—assumed command of the convoy.
He delayed their departure by two days to compile
weather forecasts and to attend to the minutiae
of a thousand logistical issues. Byrd Glacier,
the selected passage through the Trans-Antarctic
Mountains, demanded careful planning.

Food stores, excess fuel, sundry other provisions,
and sixty-eight civilian and military personnel
were sent ahead in an Air Force transport plane
capable of flying through winter's harsh conditions.
All air traffic ceased at the end of Antarctica's
brief summer season. The sixty-eight brave souls
who volunteered for air travel did so knowing their
chances of making it to Concordia were less than
those traveling by land.

Even if successful, a turnaround flight for a
second McMurdo to Concordia run would be impossible,
as Concordia lacked the airplane engine heating
equipment needed to keep the engines from freezing.
It was a one-way trip that held the promise of life
at the other end, absent a guarantee of getting
there.

The two-day delay allowed Breslin time to gather reconnaissance of the planned route, including Ground Penetrating Radar overflights. The pilot and his plane were lost in the effort before the GPR mapping of the Byrd Glacier could be completed. Breslin had hoped to avoid the immensely dangerous, below-the-surface hidden crevasses notorious in the mile-deep snow fields of Byrd Glacier. They had to accept the risk of completing only eighty-five percent of the GPR mapping mission.

After decades of a worldwide glacial meltdown, Byrd Glacier defied scientific explanation by reversing the pattern in early 2041, and the buildup never stopped. The glacier's ongoing expansion gave Breslin and the entire McMurdo cortege hopes of limited crevasse exposure. It was a double-edged sword. With new snow accumulations, old gaps would be hidden.

Colonel Breslin, the fifty-five-year-old, self-assured, tall, well-built commander, set the ETA for the convoy to arrive at Concordia Station on April 3rd, projecting travel time of six days over snow and ice. The Colonel's team plotted the six-hundred-twenty-mile course and planned for one hundred miles per day at twenty-five miles per hour, traveling only during daylight hours. That gave the convoy a window to avoid a forecasted mother-of-a-storm beginning to form off Antarctica's eastern waters. Breslin's ETA put the convoy two days ahead of the storm's arrival and well before Mother Nature turned the lights off. He expected they'd face trouble in one form or another and built in time for delays along the route.

After May 2nd, sunrise wouldn't be seen in southeastern Antarctica again until September—that is, if they made it to Concordia in one piece and lived through TQ-680 to see it.

Four days of tight quarters and no showers had the insides of the Snow-Cat Trooper smelling ripe. Tempers were short, and the trip was long. A small sacrifice if they made it to Concordia.

Warm inside the three-year-old Snow-Cat Trooper, built to accommodate sixteen passengers, Beth Green sat back in amongst the other twenty-eight escapees crammed into the vehicle and watched wind-driven surface snow whip past the windows outside. Designated Unit Thirty-Six, given all the transports in the convoy had been recast with new call signs according to their position in the caravan. The last vehicle in the long line of hopeful travelers, Beth volunteered for Unit Thirty-Six to keep watch from the rear.

At 4:50 PM local time, they still had one hour and two minutes of daylight, depending on their current location. Outside, the temperature of minus twenty-six degrees Fahrenheit would dive rapidly once they lost the sun. Shy of seven hours of daylight, they would lose more and more of it each day, and in the short span of a few weeks, all-natural sunlight would cease to reach Antarctica's Concordia Station. Daylight at the pole had an even smaller window, with the annual setting of the sun on April 9, 2089.

Wind howled outside her window while Beth fumbled

with a reddish, flattish meteorite she'd spotted and picked up lying on the Antarctic surface during their last stop. The continent was Earth's richest source of such objects, mostly due to the ease of spotting dark-colored space rocks against the all-consuming whiteness. Its near-rectangular shape, no more than six inches long, three inches wide, and less than an inch thick, was highly unusual for a meteorite.

A fellow scientist with family roots from Pakistan, sitting alongside Beth, asked, "Whatcha got there?"

"Meteorite. Found it just lying there. Look at the colors. You're a geologist. Have you ever seen one this red? Not crystals imbedded in metal, a metallic crystal."

The woman gestured with her hand out. "Let's have a look."

Beth found herself strangely reluctant to accommodate the request. Instead, she held it out in her palm for her friend's inspection. Before she could react, the woman snatched it away.

A pang of loss stabbed at Beth's heart.

She turned it over, inspecting it from every angle. With rock in hand, she motioned her palm up and down in judgment of its weight. "Never have I seen anything like this. The shape. The coloring. And it's solid, not brittle, no honeycombs, and it's almost weightless. If we make it out of this alive, I'd like to study it. If that's okay with you."

Beth, normally a very generous person, hesitated. "First, we have to get past TQ-680 and make it to Concordia. But sure, why not? I'd be interested in what you have to say about it. It's one of a kind."

"Then we have a deal," the fellow scientist said, and tossed the space rock back to Beth.

The meteorite jostled about between Beth's hands before she secured it, closing her fingers tightly around it. A sense of satisfaction and relief settled in as she stared down at the compelling object.

The woman broke Beth's concentration. "We're going to make it. Don't you worry about that. I can't believe so many stayed behind."

"You and me both. I don't understand people sometimes. Even if our chances are fifty-fifty for us to make it to Concordia, those are better odds than staying at McMurdo."

"Not sure how we're all going to fit. I know they upgraded Concordia this past year and now have almost seven hundred staying there in the summer. If we get there, along with people from the other outposts, it's going to be tight. A lot of mouths to feed. Not sure reaching out to the other stations was the best idea. Supplies aren't going to last forever."

Beth understood her point. Everyone could end up starving to death for the lack of food rations, yet what choice did she have? The world's population was on track to be wiped out—the McMurdo convoy included. Every soul had to be afforded an equal chance to survive for the good of humanity. Numbers mattered. More people, not less, would be required to repopulate civilization. Whatever would be left to rebuild from—if anything of Earth remained.

"Concordia evac'd most of the staff. I heard the

last of them flew out at the end of February. Only ten stayed behind. At least they know we're coming," Beth said, pleased with herself. She put the prospect of starvation from her mind. A problem for another day, if they saw another day.

The woman added. "I trust Breslin. He's top notch. If anyone can get us there, it's him. As for keeping us alive after that, he's our man."

Beth asked, "How well do you know him?"

"He's called me in a few times to consult with the Air Force. He's a good guy. Competent. And I mean that in a positive way. He'll get us there safe."

Beth replied, "Four days down. One, maybe two to go."

"We've made good time, only minor obstacles, and the weather's cooperated. That is, until today. Wind's picked up in the past hour. Wish we had access to the weather forecasting computers back at the station. It's getting worse by the hour."

Beth looked out one of the small, insulated windows as snow whipped past, and a gust shook the ten-thousand-pound transport. The blustery weather nearly reduced visibility to zero.

That's when trouble hit.

The leading edge of the storm's arrival, two days early, took everyone by surprise.

Beth stopped talking the second the radio squealed to life.

From the command position in the lead transport, an announcement went out. "This is Colonel Breslin in Unit One to McMurdo Convoy. Over." A pause allowed the thirty-five other transport vehicle radio operators time to assume their stations.

"… Breslin… this… position… thirty-six… can't…"

The radio crackled and hummed.

Someone in Beth's cab called out, "He's breaking up. Maybe we are too. Maybe Breslin can't hear us."

Wind ripped across the open plain, picking up snow and throwing it against every vehicle. Visibility was down to twenty feet and the blizzard-like conditions engulfing the caravan hampered radio reception the further from its source. And Unit 36 sat at the end of the line.

"This is Unit Thirty-Five. Breslin, come in. I can see Unit Thirty-Six. She's right behind us. Over."

The woman sitting next to Beth asked, "We can hear Breslin. Why can't he hear us?"

"This is Breslin. Unit Thirty-Five. Listen in and when I'm done, get someone out there and relay all info to Unit Thirty-Six. Over."

"Unit Thirty-Five. Roger that. Over."

"This… thirty-six… breaking up… say again…"

"Breslin here. Listen, all units. Storm's kicking up. Getting worse by the minute. Convoy not safe out in the open. Valley half mile ahead. We'll hunker down there. Keep engines running. Minus twenty-six out there. Going to lose the light soon. Going to get colder. Storm should pass in ten to twelve hours. Over."

"… six… say… over."

"This is Breslin. Thirty-Five. Make sure Unit Thirty-Six is up to speed on the plan. After that, lead her to join us in the protection of the valley ahead. Attention all other units, follow Unit One. Over."

"This is Unit Thirty-Five. Roger that. Stopping. You go on. We'll catch up shortly. Over."

In a panic, the woman pleaded, "Why doesn't he answer us?"

With limited sight, Unit Thirty-Six should have called an "all stop". In the confusion of radio signal failure, the vehicle's driver did not. In blinding snow, Unit Thirty-Six, the Snow-Cat Trooper at the end of the caravan, slammed into the rear of the stopped Unit Thirty-Five.

Beth and everyone inside Unit 36 careened into whatever occupied the space in front of them. Her head slammed into the metal bar of the seat frame and she was out.

Loseff gently closed the book and looked up at the dumbfounded Jaynes. "The look on your face says it all. Either this book is a fairytale, or we've all been lied to for generations."

Can't Trust Anybody

Black Haven, Concord City

Reyne

Reyne, Gina, and Red trailed Mahoney through the dirt-packed streets on their way to Concord City's central meeting house where the council awaited Red's return. An uncertain outcome left Reyne uneasy. From Mahtoney's account, Reyne figured his ability to remain in the city and gain access to Red's guy hinged on the outcome of the council meeting.

Although eerie, cloaked in ever-present despair, there appeared to be a sense of normality to the street life he observed. The hodgepodge of housing designs combined with varied construction materials gave Reyne the impression Concord City was built on a foundation of spare parts. Rows of small concrete blocks chiseled from the moss fields debris stacked up like children's playhouses. Others, of rammed earth neatly finished with thatched roofing, and elaborate two-and three-story stick construction homes sat alongside single room dome shaped mud-brick units. Most surprising were the cohune palm log cabin multi-family dwellings. Black Haven tribal life was primitive in comparison.

Reyne thought he spied light leaking out of one large structure. Pointing, he asked, "What's that?"

"Greenhouse," Mahtoney said, short and curt.

"Is that light?"

Mahtoney stopped bringing them all to a halt. "Sure is. We use it to grow very unusual plants and the like. Helps feed everyone living here."

Confused, Reyne turned to Gina. "How is there light? I didn't think..."

"You got that right. You don't think." Red laughed.

Gina asked, "How?"

Matter-of-factly, Mahtoney replied, "Bioluminescence."

Reyne scratched his head. "Bio lumo what?"

"Living things that generate their own light. In this case, bats that glow in the dark. Well, when they sleep anyway. A colony lives along the top in the rafters half the time. There's got to be thousands of them. It's pretty bright in there. They leave and return on a regular basis. Besides, bat shit makes great fertilizer out in the fields."

With a scrunched face, Reyne asked, "That don't make sense. Bats light up when they sleep? Seems it would attract things to them while vulnerable."

Mahtoney snickered, "Exactly. That's the point. They have this sense about them. Anything gets close to them, even when they sleep, something in their brains alerts them and they snatch it out of the air for a quick meal. Moths and bugs are attracted to the light. Then, when the bats fly away and hunt, they go dark. And, whatever they go after, don't see them coming."

"Red," Reyne interrupted, "your people ever do that kinda thing with glow-in-the-dark bats?"

With a shrug, Red replied, "Story is a few tribes tried it. Brought on too much attention. Tribes fought each other over them. Lots of people got killed trying to do what Concord City does. That was long ago, before my time. All the tribes just gave up on it. Wasn't worth it. You could grow more food to live on, but on the downside, you died trying to protect it. Kinda defeated the purpose."

"So why can Concord City get away with it?" Gina asked.

Red was first to answer. "Two words... Devil's Hammer. No one wants to fuck with him. Now that he's gone, who knows?" She turned to Mahtoney. "Enough with the science lesson."

Mahtoney shoved Reyne from behind. "Get a move on. We have a meeting to get to."

Along the way several passersby acknowledged Red with a warm welcome usually followed with a sneer for Reyne and Gina. The children in the streets roamed freely and seemed to look up to Mahtoney.

"Did you bring anything back for us?" a young girl pleaded as she and six companions circled the tall Concordian native.

Down on his haunches, Mahtoney rubbed her head and offered the child a warm grin. "I just went a mile or two outside the city. Do I have to bring something back every time I pass through the gate?"

"Yes! Yes!" the children all shouted as they jumped up and down.

He held out empty, open hands.

Wild excitement and childhood innocence died at the gesture.

Red reached behind and grabbed her backpack. Opening it as she walked, she threw handfuls of meadow muffins into the air. The youngsters jumped as their enthusiasm returned and a mishmash of arms flew up to snatch the prize before another could claim it. "More. More," they demanded. Red kept walking while tossing every piece of moss she'd salvaged.

Back on his feet, Mahtoney slapped Red on the back. "Thanks. You saved me once again."

Gina tugged at Reyne's shirt from behind, pulling him back a few steps. "I think we're being followed."

"Yeah, by a bunch of little kids."

"You're an idiot. No, not them."

Reyne craned his neck to scan the area.

"Don't turn around," Gina shot back.

Reyne heeded the advice and kept walking. "We're strangers to these people. Of course they're gonna be curious."

"Maybe. It's just that I swear there's someone moving, house to house, peeking around each corner, following us."

"Ever think they ain't followin' us? They're following either Red or Mahtoney?"

"Good point. Maybe you're not an idiot, but I don't think so."

Confused, Reyne asked, "You don't think what, that I'm not an idiot or that they ain't followin' us?"

Gina smirked. "Exactly."

Red stopped and turned around. "What are you two up to back there?"

Gina offered, "Just takin' in the sights."

Red demanded, "Get up here. We should talk before we get to the council."

Gina slipped her arm under Reyne's, dragging him along with her as she sidled up to Red. "I was thinking the same thing myself. I'd like some advanced intel. What's the layout? How many will there be? Are we in danger? Exit points?"

"Forget all that. They're just going to check you out. They want to make sure you don't pose a threat to anyone. If you pass, the Council will allow you free rein. After that, I'll be able to take you to my guy who might help you off Black Haven... together."

Reyne looked at Gina and offered surprised raised eyebrows as if to say, "So, you agreed to sleep with her?"

Gina shook her head.

He couldn't resist giving Gina a little payback. "What gives, Red? You forgoing the prerequisite bedding? We just gonna meet with him?"

Gina slammed an elbow into Reyne's rib cage. He doubled over.

"Not at all. Just figured the answer has to be yes. You both followed me all the way here. You want out. What else could it be?"

Reyne popped back up, and his eyes lit up at Gina.

Gina hung her head. "I hate you both."

"Listen, first things first. Just follow my lead. Don't do anything aggressive. Speak in soft tones. And if they ask you anything, the truth is the best approach. One woman on the council is pretty good at detecting liars."

Reyne asked, "What about the Devil's Hammer? This is his village... well, it was his village. They're gonna be mad about that."

"Yeah, At first. I'll make them see it my way. Just wait and see. You'll be surprised at how persuasive I can be."

Gina threw in, "What about your people? They ain't here with us and didn't show when Mahtoney made an appearance?"

"I'll cover that. Gonna ask for Concord City to accept them. They're hard workers."

Reyne observed, "You're throwing a lot at this council. Are they the kind of people who can deal with it?"

"I've done a lot for Concord City. Now I'm asking for something in return."

Mahtoney joined in. "Neladith, grab the two newcomers. Let's get this show going." He opened one side of two large double doors. "In you go. We're here."

The open portal proved too dark for Reyne to make out what awaited him and Gina inside. "Even a small lume crystal would be nice right about now," he joked.

Gina ignored the jest. "Nothing good is going to happen in that room. I can feel it."

"We gotta meet with Red's guy to get off Black Haven. No way around it. You got any other ideas?"

Gina pouted, "No."

Red stepped between them and, with one hand behind each of their backs, gave them a gentle push forward. "No need to dally. Get your asses in there. I'll be right up there with you."

"That's what I'm worried about, Red," Gina said, stepping through the door.

Reyne's vision improved once inside although only slightly. Beams standing ten feet apart lined the long, open center space. Black flames flickered from angled sconces protruding from each. Reyne wondered if the seeming lightless fire offered those born to Black Haven some advantage. He certainly didn't get any. Two massive caldrons, set off to each side and in front of the council rostrum, blazed in angry black. The outline of nine bodies, faces hidden from Reyne in the gloom, sat in a row upon the raised platform. Voices caught his attention and when he'd finally taken notice, Reyne was stunned to see at least a hundred people lining both sides of the room.

From somewhere near the nine-paneled rostrum a loud *thunk* rang out. The voices dimmed. *Thunk.* And with the second ceremonial demand, silence filled the vast space.

The shape of a man—in dark silhouette—with a staff in one hand, stepped out before the dais. "Neladith and Mahtoney, both members of the Order of Concord, protectors of our city, you have asked to be heard by the Unity Council."

The silhouetted man slammed down his staff.

Thunk.

And again.

Thunk.

"Speak your purpose."

Red stepped forward to face the nine. "Our benefactor is dead."

The crowd erupted in a collective gasp. Cries rang out.

Thunk.

Thunk.

Silhouette man roared, "Silence. I will have silence!"

Red turned to face Reyne and Gina.

Her arm shot forward, pointing at the two Tarticans.

"They killed him!"

FOOTSTEPS

Neladith

The stolen outfit that Neladith took from Mithany's leather goods shoppe had give in all the right places. The Evidar agent beamed inwardly as she ran north through the forest, laying down false tracks pointing to Topak.

Sure, they'll be coming for me as soon as the Judjurex recovers. That old fucker will never catch me. She couldn't be certain how long he'd be out. If the blow fractured his larynx, worst case for him, life threatening; if her jab to his throat resulted in a mere contusion, he'd be up and about soon. She hoped for the former yet knew she had to take action assuming the latter.

While Neladith enjoyed her little diversion into Hensdale, she held on to one regret from her brief stay; she missed her chance to see Mithany one more time. Not that Mithany would be the least bit accommodating to her visit, but Neladith regretted the missed opportunity nonetheless.

Since Mithany proved out of reach, Neladith had no reason to stick around. She needed to put as much distance between herself and whatever group of ragtag recruits Hensdale's Judjurex assembled. As a wanted fugitive for Arek's attempted murder days earlier, Neladith's taunts at evading Hensdale justice would surely motivate the townsfolk to find her. Yet gathering up a posse would take time. Time Neladith would use to create false tracks, leading Tetrip away from her true destination.

During her brief return to Evidar, the Devil's Blacksmith tasked her with tracking down Selundra Quith. Now back on Tartica, and out of range of the Devil's Blacksmith's watchful eye, she needed to put distractions aside, at least for now, and resume her mission. *Besides*, she thought, *killing Quith will be its own entertaining distraction.*

After setting down an obvious trail of broken twigs and matted footprints—props the forest surrounds offered her in creating the impression of an escape headed north—she was confident the Judjurex would follow. Once she changed direction, she'd carefully avoid creating new markers, hiding from the Judjurex her true destination once she turned east towards The Woodlands—where she and Quith burned the bodies of Dylla and Mera.

Tartica, unlike the environs of Evidar, was unfamiliar territory to the highly regarded young operative. On her only other visit to Tartica, all her time had been spent around Hensdale, Owls Neck, and Topak. Once she reached The Woodlands, afterwards turning south, everything would be virgin ground with unknown dangers.

Neladith was young, not stupid. Stopping to take a quick breather, she bent over, resting her hands on her knees. *Think, Neladith*, she told herself. *Remember your briefings. Dylla laid out details. All those shitty little villages, roads, places of interest. Ah, more importantly, safe houses and contacts.*

Rising, she tapped her knuckles against her temple. *Come on, girl, you got this. It'll take a few days for me to get there. Need food, and gotta get me a good knife to kill you with, Mister Whitetop.* A name for Quith that Mithany told her about from the trio's fortuitous meeting in Owls Neck more than two weeks ago. *I know where you're going, Quith... Dylla's contact in the Thuggery, Nails, is your best bet. If they gave me good intel, Nails is even more duplicitous than you—for the right price that is.*

The side of her index finger tapped her lips a few times. *Oh yeah, I'm gonna need some coin.*

With both hands on her hips, Neladith twisted from side to side and then leaned back, stretching her tired muscles. Speaking aloud, she said, "Well then, we have a plan. Stay off the road. Find that safe house and hit a few small villages along the way. Rob a tavern or two, after a good meal, of course, and then on to the next." She looked around. "One forest around here looks like any other. Sun's on my left in the morning, on my right in the afternoon."

After half a day and a full night, Neladith expected she'd put herself beyond the reach of whoever Hensdale sent out to find her. Youth, training, and determination had prepared her well for the otherwise arduous journey. Few individuals had the stamina to keep up with the pace she set. During a quick pause to get the lay of the land, Neladith stopped to look around. *If I got this figured out*, she raised a hand over her eyes and squinted, *The Woodlands shouldn't be too far up off.*

About to take her next step... *clopity... clopity... clopity...* faintly wafted through the forest's leafless trees. Neladith stilled, tilted her head, and aimed her left ear towards the sound. It grew louder, *clopity... clopity... clopity...* and louder... *clopity...clopity.*

Swosh, swosh, the sounds of leaves underfoot rustled along the forest floor.

Neladith crept in measured steps behind an enormous tree trunk. *Footsteps! Horses. Men.*

COMMITTED TO A CAUSE

TETH: 16TH DAY OF THE HARVEST MOON

Jerithan

Not all of Teth's population cowered in their dwellings as the Temple of Life Palace burned. The mob responsible for tearing down Tartican civilization's single most identifiable symbol of a faith embedded in the Covenant of Universal Absolute Obligations had cheered in celebration, watching from a safe distance—those fortunate enough to have escaped in time.

While the Temple Palace blazed, absent any effort to save it, Jerithan considered it proof the riotous horde was more committed to their cause than those of the faithful. Proof, Jerithan believed, human nature's concern for individual safety outweighed the desire to secure a place in the eternal Community of Souls the Temple of Life faith promised.

Night had given way to dawn and still the Temple Palace burned. Flames continued to feed off a millennium of history, treasured artworks, inspired architecture, artisan-crafted furniture, and every book in the Temple's Secret Archives. All were reduced to nothing more than fuel for combustion.

The two escapees, Jerithan and S'Leen, stopped for a breather as they sped from the conflagration. Looking back at the place from which they escaped, tears welled in S'Leen's eyes. "Jerithan, my heart is broken."

Gently, Jerithan took S'Leen's hand in his. "As is mine. It's an awful sight. I'm not only filled with sorrow, I'm filled with anger as well. This need not have happened. Serco's incompetence in protecting our sacred home is as much to blame as the idiots with torches."

Nothing to say? Jerithan asked the Voice. Silence filled Jerithan's mind. His follow up, *Are you there?* proved just as fruitless. *When are you ever there for me when I actually need you?* A reply did not materialize, nor was one expected.

"You and I are lucky to have survived," S'Leen said, looking towards the once beautiful Temple Palace. "Do you think the others made it out safely?"

"We can only hope they did... except for First Lord Serco. I am a holy man at heart, yet only human. I am ashamed to admit, the thought of Serco's death comforts me."

"Jerithan, don't let his actions against you taint your soul. The Goddess Teth teaches us forgiveness. You don't need me to remind you the tenets of our faith. Nor do you need me to judge you. What he did to you is indefensible."

"S'Leen, you are a dear friend. I do not fault you. There is hate in my heart aimed at Serco, which I know is wrong. I accept who I am. Come, let us forget the man. There is someone I know in Shantytown. We can hold up at his place."

As they made their way into the ghetto of Teth, with the spectacle of the Temple's destruction commanding the attention of anyone out this early in the morning, the alleyways of the slums were mostly empty.

Jerithan reassured S'Leen, "Disheveled, dirty, and half-dressed, I cannot foresee being identified even if we run into anyone this early in the morning."

S'Leen stopped and pointed. "Jerithan, look up ahead. It's Shantytown's Communal Temple. It still stands. Let's go in."

"I would prefer we make for the dwelling of my contact. A guy named Timble."

"You said it yourself, there is little chance anyone will notice us. Please, I would like to pray... inside."

"Little chance, maybe. Little chance does not mean zero chance. Anyone devout enough to be praying at this hour just might know who we are."

"Come on, Jerithan." She grabbed his hand and pulled him along. "We're going inside."

Those of the sparsely gathered within Shantytown's Communal Temple turned in unison as the squealing hinges of heavy doors announced new arrivals.

Jerithan stopped in his tracks with every head turned in his direction.

S'Leen yanked him forward. "It'll be fine."

Although her proclamation intended to reassure him, it didn't. He accepted the risk, for S'Leen's sake. He whispered, "No names."

To his surprise, the nave appeared intact from the effects of society's disgruntled. Overall, the temple appeared in good shape; in as good a condition as the meager offerings the poor congregation could accommodate. Standing silently looking out over the meagerly adorned holy ground, he didn't recall ever sharing any of the Temple's considerable wealth with the Shantytown congregation. It never bothered him before.

The traditional green carpet of well-manicured grass covered the expanse, sloping gently towards the altar. Low-rising shrubs and trees lined the perimeter walls. Their upper branches reached high above and intertwined as they stretched out, forming the cathedral's ceiling. Autumn claimed the right to color the leaves of every tree across Tartica orange, yellow and red, save those of the continent's various holy grounds. Jerithan looked up at the green, vibrant foliage illuminated by brilliant sunrays, like a stained-glass dome bathing the inner sanctum in a holy verdant, ephemeral glow.

"It is so beautiful, Jer... sorry, Keflin." S'Leen's face lit up with excitement. "By the grace of the Goddess Teth, this temple survives. It's a wonder... it speaks to me. It proclaims a message in these times of chaos and destruction: There's hope." With her thumb, she completed the Signum Circulus over her chest, finishing, as tradition dictated, with an open palm resting peacefully on her heart.

Jerithan didn't repeat the gesture. Instead, he bore down on the few parishioners scattered over the open seating of the green lawn... watching them... as they watched him. Their eyes followed his and S'Leen's every movement.

An older woman, wrapped in a shawl, with white hair poking from beneath her babushka, stood. Jerithan's eyes narrowed at her, and he elbowed S'Leen in the side. Not more than twenty feet away, the white-haired woman appeared to squint back at Jerithan. He gulped down the saliva gathering in his throat.

The old woman's arm raised slowly. She cocked her head to one side, held it there for a few seconds, then pointed at Jerithan. Her hoarse, loud, gravelly voice announced to the others in the Communal Temple, "I know that face." She wiggled her finger in his direction and shouted, "That's Jerithan Cree!"

BLAME

BLACK HAVEN, CONCORD CITY

Reyne

"They killed him!"

Red's words shot an arrow of betrayal through Reyne's heart. Like a tsunami of fear, waves of terror pounded against every nerve in his body, already raw from constant exposure to the unknown. Reyne recoiled at the cacophony of anger flung at him and Gina in reaction to Red's accusation. His jaw clenched, and he balled his hands into tight fists.

Thirty feet beyond Reyne's position, at the edge of darkness, Black Haven hid from him in obscurity. A moving boundary of uncertainty that followed him every step of his journey. It taunted him from the moment he arrived in the alternate reality of Earth called Black Haven. If safety existed at all, it occurred inside an imaginary bubble ten yards in every direction with no promise of finality from one heartbeat to the next. Never a moment's peace—the persistent threat of danger lurked just outside the limits of his visual perception. With Red's accusation, the peril exploded tenfold.

The monster buried deep in his soul, lusting for revenge, crazed at the murder of Daedyn, consumed by hatred for those who'd killed his baby sister, his mother, his father, yearned for release. His inner beast had been denied for too long and Reyne, having gained some measure of control over it, thought, *Do it. Let it out.*

Breaking Reyne's concentration, a resounding *thump* rang out. The hooded staff bearer's crosier slammed into the wooden floorboards. He raised it quickly and, with even more force, thrust the wooden ceremonial rod downward.

Thump.

And again.

Thump.

The momentary thought sparked inside Reyne to release the monster within died in the attention-grabbing interruption of Silhouette Man.

A hushed silence fell over the room. Reyne scanned everything within the visible limits of his sight. Hatred stared back at him everywhere he looked. Lifting his gaze to escape their harsh judgement, he spotted empty handrails of a balcony lining the upper level. What lay behind them, he couldn't tell.

Red shouted at the crowd, "The Devil's Hammer has been taken from us." Her words filled the cavernous space.

The hundred in attendance erupted. The sound was deafening. Unlike the limits Black Haven's gloom placed on his eyes, voices from angry faces and from unseen Concordians reached out beyond his thirty-foot visual perimeter to attack his ears.

His head spun from one angry proclamation to the next.

"They must pay!"

"Death to the strangers!"

"Death is too good for them."

A stone flew past Reyne. Then another.

Silhouette Man crashed his staff against the floor. *Thump.*

"Enough!" he roared, bringing an instant halt to the commotion.

Reyne's veins pulsed against their limits to hold back the blood coursing through him. His temples, his eyeballs, the arteries in his neck throbbed with every heartbeat.

Let the monster out.

The call came from somewhere deep within the anger consuming his soul, pleading for release. With the monster lurking in his thoughts, Red's voice barely touched the edge of his awareness.

"... because of them." She flung an accusatory finger in Reyne's direction. "The people of my homeland have been attacked. Killed. My tribe is no longer safe in their ancestral lands. I ask for the council's declaration... put these two to death..." With arms spread wide, she slowly turned to address every person in the meeting space. "Now, right here, with the Council's approval, I will kill them for all of you to witness."

Gina's tone spit fire into Reyne's ears. "That motherfucking cunt set us up."

On the verge of losing control, Reyne's eyes bounced around in their sockets from side to side, up and down, wildly driven in search of a target.

Control rested on a razor's edge.

While the sound of Gina's voice entered his ears, it failed to settle in his mind. The elbow she jabbed into his side, however, stole his attention.

Silhouette Man pointed his staff at the pair. Gina's jab brought Reyne's focus back. Silhouette Man raised his staff high into the air. From the boundaries of his perception, along an upper tier of the chamber, slowly a dozen arrows emerged from the blackness as though materializing as they inched into Reyne's field of perception—with bows, drawn and ready. Encircling the upper balcony, twelve archers flowed out of the ebony limits of Reyne's focus. Once fully emerged into view, they stood at the handrails with weapons angled downward, leaving little doubt as to their purpose.

Someone in the crowd screamed out, "It's the Devil's Hammer!"

Reyne's, Gina's, and Red's heads snapped in unison to face the dais.

From behind the enormous table set atop the podium, seated at the center of the Unity Council, a man stood up and stepped out of the shadows. He unwrapped the scarf covering his face. Reyne didn't have to wait until he finished. He already knew the man behind it.

Gina gasped, "Mera."

The man behind the veil's voice boomed across the room, "How dare you!"

Red's head whipped about the meeting hall as though searching for something. She opened her mouth to speak. Black Haven's Mera—the Devil's Hammer—pointed and motioned a command with a single finger.

Swosh. Swosh. Swosh. Swosh. Swosh. Swosh. Swosh. Swosh.

Nine arrows released in response to the finger's command. The balcony archers hit their target even before Reyne could cover his head.

In rapid succession... *Twack. Twack. Twack. Twack...* all nine, metal-tipped, small wooden missiles bit into flesh.

A second later, commotion broke out, up in the galley amongst the archers. A small, hooded form could be seen moving between the balustrades, running towards a bowman. A moment later, turmoil erupted. An archer, shoved from behind, spilled over the railing.

With a *thud*, the archer landed dead on the floor.

The shadowy form raced to the next archer. An instant later, another bowman was dead. From the other side of the balcony, a man pulled back his bow. His aim followed the swift moving target for a heartbeat. The snap of his bowstring filled the hall. *Twack*, the arrow found its target. The unknown, small hooded form fell to the balcony floorboards and momentum tumbled it forward. The archer, saved by his compatriot, picked up the body. He leaned over the upper railing and threw the lifeless killer over the side.

It landed with a resounding *THUD*.

A collective gasp rang out.

Reyne looked down at the remains.

He knew the face.

Sissy was dead. Her bloody blade still gripped in her small hand.

If the shot didn't kill Sissy, the fall certainly did.

Sissy's limp body landed right beside Red's arrow-ridden corpse.

Fear should have taken hold of Reyne. He wondered why it hadn't. Black Haven's Mera had planned to kill him back at the compound. Reyne expected he and Gina would be next. He turned to Gina. "How's Mera's look-alike still alive?"

Gina angled her head to one side. "That's your reaction to all this? How's he alive?"

Thump.

Thump.

"Silence," Silhouette Man demanded.

Mera of Black Haven came out from behind and sauntered down the steps. He walked up to Gina. After a momentary visual inspection, he stated, "I do not know you. Why did you care I might die? You cradled me in your arms when you thought me dead. Why?"

After a long pull through her nostrils, Gina exhaled slowly. Seconds passed. Reyne could tell she was studying his face. She smiled at Black Haven's version of Mera. "At the time, I thought you were someone else... if I'm being completely honest."

"Honesty is always appreciated. As a matter of practice, I demand it."

"Well, you're not him. He's the only person I ever called 'friend'. I watched him die. Imagine my surprise, seeing your face, thinking you were him... and alive. Lying there, dying in my arms a second time. I couldn't lose him again. I thought you were him. My emotions got the better of me."

Black Haven's Mera circled Gina in careful steps, as though evaluating her from every angle. "I am told you are an assassin. Are you here to kill me?"

Reyne opened his mouth to answer. Mera put his open palm to Reyne's chest and said, "No, young man. I want to hear from her."

Gina spun to face him, "Look buddy, me and Reyne have no interest in you or anyone on this shithole of a planet. Yes, I'm an assassin back on Tartica. You know... my version of Earth. I just want to get back there. True, I'm not here to kill you. Whether you live or die is of little concern to either me or Reyne."

He turned to one of the other members of the Unity Council seated at the rostrum. She gestured with an affirmative nod. "My associate believes you. She has a talent for detecting lies. I'm left with the question of what to do with you both."

Reyne blurted, "How are you still alive?"

Gina mouthed the words, "Soul Stone."

Reyne replied in kind, "Soul Stone?"

Black Haven's Mera had the look of surprise at Gina's presumed conclusion.

"Reyne Brenton, I am concerned about you more than I am about your assassin friend. We both made certain proclamations of death towards each other. Yet, that was when you thought this to be Evidar. You present me with a conundrum. I did not believe, nor was I interested in, your quest to reach Evidar. However, upon reflection, I may have been too hasty."

He gave Reyne a thoughtful glare, then announced to everyone in the hall, "These two did not attempt to take my life. In fact, this woman called Gina thought to save me from the real assassin, lying dead at my feet."

The Devil's Hammer looked into Red's lifeless eyes and kicked her in the face.

"This dead woman, this traitor to me and all of you, sought to blame these two travelers. The woman who shot an arrow into my chest has paid with her life and the life of her ill-advised associate." He paused. "The people of her tribe are outside the city limits, expecting salvation. They participated in her deception."

His foot struck her again. Red's head recoiled at the limits of muscle tissue to keep it from being separated from her neck. "Gather up her tribe outside the city with a promise of assistance. Escort them back to their tribal lands. Say only that their leader and her associate are to remain here. Once there, in the area they call home, hang them in the open for all the other tribes to see. Young and old alike, leave none alive. They will help Concord City by serving as a warning to others."

Reyne gave Gina a shrug as if to say, "What's gonna happen to us?"

Gina shot back wide eyes and open palms.

"Mister Mahtoney," Black Haven's Mera continued. "Escort these two to my dwelling. I have much to think about. Stay with them until I arrive. Their safety is in your hands. Do not deny me the opportunity to eliminate them if I so decide that to be their fate. I will be along shortly."

He made his way back up the platform, then stopped. He turned to address all those still alive in the meeting hall. "No one is to harm either of these two. I have yet to decide if either is to live or die. Until then, they are my guests in Concord City."

Soul Survivor

Tandure: 16th Day of the Harvest Moon

Loseff

Loseff positioned himself on his bed with a pillow resting on the headboard. He opened the book and commenced to read:

Dawn of the Third Age
Chapter: Soul Survivor
April 3, 2089

A mental haze engulfing Beth's awareness receded in slow, begrudging increments. The fog of mind gave way to full consciousness, alerting her to the radio's crackles and hums bouncing around the inside of the Snow-Cat. Her eyes opened to the sight of motionless bodies. They were her friends, her colleagues. A gasped of horror seized her.

"Oh, God! No!"

She jerked back, slamming into a frozen body. Tears gathered but froze along the path down her cheeks. Beth turned and came face-to-face with her friend, Kay. Vacant eyes stared back at her. The icy glare that would remain with her forever.

Beth screamed, "Oh, God! Oh, God! She's dead."

Beth scanned the inside of the snow vehicle. Her mind reeled.

"Oh, my God! They're all dead."

In a panic, plumes of hot breath rapidly escaped her nose and mouth to billow in front of her eyes. She tried to grab hold of the seat back's rail. As she reached out, *clunk*. Looking up at her hand, the red meteorite clutched in her grip had struck the metal bar. She realized she had been clutching the strange object. With frosted tears, Beth turned her wrist to inspect the glowing, otherworldly rock. Neither warm nor cold, it denied the conditions in the cab to affect it, as did the exposed flesh of her hand gripping the object.

Bewildered, she stared at it, only to snap back when its presence seemed to suddenly reach out to her with tendrils wrapped around her soul. Her heart thundered in her chest, her eyes sprung open wide. Fear seized her mind, and she quickly shoved it into her coat pocket. A strange sense of remorse tugged at her, putting the space rock out of sight.

Beth tried to drive it from her thoughts and focus solely on finding survivors. She shook her head, clearing it of cobwebs. "Get a hold of yourself."

Beth turned her gaze to the nearest window, only to discover the outside world hidden away by fog and a thin coating of ice clinging to the tempered glass. She cleared just enough to discover snow whipping horizontally across her view—and saw night had taken over.

In the horror of death, the confusion of being alive, the fear-inducing space rock's presence, she hadn't given any thought to the lights inside the Snow-Cat. "Thank God the batteries haven't drained."

Scanning the lifeless forms of her friends, she searched each one for the telltale signs of warm air escaping into the frigid cold. Only her own respiration continued to birth small visible clouds of breath. Nothing moved. She ached for the dead. The people she cared for.

She told herself, *This was your idea.*

Get to Concordia Station, you told everyone.

Now, they're all gone.

You did this to them.

She hated herself at that moment. Heartache washed over her, and her insides felt like a sinking ship descending into the dark murky depths of a vast, bottomless ocean. The scientist in her knew the involuntary release of norepinephrine coursed through her veins.

What choice did I have?

What choice did any of us have?

We'd all die if we stayed.

No, I can't blame myself… Unsure she believed her own thoughts.

Lifting her eyes to the instrument panel, it showed the outside temperature to be thirty-six degrees below zero. Inside the cab, only eighteen below.

How am I still alive?

Aware of the stages of hypothermia—everyone at McMurdo Station had been trained on it ad nauseam—Beth wondered if she had entered its final stages where the body feels a sense of warmth, just before death came calling. Although, absent the accompanying symptoms of fatigue, heat stress, cramps, sweating, edema, or any of the others, it didn't fit.

Maybe I'm delirious?

Maybe this is hypothermia.

I just don't think so.

What else could it be?

Fogged over as all the other windows, Unit Thirty-six's front windshield withheld its secrets of what lay beyond. It shone as a white curtain lit from behind revealing one detail: the Snow-Cat's headlights remained on. What hid behind the white curtain, Beth needed to find out. Her life depended on it. And she had to conserve whatever battery reserves the Snow-Cat's cells clung to.

Beth feared what came next; her only path to the front of the cab was over the dead. Moving forward, she squinted, not wanting to look into the faces of her dead friends. Reluctantly, she put her hand atop a man's forehead. He'd been a welcome ally in all her years at McMurdo Station. No more than twenty-nine years old, he excelled at Antarctic topography. With cloudy, frosted-over open eyes, he stared back at her. Her own scrunched face pulled back, and her stomach wretched.

She made it past him.

One by one, Beth cat-walked over body after body, as tears fell before crystallizing into a tiny breadcrumb-like trail she left behind.

Empty of its passenger, Beth slid into the Snow-Cat's driver's seat, took in a deep breath and released a plume of lung-smoke. With a gloveless hand, she attempted to clear the windshield of its grayish-white veil. Wiping free the collected remnants of the now dead exhalations, Beth came face-to-face with a white wall of wind-driven snow caked to the outside of the window. Her hand rested against it.

Shit! Can't see a damned thing.

Then it hit her. She spread her fingers, pressing her palm against what should have been an iced-cold piece of glass.

What the hell?

Beth jerked her hand away. Her eyes studied the flesh covering her palm.

Pink, not blue. Huh?

Her mind searched her fingertips for the involuntary information it should have been providing her brain. She ran her thumb over its four adjoining fingertips. Her sense of touch worked fine. Her exposed skin, at minus eighteen degrees, should have been numb at best.

"Focus, Beth," she told herself out loud. "Everyone else is gone. Okay, I should be too. I'm not. That's a mystery for tomorrow. It's night. There's a blizzard outside. It's minus thirty-six. Can't go anywhere. Think!"

The radio squealed unintelligible noise. She snapped her head at the sound. With what should have been icicles for hands, she snatched the mic, pressed the call button and shouted, "Mayday! Mayday! This is Unit Thirty-six. Come in. Anyone, come in."

She waited.

Crackle. Hum.

"Mayday! Mayday! Come in."

She waited.

Nothing.

Again and again, she pleaded with the open mic for another human voice. Dejected, she cradled the mic hook in its holder—giving up. "The storm. It's got to be interfering with the shortwave signal. Damn it!"

She switched off the headlights and looked for the internal heat controls. The toggle switch showed the heat had been set to run. Notwithstanding what her eyes told her, it wasn't. A flip down and then up failed to engage the heating unit. Slow at first, she repeated the process over and over; in frustration, she flicked it on, then off, faster and faster. "Damaged when we crashed? How do I get you to work?" She pleaded with the small metal switch. "I'm a scientist, not a mechanic."

Beth crossed her arms, leaned back in her seat, and gazed at the gray-white mass in front of her. She turned to look over at her friends and colleagues. "I'm so sorry I brought you into this."

"Think, Beth. What are your options?" She checked her watch. "Okay, 4:22 AM. Wow, I've been out for ten hours, maybe more. I should be dead… Forget that… Focus… Astrological twilight for another two hours. Nautical and civil twilight, then 9:30ish and eight hours of daylight. Storm came in early. Should pass before the sun's up. One shot at starting the engine." Reluctantly, she acknowledged the futility of venturing out, *Trapped… for now.* "Going to have to wait until sunrise." *Hum, still not feeling cold.*

Resting her neck on the seat's headrest, she looked at the ceiling and blew puffs of steamed breath into the air. "Once the storm settles, should be able to get Colonel Breslin on the radio. Can't go out in the storm. I have only one choice. Wait it out."

Beth closed her eyes, accepted her fate, and hoped for the best. She drifted off to sleep thinking of her friends and wondering if hypothermia would take her in the night.

Loseff turned back several pages to examine the handwritten words in the margins that read: *Meteorite. Red rock? What is it?*

He recognized the handwriting—his father's!

Face the Music

Teth: 16th Day of the Harvest Moon

Jerithan

The woman's words, "That's Jerithan Cree," shook him to his core.

Anger flared in Jerithan's gut. He'd told S'Leen he didn't want to stop. They needed to get to safety—to Timble's home. She insisted they explore the Communal Temple first. His stomach roiled and his body instinctively flooded with cortisol to prepare the fearful former First Lord for a fight-or-flight decision. Never really a choice. Flight was hard-wired into his brain whenever he faced physical harm.

"How dare you!" A man in his mid-thirties shot up, dressed in shabby clothes, screaming at Jerithan. "You abandoned all of us, hiding behind your palace walls. Now that it burns, you come here to hide." Spittle flew from his mouth. "You're a coward."

Everyone else not already standing picked themselves off the green grass in unison. Wild-eyed, Jerithan scanned the room. His muscles tensed, making ready to flee.

S'Leen gripped his arm before he could act. "No, Jerithan. We owe them more than just running away."

He barely heard her plea over the twenty plus voices, all shouting angry words at him. "Are you crazy?" he said, ripping his limb from her hold just as several of the parishioners stepped towards the two Prudents.

S'Leen rested her hand on his. "We have failed in our service to the flock. The Temple of Life has failed the faithful of Shantytown. I have failed them."

Sadness touched his heart as S'Leen's words drilled past his defenses. Never one to give great concern for the wellbeing of others who did not serve his purpose, his tenure as First Lord had always been about power, not about caring for the faithful masses. Yet here they were, only twenty or so true believers—a pitiful showing—gathered in a house of prayer, choosing faith as their only defense against a riotous mob.

S'Leen continued, "... and yes, you have failed them, too."

Jerithan recoiled, flabby and bare-chested, his soul as exposed as his flesh to S'Leen's accusations. Of course, she was right. They were all right. He was a coward. He didn't deserve their respect. Their devotion. Their adulation. Their sympathy.

... or their help.

He flung his arms back. His paunchy belly thrust forward. He yelled at them, "Yes! You have the measure of the man I am."

One shouted, "There, you have it. He admits it."

Another threw in, "You're pathetic."

Jerithan's voice dropped to a hushed whisper, "I *am* pathetic," and he hung his head.

A hand, S'Leen's, gently rubbed his back.

An instant later, a ruckus of accusations and condemnations were hurled at Jerithan. Perhaps the loss of his beloved Temple Palace awakened the faith inside him long denied—or was it the degradation, the humiliation he shared with the motley parishioners?—yet whatever the cause, he understood their anger. It was his own anger.

It tasted like betrayal.

When the call came to end the Covenant of Absolute Universal Obligations, the foundation of Tartican civilization, the Temple of Life Prudents all cowered inside the safety of the palace, leaving the faithful to fend for themselves.

They were betrayed by Temple leadership.

He was betrayed by those very same people.

For the Shantytown faithful, it was the institution of the Temple of Life, its leadership, and even himself as First Lord, who had failed them. Jerithan's own sense of abandonment mirrored the pitiful few before him, and he connected with their plight.

They were abandoned by the Temple of Life.

He's been discarded by the very same.

They yearned for salvation.

He yearned for redemption.

In that realization… in that moment, in the aftermath of the Temple Palace's ruination, he faced the fraud of the leader he had been. A tiny spark flared in his heart, struggling to ignite the dry wick of his faith's long-dormant, internal guiding light.

He snapped to attention. "Who leads this service?" he demanded. They weren't listening and continued their verbal assault.

His voice boomed, "Enough!"

Silence fell over the hall.

Respectful and commanding, he asked again, "Now, tell me. Who leads this communal service?"

Heads turned from side-to-side without speaking. White-haired-babushka woman answered, "No one. There is no service. Our Communal Leader has fled us in our most dire time of need… like all the other Temple cowards."

Jerithan accepted her sting and offered a gentle smile in return. "You deserve better. You gathered here to pray before Second Lord S'Leen and I interrupted your devotional offerings. If you will have me, and I know I am not worthy, I ask that you allow me to deliver a traditional Temple of Life service. I have a lot to make up for. I would like to start that journey, here… with you… today."

Tears welled up in S'Leen's eyes. In a soft, warm tone, she remarked, "The Goddess Teth surely works in mysterious ways."

A voice from the back of the small crowd rang out, "Why should we let—"

White-haired-babushka lady spun around to face the man with her arms crossed over her chest. He, like all the others, went silent.

A peaceful quietude hung over the room. The older woman looked Jerithan up and down. "You ain't much," she sneered, then turned to everyone else, "but he's all we got." She swept an open arm toward the empty altar. "Go ahead. Give it yer best."

No one else spoke.

Taking S'Leen by the hand, Jerithan said, "We must do this together. I would be honored to have you at my side."

After securing vestments from the antechamber for himself and S'Leen, as giddy as a schoolboy, Jerithan delivered a heartfelt service, one that touched even his own tainted soul. As they progressed through the liturgy, additional stragglers found their way through the open doors.

Word quickly raced through Shantytown the former First Lord was delivering mass in the slums of Teth while the Temple Palace burned to the ground. By the end of the ceremony, over two hundred sat upon the open field under the green cathedral canopy above.

Jerithan's heart swelled in ways he hadn't experienced in years. He probed his mind for the presence of the Voice seeking praise for a job well done. The Voice was nowhere to be heard. *Why should this be any different? You are never here when I need you.* Jerithan didn't allow the absence of the Voice to detract from his first footsteps on the path towards reclamation.

As services ended, a man stood up. Tall, with orange hair, and in a voice that belied his massive size, the man squeaked out, "Jerithan, you's the man we needs to lead us."

ATTACK OF THE FLOWING RIVER

NORTH OF HENSDALE: 16TH DAY OF THE HARVEST MOON

Neladith

As the host drew near, Neladith's best guess put the number of horsemen and infantry at about two hundred. All dressed in oddly colored matching uniforms. She'd never seen clothing speckled with small patches of multi-shaded browns and grays. This wasn't some haphazard posse Judjurex Tetrip would have hastily thrown together. These were soldiers.

Crouched behind the base of an enormous tree, Neladith turned away from the approaching horde. Resting her back against the huge concealment, she pondered the implausibility of it all. *Soldiers? Ain't no armies on Tartica. And in the middle of a forest traipsing in and out of trees. Doesn't make sense.*

Horses didn't exist on Evidar, the version of Earth from which she hailed. However, she was familiar with the creatures, having seen them in and around Hensdale during her prior visit to Tartica. She admired their beauty, their grace, and their willingness to serve people. It added to her desire never to return to Evidar. Yet, more than anything, Neladith understood her goal to remain on Tartica was a fool's dream. Instead, she imagined the damage she could do to the other tribes of her home world if she could just bring one horse back with her. Getting a dumb beast through the Void, well, that too was impossible.

With one hand, she reached around to rub her neck while recalling a briefing. *Soldiers shouldn't exist. Not on Tartica. This place ain't like that. Things are changing fast around here.*

As a trained operative, she needed intel on this recent development. It held the possibility of fucking up her plans, and that wouldn't do. Turning back, she peeked out from her vantage point, careful to remain hidden. Still a hundred paces out, moving between the trees, the unit appeared scattered about and lacked cohesion, being forced apart to pass through the dense woodlands.

Spread throughout the leafless timbers as they approached her position, they looked like checker pieces dropped from atop a child's board game she recalled seeing in the home of two dead apple farmers—each piece, each soldier randomly sifting from one peg, one tree, to another as it drifted downward, onward, to-wards their goal. They were loud, noisy, and appeared to have little concern of being discovered. She figured, *Who'd be looking for soldiers who shouldn't exist... and, in the middle of fuckin' nowhere? What reason would they have for stealth... none.*

The unit was moving south and Neladith wondered, *Where'd they come from? Who sent them? To what purpose?*

Two of the uniformed troopers veered in her direction, appearing to go around a tight grouping of trees, randomly peeling off from the central host. Realizing she'd be exposed if they stayed on the current route, with no way to move without being discovered, Neladith covered herself with the fallen brown foliage densely littered across the forest floor. The leather outfit she'd stolen while in Hensdale matched well with the abundant dead vegetation.

Buried under her makeshift covering, the voices grew louder, closer, while the clomping of horse steps remained farther off. While lying flat, one side of her face pressed to the ground, with only her eyes narrowly exposed to keep watch, Neladith spied two of the mystery soldiers approaching. Closer the pair came until they were right on top of her position.

Breathing shallow to prevent her leaf pile from moving up and down, giving away her position, Neladith stilled her body. Just then, a boot swept under her ankle, her leg muscles locked, and one of the uniformed strangers tripped forward. The other caught an arm and prevented the fall.

With only her eyes moving, Neladith looked up at the pair standing together only a few feet from where she lay hidden.

In a man's voice, one of them said, "You alright?"

A woman replied, "I'm fine. Got my foot snagged under a branch."

"Walk much?"

"Almost forgot how funny you are."

Relief washed over Neladith just as her calf gave her a new problem; it itched and demanded immediate relief. The sooner the foreigners got out of there, the sooner she could attend to the nagging irritation screaming for attention. Just moments from relief, the man grabbed the woman's arm.

"Hold up, Shally, I gotta take a piss."

Shit! Neladith grit her teeth and pushed down the auto reflex her body demanded of her to scratch her leg.

The woman replied, "Don't let me stop you."

With two eyes peering out from behind an opening in the leaf pile, Neladith observed as the man unbuttoned his fly, freed his member, and let loose a river of steaming urine against the massive trunk she'd previously hid behind.

The uniformed woman leaned in, rested one hand on the tree, bent forward for a better view, and joked, "That thing in your hand looks like a dick, only smaller."

Neladith pressed her lips tight to keep from laughing, thinking the woman nailed the assessment.

"It's a grower," the man said casually as he shook out the last drops. He gave no offense in his reply to being watched as he relieved himself or to the woman's jibe at his manhood.

"If you say so." The woman's response sounded skeptical to Neladith's ears.

"Only one way to find out. Want to take it for a ride?"

"In your dreams, soldier boy."

A thought occurred to her. *This is Tartica. Covenant and all that repopulation bullshit...* Her reflection was interrupted by hot liquid along the side of her face. *Agh, you fuckin' asshole,* rattled around in her head realizing from whence it came. Fighting back revulsion, she squeezed her lips tight and remained motionless as more of her cheek experienced the attack of flowing urine. Her itch continued its demand to be rubbed.

While stuffing his undersized bits back into his pants, he complained, "We've been marching for two days since we found that birthing farm abandoned near Topak. And Topak itself was a complete waste of time...burned to a husk. Now we're supposed to sneak up on Owls Neck and Hensdale. This is a fool's errand."

"The Peoples Republic of Kantos is paying us well. Who cares if we don't find any Samers? Less work for us that way. Fewer quarters to build. Fewer prisoners to keep track of. Besides, you got somewhere else you're supposed to be? Got someone waiting for you back in Port Royal?"

Fixing the last button of his fly, he said, "And what if I do? You jealous?"

"Not after getting a look at what you're working with. I'm good."

"You know, I got other skills," he laughed, flicking his tongue.

With a shudder, her face contorted, and she shook her head as though biting down on sour fruit. "With a blessing from Teth herself, I hope to never find out."

Tugging on the front panel of his pants, making sure everything settled in the right place, Neladith watched and wondered, *I don't know how guys walk around with those things stuffed in their pants all day.*

The man tested the fit, moving his hips side to side, and added, "We're going to be at this Samer round-up assignment a long time. Gets lonely. You'll come around."

As the duo walked away, Neladith heard the woman's last thoughts on the matter when she said, "Can't imagine it so. If I ever get that desperate, maybe I'll get lucky and one of them Samers will kill me first." The pair's laughter drifted away on a breeze as they strode off.

Still concealed out of sight, Neladith held her position, intent on waiting in place until she no longer heard or saw movement from any of the two hundred. Yet, it didn't stop her from rubbing her boot against the opposite leg or lifting her face a few inches off the ground out of the puddle of piss.

A short while later, confident the host had departed, first turning her head from side to side for a better sweep of the area, and finding herself alone, the youthful

Evidar agent stood, brushing herself off. "Agh, you fuckin' dick," she spat aloud, wiping her sleeve vigorously against the offended cheek.

Crossing her arms over her chest, she tilted her head back while putting the pieces of conversation together. *Alright. They're moving south towards Hensdale. Good. I continue into the Woodlands, then south, I should stay out of their way. Huh, this Samer round-up they're on... prisoners... wonder what that's about?*

"Agh," she spat aloud and drove her cheek into her shoulder... and wiped again.

Survive

Tandure: 16th Day of the Harvest Moon

Loseff

Still angered at the revelation his father, the Chancellor of Adelle, had read *Dawn of the Third Age*, Loseff seethed looking down at the unopened tome. The notes his father left in the margins gave proof to Loseff that his father had taken the account described in the book as factual. Yet, never had Adelle's Chancellor shared any of it with him. His own father denied him the knowledge that Tartica's way of life was built on a lie. The Covenant's demand to reject technology, to embrace Nature as the only path forward for the betterment of humanity, was all a hoax; a way of controlling the population. The end of the Second Age had not been brought about by the overconsumption of the planet's natural resources, as everyone in the Third Age was taught to believe, but by a gigantic space rock.

Pacing back and forth, his insides roiled. *Fuck you, Father. You couldn't trust me? I'm your son.*

Alone in his room, Loseff stopped moving and contemplated aloud, "Yeah, I get it. It's all about power. Still, that's no excuse. You should've trusted me."

He wondered if the big lie helped his father to embrace electrics or to so easily toss off the Covenant as a means to tighten his grip on Adelle. "I guess the Covenant is an important tool until it's not."

He asked himself: *Did you share Dawn of the Third Age with Derr? My dear sister, Tane? ... Mother?*

Loseff's heart sank at the thought his mother withheld it from him, while feeling only bitterness at his father's duplicity—a deep, seething resentment settled over him.

That Tane might have been brought into their secret circle fed his lifelong animosity as the Kingdom's spare; Tane, the eldest child, would be the next Chancellor of Adelle. For him, only scraps.

Picking up the delicate manuscript, Loseff's fingers rode over the ancient cover. "Alright, let's see what else you haven't told me... *Dad*." Fury washed over him as he opened the book and read:

Dawn of the Third Age
Chapter: The Long Night
April 4, 2089

At 9:55 AM on April 4, 2089, the sun broke over Antarctica's horizon at a latitude of -76.09996 and a longitude of 133.333332, lighting up the snow encrusted windshield of Unit Thirty-Six. Minus twenty degrees Fahrenheit inside the cab, Beth pondered why she hadn't frozen to death through the remains of the night.

She scraped free the crystalized breath clinging to the window, yet realized to see anything outside, she needed to get outdoors to remove the remnants of what Mother Nature threw at the McMurdo Station convoy the day before.

Whatever they'd crashed into late yesterday afternoon remained concealed behind the encompassing white veil blanketing the Snow-Cat's windows. Also denied her: the status of the entire McMurdo Station caravan. With eyes squeezed tight, Beth paused. "Please, let it all be a dream."

Warm fingers, huddled inside battery-powered, electrically heated lined mittens, Beth balled her fists in anticipation of what she hoped not to see. From the driver's seat, she turned her head—and her attention from the mystery of what awaited her outside—to the friends and colleagues inside. Slowly, reluctantly, she forced her eyelids open. Horror filled her with dread.

They're all still dead.

Her chin dropped to her chest. Her heart sank at the plight of her deceased fellow travelers, mixed with self-pity for her own plight. She slapped her exposed face. "Pull yourself together. Mourn later. The daylight won't last long."

With clenched fists, she hammered against her temples. "Think Beth. Think."

One thought after another danced about in her head. As though speaking to a friend, she said aloud, "You have about nine hours of daylight. The last GPS readings put the convoy half a day out from Concordia. That's at 25 MPH. If I've got to walk it, it'll take days. You'll never survive. Where's the rest of the convoy? Okay, get Colonel Breslin on the radio, then get a look outside. Figure out how bad this thing's damaged."

Slipping off one mitten, Beth's hand snatched the radio's cold, plastic mic, pressed the call button, and pleaded, "Colonel Breslin, come in. Over." She waited. Silence. "Breslin, come in. Over." Nothing.

She screamed, "Dammit! Come in!" The crackle and squeal of the shortwave hissed back at her, absent Breslin or any other human sound. She erupted, "Ahhhhh!!" repeatedly stamping her boots against the Snow-Cat's iced-cold metal floor. "Anyone! Answer me!"

Dejected, Beth sat back. "Alright. I've got to do this on my own. Can't be any worse outside. Let's see what's out there." She flung her hand to the door handle, pushed hard against it. It failed to give. With her foot, she kicked it open, and a gust of even colder air swept into the cab. Frigid air slapped her face. How she was alive and not frozen to death played on her thoughts. "Let it go," she said aloud. "Figure it out later, if I live long enough."

She remembered seeing several of the frozen wearing ColdAvenger face masks. Hers was packed away wherever her belongings had been stashed. Determined to give herself every advantage to survive, Beth cringed at what she had to do next.

"I'm so sorry," she told a familiar face as she slipped the ventilator-assisted cold weather breathing mask over her dead friend's head. Beth pulled back her hood and slid the ColdAvenger over her face. Grabbing snow goggles hanging on the dashboard, Beth secured the one-piece unit over the upper half of her exposed face and pulled her hood back on. "Ready to go."

Outside the Snow-Cat, it became apparent to Beth what happened. The front of Unit Thirty-Six embedded itself into the rear of Unit Thirty-Five. Her thoughts raced to the fate of those inside. Her heart thundered in her chest. *Oh, God, no. Please, not them too.*

Through everything protecting her head from the cold, a distant hum poked at her ears. *Lord, I know I should be dead. Please let me have this.*

The hum grew closer. *You protected me through the night.*

Beth stilled and waited. *You must have a purpose for me.*

The louder it became, the hum turned into a repeating clank and the rattling sound of another snow vehicle filled her with hope. Beth raced around the entwined, disabled Snow-Cats. Snow crunched underfoot with each step. She stopped.

"Yes!" she shouted, pounding her fists high into the air.

Slow to close the book, careful not to cause damage to its delicate state, Loseff sat back to consider what he'd read. *Good for you, Beth, whoever you are.*

CHANGE OF PLANS

THE WOODLANDS: 16TH DAY OF THE HARVEST MOON

Mera

A tall, slender, middle-aged woman whose facial lines spoke of a hard life, dressed in an all-leather black journeymen's outfit adorned with knives on either side, casually strode into camp.

A light rain that had been rolling through on and off all morning, collected atop Mera's makeshift lean-to as the wet forest floor muffled the woman's approach.

Mera heard someone call out, "Welcome back, Kess." Mera jumped up and stormed out from under the lean-to. "Where the fuck have you been?" he demanded.

The crow's feet around her eyes pulled in tight. "That's how you greet an old friend?"

"You've kept me sitting here for days. You may have doomed Tartica!"

She pulled Mera in a bear hug and spoke into his ear. "I've so much to tell you. I'm sorry for making you wait. It couldn't be helped. As far as saving Tartica goes, that ship has sailed."

Mera stepped back. "You don't know what you've done."

She pulled back her hood and let the raindrops attack her scraggly mess of graying-blond hair. "What I've done, old friend, is collected information. And, by the way, my people made sure one particular assassin from Evidar didn't find you."

"Hmmm."

She slid her arm under his. "Oh, don't pout. Come on, let's get inside. I'll tell you everything."

Although the small stick-built structure was cramped, there were two stumps for chairs, a third masquerading as a side table, and it kept the rain off them both.

Mera pounded his fist on the open stump. "You fucked me, Kess. I didn't have time to sit around here with a thumb up my ass waiting for you to mosey in like it was a holy day of fun and games."

"It's been a few years since I fucked you." She scoffed. "Or, if I remember correctly, you fucked me. Yeah, you were the one on top..." With a shrug she prodded, "Did you miss me? It's been a while."

"I wish I had time to reminisce."

"Alright, alright. You're no fun anymore, so I'll get straight to it. You were spotted by one of mine a few days ago. And not far behind you was a guy with the telltale eye-shine. One of Evidar's, no doubt. He was on your trail... and getting close."

"I know all about him. His name is Quith."

"One of my scouts steered him away by picking up your trail and leading Quith away to follow him. This Quith guy is now headed south to Teth... You're welcome."

"I had it under control, Kess. You put me back days from where I need to be."

"You had it under control? Did you know there are two more Evidar agents coming up from the south, probably heading for Teth? Those two are asking around about some nut farmer from Hensdale and the Quith guy you mentioned."

"No, I didn't know about the other two. Reyne's one of mine, and they won't find him."

"Well, let me catch you up on the rest of it. You're gonna need a new plan."

Mera crossed his arms. "Let's hear it. This better be worth it."

Kess rose, went to a box stashed in one corner, and pulled out a jug along with two wooden cups. "How about a drink first?" She set the cups on the would-be table, filled them both, and handed one to Mera. "Drink up, old friend. We've known each other for decades and it amazes me you haven't aged one day. And look at me," she said, running her fingers through the tangled mess on her head. "My once-beautiful, long, blond, silky hair is going gray. How do you do it?" She held out her drink, nodded at Mera, and gulped it down. "Ahh, gotta love the burn."

Mera ignored her question and downed his drink. "Shit, that's rough... Another."

Kess poured a second round.

"Would your people really have shot me if I made a run for it?"

"No doubt about it. You made the right choice staying put. Besides, you're gonna agree with me that what I'm about to tell you was worth the wait."

"Enlighten me, then."

"It's a shit-show out there. You know I keep tabs on things. That's why you pay so well. I met up with a bunch of my scouts. Several were late."

"Are you going to keep me in suspense?"

"Teth is gone."

"I know that."

"Did you know the Temple Palace burned to the ground? Jerithan's been stripped of his First Lord title. Serco took over as the Temple of Life's head honcho. That didn't last long. He's nowhere to be found. Everyone figures he died in the Palace fire. Nails is missing. The Thuggery's got no clue where she's gone to. Kantos and Greenlin are all that remains of the United Front. Both are having a hard time recruiting soldiers. There's a new Prime Minister in Kantos and she's rounding up Samers, licensed and otherwise. Kantos set up half a dozen holding camps to keep the Samers from defecting to Adelle. Tomelai's putting together a massive army. The Hidden Hand, the wealthy elites working against Tomelai from the shadows for their own financial gain, are playing both sides. The Covenant is dead. Should I go on?"

Mera took in a deep breath then leaned forward, holding out his empty cup. "I'm going to need another. And keep them coming."

SEEDS IN A VAULT

TARTICA: 16TH DAY OF THE HARVEST MOON

Loseff

After leaving his father, Derr, Kiple, and the rest of the War Council, following the briefing, Loseff was eager to explore more of *Dawn of the Third Age*. In the aftermath of discovering his father's handwriting in the margins of the ancient manuscript, the ties binding Loseff to the Tomelai dynasty began to fray at the edges.

What other secrets the book had yet to reveal, Loseff yearned to get at them. He contemplated its impact on him and understood his future, and his father's, rested at the tipping point of a fulcrum. The answer to which way it would fall awaited Loseff inside the pages of Earth's true history. A history withheld from him by his own father that he was never supposed to know. He swallowed the bitterness of family betrayal and tainted parental love.

Light streamed in through his bedroom window. He lifted the book off his lap.

Dawn of the Third Age
Chapter: Seeds in a Vault
April 19, 2089

Beth Green and Janek, along with nine hundred and three other souls, were securely packed inside the Concordia Station World Seed & DNA Vault Repository.

It had been dedicated in 2078 to coincide with the research station's total rebuild. Sitting deep below the Antarctic Plateau's East Antarctic Ice Sheet, the seed vault was humanity's last best hope to deliver survivors into the future—after T-680.

The emigres from McMurdo Station, along with Concordia's winter inhabitants, prayed, cried, and huddled together on the morning of April 19, 2089, facing down the day of Earth's predicted destruction. Hope for a miracle had been abandoned.

Beth thought of her parents and her sister. She loved her family, and even with Janek in her arms—who completed a harrowing trip to arrive at Concordia only the day before—her heart was filled with sorrow knowing they would all die. She'd spoken with her mother, father, and sister only once after the news hit that the end of the world drew near—before all communication options to reach them went out.

Tears filled her eyes and a profound sadness drained her. Beth's family, along with the rest of humanity, were only minutes from being wiped off the face of the Earth—or whatever would remain of the planet's surface.

Janek looked down at the time on his sleeve; 10:46. At 10:49 Coordinated Universal Time, Asteroid TQ-680 was predicted to crash into Earth, just north of the Russian land mass. All of civilization, all of history and the future of life on the planet, had less than three minutes left. His thumbs wiped away the water seeping from Beth's eyes.

"I know," was all he said to her.

Inside the seed vault, its occupants, wrapped in blankets and coats against the cool temperature—required for the preservation of humankind's raw materials—hunkered down within its fifteen-foot-thick walls. The impenetrable ten-foot-thick, solid steel blast door closed without a sound.

The vault had been built to survive earthquakes, floods, fire, a slowly moving ice sheet, and just about anything Mother Nature could throw at it. Unfortunately, Asteroid TQ-680 went beyond anything she could cook up. In the enclosure, packed with frightened scientists, the collective mindset put the odds of the seed vault holding at 50-50.

Janek stared at the time instrument radiating from his shirt's cuff. Beth held her breath as 10:49 AM came and went without a sound, or without a single manifestation signaling the world had just ended.

Hushed silence hung over every corner, curve, and ceiling beam of the hallowed enclosure. The yellow lights of the emergency power supply glowed against the cold gray concrete walls. All other energy sources of Concordia Station had been shut down out of concern for the plethora of destructive forces TQ-680 would throw at them. The numbers ten and forty-nine consumed Beth, as they most likely did for every other mind on the planet.

"Beth"—choking up, Janek cleared the phlegm building in his throat—"a reminder: it will be at least thirty minutes before the effects reach us."

Colonel Jase Breslin rose. "It is now 10:50 UTC. It's done." He paused. The matter-of-fact military man trained in war, hardened against its destructive consequences, wept openly. "My heart longs for my wife, my children, and my granddaughter, whom I will never see again." He rubbed the heels of his palms against watering eyes. "My heart is broken as am I… the man before you. My heart goes out to all of you, your children… your spouses… partners… your parents, and loved ones. And for lost friends whom none of us will ever again speak to."

Breslin bowed his head and appeared to collect himself. After a long pause, he continued, "I don't know if we'll survive today. I *do* know that each of us owes a commitment to every man and woman in this building, that should God so decide we endure this day, we must commit our lives to each other. I don't have the words for this moment. I don't believe there're any in all of human language to adequately address the profound meaning, the depth of emotion, the unfathomable loss of love on a global scale. Words fail us all. Our souls understand what words cannot express."

A man stood, who Beth didn't recognize and assumed him to be a winter resident of Concordia. He spoke in a heavy French accent. "Colonel." The voice came void of emotion. Beth wondered if the thought of the world ending overwhelmed his ability to process it. "If the asteroid struck near Russia just moments ago, over twenty-five thousand miles from us, that means a shock wave traveling at perhaps one thousand miles per hour is going to sweep across Antarctica in minutes."

Once composed, Breslin assumed a military at-ease posture with both hands clasped behind his back. The sorrow flowing out in his voice hadn't followed the lead his body stance projected. "Yes, that's been covered in all the prep briefings."

The Frenchman continued outlining his dire prediction for the seed vault's occupants. "Not just a shock wave, a plasma wave approaching temperatures matching the surface of the sun. It's going to race across the planet and over the top of us. How can we possibly survive?"

Breslin shrugged. "Maybe you're right. Consider, though, we're a bit below ground. The ice sheet above the vault might be all that saves us. I don't think we need to discuss this right now. Let's just focus on surviving."

The Frenchman would not relent. "Even after the plasma wave has done its worst, a trailing pressure wave will roll over us. And later a conflagration, in an ever-growing ring of fire, expanding outward from the center of impact, faster than the human mind can comprehend. It has already likely overtaken Russia as we speak. The firestorm will either run out of steam or make a run at Antarctica.

"After that, the asteroid will throw off millions of tons of earth into the atmosphere and pieces of it will rain down on the planet as screaming, molten-hot pebbles, rocks, boulders, and these missiles of destruction will set ablaze whatever they touch. The air will become super-heated and will be carried on winds, reaching speeds no hurricane has ever matched. Earthquakes will shake the pillars of the earth; volcanos will erupt, and the oceans will rise in a global tsunami one to two miles high."

Breslin replied with conviction in his tone, "Even if you're right, we owe it to those we love and to the future… to hope."

"Colonel Breslin," Beth stood. "Would you mind if I speak?" She rubbed the tears from her face. Without waiting for his approval, she spoke. "I've lost everyone I loved today." She looked down at Janek. "Save one." She offered him a sorrow-filled smile. "As have all of you. While we might all be dead in the next few minutes, I believe in those who built this vault, and I believe in humanity. I will mourn and I will grieve and I will fight with every ounce of courage that every single one of you here in this place will live and will, with me, begin the process to rebuild civilization, whether it takes a decade, a lifetime, or a millennium."

She looked around at all the faces. "We have all lost everything. Family, friends, those we hold most dear to us, are gone… or soon will be. There is a gaping, wide chasm in my soul that nothing will ever fill. I say to all of you. You are now my family. Every single one of you. I will hold you in my heart and love will be my gift to you."

Shaking, Beth sat and wrapped herself around Janek. He gently stroked her hair and rubbed her back.

Colonel Breslin pursed his lips. "Thank you, Beth. And I will honor your gift of love… however long I live." He nodded to her. "Listen, everyone, we have four things going for us. Our elevation puts us over ten thousand feet above sea level. The air is thin and it just might tamp down the pressure wave. An oceanic tidal wave isn't likely to reach us, given how far inland we are and how high up we are. The air temp, constantly at somewhere between twenty below and eighty below, enveloping the entire continent, will be like a break wall when the plasma wave slams into it. A ring of fire will sweep over and consume the land masses of the Americas, Africa, Europe, and Asia. I'm betting it won't survive the journey across the ocean surrounding Antarctica.

"Let's not overlook the fact we're on the other side of the planet. Many of those aftereffects may not even get this far and if they do, they'll be weaker than at the epicenter. Let's not forget, we're one hundred feet underground surrounded by fif-teen-foot-thick concrete walls and floors, secured by state-of-the-art pylons drilled into the rock bed almost a mile down, designed for a structure buried in a crawling ice sheet. The seismic dampers built into this structure to steady it against earthquakes are beyond any technology I've ever seen. Are we going to make it? I know this. We have a better chance than anywhere else on Earth."

For how long they gathered huddled in silence except for the sounds of those crying, Beth didn't know, when she reached for the red meteorite in her coat pocket. Her fingers wrapped tightly around the otherworldly rock. Still snuggled with Janek, she glanced down, noting the time displayed on his shirt cuff, 11:13. She pulled her head off Janek's shoulder to look up at Breslin. "We are going to find out in about six minutes."

Seven minutes later, all eighty-five million pounds of the concrete seed vault started to rumble.

Loseff closed the book and set it on his lap. With his heart pounding, staring blankly at nothing, his jaw hung open. *Holy shit!*

Trust, It's a Bitch

Derr

Derr and Chancellor Tomelai left the War Council behind where Tomelai had directed to develop a comprehensive defense strategy. Derr had other issues on his mind. "Rotti, Loseff's found the book."

"That meeting proved disappointing," Tomelai said, ignoring Derr's effort to change topics.

"Rotti, listen to me. This is important."

Tomelai shot back, "And not having a coherent strategy for the defense of Adelle isn't?"

"Of course it is. There were bright spots in that briefing. Recruitment is far outpacing anything the United Front's put together. Samers are flocking to our cause and Loseff has put together two special forces units. One exclusively made up of Samer men who've joined our ranks and the other of like-minded female Samers. He believes they're bonded by a unifying cause and will perform better than the general population of recruits. He could be right. They're developing into tight, cohesive, highly motivated units. Related to that, the KCG has culled several spies planted amongst our troops. And General Kevine has made significant progress on securing our burgeoning military with a steady stream of supplies. It's moving ahead as well as we might expect. No one alive in Tartica has any experience at war. Give them a chance to succeed. The UF isn't anywhere near ready to launch an attack, so we have time."

"That is all well and good, Drew. We cannot rely on a defense strategy of the UF remaining dysfunctional. And this coming from you? You are always preaching to plan for the worst."

"Fair enough. However, my advice to you, Rotti...let it play out. Commander General Kiple needs to establish his authority over the War Council. Once this war gets going, you're going to rely on him. And yes, this is coming from me, the guy who never thought that much of Kiple. You and I can't be everywhere. You're going to need a firm hand for those times. We are pulled in too many directions to handle everything this war will throw at us. Give him a chance. If he fails... can his ass."

With arms held tight across his chest, Tomelai said, "For now... but my patience has its limits."

"Good. That's settled. Back to Loseff. My source tells me he's found the book you hid."

"The book?"

"*Dawn of the Third Age.*"

"Oh yeah"—Tomelai nodded—"that book. How the hell did he find it?"

With raised eyebrows, Derr reminded Tomelai, "You sent him into Adelle's Secret Archives to read up on generals from the Second Age. My source tells me it dropped out of that secret compartment you shoved it in."

Tomelai grabbed Derr's arm, halting them both in place. "Who is this source of yours?"

With a gentle pull, Derr released Tomelai's grip and Derr continued walking. "You know I can't share that with you. It's for your own protection. If it ever slipped out that I've been sharing their identities with anyone, the intel well will dry up. I need that intel flowing to do my job. You know, keeping you alive."

Tomelai flapped his gums, then asked, "Has anyone else seen it?"

"So far he's keeping it between himself and that friend of his, Jaynes."

"Drew, that book cannot get out. You need to put a lid on this. Since the day my ancestors found it, it's been passed down from generation to generation of Tomelai Chancellors. I'll not be the one to break the chain."

"I'm keeping close tabs on Loseff and Jaynes. The problem is that I can't just have him turn it over without exposing my source. That would have a devastating impact on our ability to monitor General Loseff from close range. At this point, he doesn't seem inclined to let anyone else in on his little secret."

"Has your source provided any feedback on whether Loseff believes any of what he's read?"

"From what Loseff's gleaned so far, it's got him thinking."

"What of this source of yours? That is one more person with knowledge of the book. How do I trust this person not to leak what he or she's learned?"

"Rotti, it's going to be a problem. You, more than anyone, know my methods don't allow for loose ends."

"Alright, Drew, I can accept that you have a tight lid on this source. Yet, what if Loseff shares any of it beyond Jaynes? You can always take care of Jaynes later. Loseff's my son. I cannot just have him disappear. Is this going to be a problem?"

"The situation is fluid. The short answer is, maybe. I'm keeping close tabs on how it's progressing. On the plus side, have I ever failed you?"

Freedom's Not Enough

Black Haven, Concord City

Reyne

Thoughts of Mithany danced in Reyne's head while awaiting Black Haven's doppelgänger of Mera to arrive. The Many Worlds Theory explained how independent dimensions of Earth and copies of the same people in each of the distinct realities could exist—or some gibberish like that, if Reyne recalled correctly what had been explained to him. However, his own death remained a real possibility, depending on the whims of his host. Whether multiple anythings actually existed didn't mean shit; dead was dead.

As they waited, he and Gina were not alone. Mahtoney stood nearby with one leg bent at the knee, and a foot resting flat against a wall at the home of Black Haven's Mera.

Reyne asked, "Gina, I know it ain't worked since we went through the Void. Is there any chance you can get that special talent of yours up and running? We gotta get out of this mess."

"Wish I could help, farm boy. Nothing there. It's gone."

"That's a shame. Doesn't seem like Red even knew a guy who could help us. It was all a setup. She kept us around as scapegoats."

"True enough. And all her shit about trading sex for access to this mysterious guy who could help was nothing more than a brilliant diversion. Kept me thinking of a way to get out of fucking her instead of what she was planning. I admire how she played it. I should've seen through the deception. I should've known better. The blame's on me for our current predicament."

"I remember you told me you were better than most, even without your gift. What do you think?" Reyne gave a nudge in Mahtoney's direction.

Mahtoney piped up, "You know I can hear you two idiots."

Gina ignored the Concordian's comment. "Listen, farm boy; yeah, I could take him out easy enough. After that, we'll still be in the shit. This Mera look-alike will send out his minions to hunt us down. I can handle two or three at a time. Against a small contingent armed with weapons, which we ain't got, we don't stand a chance. The best play we got is to hear him out. If it goes bad, I'll do what I can. Until then, we sit and wait."

Mahtoney added his assessment. "Listen to her, farm boy. Sounds like good advice... And you got a major hole in your plan. Taking me out... not gonna happen."

Gina winked at Reyne, curled her lips upward, and gave him a thumbs-up as if to say, "Mahtoney doesn't stand a chance."

What hid behind the dark veil that followed Reyne as he sat waiting for a proclamation of judgement added to his anxiety. For all he knew, he was being observed and evaluated from the shadows. The room's perimeter reached beyond his sight, except for the wall holding Mahtoney's foot. He existed in what seemed like an air pocket in an ocean of charcoal gloom.

"Gina, we've wasted enough time in this place with Red's empty promise to get us off this rock. Teth was in chaos when we left, and the rest of Tartica has probably gone to shit by now. The Devil's Blacksmith is still on the loose on Evidar and I'm no closer to getting back to Mithany."

"Sums things up about right, except you left out the bit about me holding you back from getting off Black Haven."

"Gina, I don't see it that way. Sure, I hated you at first. Things changed. We gotta get back to Hensdale together."

"What about Evidar? We have a mission to take out the Damus and, if possible, the Blacksmith guy."

"Not sure I can get us to Evidar. I fucked it up the first time. That's how we ended up on Black Haven. You want to chance it again? Better off setting our sights on Hensdale."

"Chalk it up to serendipity. You got to see the dead body of a woman that looks exactly like the one who murdered Daedyn. That had to give you some pleasure. Serendipity is a big word. I haven't used it in quite a while. You like that one?"

"I know what serendipity means. Don't be a wiseass. And, no, seeing Red lying there dead didn't do a thing for me. Yeah, she screwed us just when I was just starting to like her. She ain't the version of Neladith I want to see dead."

"You're a better person than me. She fucked us both. Double-crossed us. I'm glad she's dead. Fuck her."

"Fuck her?" Mahtoney threw in. "Fuck you. She was a better person than you'll ever be."

"Fuck off," Gina shot back. "Stand there and shut up, errand boy. This don't concern you."

Mahtoney crossed his arms. "When he returns, I can only hope he gives me the pleasure of gutting you both."

Gina jumped out of her seat. "Bring it on... errand boy."

From somewhere in the engrossing darkness, Reyne heard a familiar voice. Calm words flowed out of the encircling gray despair, "That will be enough. Mahtoney, you can leave. There will be no gutting today. We'll see about tomorrow."

Reyne grabbed Gina's hand and pulled her back.

Black Haven's Mera moved out of the gossamer gray veil into Reyne's sphere of vision. The man pointed at Mahtoney. "Leave."

Sarcasm dripped from Gina. "Bye-bye, errand boy." And she waved her fingers at the departing Mahtoney.

Mera asked, "Is that necessary?"

Reyne ignored the exchange. "What do we call you? The Mera I knew is dead back on Tartica. Don't seem right, me using his name here and now."

"Well, Mister Brenton, Mera is my name. Perhaps I share it with a man who looks like me. You never knew anyone two people with the same name before?

I find that highly unlikely. You think you are the only person in all of Tartica named Reyne?"

"I suppose. Alright, Mera."

Black Haven's Mera slapped his hands together. "Great. We are off to a good start."

Gina asked, "You're not worried... alone with the two of us?"

"Why? Should I be? You told me a short while ago you did not care if I lived or died. Was that a lie?"

"No."

"There. You see, I have nothing then to worry about."

Mera, apparently reading Reyne's face, asked, "What is on your mind Mister Brenton?"

"Just Reyne will be fine... How are you alive, and how did you get here before us?"

"I think your friend Gina knows the answer to your first question. We'll talk about that shortly. As for getting here before you, my travels were not encumbered by avoiding enemy tribes or evading hostile territories, as was the now-dead woman's who led you here."

Gina started to say, "Soul—"

Mera cut her off. "Where are my manners? May I offer you something to drink? Or a snack, perhaps?" He raised one arm and snapped his fingers. Immediately, two women flowed out of the darkness, each carrying a platter. Reyne's mouth watered at the sight of trays laden with fruits, nuts, crackers, and cheeses placed on the table before them. In unison, the two women poured water into metal goblets, set down the metal water pitchers in practiced synchronized movements, then turned and walked away.

Reyne lifted a piece of cheese, raised it to his nose, and delivered it to his waiting mouth. "Delicious. Gina, you gotta try this." With little concern for manners, Reyne dug in, exploring a piece of everything put before him. With a mouth full of food, he mumbled, "How? Cheese? Nuts?"

"Do not look so surprised, Mister Brenton. We do have animals who produce milk and have adapted plant species to do well in the absence of sunlight. Don't forget about the bat sanctuary. We have several like it. I am pleased to see you appreciate our efforts. Those tribes who've chosen to decline my help struggle to live off the land minus the innovations I have developed over all my long years."

Gina appeared more reserved. "Fattening the cattle before the slaughter?"

"Not at all, Miss Gina. I am sorry, I do not know your last name."

Gina said nothing.

"Well, Miss Gina..."

"Please, just Gina... no Miss."

"As you wish... Gina. To answer your question, that will depend on our conversation. You can look at it as a last meal for the condemned or fuel for your journey to freedom. Shall we find out which applies?"

Reyne scooped up a handful of nuts and rolled them in his palm. He examined them and found them different from the alphens he and Daedyn produced. His heart sank thinking of his brother. With an effort, he shook it off. "What is this place? Concord City. Looks like it's been pieced together."

"Mister Brenton—" Mera from Black Haven started.

"Just Reyne, please."

"Reyne, it's quite simple. Many of us huddled together at this isolated research station in the belief it could survive the devastation that threatened Earth. Sadly, the rest of humanity did not make it through the asteroid's destructive impact to the planet. Almost two thousand of us gathered across a handful of fortified locations. This place was once the Concordia Research Station. Generations of progeny have called this place home since the time of the Great Destruction."

Reyne's eyes narrowed, looking back at Mera. "You said, *many of us.* You're sticking with the story you lived through the Great Destruction fifteen centuries ago? Impossible." And he shoveled a handful of nuts into his mouth.

"No, Reyne, not impossible. Yet, I can see how you would think so. Your friend knows something about that. She mouthed the words *Soul Stone* back at the Unity Council gathering. It earned you this reprieve. I wish to learn more of what you both know."

Gina picked up a cracker from the tray, took a bite, and said, "Why should I share anything with you? You're just gonna kill us after you find out what you want to know."

Black Haven's Mera rubbed his chin. "I could have you both killed now… before we talk. You will not have much to say afterwards, nor will you have the opportunity to earn your freedom. Gina, which approach would you prefer I take?"

"You're holding all the cards."

"Yes, I am. This way, you might just get lucky. Shall we play?"

Without hesitation Reyne blurted out, "No."

Mera angled his head to one side, looking quizzically at Reyne. "No?… I did not expect that. Can I change your mind, or do you want to die?" His polite manner and tone rang of certainty to Reyne's ears.

Gina jumped in. "That's right. No, we won't play your game. Freedom's not enough."

Reyne curled his lips and nodded as if to say, *You go, girl. Exactly what I was thinkin'.*

Reyne stopped chewing, swallowed, and said, "Look, me and Gina ain't here to kill anyone in this version of Earth. I need to get to Evidar or back to Tartica. There's a hitch… I don't know how to pull Gina through the Void with me. She can't do it on her own. In your office, the day Red shot you, you told me Beth somebody knew how to bring another person through the Void. You tell us how it can be done, and we'll tell you whatever you want to know. That's the deal."

A smile broke across the face of Black Haven's Mera. "What if I do not agree to those terms? And I gather neither of you holds a Soul Stone. You will both be dead rather soon."

Reyne looked at Gina, who nodded in agreement, then he turned to Black Haven's Mera. "Then we die. If I can't get us both home, we're stranded here forever, and that's as good as dead. Take it or leave it."

Black Haven's Mera didn't say anything for a dozen heartbeats. He studied Reyne. He looked at Gina. With his arm raised, he snapped his fingers. "I choose to leave it." Immediately, twelve large men emerged from the shadows into Reyne's perception.

Reyne didn't hesitate. He jumped from his seat and charged.

Gina was one step behind.

Against six men each, the struggle ended quickly.

Pinned against a wall, Reyne's arms were held behind his back. A massive forearm pressed into his neck. It crushed against his Adam's apple. Gina lasted only a few seconds longer, trapped beneath a pile of man-flesh with her back pressed to the ground.

Black Haven's Mera hadn't moved. "Would you like to change the terms of your proposal? Perhaps something less final that gives me more options?"

Reyne, in a hoarse voice, spat, "Fuck you."

With the slightest movement of his index finger, *Bring them here*, Mera commanded.

Half a dozen men jostled the six-foot Reyne across the room. He squirmed, spit, stumbled, and resisted with all his might. It wasn't enough. He reached into the depths of his despair, hoping to awaken the beast within.

It stirred in his core.

The monster inside coveted retribution for Daedyn's murder.

Fury roared in his soul at his baby sister's sliced-opened throat.

It despaired at the slaying of his mother at the moment of his birth.

It raged at a knife buried in the heart of a father he never knew.

It salivated for payback against those threatening Mithany.

The beast within hungered for vengeance against them all.

The monster lurking in his soul craved for the freedom to deliver pain.

In the despondent, hopeless, disheartened misery consuming him, words unable to match the depths of his anguish, sparked... *Let the monster out.*

... And in that instant, it was free.

His eyes rolled back into his head. He erupted in a guttural moan. Reyne, no longer in control; the beast took over. With the monster unleashed came a source of strength unknown to Reyne. His right arm threw off one of his captors.

His foot slammed backwards, shattering the kneecap of another. He crashed his forehead into a third.

Three were down. Reyne roared like a wild animal. The men attacked, pounding him with body blow after body blow. The beast controlling Reyne felt no pain. He ripped his left arm free. Balled his huge hand into a fist and, like a hammer, drove it into the face of another.

Two of Gina's captors jumped into the fray. One slammed his fist into the back of Reyne's neck and at the same instant the other drove his foot into the back of Reyne's knee. Reyne went down.

A terrifying war cry rose out of his core. He shot his elbow backwards, driving it blindly into the nose of an opponent. With an awful crunch, the man dropped. The two enormous men who were left struggled to hold Reyne down.

The beast within gathered all its primeval strength.

What Reyne had become, bent one leg at the knee, and pushed off the ground. "Arrrggg!" Almost standing, he flew open his arms, throwing off his last remaining assailants. The metal water pitcher from the tray of nuts crashed into the back of his skull. Water splashed across the room.

Reyne fell forward, flat on his face.

He came to with his ankles tied together, as were his wrists behind his back. Gina appeared to be in the same predicament.

She frowned. "Nice try."

"Welcome back, Mister Brenton." Mera gave a nod and two women appeared from out of the ebony gloom, each holding a knife. Two men took hold of Reyne's arms, as did two others to Gina's. The knife-wielding women took up positions behind them both.

Another nod from Black Haven's Mera and Reyne felt the edge of cold steel pressed to his throat.

"Last chance, Mister Brenton."

"For the last time, it's just Reyne... asshole."

"And what about you, Miss Gina?"

"Fuck off."

Reyne observed Black Haven's Mera raise one finger. It pointed upward, and hung there, motionless, for what seemed like an eternity.

Reyne accepted his death.

He recalled what Tartica's version of Mera had confided in him when this all began. "If you die, there will be no reason for Evidar agents to go after Mithany to get to you." With his own death, he could at least secure safety for the woman he loved. Strangely, he was at peace. Mithany would be safe; that's all that really mattered. Tartica would have to fend for itself.

He looked at Gina and confirmed the same commitment in her eyes.

They would die together.

In a soft tone, Reyne stared straight ahead, watching for movement from Mera's finger and said, "Go ahead. I'm ready. Do it."

A Horse to Water

Teth: 16th Day of the Harvest Moon

Jerithan

Jerithan no longer considered himself qualified to lead a flock of true believers. Before the vote stripping him of his position as First Lord, he could have. That was a different Jerithan. The degradation he'd endured since that fateful day purified his mind of any such nonsense.

Tartica now existed in a state of chaos, and Tartica appeared to be in better condition than his soul.

Jerithan opened his arms wide. He stared up at the man with orange hair and a high, squeaky voice that belied his enormous size. "Timble, my friend, my betrayer, and yet, my redeemer, I am pleased to see you unharmed."

He turned to face S'Leen. "May I introduce you to the man who saved me from the clutches of certain death by means of Thuggery justice, only to step aside when Derr's KCG took me into custody."

"I seen ya look better, Jerithan," Timble replied, rubbing his chin. "Not by much. And I ain't no betrayer, Miss S'Leen, like he says. Nah. Didn't happen that way. Did what I hadda. He wouldn't be standin' here if I didn't. Glad ya are, Jerithan. Me and all these folks needs ya now."

Looking down at his feet, Jerithan cupped his hands together inside the adjoining sleeves of his vestment. "I am not the man I was. You need someone else. Not me." Lifting his eyes to meet the onlookers all staring at him, Jerithan reiterated, "Not me."

The words escaped sad and weak.

A woman with a babe on her hip and another child gripping her calf asked, "Timble. What makes ya think this jamoke can do anythin' for us folk? He's one of 'em. When he was First Lord, never seen him here. Think he gives a fuck about us? Then... or now?"

"Maybe so, Stella. By the way, ya boy's lookin' better. Glad for it. And this guy here, Jerithan, I believes in 'em. He grew up on the streets like us. He's seen both sides. The Green Robes fucked 'em over. Sent him back to the gutter. He ain't one of 'em anymore. He's one of us now. I'm pretty sure he'd like the chance to fuck 'em right back."

With a quick nod, Stella added, "Thanks, Timble. Appreciate the medicine ya found for my boy. He's okay now. Let's get back to this Jerithan. Let me ask ya, ya trust 'em? Ya sure he ain't gonna fuck us over?"

The boy at her leg objected. "Ma, ya used a bad word."

"Hush now," she told her son with a gentle smile. "Ma's gotta talk with the big folk."

"But Ma..."

"I says hush," she scolded the boy with a gentle tap to the top of his head.

Timble scratched his ear. "Lookin' more like his pa every day."

"Yeah, and like his pa"—she looked her son in the eye—"he don't know when to shut up."

One of the other women shouted, "You's got that right, Stella!"

The crowd, a tight-knit group who all apparently knew Stella's husband, broke out in laughter. Jerithan didn't.

Stella returned to her question for Timble. "Didn't answer me. Ya trust 'em... this Jerithan guy?"

With flapping lips, Timble let out a gush from puffed cheeks. "Hard to trust anyone when ya gotta struggle to live day to day." After a moment of silence, he added, "Yep, guess I do."

Stella shook herself free of her son's hold on her leg and handed off her daughter to a man standing next to her. She backed away a few steps to address everyone in the room. "Can't say I know this Jerithan. I do knows Timble. We all do. He ain't no saint." She rolled her eyes, and the crowd laughed as one. "But Timble's done right by all of us. Been there for all of ya. May, you's remembers when ya ma needed help. Who got ya the coin? Timble here." She swiped a thumb in Timble's direction. "I sees ya Margly." She squinted and pointed at the man. "Yeah, we alls remembers it was Timble who pulled you's cahones outta the fire when you's was in trouble with Nails. She was gonna have your balls. And we knows how much she like balls."

Someone yelled out, "Stella, ya do likes to talk. Just get to the point."

"Ya better pipe done over there, Harmmy, I saw whatcha did last night. I'm sure Jeyne would love to know. So ya hush up right now."

The man lowered his head, stepping back.

"So ya's all get the point. Timble's been lookin' out for us all here in Shanty-town for as long as any of us can recall. I trusts 'em. Maybe not this Jerithan fella, but I trusts Timble. He says Jerithan's the guy to lead us, I'm with Timble." She paused, held out her finger, and pointed it around the room. "And everyone of ya fuckers better be too."

Harmmy shouted, "Stella, I'm with you!"

"Of course you are," the man holding Stella's daughter replied. "Just as long as Stella don't tell Jeyne whatcha did last night."

Another round of loud laughter filled the chamber.

S'Leen leaned in close to Jerithan's ear. "These people are amazing. Consider all they've been through. The lifelong, day-to-day struggles they face to survive, and they can still laugh. They can find joy amidst this chaos. Jerithan, these are special people. If they asked me to lead them, I'd be honored and proud to be their chosen one. They didn't ask me. They asked you. You have to do this."

"S'Leen, I mean no disrespect. Lead them... where? What do they want from me?"

"You just delivered your most passionate sermon in years. I heard it in your voice... in your tone. It's been a long time since I've heard you sound like that. It's apparent to me; you have found your faith and your purpose once again. A purpose Serco stole from you. *Now is your chance.* Be the First Lord you were born to be. Even if it's only for Shantytown. Seize this opportunity to make a difference in these people's lives."

"I don't know what they—"

"My friend"—S'Leen didn't wait for Jerithan to finish his thought—"there's only one way to find out." And with one hand on his back, she shoved him forward.

Farewell My Love

Black Haven, Concord City

Reyne

Bound at the ankles and wrists, Reyne stood in silence. A woman behind him with a knife to his gullet and two hulking Black Haven natives secured him from any further escape attempts. Gina loomed at his side similarly accompanied by her own host of executioners, ready to fulfill their purpose. All waited on a simple finger-twitch—that held the promise of death.

Seconds passed.

Then minutes.

Reyne should have been scared. His heart should have been pounding. He should have been pleading for his life. Except Reyne was at peace with dying; Mithany would finally be safe from enemies trying to get to him. Though, thoughts of what a life with her could have been evoked sadness. While awaiting the finger's deliverance, he imagined the children he and Mithany would have raised together at their orchard homestead. It was all he ever wanted out of life; a simple existence with the woman he loved, little kids scampering about, and his brother at his side.

He thought of Daedyn and recalled a time as boys, only five years old each, they'd run off to go fishing and got lost on the return home. His adopted mother, unable to locate her sons as night settled in, was frantic to find them, yet upon their return, she didn't yell, didn't admonish, just embraced them in her arms with tears in her eyes. A sense of peace tinged with sadness washed over him reminiscing about the many times he and Daedyn came to blows, as youthful brothers often do, only to bond even stronger in reconciliation. He loved Daedyn. And he missed him.

The opportunity to save himself by transfiguring through the Void had been lost. During his time on Black Haven, he considered returning to Tartica, hoping to find an answer. He needed to bring Gina back safely. He believed Tartica's version of Mera was dead, and nobody alive on Tartica could provide him information on navigating the Void with another consciousness in tow. And if he left Black Haven for good without Gina, it meant leaving her in its ever-present gloom, alone and without hope. A choice he couldn't live with.

He considered giving Black Haven's Mera the information he demanded. Yet, he thought of Red's tribe and the promise of help from the same man who had Red killed. A hangman's noose for everyone in Red's tribe hid behind Mera's false words of help—to be delivered to one and all, children included, as the price for their collective trust in the man. Just as Red had double-crossed them, Reyne expected Black Haven's Mera to do the same, regardless of what he promised.

Reyne never really had a choice. All roads led to death.

And still, the finger didn't move.

As he waited, Reyne reflected on his time in the Void when he had once touched Mithany's mind. He wondered if he could reach out to her again before dying. Did he have time? His heart ached to say goodbye.

He recalled the day he and Tartica's Mera broke camp while on the run, the morning after Daedyn's murder. In the cold damp dawn, he experienced lucid dreaming, wide-awake. Could he do it again? And if so, could it lead him into the Void? What did he have to lose? It was now or never. One last chance to tell Mithany he loved her, and that he'd never be coming home.

Reyne closed his eyes and repeated in his mind the hypnosis session he recalled while lying in an open field on his first journey into the Void. As he did, his heartbeat slowed, and Reyne experienced peace wash over his mind and body. Much to his surprise, he found himself able to relax. He repeated every step he recalled.

He focused on Mithany, cuddling together in his bed. Slowly, his body entered a strange state of sleeplike restfulness while his psyche remained alert.

He'd given away control over his muscles; they did not respond to his commands. As a child, he called them night terrors—lying in bed, his mind awake while in a dream-state, his body nonresponsive. But not this day. Fear had no hold on him. With his mind untethered from his body, his consciousness floated above. His state of being existed without physical form. He looked down at himself and Gina, both bodies bound and secured below him. Reyne's nonphysical awareness observed Black Haven's Mera staring at him as though deep in thought himself.

Quickly, Reyne turned away as Tartica's Mera taught him to do and he let his mind drift towards the empty blackness at the edge of his non-corporeal awareness. He slammed into nothing, the metaphysical boundary between reality and the Void. It held him tight. Determination, resolve, and love powered his will as he struggled against the forces holding him back.

He would not be denied.

His will to connect with Mithany one last time before dying was stronger than anything the noncorporeal world could throw at him. All at once, his mind, free of its physical body, exploded through the barrier into the Void. Even darker than Black Haven, ebony nothingness enveloped him.

Threads of countless lives playing out in Probability Waves crashed into his consciousness. Thousands upon thousands slammed into him. He experienced individuals whose life-path diverged into untold alternate futures that might never materialize. Some he recognized, most others he did not.

No!

Focus!

And he searched the myriad Probability Waves for the only one that mattered. He locked Mithany in his thoughts. He searched for her taste, her smell, or just an improbable glimpse of her in the utter absence of light. All his senses fired, expanding wildly in every direction into the Void, craving the slightest tingle resembling Mithany's life-force.

He pursued a Probability Wave to Brenal's death, and another that flowed along a path ending in Arek's passing. "No, these gotta be false futures that will never happen," he told himself. He had to believe Brenal still lived, and that Arek was not dead.

He followed Arek's life force to another of his Probability Waves along a path where Reyne's thoughts witnessed Arek making love to Mithany. Reyne reeled—revolted at the thought. Despite the appalling imagery along the incestuous tendril of Arek's possible future, there it was, the aroma of Mithany's essence. The sweet rose-petal fragrance of her skin. The delicate, apocrine aroma of her hair. The intimate musk of her womanhood infused with a hint of molasses. The savory honey-like whiff of her love for him captured his non-material heart.

He quickly discarded Arek's connection and clung to Mithany's life force. Thousands of Mithany's alternate futures exploded into his mind. As before, so many divergent timelines led her to exist without him. It pained his soul to experience each one. His consciousness swept through them all. Despite the voluminous choice, he knew her heart and locked on to the Probability Wavefunction he divined to be Mithany's true timeline. With all his focus, he concentrated on it.

An oasis started to open in the Void. In small increments, the pure blackness of the Void gave way. Mithany was crying. It shattered him to see her in such pain. A pillow held tight to her chest. His pillow. Light flooded into the oasis. There she was before his non-physical sight. His love for her overwhelmed his soul. His thoughts reached out to hers.

Mithany, he called to her.

To his surprise, her head snapped to look up.

He called out again, *Mithany.*

"Reyne?" she whispered, scanning the room.

It's me, my love.

"Reyne? How? Where is this coming from?"

I love you. I miss you so much.

"Reyne, I miss you too. I need you. Come home to me."

I'm sorry, my love. I won't be...

In an instant, everything shattered.

Reyne felt a slap across his face.

The oasis collapsed.

His eyes shot open. His mind and body were back as one... on Black Haven. He screamed, "NO!"

A woman with a knife to his throat stood before him.

She whispered, "Don't move." And pressed the blade into his flesh just enough to draw a droplet of blood.

"Mister Brenton, where have you been? You have not responded to any of my queries."

Reyne closed his eyes. Mithany was gone. His heart sank. He hung his head. "What else can you take from me? Just get it over with."

"Well, Mister Brenton, that's the thing. As I was about to open your throat—or more precisely, the woman before you was, I attempted to bid you a final farewell. You failed to respond. I have been trying to get your attention for some time now. You were somewhere else. Not in body. In thought."

Reyne took a deep, slow breath. "You talk a lot. Maybe I was just ignoring you."

"I do not think that's it, Mister Brenton."

"Enough of the Mister Brenton crap... Oh, I give up... Call me whatever you like."

"Good. We have that settled, Mister Brenton. Now, answer me. Where had that mind of yours escaped to?"

Reyne turned to his right. Gina stood just as he left her: bound, manhandled, and alive. She squinted, looking confused. "Reyne, you've been unresponsive for like an hour."

"Sorry, Gina. Seemed like only seconds. Are you okay?"

"Mister Brenton, enough chatter," Mera demanded. "I have questions that need answers."

Reyne's lips curled in a deliberate sneer. "Mister Mera, does it really make any difference where I been?"

"Mister Mera? You are mocking me. Not helpful, young man."

Reyne found peace in saying goodbye to Mithany. Although he'd been cut short, he touched her soul and told her he loved her. It had to suffice. As for Black Haven's Mera, Reyne now held the advantage. Mera could do with him what he liked. The gloom of Black Haven had been driven from the ever-present weight bearing down on his soul. The simple, brief encounter with Mithany filled him with her love. Reyne's heart was free.

Almost effervescent, Reyne responded, "Not helpful to who? You? Not really a big concern of mine at the moment."

"Mister Brenton, it should be. Your demonstration has given me pause. If what I think I have just witnessed is, in fact true, you and your friend may just survive this day. Are you concerned now?"

Confidence flooded through him. The burden of remorse had been removed. "I'll bite. What's on your mind, big fella?"

"Mister Brenton, insolence does not suit you. You are trying my patience. I have had others put to death for less."

With a wide grin, Reyne said, "That might be true. You keep saying you're gonna kill me. Here I stand. I must have something pretty big that you want. Untie me and Gina, then we can sit down and negotiate terms."

"Here is the problem with your proposal, Mister Brenton. You have demonstrated two unique skill sets I have rarely witnessed in all my years. The one earlier today, where you incapacitated several of my associates, gives me pause at having you unbound."

"Mister Mera, how about I just promise you not to go into psycho mode?" He followed his offer with a big, toothy grin.

"You are more clever than your outward rustic persona. You do not trust me to keep my word, and so you challenge me to accept yours."

Reyne continued in silence, extending Mera a grin from ear to ear.

Black Haven's Mera waved off the knife-wielding woman and with a nod, the brutes holding him and Gina took three steps back. "There. Does that help?"

Reyne shook his head. "Nope. Untie us both."

Black Haven's Mera tilted his head back, pulled in a long slow breath through his nose. When he returned to face Reyne, his lips formed a circle and he let it out. "Alright. I will trust you as a sign that you can also trust me."

"Oh, you can trust me. Yet, I'm not sure there's anything you can do or say that'll ever get me to trust you."

"So be it." With a casual wave as though a command, the knife-bearing women reappeared, drew their blades, and with the same synchronicity as they did pouring water earlier, slit the ropes free from Reyne and Gina.

Reyne wiggled his ankles one by one and rubbed his wrists, as did Gina. "Okay. So far, so good. What's on your mind?"

"Mister Brenton, did you just now access the Void?"

"Sure did." Reyne shot Gina a one-eyed wink.

"Tell me, Mister Brenton, how your consciousness drifted off while wide-awake."

"Sure. Right after you agree to two things. First, when we're done here"—Reyne wiggled his finger back and forth between himself and Gina—"we go free. And no horseshit word play. I know I'm makin' a deal with the devil."

"And the second?"

"Second, I just want off Black Haven. Tell me how to piggyback Gina on a trip through the Void. You've seen it done before."

"The first is easily accomplished. You have my word. As for the second, it is no simple task. I have only known one other person capable of such a feat. You imagine her as your Goddess Teth. She has been gone from my life many years. Frankly, I am amazed you accomplished it to bring Gina here with you."

"Sounds like we don't have a deal."

"We do have a deal, Mister Brenton. I will share what I know. Whether you can achieve the piggyback, as you called it, that is on you. I am willing to gamble that you can, now that I have witnessed the rarest of talents; you enter the Void from a waking state. It is the only reason I have to accept this compact: your ability to communicate with others through the Void. I will require your use of this talent, one time, for my benefit, as a condition of our agreement."

Reyne walked over and stuck out his hand. "I can accept those terms. Agreed."

Gina raced to Reyne's side. She grabbed his wrist, pulled it back from its offering, and spun him to face her. "You sure about this? What services? You don't know what you're getting us into."

Touching Mithany's soul filled Reyne with a growing sense of optimism. He'd been ready to die. Now he was ready to live. He'd been given a second chance at life and hope grew in his heart. The deal before him offered a pathway to be with Mithany again. "It'll be okay, Gina. I'll do whatever I have to... so I can get you back to Tartica." Not wanting to give Black Haven's Mera information to use against him, Reyne left off his true purpose: *and to see Mithany again.*

From his seat, Black Haven's Mera grinned up at Reyne. Reyne grinned right back at him, thinking he'd come away from their negotiations as the victor. He lifted Gina's hand off his wrist, then stuck it out once again.

"Mister Mera of Black Haven, we gotta shake on it, you know, to make it official."

Pity No More

Hensdale: 16th Day of the Harvest Moon

Mithany

Mithany neglected Arek in a way she never had before. They'd always been there for each other, no matter the obstacles life threw at them. Santander's thoughtful intercession into her own self-pitying isolation in the bedroom she and Reyne shared pulled her head above water if only for the moment. So consumed in her own sorrow, struggling with the orchard's destruction at Neladith's hand, enduring separation from Reyne, struggling with Daedyn's murder, and profoundly sad at Hollid Brenal's death, Mithany had tuned out everyone in her world, Arek included.

Santander closed the door behind him, leaving Mithany alone in the room.

She wiped away her tears and hung her head. With legs crossed, sitting on Reyne's bed, shock gripped her heart when Reyne's voice slammed into her thoughts.

Mithany, he called to her.

Confused, Mithany's head spun wildly, searching the empty room.

He called out again, *Mithany.*

"Reyne?" she shouted. Her heart pounded.

It's me, my love.

"Reyne? How? Where is this coming from?"

I love you. I miss you so much.

"Reyne, I miss you too. I need you. Come home to me."

I'm sorry, my love. I won't be...

Then silence.

"Reyne!"

She waited.

"Reyne, speak to me." She pleaded, "Don't leave me."

She screamed, "REYNE!"

Santander flung open the door and shot into the room. "Mithany!" He looked around. "Are you okay, dear?"

With puffy eyes, drooped lids, and a quivering lip, Mithany whispered, "Reyne was here. I don't understand how." Her volume slowly rose. "I'm going crazy. I can't take this anymore." Lost in confusion, she looked up into the pained eyes of the grizzled Santander.

"Oh, my dear, I'm so sorry." He opened his arms as an invitation.

Mithany shot up, buried her head in his chest, and wrapped her arms as far as they would go around his ample gut. "I know it was his voice. It was him. Am I losing my mind?"

Santander laid his head atop hers. "No, dear, you're not going crazy. You've been through so much."

Hearing the squeal of the bedroom door, Mithany peaked around the side of Santander's waist. "Arek," she cried out as he hobbled through the doorway. She opened one arm for him to join them.

As Arek nestled his body into the shared embrace, Mithany laughed to herself, imagining the look on Santander's face at the uncharacteristic position he found himself in. She lifted her eyes to meet the old man's. His one-eyed wink did more to lift her spirits than anything she'd experienced since Reyne's departure.

Stepping back, Mithany rubbed the heels of her palms into her watery eyes and announced, "You both have lifted my heart. I can't go on in pity anymore... Thank you... I love you both." She leaned forward, raised up on her tiptoes, and kissed Santander's cheek. She reached out for Arek's hand and pulled him in tight, whispering in his ear, "Can you forgive me?"

Arek pushed her away, grabbed her face in his hands, kissed her forehead, and said, "Forgive you for what, Sis? I could never be mad at you." A tear dribbled down his cheek.

With a thumb, she wiped away Arek's telltale sign of devotion. "Big boys don't cry," she teased him.

Arek wrapped his arms around her slight frame and squeezed her tighter than she'd ever been hugged before. "You're killin' me," she giggled and looked to Santander for help. She spied the hardened general manager wipe away a single tear of his own.

Amused, she tracked the movement of his wagging finger: its message: "Tell no one you saw that."

After Arek released her from his bear hug, Mithany stood between the two men. She took them both by the hand. Rejuvenated with love in her heart and joy in her voice, she told them, "No one can replace Reyne, but you two come close."

Santander's heavy arm landed on her shoulder, and he pulled her in tight.

She looked up at Arek, then to Santander, "You guys might think I'm crazy. Reyne just spoke to me."

Santander said, "Well, I did hear you saying something to someone. I didn't hear them. If you say it was Reyne, I believe you, dear."

"He touched my thoughts. I don't know how. I think it happened once before. I can feel it in my soul. It was him. He's alive. And with you two wonderful men by my side, knowing Reyne's alright... I'm gonna be okay."

"Good," Santander added. "Then get your ass out to the southern orchard. Those Topakers are screwing everything up." He winked, shrugged, and said, "I got a reputation to live up to."

She laughed and hugged him in a daughterly embrace. Santander looked around the room, as though not sure what to do. After a few seconds, Mithany stepped away and took Arek by the hand. "Come with me. We'll do it together."

Beginnings

Reyne

Reyne squinted, hoping to peer deeper into the ever-present gray-black veil enveloping him. He watched the two knife-wielding women—who'd just cut him and Gina loose—and four large Concordian brutes fade into the darkness. They all departed at the command of Black Haven's Mera.

Frustrated at his lack of visual acuity, Reyne turned his attention to fulfilling his end of the bargain. He agreed to perform a service and to provide information to Black Haven's Mera. "I get the idea of this two worlds stuff—well, now three worlds. What did you call it, the Many-Worlds-something-or-other?"

"The Many-Worlds Interpretation, to be correct, Mister Brenton. Consider the myriad Wave Functions you and Gina encountered in the Void. You experienced many divergent futures of the life forces you touched, thinking a person has only one true timeline hidden in the mix. The Many-Worlds Interpretation of that situation is quite different. It theorizes that all the other possible futures from that single point of your inspections do exist in alternate dimensions at the same time... like the three distinct realities of Earth we are aware of: Tartica, Evidar, and Black Haven, as you call them."

"Wait a second," Reyne demanded. "I'm confused. Didn't you say previously that reality split off the instant some big space rock smashed into Earth? You said that's why Tartica didn't get all the damage Black Haven did. Evidar and Black Haven both ended up as shitholes."

He looked over at Gina, then turned back to Black Haven's Mera. "I ain't no genius. Doesn't that mean the dimensional split between Evidar and Black Haven had to fragment after Tartica already existed? Evidar and Black Haven had to split into different dimensions after the Great Destruction, not at the very instant it happened. That's if any of this multiple-realities-shit is real."

"Look at you, farm boy. Maybe you're not as dumb as you look. You put all that together by yourself." Gina bobbed her head up and down, adding, "I'm impressed."

Behind a fake smile, Reyne replied with a single raised middle finger.

Black Haven's Mera disregarded Gina's comments. "Until you showed up, Mister Brenton, Evidar existed outside my scope of knowledge. When I returned from an unsuccessful venture into the Void, I assumed I had returned from whence I left. Since time in the Void is uncertain, I assumed Beth returned before I emerged from the Void and had since transfigured to Tartica with all those not there upon my return."

Gina quipped, "You know how the saying goes when one assumes?"

"Mister Brenton, if Evidar does exist, then you are correct. The divergence between Black Haven and Evidar most likely occurred after the Great Destruction in order to create two identical, post-apocalyptic Earths."

"If it helps," Gina began, "from what I gather, they're not much different. I mean, Evidar's supposed to be as miserable as Black Haven. Plus, it's got a guy everyone calls the Devil's Blacksmith. They call him that behind his back, just like people here got a name for you... behind your back. No offense intended; I hear you're a wee bit sensitive about being called the Devil's Hammer. Evidar and Black Haven got a lot in common."

Reyne piled on, "Yeah, don't forget, the nicer version of you ended up on Tartica. Then again, to be honest, that other Mera ain't all that much nicer."

Gina smacked Reyne's arm. Picking up on his line of thinking, she added, "If this crap is to be believed, and if farm boy over there is correct, the separate dimensions of Black Haven and Evidar may have come into being when the real Mera, the guy I knew on Tartica, went through the Void."

"That is quite astute of you, Miss Gina. I would agree, given I what know of Tartica. Although I knew not of this other version of myself existing in your reality."

Smacking Gina with the back of his hand, Reyne said, "Imagine that, big scary guy hands out compliments."

While rubbing her arm, Gina kept talking. "Hear me out. It seems to me our Mera made it through the Void into Tartica, but Fake Mera didn't and ended up here. It's possible the dimension of Black Haven came into being that very instant. You figure out when that happened, you got your two alternate dimensions of the same shithole, Black Haven and Evidar." She held out her hands as though weighing imaginary objects.

Reyne ran his hand over the back of his neck. "My Mera, the one from Tartica, sent me to Evidar hoping to stop something terrible from happening. He thinks the Devil's Blacksmith from Evidar has figured out how to merge Tartica and Evidar into one dimension... or something like that. Even though he never explained how, it would mean Tartica's fucked. He thinks it could happen soon."

She added, "I don't recall the man I knew as Mera ever portrayed an alternate version of himself as the Devil's Blacksmith. The Devil's Blacksmith from Evidar has to be a different person. In fact, Real Mera gave me the impression he knows the Devil's Blacksmith from his past and they had some falling out. Too bad he never told me who. I'm guessing it's someone close. And since you two Meras were the same guy before this supposed divergence, maybe you got some idea who this Devil's Blacksmith fella could be."

With her head to the side, Gian studied the face of Black Haven's Mera. A few seconds passed before she went on. "Since this Soul Stone exists in all three alternate versions of the same staring point, Earth—Tartica, Evidar, and Black Haven—then you, the Devil's Blacksmith, and Tartica's Mera are all as old as fuck. And you all had to put your hands on this Soul Stone before all these timelines fractured."

"You usually have a lot to say. Why so quiet?" Reyne asked of Black Haven's Mera.

"Mister Brenton, I am contemplating everything you and Miss Gina are discussing. I am also reflecting on the death of Tartica's version of me... who you have reported has died. It is reasonable to speculate that myself and this other Mera were the same individual in the past. However, I must ask, why do you think him deceased? If we are the same, does he not possess a piece of the Soul Stone?"

Answering for them both, she said, "I witnessed him die. It looked like an arrow pierced his liver. He was unresponsive and bleeding out when this knucklehead"—she motioned her thumb at Reyne—"swept me up into his trip through the Void, dumping us both here... in a realm we assumed to be Evidar."

"Miss Gina, you have demonstrated knowledge of the Soul Stone's restorative capacity. Why do you presume this other me to have succumbed to death? The Soul Stone's ability to heal whoever bears it is powerful. Unless you remained with him longer than three days after his injury to confirm he did not recover, you should not assume him dead."

Reyne's head whipped to face Gina. "Three days? You know anything about that?"

Black Haven's Mera held up one finger. "Mister Brenton. Miss Gina. There is a bond between Soul Stone and its possessor which I cannot explain. It has a presence of its own and it has entwined itself with me. The Soul Stone is a source of comfort and healing beyond what the body itself can achieve. I feel its presence at all times, and it experiences mine. There is an energy within it I cannot account for, and once it has bonded, it craves to experience life through its host. The Soul Stone is highly motivated to effect bodily repairs to ensure its host continues living. That has been my experience, anyway. I have not aged from the point of The Bonding."

Gina's eyes bugged out. "Reyne, you know what this means? He might be alive." She wrapped her arms around Reyne's neck. "He's alive."

With her face buried in his shoulder, Reyne asked, "Why three days?"

"Mister Brenton, the Soul Stone can help repair its host from injury rather quickly. Much faster than the body can do on its own. However, it cannot perform miracles. It has limits. I have been fortunate not to have exceeded them.

Although, I have myself been thought dead by others more than once, only to come around as good as new. As you have witnessed, I healed quickly from the arrow in my chest delivered by the now-dead woman. The Soul Stone's regenerative properties enabled me to meet you here in Concord City after appearing to have died."

While lightly pounding on Reyne's chest, Gina declared, "Mera's alive! My Mera's alive!"

Black Haven's Mera placed a hand on Gina's back. "Maybe."

Gina spun and snapped, "No! You can't do that. Give me hope, then steal it away... He's alive." She pointed her finger at the Mera look-alike. "Not another word about it." She wiped away her tears. Her voice trailed off, "He's alive."

"The prospect of such, Mister Brenton, brings up an interesting opportunity. If this other version of me still exists in the reality of Tartica, I would like to connect with him."

Reyne shrugged. "So, go ahead. Connect with him."

"Mister Brenton, you puzzle me. Sometimes you show great insight, albeit unexpectedly. Others, the obvious appears to elude you."

"Hey farm boy, I think Fake Mera just insulted you."

With a deep breath, Reyne held back a reply, and Mera continued, "If my timeline split into two divergent dimensions when I attempted to traverse the Void, this other Mera made it to Tartica, whereas I did not. If this is the true genesis of where Evidar and Black Haven split, and the point at which my one life became two, I will require your help."

Disregarding Gina, Reyne asked, "You think I can get you through the Void?"

"I wish it were so, Mister Brenton. Beth could not do it, and I harbor no illusions a novice such as you can do what she could not. Success is more likely if you reach out to this other version of me on my behalf."

Reyne shot back, "Who's Beth?"

Her face scrunched; confused, Gina probed for more. "I don't understand. Are you asking Reyne to go back to Tartica and leave me here so he can have a chat with real Mera? Fuck that."

"No, Miss Gina. Your associate here did something quite amazing today. He made a connection to someone on Tartica when he entered the Void earlier today. They communicated with each other. Isn't that right, Mister Brenton?"

Gina pushed off Reyne and locked eyes. "Reyne, what's he talking about? Is that even possible?"

"Miss Gina, your friend here is more talented than he lets on."

Running a finger over his lips, Reyne said, "We haven't had a chance to talk. I was gonna tell you. Honest. For a very brief second or two, I reached out to Mithany. Never connected with her in the Void like that before. Well, just the one other time. I swear, when you and me were alone, I was gonna tell you about it."

Gina slammed her fist into Reyne's chest. "You're a dick."

"Fuck. That hurt." He rubbed at the point of impact. "I'm sorry, Gina. I didn't have a chance to tell you."

"Maybe you didn't have a chance today, but what's this *once before* bullshit?"

"It's not like that. Remember when we were in the Void together? You said you felt Mithany's presence at the same time I did."

"Yeah, so what?"

"Well, since this jerk over here was about to kill us, I tried it again. I didn't even know if I could do it. I had to try. And I got to say goodbye to her. It lasted a few seconds. And by the way"—Reyne turned to Black Haven's Mera—"how did you know I connected with someone in the Void?"

"It was obvious, Mister Brenton. I did not know with whom, yet I surmised your purpose. You accessed the Void. And while there had the opportunity to continue your journey to Tartica. You could have left your partner to die on Black Haven. You did not. Ruling out a complete body-and-mind transfiguration escape, what other reason did you have to enter the Void, unless to connect with another? Again, something only a very few achieve."

Confused, Gina reacted. "I didn't know such a thing was possible."

"Gina, you know I won't leave you behind. I just had to reach out to Mithany." Turning to Black Haven's Mera, Reyne continued, "If I do this with you, connecting with Tartica's Mera, it's a onetime service you get from me. And that includes the fact none of us knows if Tartica's version of Mera is even alive."

"Perhaps."

"Bullshit with your *perhaps*. You get one shot at it. Then our deal is done."

"Yes, I agreed to those terms, Mister Brenton."

"Then what's this *perhaps* nonsense?"

"Once you hear what I am considering, Mister Brenton, you may change your mind."

"Tell me what's brewing in that evil brain of yours or I ain't doin' shit for you."

"It is really very simple, Mister Brenton. Only three people own a piece of the original Soul Stone. And yes, Gina is correct in her assessment; we who bear the Soul Stone are 'as old as fuck' as she has so eloquently pointed out."

"What's your point?"

"The Soul Stone came to us before the Great Destruction divergence, not after. I am aware of all three individuals who held a part of the original object. Myself, and that includes the other version of me on Tartica... one. The woman your world imagines to be the Goddess Teth... two. And the third is in the hands of a man who can't be trusted. You refer to him as the Devil's Blacksmith of Evidar. If Evidar does exist, I know who the holder of the Soul Stone must be. The true name of the man you call the Devil's Blacksmith is Janek. If he succeeds with a convergence affecting Tartica's reality, Black Haven will likely be pulled into the convergence of all Earthly dimensions."

Surprised, Reyne looked skeptically at Black Haven's Mera, "Until I showed up, Evidar didn't exist to you. Now you're tellin' me you know this Devil's Blacksmith. Don't seem possible."

"The Devil's Blacksmith... his name is Janek... and he is my brother. If this other version of me from Tartica sent you to Evidar to stop Janek, I trust your Mera to have a good reason for putting your life at risk. Janek must be stopped."

"Why?" Reyne demanded. "Why is it so important to you to save this shithole of a planet?"

"Because it's *my* shithole... and there is no way of knowing what convergence will do to it."

ROUNDUP

HENSDALE: 17TH DAY OF THE HARVEST MOON

Mithany

Thud... resonated through the treestone home of Reyne Brenton where Mithany lay asleep in his bed—alone.

Thud...

Thud...

Thud...

The pounding at the door shook Mithany from her dream. A dream of her and Reyne sitting at the orchard's burn pit, watching the flames and laughing with Daedyn. Her heart sank upon waking, recognizing the real world withheld both men from her. Daedyn was dead. Reyne was gone.

Thud...

"Alright! I'll be right out!" Annoyance fed her soul, wanting to enjoy the peace of her imagined reality of Daedyn and Reyne at her side once again.

Thud...

Mithany threw on a robe and secured the tie around her waist. "I'm coming! Hold your horses!"

She stamped down the hall, then threw open the front door. Before even seeing the face of the intruder, she spat, "What's so—" The sight of a uniformed soldier, sopping wet, sword scabbard at his side, stopped her mid-thought. Fear fixed her in place. She froze.

Rain poured down and ran off the porch roof.

Dressed in an odd multi-shaded patchwork of browns and grays as though to blend into a leafless forest, the soldier appeared to give the downpour any notice. "I'm sorry to wake you, ma'am. You and all the townsfolk of Hensdale are required to meet with my superior at the village square."

"What's this about?" Mithany demanded, looking up at the much larger man.

In a polite, yet direct tone, the soldier stated, "He'll cover all that. Now, if you'll please come with me."

Wrapping her arms around her robe, Mithany curtly replied, "I'm not going anywhere with you until you tell me what's going on."

"Ma'am, I mean you no harm. We are a unit from the Peoples Republic of Kantos... your government. Prime Minister Hermens has ordered your attendance."

"What, just my attendance?"

"No, ma'am, your entire village. And all those in Kantos will eventually be called to attend similar gatherings, in time."

In a huff, Mithany acquiesced. "Let me get dressed."

With one hand on the door, Mithany pulled it closed. Just as quickly, the soldier grabbed onto the side of the door and held it open.

"Again, I'm sorry, ma'am. Now."

"It's pouring out there. I'm barefoot. It's cold. I'm in my nightclothes and a robe."

"Alright. Get your shoes on and grab a coat. Leave the door open where I can see you."

Most of Hensdale's population had already arrived in the village square by the time Mithany arrived. The agricultural community of farmers, laborers, and supporting trades were early risers by nature. Also joining the locals were the displaced Topakers who had remained to assist with the Brenton Family Orchard resurrection following the fire that nearly destroyed it. All stood in the center grassy median separating both sides of Hensdale's quaint marketplace, facing the Communal Temple that anchored the square. Everyone appeared as annoyed as Mithany.

Heavy rain pelted all in attendance save the few who found cover under the leafless trees that lined the small park on either side for whatever little protection it offered.

Mithany spotted Arek standing near Judjurex Tetrip, and she made her way to her brother's side. With a kiss to his cheek, she said, "Morning, Arek, what's going on?"

"Hi, Sis. No idea. Me, Tetrip and the posse he put together were just about to round up the horses and head out to find Neladith when these guys showed up."

"How's Tetrip doing? Is his throat better?"

"Yeah, he's fine, Sis. Took longer to get volunteers than he expected. A few Topakers volunteered as well."

Mithany slipped her arm under Arek's and pulled him in tight. Arek jostled his cane in his other hand to steady himself in the throes of Mithany's embrace. "Careful, Sis, remember, I ain't what I used to be." He looked down and kissed her on the forehead. "Gonna miss you, Sis. Don't know how long we're gonna be out there lookin' for her."

Tetrip interrupted, his tone harsh. "Quiet, you two."

Mithany squeezed her brother and laughed. "There's the Tetrip we all know... and love."

"Hush young lady," Tetrip shot back.

"And good morning to you, Judjurex," Mithany offered with a polite nod.

"Yes, good morning," Tetrip replied matter-of-factly. "Now, be quiet."

Arek leaned in to whisper in his sister's ear, "He'll never change, Sis."

Clang... Clang.

The steeple bell atop the Communal Temple stole everyone's attention when it rang out. Soldiers from behind, Mithany guessed around fifty, forced the Hensdale townsfolk forward towards the temple.

Rain continued to drench the gathered villagers as they moved in unison. As they walked, Mithany told her brother, "At least it's not snowing."

Her hair was soaked, matted to her head, and the cold morning air stole every ounce of warmth her petite frame generated. Just like everyone else, her bones were chilled to the core.

Random voices could be heard calling out, "What's this all about?"

Angry shouts bandied around, "Get to it already!"

The crowd, pressed closer and closer together, started pushing and shoving.

Clang...

Clang...

Clang...

The pushing stopped, and the crowd came to a sudden halt. A short man with a gray beard, dressed in a fancy uniform different from the other soldiers, stepped out from inside the Communal Temple and held up both arms.

A hushed silence fell across the square.

From somewhere in the middle of the tightly packed townsfolk, Mithany heard the voice of Spetzer Bellsek—the foul-mouthed, arrogant, unrequited admirer of hers since childhood, who Mithany avoided whenever possible—joke to his small band of followers, "Who's this clown?"

Almost instantly, a soldier forced her way through, heading straight for Spetzer. Unable to see all the commotion, given her short stature, Mithany asked, "Arek, what's going on?"

"Spetzer's gettin' pulled aside, Sis. No loss there."

Spetzer yelled out, "Get the fuck off me!"

Another soldier, a big fellow, came up behind Mithany, pushed her aside, and marched straight towards Spetzer.

"Arek, can you see what's happening?"

"Looks like the wiseass ain't gonna wiggle himself free of that brute." Arek continued his play-by-play account for his sister's benefit: "Spetz is trying to stand his ground, Sis... Ah, he lost. Soldiers on either side got him by the arms."

Escorted out of the crowd, Spetzer stood quietly between two armed guards.

A man came to stand next to the leader, dressed in similar formal garb. Yelling, he asked, "Does anyone else have anything to say?"

No one spoke.

"Alright then. Let's begin." He turned to the leader, then stepped aside. "They're all yours."

"My name is Colonel Mac Ardle. I am sorry to have pulled some of you from your beds and others from attending to your chores. As citizens of the People's Republic of Kantos, I have grave news for you all. The Kingdon of Adelle has withdrawn from the Covenant of Absolute Universal Obligations."

A voice shouted from deep within the crowd, "Big fuckin' deal. We all know that."

The man standing near Ardle pointed to one soldiers, then aimed his finger toward the anonymous speaker. Ardle held up his open palm as if to say, "No. Let it go."

The Colonel continued, "That's good. Then you know how important it is to all of us that these actions cannot stand. The foundation of our civilization rests on universal adherence to its principles. Yet, what you do not know"—he paused, raising his arms high over his head with clenched fists—"Adelle has declared war on our great nation!"

A roar erupted. Villagers from everywhere in the huddled mass were shouting. Mithany found it hard to make anything out with so many people screaming angry, vile things. She pulled on Arek's arm, bringing his head down so she could be heard. "The rumors are true. Oh, Arek, this is bad."

"Don't worry, Sis. I can barely walk. Can't imagine they'll want me to join the cause."

"I'm happy they won't want *you*. What about me?"

"Well, Sis, let's just hope they don't have a uniform small enough to fit you."

She kicked him in his good leg. "You're a dick."

"Hey, that hurt. I'm bein' serious, Sis."

The incessant, random yelling came together as a cacophony of a single garbled sound, drowning out any comprehension of coherent meaning.

Clang...

Clang...

Clang...

With both arms raised high in the air, Ardle waved them back and forth, demanding silence.

No one listened to his command.

Clang... Clang... Clang... Clang... Clang... The temple bell pounded against the boisterous villagers' ears and went on and on until, finally, the mob realized nothing could be heard over the resounding bell. Colonel Mac Ardle had the silence he'd requested.

Ardle's tone softened. "What this means for all of you, for all of Kantos, is that our nation seeks volunteers to defend our way of life. Prime Minister Hermens is hopeful that we will muster an army sufficient for its purpose. My Captain, here to the right, will enlist those of you willing to serve."

Several of Hensdale's finest shot up their arms as if to say, "Take me."

Most did not.

Ardle pointed at each of the waving hands. "Your country thanks you. You can make your way to the front."

As they did, the Colonel added, "There are several of you Prime Minister Hermens is concerned for. You are at risk, as war will soon be upon us, and you will require our protection. May I please have the following step out to the left and join the sergeant standing on the park bench?"

As Colonel Ardle read eighteen names of young and old alike, Mithany again pulled on Arek's arm. "They're all Samers. They're rounding up the Samers, Arek. What do you suppose they're up to?"

"I don't know, Sis. After what happened at the birthing farm and what happened in Topak, I'm guessin' Miss Fancy-Pants Prime Minister is worried what they might do to the rest of Kantos. This ain't good."

"What's this all about?" someone shouted.

"I ain't goin' nowhere," came another.

Just then, Spetzer yanked his arm free and raced towards Colonel Ardle with his two guards chasing after him.

With one hand held out, commanding the soldiers to end their pursuit, Ardle addressed Spetzer. "Young man, do you have something to say to me?"

Spetzer turned his back to Ardle. "Yeah, I got something' to say." With an open hand above his brow, Spetzer scanned the crowd as heavy droplets pounded everyone, waiting on his next words. Leaning forward, his visual search came to a halt. Spetzer aimed his stare in the direction of Arek, where Mithany stood. "Colonel, it's obvious you're rounding up Samers. Why, I got no idea. Since you are, you should know"—he flung his arm, pointing straight at Mithany—"that girl there's been havin' unlicensed sex with another woman, and I walked in on it. So, if you're takin' Samers, you better take her too."

FAIR ENOUGH

TETH, SHANTYTOWN: 17TH DAY OF THE HARVEST MOON

Jerithan

After only one day following S'Leen's insistence on a quick stopover in Shantytown's Communal Temple, it had transformed into a refuge for Jerithan to lay his head and a gathering place for the de facto resurrected First Lord to hold court. With the whereabouts of Serco uncertain, along with the other Prudents caught up in the riot that saw the millennium-old Temple Palace burned to the ground, the faithful of Shantytown had proclaimed Jerithan Cree First Lord, at least by those in attendance the night before. Support from the rest of Shantytown had yet to be earned.

By most accounts, if word of mouth was to be believed, neither Serco nor any of the Green Robes survived the attack on the Palace. Notwithstanding Second Lord S'Leen's acclamation of Jerithan's faith reborn, news of Serco's likely death sparked joy in his heart. Although he lamented, no one had actually seen his tormentor's dead body. It mattered not given the sheer destruction the fire caused, and the expectation that nothing living could have survived the flames. For those who tried to escape their fate, the inciting mob made sure none did. He and S'Leen were lucky they slipped through. The presumption of Serco's demise was good enough for Jerithan... First Lord Jerithan.

With huge hands gripping the lintel above his head, Timble stood at the opening of the antechamber just off to the right of the altar. Inside the small room, Jerithan splashed water on his face while S'Leen pulled a green vestment off the rack. In a voice that belied his massive stature, Timble's tone resembled that of a teenage girl, as it always did. "Got us some figurin' to do today there Jerithan... guess I should be callin' ya First Lord Jerithan." The orange hair and orange eyes added to the incongruity of the big man. Although Timble gave off a gentle persona, Jerithan experienced firsthand what Timble proved capable of when pushed. Inside the slums of Shantytown, the ghetto of Teth, he knew what any of its inhabitants were capable of in their struggle to get by from day to day.

Wiping his face dry, Jerithan mumbled through the hand towel, "That we do, my friend. That we do." Tossing the rag aside, he said, "I'm still not comfortable with these new arrangements. Giving one sermon to a handful of people does not make me the First Lord of the Temple of Life."

The Voice broke into Jerithan's thoughts. *"This is the opportunity we have been building towards... your return to power."*

If I do not play this just right, I will be back in the gutter soon enough, Jerithan replied to his internal companion. Once thought to be the voice of God, Jerithan now knew better. Recent events exposed the falsehood in that assumption.

Poking her head through her newfound vestment, S'Leen added, "Destiny has delivered you here to this place and this time to begin the rebuilding of our flock. Of what I saw in you last night, you have been chosen by Teth herself to lead us." She ran her hands down along the front flowing panel. "It feels right, Jerithan."

"Destiny... I think not. We have worked hard, you and I, to put you in this position to take advantage of this opportunity. Do not tell this nice lady such things."

Stay with me. So much will depend on my first day.

"Get ya self presentable, First Lord," Timble began. "There're folks out there wanna meet ya. Yeah, I get ya concerns about bein' called the Temple's top dog, but consider this, ain't nobody left. Serco's dead, along with the other Green Robes. At least that's what everyone's sayin'. Besides, whether Serco's dead or not, you're still the right man for the job. You're one of us. Were at one time, anyway. Can be again. Folks I talked to are countin' on it. Countin' on you. Just gotta get 'em to trust ya."

Jerithan closed his eyes, tipped his head back, and took in a deep breath.

"Take it all in, Jerithan. It smells like success. You are back. Revel in it."

"Thank you, Timble. Your kind words are very much appreciated. I will stick my toe in the water as the interim Temple of Life leader. Let us see how today goes."

"Good enough for me." Timble nodded and threw his arm around Jerithan's shoulder.

"S'Leen, if I am going to regroup the Temple of Life faithful, I need you by my side. The Temple Palace is gone. Prudents stationed in Greenlin and Kantos are not likely to be coming home to Teth anytime soon, and the Prudents from Adelle who haven't been deported are probably in hiding with the declaration of war hanging over their heads. Those that were at the Palace the night it burned down... are no more. May they rest in peace."

S'Leen made the sign of the Signum Circulus over her heart. "May Teth welcome them all into the Community of Souls." After a reflective pause, she continued, "Of course, you have my support, Jerithan. You've always had my support."

"Thank you, S'Leen. And I think you will agree, we cannot return to the old ways. This opportunity to rebuild the Temple of Life must reflect our current circumstances. The faithful in Teth outside of Shantytown have either abandoned the city or have gone into hiding. The city itself is in ruin. The Temple's leadership structure has been decimated. We are cut off from our flock in Greenlin, in Adelle, in Kantos. War has been declared. And it is the overlooked, neglected, dedicated believers of Shantytown upon which the future of our faith now depends. They will be the rock upon which we build our new Temple."

"Not bad, Boss. Oh, sorry... First Lord," Timble said, shaking his head in agreement. "These're good folk. Won't do ya wrong. Just gotta treat 'em right. Always treat 'em right."

When Jerithan turned his attention back to S'Leen, he was taken aback. For a brief moment, he saw more than mere admiration in her eyes. She had the look of a smitten teenage girl. Planning the resurrection of the Temple of Faith aside, the opportunity to bed S'Leen brought a smile to his face and a burgeoning desire to his loins.

"Some things never change, my friend. This desire for her is a positive sign that your confidence is returning. When was the last time you considered having your way with a woman? This is good. She can be yours. Yet not today. We have more important hills to climb. These people of Shantytown do not need a First Lord, or any lord for that matter. These economically repressed followers are the foundation of your new flock. They do not seek a 'Lord' to put himself on a pedestal above them."

Thank you. That is something useful I can use. Good advice.

Rubbing his chin, Jerithan reflected, "The title of First Lord does not seem right anymore. It suggests that the officeholder, the steward of our faith, is better than those of the flock. I am merely the first amongst equals and my title, all our titles, should make the statement we are of the people, not above the people."

With a tilt of his head, Timble appeared to be considering Jerithan's suggestion. "Call yaself whatcha like. Can't argue with the point, though. Sounds about right."

"S'Leen?" Jerithan asked.

Nodding, S'Leen replied, "You'll be standing tradition on its head. Maybe this is the exact moment to do just that. I say seize the opportunity."

"Jerithan, may I suggest the title of Princeps? It had once been used by a great man of long ago to denote himself as First Citizen of a great empire. Although, he was, in fact, the first emperor of a once glorious republic. A position that you may one day lay claim to over all of Tartica."

Jerithan reflected, *Princeps sounds too much like 'prince'. I am not going to gain favor amongst people living in a ghetto by calling myself a prince.*

"Very perceptive of you, Jerithan. As for Princeps, the word prince is in fact, a derivative. No matter, your point is well taken."

S'Leen added her insights. "Breaking from the past and bringing our order down off its pedestal will go a long way towards building trust."

"We will figure out our new titles later. We have more important issues facing us. Timble, let's meet these people."

With a jolt, Jerithan felt Timble's arm, once again, come down on him as the big man pulled Jerithan along. Stepping through the antechamber door frame, Timble called out, "Listen, you mutts, this is the guy."

"He don't look like no leader," one of them called out.

"Looks ain't everythin'," Timble shouted back. "At least that's what your wife says."

"Don't ya talk about my wife, Orange Man."

They all laughed. At least everyone did except Jerithan, being preoccupied with sizing them up.

Looking over the twenty or so Timble had gathered to introduce Jerithan to, their clothing was worn, frayed, dirty, and whether donned by man or woman, all wore skeptical faces. Timble had prepared Jerithan, telling him these were the unelected leaders of Shantytown by choice or by reputation.

Taking his place behind the altar, Jerithan stationed himself to assume a position of authority. He aimed to reinforce the visual message that he was a leader. Yet, when he spoke, he intentionally toned down his words. "Thank you all for coming at my friend Timble's invitation. I know this is short notice."

A woman approached the altar. "You don't look like nothin' special."

Intentionally adding contractions to his delivery, intending to avoid sounding overly pompous, Jerithan simply said, "I'm not. I'm just like everyone else."

"Like fuck you are," she shot back, flittering her hands, wiggling her fingers as she mocked, "Ain't you the First Lord? Well, was once. Now wants to be again."

Aided by years of practice, Jerithan curled his lips upward, offering a friendly visage while he methodically searched each of their faces, unsure what he'd find. After a brief pause, Jerithan said, "There are no lords here. We're all just people who've got to figure out how to survive what's coming. The Temple's in shambles. Together, we can put it back together in a way that supports the people of Shantytown like it never has before... and saves Teth from being overrun by the Thuggery and by an army that's coming our way. Sooner rather than later, soldiers from Adelle will storm Teth."

The large open space of the Communal Temple, its short-cut green grass gently sloping downward towards the altar, seemed to gobble up the attendees as they moved in unison towards Jerithan. "Big words from a little man. You didn't give a shit about us when ya was First Lord before. Why trust ya now?" a voice from the crowd called out. The others all shook their heads in agreement.

Timble stepped between them and Jerithan. "True enough." He turned to eye Jerithan up and down. "Wouldn'tuv gave him the time of day when he was First Lord. Never seen him here back then. None of us did. Gotta admits, he was an asshole as First Lord."

Jerithan turned to S'Leen, who had replaced her look of love with one of fear.

"I seen him get yanked off his pedestal. Watched him survive the streets, just like us. Did ya know he grew up in the gutter like most of yous?"

"Bullshit," came the collective reply.

Jerithan gathered his courage and jumped in before Timble could answer. "I did. I stole more food than I paid for. Wrestled dogs for scraps and I lost more times than I won. I slept where I could. However, you're right. I've forgotten that life long ago. These past few weeks I've been reminded of where I came from, of what the good people of Shantytown live through every day. If I were you, I'd be skeptical too. Being stripped of my position, being forced to return to the life I once endured, has made me a new man. With me, you have someone who knows what goes on in the halls of power and knows what goes on in the streets."

The woman standing at the lectern near Jerithan asked, "So what? You is still an asshole."

"For what I did as First Lord, for how I treated others, I will always be an asshole. And now, I'm the asshole who cares what happens to you and cares what's about to happen to Teth. And let's be honest, on your own, you're all fucked. Troops from Adelle will come pouring into our city. And you are not the least bit prepared to repel them. I can help with that."

A short woman breastfeeding a baby in her arms stepped forward. With her hair pulled back in a bun and looking exhausted, the woman lifted her eyes from the newborn to angrily stare down Jerithan. "I'm a regular here at Temple. One ya call a member of the flock. Ya never did nothin' for me in return. So how ya gonna protect my boy now? With all these troops ya scare us with. I'm listenin'. Speak... asshole."

Jerithan stepped out from behind the altar to come face to face with the breastfeeding woman. He looked down at the babe in her arms, ignoring her exposed heavy bosom. "How old's your boy, ma'am?"

"Three weeks. Gonna have a hard life ahead of him. How ya gonna change that?" There was a sadness in her voice that touched Jerithan. He turned to look back at S'Leen. He hoped to find something akin to forgiveness in her eyes—for the lack of support the Temple failed to provide to its neediest. S'Leen only looked away. She'd failed the people of Shantytown just as much as he had.

With his hand on the babe's head, Jerithan spoke softly, "I don't deserve your forgiveness. I won't ask for it. Nor can I make amends for my actions in the past. As for your child's future, there is only today. We all must come together to secure a tomorrow for him and for all of you. If we succeed"—he moved his hand over his heart—"I promise you, with my life, if given the opportunity, we will survive today and make a better tomorrow for him and everyone in this community. I'm not the man I was. I know in my heart I *am* the man you need now."

Water welled in her eyes looking down at her son, and after a quick sniffle, she said, "Not much choice, I suppose. Guessin' I can do that." Lifting her gaze to Jerithan, she added, "But gonna hold ya to it. Ya know, givin' your life and all."

Jerithan smiled back. "Fair enough."

Just One Flaw

Black Haven, Concord City

Reyne

In a dark room, sequestered inside the dwelling of Black Haven's Mera, Reyne had been tasked with connecting with Tartica's version of Mera through the Void. Gina took up a position on a nearby chair their host graciously provided.

"Can you do it, farm boy?"

"I got no idea."

"Seems to me you're good at it. You touched Mithany's mind in the Void and once from a waking dream. You're a natural."

Reyne's head jerked back. "Natural? Are you crazy? I fuck it up every time I enter the Void. We're supposed to be on Evidar... I fucked that up. Then, somehow, I transported you along with me... I fucked that up. I connected with Mithany by chance the first time and had no clue how I did it. Today's the only time I got it right. So, no, I don't know if I can find Tartica's Mera in the Void. He might not even be alive."

Her words came out softly. "Don't say that."

"And what's all this about a Soul Stone?"

"Sorry, farm boy." Gina perked up. "Mera never shared a lot about it. It's got some sort of healing power is all I know. Once, while we were hunting Evidar agents, I thought they'd killed him. A day later, he's up and about, as good as new. He told me a little about it then. He never spoke of it since. I've asked for more details a few times. He clams up."

With a sneer, Reyne exclaimed, "That's just great!"

"Lighten up, farm boy. We're alive and Red's dead. Could be the other way around."

Reyne locked his hands behind his head. "Guess the good news is I'm gettin' better at controlling the Crazy-Reyne episodes. Triggered the last one all by myself. Not sure how I did it, though."

"It's a start. If you can call it up at will, we'll both be a lot better off."

"Another plus... you've given up on all that sex talk."

"Get over it, farm boy. Told you it was necessary. Had to do something to get your head out of your ass. Worked, didn't it? Got you ready for the mission."

"You never said you were sorry."

Gina frowned. "Sorry for what? I'm not sorry for a single word of it. I had a job to do... You."

With a clenched jaw, Reyne shot back, "Fine."

"Oh, don't pout. We have bigger problems. I still think we should shoot for Evidar."

Reyne's face scrunched. "Are you crazy? You think I can land us on Evidar?"

"You can do it. After you connect with Mera's thoughts, get him to give you some tips. We're on a mission. We have a Damus and a Devil guy to put down. Tartica's counting on us. Can't walk away from that," she said, shaking her head.

Reyne rubbed his fingers across his chin. "We'll see. If I can find Mera in the Void, you and me can talk after."

"Look, I get it. You miss Mithany. You think you have one chance to make it back to Tartica. But consider this: you touched her thoughts twice now. If you can do it at will, you solve the whole, 'Oh, I miss Mithany so much'..." Gina wrapped her arms around herself and puckered air kisses in Reyne's direction. "And we can attend to the business of killing people."

"You can be such a—"

Gina cut him off, waving her finger at him, "Now, now, farm boy. Don't go saying something you're gonna regret."

Reyne let several seconds pass. "I suppose it's possible."

"Well, there you go. We're on a roll. You control that berserker shit. Talk to Mithany in the Void every now and then, and if we can figure out how to get my quickness back... nobody will stop us."

"Yeah, only one flaw in your plan."

"What's that?"

Reyne hung his head. "Me, getting us both to Evidar."

What're You Gonna Do About It?

Tandure: 17th Day of The Harvest Moon

Loseff

Five battalions of one thousand soldiers each assembled near the banks of the river just outside Tandure, awaiting the arrival of their leader, General Loseff Tomelai. Commander General Kiple settled on a streamlined structure for the Grand Army of Adelle, assigning five battalions to each of the two divisions they'd mustered so far. The early morning sky delivered heavy, dark clouds with a promise of rain, or snow if it didn't warm up.

Each soldier under General Loseff's command stood at attention, dressed in their recently issued leather brigandine combat uniforms. Two of the battalions equipped each infantryman with short swords secured in back scabbards. Positioned on either the right or left hip a short oak cudgel slipped into the troopers' specialized pant leg pocket, as a weapon of last resort. Two other of General Loseff's battalions were outfitted with eight-foot-tall halberds. A single battalion of archers held bows in place of pikes, and arrow-filled quivers instead of back scabbards and swords.

The Hidden Hand's de facto leader, Jah'Rou Chamette's effort to ensure his confederates manufactured enough uniforms to meet the demand of Adelle's burgeoning military, along with the requisite battle gear, was in all-out production mode. Chain mail and helmets had yet to roll off the assembly line, and even then, Loseff expected availability to be limited.

As per Derr's demands of Chamette, failure to deliver came with serious consequences to the semi-legitimate businessman.

The division under Loseff's command drilled for weeks with hastily made wooden stand-ins for weapons before the real armaments were distributed only the day before. In proper military dress and armed for battle, General Loseff intended to inspect his newly outfitted recruits.

Loseff poked his head through the flaps of his command tent and called behind him, "Jaynes, you're with me. The rest of you wait here."

The pair made their way through the rows of tents shared by those of his battalion set up the night before. It would be home for Loseff and all those under him. He was determined to toughen them up for the hard road ahead. In General Loseff's reckoning, that road led to war. He couldn't afford pampered soldiers.

"You know, Jaynes, whether my father wishes us to defend or attack, I don't plan to sit around here forever playing soldier waiting for him to decide."

As an officer, Jaynes wore his sword at his hip and a small blue insignia above his left breast designating his rank. With his hand on the hilt as he walked, Jaynes asked, "How are things between you two? You've been even more resentful towards him ever since you started reading that stuff in *Dawn of the Third Age*."

"You're probably right. I can't get it out of my head that the Third Age is nothing more than a means to keep everyone subservient to a simple way of life where the few who hold power control everything. And my dear ole Dad knew it all along. He never shared a word of it with me. So, fuck him."

"That's what I'm saying. Hey, anything else in that book you haven't shared with me yet?"

"There's a lot of it I can't make out. Through the entire middle section of the book the ink's faded too bad to read most of it. I did pick up pieces here and there. The last few chapters look legible. I haven't read them yet."

"Well, hit me. What have you pulled out that you haven't told me already?"

"Okay, so the asteroid crashed into Earth like I said it probably would. The people in the cement seed vault buried under the ice sheet made it through. Most of them anyway. One guy got nearly crushed under a part that broke off when the entire structure rumbled. His head wasn't right after that. A few others died. Most of the station on the surface got destroyed."

"Sounds bad. Can't imagine it."

"I can't put all the pieces together with certainty. It reads like there was some kind of engine or machine that produced energy. They called it a nuclear reactor. I didn't read anything about how it functioned. The machine kept everything that survived working. Good thing, otherwise they would've all starved to death."

"Get to the good stuff."

"You remember the woman named Beth?"

"Yeah."

"Turns out, she started having dreams she was on another version of Earth. A version where the asteroid strike never happened. At first, she thought they were hallucinations caused by hypoxia. Turns out, she didn't imagine it. This Beth woman discovered another Earth, in another dimension."

"That's where you lose me. Another version of Earth that somebody can get to in their dreams. Can't be real."

"I believe every word in the book is true. The other version of Earth this Beth woman found in her dreams is this place: Tartica."

"No way. Two Earths. How's that even possible?"

"Yes, way. Then Beth started pulling others along with her in her dream world, dumping them off, one by one, here on Tartica. Even though they didn't call it Tartica, it's clear enough to me it is. The people who survived in the cement bunker escaped what was left of Earth and started a new path for humanity, under their rules, right here. I believe they were the seventeen hundred forty-two signers of the Covenant. Those same people set up a fake religion because they said there were too many wars in Earth's history fought over competing belief systems. Don't you get it, Jaynes? Our beloved founders, the Covenant, devotion to Nature, the Temple of Life—it's all a con."

"And you believe every word of what you've read?"

"Absolutely. All the pieces fit. The author, some guy named Albert "Mera" Meraturoc, left it behind as the true telling of how the Third Age came to be.

It's the only book like it and it's been hidden away. If people knew the truth, do you think we'd all be willing to follow the Temple of Life, devote themselves to Nature, and all that BS? Do you think the Covenant would have any meaning? Of course not. This Mera guy wrote it, maybe for himself. Who knows why? One thing's certain, my father got his hands on it, and now, it's mine."

"If you believe the Third Age is a con, and I'm not saying it is... since you do, what're you going to do about it?"

"What do I gain by pretending anymore? Why do I have to play along? If it's all horseshit, I've been thinking... what stops me from stealing it all from Father? Or from the rest of them?"

"You're on a roll now," Jaynes jibed.

"No. I'm serious. Listen to me. If the rules of governing, if the basis of our civilization's morality, if our religion worships a fake god, if it's all made up, why do I have to honor it? If the Covenant of Absolute Universal Obligation is built on lies, none of it holds legitimate authority. Why shouldn't I just grab what I want? I've lived my entire life as a backup in case anything happens to Tane, believing it meant something. After reading that book, I feel like a weight's been lifted off me. The shackles have been thrown off. I'm free... and I have an army behind me."

Jaynes slapped Loseff across his shoulders. "I've known you a long time, my friend. Your mind's already made up. Let's just say you succeed at whatever it is you're contemplating. Have you thought about how ripping the reins of power from your father would affect your mother? Worse... Derr?"

Loseff let out a sigh. "I know. That's going to be a problem."

"I don't know which of them is more devoted to your dad. And you can't deny the fact your mom loves her family. You'd be fuckin' with her husband. You'd be fucking with her daughter's inheritance. Your mom can be one scary bitch when you get her riled up if anyone threatens her family. Don't get me started about what Derr will do to you."

Jaynes' words stopped Loseff in his tracks. "It's all that keeps me at bay. I do love Mother... I can't imagine Father didn't read her in, or Derr, for that matter.

They're both part of Father's deception."

"Well, whatever you decide to do, I'll be right there with you for however long Derr lets us live."

Loseff spat back, "Fuck Derr."

After a quick, derisive flap of his lips, Jaynes shook his head. "Sorry, my friend, you don't fuck Derr. Derr fucks you."

Secrets Kept from Friends

Tandure: 17th Day Harvest Moon

Derr

The Agents of Derr, Derr's Grays, as they came to be known across Tartica, fed the KCG Capitan with a constant stream of information, be it fact, rumor, conjecture, or just an unknown piece of a puzzle yet to be figured out. The key was in its classification. Knowing a thing to be a rumor didn't warrant Derr's dismissal of it or even dissuade him from acting on it. Risk measured against reward, and the threat level attributed to each morsel of intelligence guided Derr's hand. Lieutenant Ferpratt, Derr's trusted second-in-command, dutifully put into action and directed whatever KCG resources the circumstances required. Only the most sensitive of issues Derr kept from his team, and even from his Chancellor. Derr's risk assessment measured a single danger point: the threat level to Chancellor Tomelai's life. Loseff Tomelai was one such data point that Derr recently moved up the scale.

While knowledge of Derr's Grays proved ubiquitous, who any of them were, how many there were, or how they shared their secrets with Derr would remain Derr's secret long after his final days on Earth had come and gone. Of their secret identities, even his close friend—his only friend—Chancellor Tomelai was not privy, although Tomelai freed whatever coin Derr required from Adelle's Treasury to keep Derr's sources of intel flowing.

How many Grays served in the dirt-gathering apparatchik feeding Derr's unquenchable thirst for information? No one save Derr had a clue. An Agent of

Derr might be the local barkeep, the laundry lady, a foreign dignitary, a constable, or anyone from any background, even someone's closest friend. Why an army of anonymous informants chose to be Derr's eyes and ears across the realm depended on individual circumstance; coin, revenge, a sense of importance, all such reasons played a role. Not surprisingly, being blackmailed by Derr proved equally as effective as any voluntary motivation to spy for the KCG leader. Such was the reason Loseff Tomelai's closest friend, Verek Jaynes, reported to Derr on a weekly basis: blackmail.

While most public interactions with one of Derr's informants required the requisite dark gray, loose-fitting, gender-concealing, face-hiding attire—which gave rise to their collective monicker—Derr's seemingly casual conversation with Lieutenant Jaynes, as Loseff's battalion drilled in an open field just outside Tandure's city limits, was such an ordinary and expected circumstance, it was beyond suspicion. Onlookers, even Loseff himself, would assume Derr to be gathering input on Loseff's leadership, the battalion's progress, and its readiness for deployment. Derr was careful to offer onlookers only Jaynes's back, reinforcing what they all knew down to their core, what they all feared. Derr was watching them... he was always watching.

"Salute me like you always do. Like I always tell you not to. This conversation needs to look like any other," Derr commanded Jaynes.

With a snap of his hand to his brow, Lieutenant Jaynes complied. "I fuckin' hate you."

"I would imagine you do. Everyone looking on will think I just told you to put your hand down," Derr said, shrugging off any concern for the young man's obvious internal conflict over spying on a man he called his closest buddy. "Now, with that out of the way, as it's of great concern to the future of Adelle, I expect your complete cooperation once again. Should you hold back or hesitate to be forthcoming, may I remind you..."

"No. I don't need a reminder. How about this for a reminder... fuck you."

Derr quipped, "Feel better? Does that help swallow your betrayal? Don't answer. It's not necessary. Just give me the update."

"Did I tell you I fuckin' hate you?"

"No need to be repetitive," Derr said nonchalantly. "I have almost perfect recall. You fuckin' hate me. Join the club. I got it. Move on."

Jaynes crossed his arms in a pout. "What do you want from me this time?"

"Let's continue from where you left off in your last report. Tell me more about this book he found and his more recent reactions to the new passages he's read."

"Have you ever seen this book? Have you read it? What did you think?"

Like a stone, Derr gave nothing away. He shifted his focus from the troops drilling off in the distance to deliver narrowing eyes in a harsh glare aimed at Jaynes.

With apparent reluctance, Jaynes paused... "It's hard to imagine anything in that book is true. Loseff believes it is. Every new chapter he reads just gets him more riled up."

"Do you believe the things he's read to you or told you about *Dawn of the Third Age*?"

"I don't know. Maybe. What's it matter what I think? This is about Loseff, and he soaks up every word he reads."

"What's got him so agitated about its contents?"

"It's the message. The theme. Our religion. The Covenant. The foundation of Tartican civilization. It's all built on lies. At least that's how Loseff reads it."

"Flap your arms. Make them all think you're angry, arguing with me," Derr commanded.

"What?"

"Just do it."

Jaynes threw his arms in the air and gestured with them several times before settling his hands on his hips. "How's that?"

"It's for your benefit, Jaynes. You wouldn't want your bestie getting suspicious."

"Did I say I hate you?"

"Of course you do. Just tell me why Loseff thinks this '*big lie*' matters to him. Now, cross your arms over your chest like before. Stick out one leg."

"Whatever," Jaynes complained, yet complied. "Anyway, to Loseff, it means all the rules are meaningless. It makes him question why he needs to comply."

"What does noncompliance look like to him?"

"I don't know. We didn't get that far."

"You've known him all your life. Take a stab at it," Derr demanded with a touch of annoyance.

"He's complicated. He could walk away. Give up. Or he could rebel. We both know he never much liked the idea that his purpose in life is that of a spare part. You know, being second in line. He's always resented it. He'll probably never get to have any of the power that's been promised to his sister by her rite of succession and all that."

With a *tsk* of disappointment and the encouraging repeated rolling motion from his hand, Derr prodded, "Which way is he leaning?"

"Can't say for sure."

"Come on now, you're not that stupid. Take an educated guess."

"Fuck you"—he paused—"it could go either way. What I can say is, he likes being General."

In the distance, Derr spotted movement from Loseff. "Session over. He's coming our way."

Jaynes turned his head towards the approaching Loseff. "Great."

Derr reacted quickly. "Look at me. Don't turn around. When he asks you, tell him we discussed his performance as a leader. You gave him glowing reviews."

"He's not going to like that you're asking about him."

"No, he's not, but it's what he'd expect from me. He thinks I'm checking up on him for his father. How he's performing as Adelle's youngest general. It's the only thing he will believe. Now, start talking about problems in the unit. He's getting close."

Jaynes rubbed the back of his neck. "There's this one guy, a sergeant that's been riding his unit pretty hard. A few of the men came to me complaining..."

Loseff interrupted the two men's conversation by shoving Jaynes playfully from behind. "What are you two talking about? Me, no doubt."

What Goes Around

Mithany

Heart-pounding fear pulsed in waves against Mithany's temples. Mithany, along with everyone else, was struck dumbfounded by Spetzer's accusation. It failed to register the rain had let up, now coming down only as a drizzle.

What she did was wrong, and she knew it. Now everyone else did as well. Not because she violated laws governing the approval required for same sex couplings, which she wasn't, but because she violated the trust inherent in the bonds of love between herself and Reyne. Engaged to Reyne, townsfolk would label her unfaithful, untrustworthy, and even worse, a cheater. In the small religious community of Hensdale, all were unforgivable offenses, as all carried a life sentence of scorn. Most damning of all the repercussions she'd face was for infidelity, and Reyne would learn of her betrayal.

The broken little girl inside her wanted to rage against Spetzer's revelation. Her dalliance with Neladith, now exposed to the entire village, and to Colonel Mac Ardle, proved more than a mere embarrassment. Drained of every ounce of energy, all she could do was surrender.

With Spetzer's accusing finger still pointed directly at her, Mithany's head spun as she caught movement out of the corner of her eye. Two soldiers broke away from their posts and pushed through the gathered Hensdale townsfolk, headed straight for her.

As the troopers approached, Arek put himself between Mithany and the on-coming military escorts. He held out his hand as if to command the pair to stop. They didn't.

Tetrip, who'd been standing next to Mithany, spoke up, "I'm the Judjurex for this village, and any accusation against this young lady concerning Covenant violations falls within my jurisdiction." Without a word, ignoring his authority, his position as Judjurex, and his protestations, the soldiers shoved Tetrip aside.

Arek grabbed the shoulder of a trooper as she passed. The woman immediately spun around, grabbed onto Arek's offending hand, and bent it back ninety degrees in one seamless motion. As Arek dropped to a knee, the trooper released her grip. He pushed up on his cane to stand.

Mithany reached for her brother's hand and squeezed. "Thank you for trying."

"This ain't over, Sis."

With military personnel on either side of Mithany, they took hold of the petite shoppe owner to escort her through the mass of bodies.

Colonel Ardle held out an open palm. "There's no need for that. Release her." The subordinates did as commanded. Colonel Ardle directed his words at Mithany and respectfully requested, "Young lady, would you mind please stepping forward?" He spread his arms and added, "Everyone, please clear a path for her."

While Mithany navigated her way forward with her gaze fixed downward in disgrace, Ardle called out, "As for the eighteen names that have been read off, all please make your way forward." It sounded like a request. Mithany and everyone else understood it to be a command.

Within minutes, Mithany and sixteen others lined up near Colonel Ardle, looking back at the gathering of confused townsfolk.

"Seems we're two people short," Ardle observed.

"What's this all about?" came an angry voice from deep in the huddle of bodies.

"In due time. First, the two missing. I ask for your cooperation. Please step forward."

Four hundred plus heads moved in every direction, searching for the missing pair, yet Ardle's request went unanswered when no one stepped forward.

Mithany looked up and down the line of the sixteen and quickly surmised that two older women, Vallilia and Doranna, were Ardle's missing Samers. The two women lived together for as long as Mithany could recall. The duo were notorious busybodies who made it a point to stick their noses in everyone's business. That never bothered Mithany. She liked them both, regardless of their penchant for gossip.

The military personnel stood several feet beyond the confined townsfolk, as though outlining the boundaries of Hensdale's Market Square. No one would get out unless allowed to do so. As one, the unit personnel looked to Ardle, awaiting their next orders. Ardle offered a subtle nod, telling them to hold their positions.

Mithany locked on Ardle's eyes and told herself, *It's always in the eyes. What are his telling me?* As she studied the leader, Ardle showed no signs of aggression and even portrayed kindness in his visage. She didn't know the man to compare any of his facial expressions from past situations, yet his current reactions appeared more gentle than demanding.

"Sergeant, please ask each of these nice people their names, and after you've checked them off, bring the list to me."

Several brief minutes later, the sergeant presented Colonel Ardle the list. Ardle looked up from the wet piece of paper attached to a clipboard. "We seem to be missing two older women named Doranna and Vallilia, if my list is correct. Would you two ladies please join us?"

Again, heads turned in every direction. After a long moment of waiting, nobody stepped forward. As Mithany studied Colonel Ardle, she took note that he remained unflustered.

"I'm told there is a Judjurex amongst you named Tetrip. Wherever you are, please come up here and join me."

Tetrip yelled out in his familiar stoic manner, "What do you want?"

Colonel Ardle politely replied, "Sir, I ask only for your help."

"Help with what?"

Ardle tipped his head back, puffed his cheeks, and released a gush of air. "Alright then. I see this issue is impeding our progress." His gentle tone evaporated at that moment. "I say to all of you, Adelle has declared war on Kantos, Teth, and Greenlin. Chancellor Tomelai of Adelle has withdrawn from the Covenant and our intelligence has determined agents of Adelle have kidnapped Samers from Kantos, both licensed and otherwise. These abducted individuals are being forced into conscripted service for Adelle. It is our government's assessment they will be nothing more than sacrificial fodder when fighting begins."

The crowd gasped in disbelief. Angry anonymous voices spat out vile condemnations of Tomelai. Mithany listened while keeping her gaze fixed on Ardle. She noticed his eyes aimed down and away as he testified to Tomelai's plans for Kantonian Samers. And as Ardle finished his speech, she noticed his fingers linger across his lips as though unconsciously hiding something.

She cocked her head to the side like a quizzical puppy as she analyzed the data she'd collected on Colonel Mac Ardle. A childhood spent learning to read her mother's every countenance, hoping to avoid the next beating, necessitated by years of exposure, taught her the meaning of myriad eye movements and facial expressions. Her assessment of Colonel Mac Ardle, rooted out from his look down and away, and in the words he spoke hidden behind his fingers, led her to an obvious conclusion: *He's lying.*

Colonel Ardle removed his hand from his mouth and pointed to the Samers. "As good citizens of Hensdale, you require your country's help. I am here to protect you. I am here to make sure you all remain safe. These seventeen people up here are in danger of Adelleian kidnappers. From bigoted neighbors. Yes, Samers from other nations are joining up with Adelle's military. Suspicion will grow about our licensed brethren even within this peaceful community. In time, you'll question whether the friends you have known all your life are secretly working with Adelle against our beloved country to subvert the Covenant... just because they bear The Mark. When the fighting begins, some of you here today will turn on your licensed neighbors."

"You're nuts!"

"Never!"

"Leave us alone!"

Through the shouts and jeers from people Mithany knew her entire life, she considered Ardle's last point: while hard to accept, it rang true to human nature.

Ardle motioned his outstretched arms up and down to quiet the crowd before continuing. "Our Covenant demands of all of us to ensure that no harm comes to another. Our Prime Minister believes these actions we take here today are the only way to ensure our government fulfills its sacred obligation. The government of Kantos must do whatever is necessary to protect those at risk."

Mithany continued evaluating his every look, gesture, eye movement, and thought to herself: *Colonel, you're hiding something. There's more you're not telling us.*

A friend of Doranna's shouted, "Well, if that's the case, nobody's ever gonna make Doranna or Vallilia fight in no army. Them two barely take care of each other. And it's crazy if you think either of them could be a spy. Hah! Neither can keep a secret longer than five seconds. Let 'em be."

Another voice rang out, "If there's a war, ain't we all in danger? Don't just protect Samers. Protect all of us."

Still another, "Where are you taking them?"

In a heartbeat, Mithany observed Ardle's face sour. His eyes drew back, his fists clenched, his body tensed, and he exploded, "Enough!!"

The troops all snapped to attention.

The Colonel's politeness gave way to harsh demands. "I will have your co-operation willingly or forcibly. Sergeant, there are more people here than just Hensdale's population. Check every arm. Round up everyone who bears a license tattoo." He pointed at Mithany, and the stern look on his face shook her to her core. "Take this little one, too."

Arek screamed, "STOP!"

Ardle shot a hard look at one soldier, who reacted immediately by shoving his way through the crowd, grabbing Arek, and dragging him to where Ardle stood.

Mithany pleaded, "No... Arek... Don't."

With a comforting tone in his words, Arek leaned in for only her to hear and whispered, "Got to, Sis."

A second before Colonel Ardle started to speak, Arek cut in before he could. "Colonel, if you're roundin' up Samers, unlicensed ones too"—Arek's arm moved slowly forward as he aimed a finger at Spetzer—"better take that guy and me. We're gonna need protecting like the others."

Spetzer erupted, "WHAT? NO! HE'S LYING!!"

Without being ordered, one of the troopers snatched Spetzer from where he stood and yanked him every step of the way to stand next to Ardle. Spetzer wiggled and squirmed. The soldier's grip held him firm.

Spetzer pleaded, "Let me go!"

Ardle demanded, "What's this about?"

Spetzer yelled out, "He's lying. I told you he's lying."

Ardle raised one finger to his lips. "Silence. I want to hear from the cripple."

Mithany tensed at Arek being called a cripple, a harsh slur nobody ever deserved, especially the brother she loved. Even worse, she surmised what Arek was up to. Mithany understood her brother all too well. He'd protect her at all costs, and there was no stopping him. Wherever Ardle intended to take her and Hensdale's Samers, Arek would make sure he'd be right there with her. Tearing down Spetzer in the process, well, that was just an added bonus.

She leaned in and whispered, "Don't do this."

Ignoring his sister's plea, Arek continued. "Colonel, sir." His tone came off flippant. "This guy here, his name is Spetzer Bilseck. Me and him need to be protected."

Spetzer screamed, "He's lying!"

"Colonel, sir, it's been going on in secret for years. Neither of us is licensed. He likes to do stuff to men when he's drunk, and well, I let him. A mouth's a mouth… you know what I mean."

The front row, standing close enough to hear Arek's account of what the two men shared, broke out in laughter.

Someone shouted, "I always knew you had it in you, Spetz!"

While frantically scanning the onlookers for his buddies, Spetzer's face burned red. His eyes bulged as they shot madly from side to side. "Trell, where are you? Tell them Arek's full of shit! Crip, tell them. TELL THEM!"

Colonel Ardle glared at Spetzer. "One more word out of you and I'll have you gagged. Now shut up."

Arek lied, that was obvious to Mithany. Her brother never spent a minute alone with Spetzer. He hated him. The siblings shared everything, including Arek's stories of every individual he ever bedded, not a man amongst them. She never judged him for his womanizing. She knew he was broken. Mithany understood his unquenchable philandering as a consequence of the brutal childhood they'd endure together. She recognized his obsession with women grew out of his craving for love denied him by the one woman who never gave him any—their mother. As a wanting child craving a mother's affection, the brother she loved manifested his unrequited affections in the arms—and in the beds—of all the women he'd ever met as a surrogate of the maternal love he never received.

And Mithany knew she was just as broken as Arek. It's what delivered them both into Ardle's grip, her bedding of Neladith.

Ardle pointed at Arek, "You. Speak."

With a smug look on his face and open arms, Arek replied, "What else is there to say? You're roundin' up people like us for our own protection. Take me away." Then Arek snapped his head in Spetzer's direction. "And don't forget about him."

After a quick glance from Ardle, two soldiers reacted to the silent command and seized Spetzer. He screamed with all the force his lungs could muster, "NO!"

EVIL WITHIN

BLACK HAVEN, CONCORD CITY

Reyne

Black Haven Mera said to Reyne, "Mister Brenton, we have a common goal. To stop the Devil's Blacksmith, my brother Janek, from affecting both Tartica and what you call Black Haven."

"That don't make us friends." While Reyne had no way of knowing whether the order given by Black Haven's Mera to terminate Red's tribe had been carried out, the order itself was a heinous offense. "You had Red's people killed after telling them you'd help them. For what, spite? It's impossible for Gina or I to trust you. After I take this trip into the Void to find Tartica's Mera... if I can even do it... what assurances do either of us have we will walk away?"

"You have nothing, save my word, Mister Brenton. It is all you get. We could put it in writing, yet that is another illusion. No, my word will have to do."

"That's the thing. I do this and tell you what Tartica's Mera shares with me, that's if he is still alive, and you get what you want immediately. What's to stop you from reneging on our deal right then and there?"

"Again, Mister Brenton... nothing. However, I assure you both, freedom is on the other side of your trip into the Void. This discussion has no point. Trust me, connect with this other Mera, and you will, thereafter, be free. Do not, and you will die here today. Trust is immaterial. Death is not. I have had enough of this discussion. Either do it, or waste no more of my time."

With vacant puzzlement written across Gina's face, she shrugged and said, "Listen, Reyne, just do it. If you don't, we're dead. It's fifty-fifty that we live if you do what he wants. The odds of survival only go up from zero chance we live, only if you do it."

"Duh, I know. I just don't want to give this guy anything he can use against Tartica. Mithany's there. I can't put her at risk."

"I assure you, Mister Brenton, I have no designs or concerns for this Tartica of yours."

"Same argument as before. How can I trust you won't try to fuck up my world, too?"

"Mister Brenton, haven't I shared with you the full extent of my knowledge to assist you and Miss Gina to affect a double transfiguration so you can depart my world together?"

"Reyne. We now know how to piggyback into the Void. Fake Mera explained it. After you do this, we're outta here." Gina said again, "Just do what he wants."

Reyne closed his eyes, took in a deep breath, opened them, and in a huff, said, "Fine."

"Then I will leave you here, Mister Brenton. Miss Gina, you will accompany me. We will return when Reyne has finished. I cannot permit you both to employ your newly gained knowledge in a foolhardy escape attempt back to Tartica... Now can I?"

Reyne smirked. "That's not necessary. You can trust us. Trust, it's a bitch."

"I wish it were so, Mister Brenton. Enough. We will take our leave."

Black Haven's Mera signaled to a lackey standing nearby, who promptly grabbed Gina's upper arm to escort her from the room.

As they walked away, Reyne protested, "How do you know I can even find Tartica's Mera in the Void and connect to his thoughts?"

"You have demonstrated extraordinary Void-talents in the short time I have known you. You will find a way, Mister Brenton. Although, if you fail, Miss Gina will be dead before you leave this room. Enough talk. Knock on the door when you are done."

Human shapes faded into silhouettes before being enveloped in total darkness. The squeal of a hinge followed by a *thunk* told Reyne they were gone. He was alone.

He'd always understood he had no choice. He had to try. He had to succeed. The small problem left to him—how?

He laid down across the sofa, folded his hands behind his head, crossed his feet, and thought through the process. He'd done it before to reach out to Mithany, yet that seemed different. Love connected his soul to hers. He would forever know the essence of her. His heart would know the true love that bonded them together. Finding Mera in the Void wouldn't be the same as finding Mithany.

Dread filled his thoughts at the prospect of encountering an untold number of the Probability Waves of hopeless souls as he had experienced on his first venture into the Void. He feared being consumed by their unfathomable sorrow. He barely escaped their hold on him. Yet, he had no choice. Gina's life hung on the strength of his will to endure it. Reluctantly he acknowledged his own death as the price of failure. Yet, as hard as he tried to accepted Gina's death laid at his feet, he couldn't.

Girding himself for what was to come, Reyne closed his eyes and locked an image of Tartica's Mera in his mind.

Sleep soon took him to the astral plane.

The metaphysical barrier between the physical world and the Void proved as difficult to penetrate as before. Yet through sheer willpower alone, he persevered through it. How long it took—unknowable. The absolute absence of light slammed into Reyne's free-floating, non-corporeal consciousness the instant he entered the Void.

As expected, millions of Probability Waves representing hundreds, maybe thousands of lives slammed into his free-flowing consciousness. Sorrow, pain, joy, terror, and hopelessness flowed into his soul from the multitude of anonymous lives. Without a body, existing in the Void as conscious energy, Reyne's essence was tossed about the ebony expanse like a single flower pedal inside a tornado. How long it went on, there was no way of knowing. Time's passage inside the

Void eluded comprehension. His mind wandered for days, or maybe only seconds.

A craving to search out Mithany consumed his thoughts, pushing aside all other attempts to invade his mind. If he found her, he wondered if he'd have the strength to move on to Mera.

Focusing on Mera, suddenly thousands of the man's Probability Waves crashed into his consciousness. It was as though Mera's life spanned untold years, and so many paths branched off into exponential futures. He bore down on the moment Mera slapped the poison dart on his kitchen table. He followed that single timeline of Mera's life.

An oasis opened coming from the Probability Waves flowing from Mera's life force. A singular aroma he'd never experienced, a mixture of ancient flesh and burned hair stole his attention. How Reyne knew its age or origin eluded comprehension. With his non-physical sense of smell, Reyne drew in the odor. It fed his mind with even more images of Mera. From which variation of Mera's life it emanated, Reyne struggled to discern.

With intense concentration, one Probability Wave flowing off Mera standing in a forest took shape as it undulated up and down. A moment's hesitation later, hundreds of alternate timelines of the life Mera might take from that point in time poured off Mera's solitary figure. Reyne struggled to focus through all the possibilities. The oasis opened wider, pushing back the ebony of the Void if only inside a small bubble of reality surrounding the image of Tartica's Mera. The edges rippled and pulsed in pitch-black globs, threatening to destroy the field of light Reyne had created.

Mera stood, looking away. Reyne's thoughts reached out to touch Mera's. Like a jolt from a lightning bolt, electricity shot through him. Reyne's mind snapped to attention. *Mera, is that you?*

Startled, Mera's head whipped around. Mera paused. He looked about in every direction.

Mera. It's me, Reyne. I'm in the Void.

Mera froze. "You're alive. Thank goodness."

And so are you. Gina's with me. We thought you were dead.

"She's alive as well. What a relief."

We ain't on Evidar. It's a different version of Earth. Black Haven. A lot like Evidar. Dismal. Dark. Miserable.

"How is the mission proceeding?"

Before that, have you followed Mithany?

"Yes, she's safe."

Promise me you'll go to her. Tell her the truth. Where I am. What I'm doing.

"Can't do that, Reyne. It's too dangerous."

Reyne erupted. *I DON'T CARE. DO IT!* and the blackness of the Void closed in on his vision of Mera.

"Reyne, you have to under..."

Do it or I'm out. And I won't get Gina to Evidar either.

"Tartica is falling apart. War's coming. I need to stop it before it happens. I don't have time."

Then I'm done. I'm out. Kill the Damus and the Devil's Blacksmith without me.

"I can't. You know that. Don't ask me to do this."

I'm not asking. I'm telling you.

"If I do this, I'll have to take her with me. It will be dangerous."

You promised me you'd protect her. Promise me you'll do what I ask, and I'll finish the job.

"Fine. I'll do it under protest."

Just do it. Promise me.

"I promise."

Good. On Black Haven, there's another version of you. His name is also Mera. He says you two are the same person and at some point, when you made it through the Void to Tartica, a version of you did not make it...him. He stayed behind. Your life's timelines split at that instant. He's got the same Soul Stone as you. Says the Devil's Blacksmith on Evidar is your brother Janek. Janek's a bad guy and he's on board to s top him.

"Fascinating."

That's all you got to say? Fascinating.

"I've always known my brother is the Devil's Blacksmith. The existence of Black Haven and another me, now that is fascinating. As far as the Soul Stone is concerned, mine is under a layer of flesh where it can't be lost. It's also the only way I could get it through the Void. If he has the same Soul Stone, since we're the same guy, it's under the skin of his chest."

Good to know. This other Mera sent me into the Void to find you. Wants to know one thing. Where's Beth? What became of her?

"I wish I knew. She got me through the Void that one time. I'm guessing in a way similar to how you and Gina made it together. Beth and I arrived in this realm we now call Tartica after she took seventeen hundred others here. She said she was going back for Janek. Janek never arrived, and I never saw Beth again."

Who is this Beth?

"Not important to you. Just tell him what I told you."

Mera, I need your help. Gina lost her ability to move fast ever since she ended up on Black Haven with me. How can it be fixed?

"My guess, something affected her Third Eye when she went through the Void. She could never penetrate the Void's metaphysical barrier. I tried to coach her through it many times. All failed. When you somehow pulled her through it, it changed her. It's only a guess. I might be able to help her, except I can't do it while she's in another dimension."

That's just great.

"You're both…"

Stop. Mera! You feel that? Oh my god, what is it?

"Yes, I sense it too. You've got to get out. Now!"

A malevolent entity. It's pure evil… It burns!

"Get out, Reyne!"

What is it?

"It senses the Soul Stone. I have it. It's why I won't enter the Void. Now it knows you as well. Our minds are connected. Get out of there!"

Agghh. It's reaching into my soul! It's tearing at my consciousness.

It hurts!

Make it stop!

"Reyne. You have to get out of the Void."

How?

"Just get out!"

Oh god, it burns.

It burns. Ahhh.

Help me, Mera.

I beg you.

Mera screamed a command into Reyne's thoughts, "REYNE, WAKE UP!"

Reyne's eyes popped open. *Awake. Free of the Void.*

The agony perpetrated by the malevolent entity quickly faded the second his consciousness rejoined his body. From his core, soft, low rumbles quickly built to a crescendo. His inner beast spewed its condescending laughter at him. The monster that lurked in his soul, struggling to get out, that craved to inflict harm on others—payback for Daedyn's murder; for his baby sister's slaughter; for his birth mother's slaying; the beast he'd released into the physical world several times before, the beast within Reyne who yearned for vengeance—just kept on laughing at him.

Reyne rolled off the sofa onto the floor with a loud *thud*. He curled up in a ball, wrapping his arms around folded knees. He wondered if Mera had planted a subliminal command in his mind during the hypnosis session, preparing him for his first trip into the Void. It saved his life. Mera had saved him... again. Rocking back and forth, his mind reeled at the existence of pure evil. An evil that touched his soul.

And still, the beast within continued laughing.

Betrayal in Promises Broken

The Woodlands: 18th Day of the Harvest Moon

Mera

Pain from the encounter with the unknown malevolence in the Void, excruciating at the instant it struck, dissipated just as quickly the moment Mera's connection to Reyne's consciousness broke off. Tartica's version of Mera set aside the traumatic encounter. He'd experienced it when he entered the Void with the Soul Stone embedded in his flesh, yet never as swiftly did the entity attack.

An impossible choice had been laid at Mera's feet: honor his promise to Reyne or stop a war.

War appeared a certainty for Tartican civilization. Mera believed events across the continent had been manipulated somehow by a brother he once loved fifteen hundred years ago. A brother he had known as Janek, now called the Devil's Blacksmith. Both bore a piece of the Soul Stone Beth had shared all those years ago with Janek, her husband—not with him. He stole a fragment of the all-important Soul Stone from Janek. It almost cost him his life. The scars of Beth's choice of Janek over him and of Janek's refusal to divide the Soul Stone between brothers still stung a millennium and a half later.

Mera set aside the past, set aside thoughts of the malicious entity, set aside the guilt growing in his gut, knowing he had to deny Reyne the promise he made to watch over Mithany.

Mera shook it off and continued on his way to Teth. Coming upon a crossroad, he looked down the well-worn dirt thoroughfare leading to Mithany's village.

Stay put, young lady, I'll be back for you after I meet with Temple leadership.

Mera's persona as a humble hobo showing up in Hensdale, occasionally checking in on Reyne's life over the past twenty years, was one of many he'd donned. Under a different guise, he was a frequent visitor to the four Tartican capitals and a welcome guest in the halls of power. Tartica's long run of peace—since its founding—had not been achieved without his occasional thumb on the scales. Careful not to overstay his welcome, Mera went decades between administration visits when he was not needed, re-emerging, when called for, with a new identity each time.

He planned to work through Temple of Life First Lord and Chancellor Tomelai to find common ground both could live with. Mera lamented, *The time of the Covenant of Absolute Universal Obligations as the unifying force governing civilization is over.*

Mera reflected as he walked; getting everyone's agreement to the creation of the Covenant he'd written in the year 86 of the Third Age had strained his diplomatic skills to the limits. That was in the past. In the present, he would have to discover a new path to peaceful coexistence these fifteen centuries later. Until he sat down with all the players, a way out of war and a renewed era of peace would remain out of reach. He feared thousands would die until he did.

While he sought peace on Tartica, he counted on Reyne, and now Gina, to eliminate the threat from Evidar. A threat even greater than the impending Covenant War between the nations of Tartica.

Betrayal lingered in his thoughts. Beth's betrayal: choosing his brother Janek after her secret affair with Janek had been discovered. Janek's betrayal, sleeping with Beth, Mera's own fiancée. And Janek, his own brother, denied him a piece of the Soul Stone. Obtaining that piece almost cost Mera his life when he fought Janek for it. He'd gained the Soul Stone, lost a brother, and soon thereafter, never saw Beth again.

Although centuries separated Mera from those events, time did little to dull his anger. He thought of his promise to Reyne and of his own betrayal to a man he entrusted with Tartica's future.

Mera stopped in his tracks. One road led to Mithany. He promised Reyne he'd protect her. One road led to Teth.

He didn't move for several minutes.

What's one woman's life worth measured against the world?

Sorry, Reyne, I hope you can forgive me. I've got a war to stop.

A Warning Nonetheless

Mithany

With Arek at her side, Mithany arrived at the western end of the foothills of the Razors, along the border of Kantos and Teth, a location Prime Minister Hermens selected as the first of six Samer internment camps. As the image of a wooden stockade rising up from the ground came into view, Mithany and all seven hundred twenty-two licensed and unlicensed Samers stopped dead in their tracks. Guard towers dotted the façade while twenty large timber roofs peaked out over the top of the encircling fence.

Colonel Mac Ardle's unit had swept through Topak, Hensdale, Owls Neck, and dozens of other small towns rounding up licensed Samers along the way. For those who never sought the official sanction of The Mark, Ardle accepted hearsay as just cause to include them—for their own protection as they were told—amongst the populous to be resettled in a safe location. Recruits from every town who'd joined Ardle's military unit, although not properly outfitted, willingly took part in the effort to move the detainees to their new home... for their own good.

Mithany, amazed at the sight before her eyes, said, "Arek, that doesn't look like a place to keep Adelleian fighters out."

"Gotta agree with you there, Sis. No doubt about it, that big wooden fence looks like it's there to keep us in... Them guard towers can't be good. But, hey, look on the bright side, you got me. Whatever 'in there' holds for us, we're goin' to face it together."

Snuggling in against Arek's side, Mithany wrapped her arms around his waist. "Don't get me wrong, I'm happy you're here with me but you shouldn't be"—she jabbed him in the gut—"and I don't think there's any bright side to a place with a giant fence and guard towers."

"Sure there is, Sis. Look at Spetz over there, arms waving, yelling, hemmin' and hawin' to anyone who'll listen. That almost makes this worth it."

A wide smile broke across her face. "Yeah, couldn't happen to a nicer guy. By the way, how's your leg holding up?"

"Nah, don't you worry about me, Sis. I'm doin' just fine."

The grimace Arek wore on his face, the one he tried to hide from her every step of the way, told Mithany a different story. He lied.

Neither sibling fared well on their journey from Hensdale to the border. Short legs held her back while Arek's reliance on his cane kept them both at the rear of the pack. With her arm under his most of the way, Mithany did her best to provide unspoken support to her struggling sibling. Though Arek never uttered a single complaint, Mithany's heart ached for the obvious suffering his sacrifice to protect her cost him. Frequently, he offered to carry her backpack. As much as she felt the weight of it against her slight frame every moment of the long march, Mithany declined each time he asked.

One trooper yelled out, "Come on, all of you, get moving!" Other pike-wielding soldiers took their cue and lowered their tall spears lengthwise across their chests, using the repurposed weapons to push those at the rear of the pack forward.

Those who felt wooden poles shoving them forward reacted as intended. The message hadn't carried very far and Mithany found herself pressed into the back of a large smelly man who hadn't moved. With her face squashed into the man's sweaty posterior, her nose curled, and she recoiled at the ungodly smell. A soldier from behind jammed the horizontally angled spear into her, forcing Mithany once again into the man.

Arek grabbed the pike and yanked it from the soldier. "Knock it off," he demanded, holding it out as though offering its return. Soldier-man's arm shot forward, snatching the pike back from Arek. The soldier then twirled it around in the air and jabbed the short nob end into Arek's gut. The cane keeping Arek propped up dropped from his grip as he doubled over in pain.

"Do that again, Gimpy, and it'll be much worse for you next time. Now, eyes forward. Move your ass."

Mithany's jaw clenched at the slur hurled at her brother. Nobody, let alone her only sibling, deserved to be treated in such a manner. Without concern for her own safety, Mithany jumped between Arek and his assailant. He'd done the same for her so many times as children protecting her from their mother's rage. Without giving it a second's thought, she fired her hand forward onto the offending weapon firmly in the soldier's grip. Anger leaked out in her tone. "There's no need for that."

With a wave of his free arm, directing others in his unit to take notice, he laughed. "Hey guys, get a load of this pipsqueak."

Letting go of the pike, Mithany helped Arek up and pushed down her fury, knowing it would only make matters worse. As hard as she tried, she couldn't stop the words leaving her mouth. "Must you be such an asshole?" she said, looking up at the man. "And do you have to insult everyone?"

None of the nearby non-prisoner-prisoners took another step. Stopping where they stood, frozen in place by the insult Mithany aimed at their non-captor-captors, everyone appeared fixated on the petite woman's brazen challenge.

Mithany wanted to reach out and pull the words back the second they escaped. Of immediate concern was the rage she witnessed in Soldier-Man's eyes. Thanks to Mithany, a man armed with a sword at his side and a sharp-ended pike in his hand was made to look stupid.

He gripped the pike with both hands, drew it back, and whipped it forward.

Mithany saw it coming. There was nowhere to go. She threw her arms up to block the blow. Both eyes squeezed shut. She braced for the impact. Just then, another soldier's massive-sized hand shot forward. The sound of wood slapping against flesh rang out. One eye popped open. Just inches from her face, Mithany saw an enormous hand gripping a wooden shaft.

After taking possession of the pike, Mithany's savior quickly handed it back to the soldier-man she'd insulted. The very large soldier with the massive hands shook out his reddened palm as he joked, "She's a feisty one. Too bad she likes the ladies."

The two soldiers stared at each other for several tense seconds. Neither appeared willing to stand down. The one who interceded, no longer joking, commanded, "Let it go. She ain't worth it."

Still furious, soldier-man slammed the nob end of his weapon into the hard dirt. With his free hand, he aimed two fingers at his own eyes, then turned his hand around, aiming one finger at Mithany. After the angry trooper turned to walk away, Big Hands gave Mithany advice. While his tone sounded soft and comforting, his message was a clear warning, nonetheless. "Miss, our unit is off to gather up more like you, and while you'll not see that soldier again, there will be others like him in the compound you're about to enter. Folks like me won't always be around to stop folks like him. Little lady, I'd suggest you watch your tongue." With a wagging finger, he added, "Behave yourself in there, both of you, or it's not going to be pleasant."

What Lies Beneath

Tandure: 19th Day of the Harvest Moon

Derr

Inside Adelle's yet to be tested war room, Tomelai gathered his Senior Military Command, along with Derr, for a review of troop preparedness. The meeting threatened to sputter out of control when a verbal confrontation broke out between Kiple and Loseff.

"Commander General Kiple," Loseff began.

Derr studied them both throughout the tense exchange with a keen interest in Loseff's aggressive posturing.

Loseff curled his hand into a fist. Lightly striking the table for dramatic effect, General Loseff continued, "I'm aware of your order to stand down until every unit, every battalion, every squad, and every man and woman in the entire Grand Army of Adelle is battle ready. With new recruits flocking to our cause daily from Kantos, Greenlin, and Teth, we begin each day at a new starting block. We will never meet the conditions you'd established."

Derr's eyes shifted to Tomelai. The chancellor gave no indication of stepping in. Derr figured his friend Rotti took a measure of each man throughout the confrontation, as did Derr. Did the man selected to lead the army, Commander General Kiple, have the requisite leadership skills to put a subordinate in his place, and did General Loseff respect Kiple's authority? Given the lack of any threat from the United Front, with no battles to be fought in the immediate future, taking time to evaluate Adelle's military command structure was a luxury Derr and Tomelai could afford—and they took it.

The older Kiple, experienced as the leader of Adelle's National Civil Peace Administration for the past few years, wasn't accustomed to having his orders challenged. Derr never cared for Kiple, believing the man's self-assured, insufferable arrogance lacked credibility. Derr could accept arrogance, that didn't bother him, yet Kiple hadn't proven himself worthy of arrogance. He was nothing more than an empty suit.

Against Derr's advice, Kiple was Rotti's choice. Because of his loyalty to the Chancellor, Derr accepted Kiple's selection as Adelle's Commander General once the decision was made. However, that didn't prevent Derr from offering Rotti his objective assessment of Kiple's performance as circumstances warranted... or that of Rotti's son, General Loseff. Neither performed up to Derr's standards, albeit getting an army prepared for battle was virgin territory.

The tallish Kiple stuck out his squared-off jaw, folded his arms across his chest, and gave Loseff a direct order, "Stand down, General."

A man accustomed to being obeyed, Derr saw Kiple's order as a lack of leadership skills. As much as Derr didn't like to, he recognized sometimes one needed to provide reasons for subordinates to effect buy in. The Loseff-Kiple standoff proved to be one of those times. Loseff's position challenged Kiple's command. As Derr assessed the others in the room, several looked skeptical of their commander General's position on the matter. Derr concluded that proving Loseff wrong before the entire War Council was the better play for Kiple.

Except Loseff didn't stand down. "Commander General, may I speak freely?"

A knowing huff shot through Derr's nasal passage in response to the gears turning in his head. *Got yourself in a pickle with that one, Kiple.*

"Permission granted."

"Sooner or later, the UF will attack. The KCG's intel and the last words spoken to our newly appointed Vice-Chancellor Tane Tomelai at the failed peace conference last month make that clear. We have the advantage at the moment. Every day we continue to wait, UF recruitment improves. This delay will cause more deaths to our men and women."

Through stern eyes, Kiple listened. When Loseff finished, Kiple said, "This is the position of our Chancellor. Now, you have your orders, General Loseff."

As Derr observed Loseff turn to face his father, he thought, *That's right, young Loseff, Kiple just told you he's not really in charge. And Kiple, you're a fool. You undercut your own authority in front of everyone in this room. You should've just explained it to him.*

The meeting continued for another hour and, as it broke up, Loseff approached Derr. "What's on the old man's schedule? I need to speak with him."

"You may be his son. When you're in this room, and when you're acting as a general in his army, you will address him as Chancellor. Are we clear?"

"Whatever."

"Are we clear, General?"

"Yeah, we're clear. When can I speak with him?" Loseff asked, looking over at his father, who was speaking with General Kevine.

"The Chancellor has a few minutes. Let's do it now."

"Good."

The response sounded more like that of a petulant child than one Derr expected of a military officer. Derr looked at Tomelai, gave him a knowing nod, got one in return, then announced, "Thank you all for attending. The Chancellor requires the room."

Expectedly, the room full of generals emptied quickly at Captain Derr's command. Grabbing hold of the knob as the last of them exited, Derr closed the door and gave Loseff a direct order of his own. "Sit."

"Son, you know how proud I am of you. You have come a long way and I especially appreciate how you push us all to see this coming war from a different angle."

"Yes, Father. Thank you. I asked Derr that I might have a few minutes because—"

Getting up from his seat at the head of the table, Tomelai sat down in the open chair next to Loseff. "I understand your position, Son. However, I ask you to consider my reasoning for taking a different approach."

"Go ahead. I'm listening."

"You are correct. Adelle has superior numbers. Although our troops are far from being battle ready, so are the few forces the UF has mustered."

"Yes, you see my point."

"There is more, Son. I am reminded of a joke that will best explain my position. It goes something like this: A young bull and an older bull looked out over a pasture filled with grazing cows. The young bull said, 'Let's run down there together. We can each have our way with a cow of our choosing.' The older, more experienced bull replied, 'Why don't we walk down there and have our way with them all?'... You see my point, Son?"

Frustration bloomed across Loseff face. "Father, we aren't bulls or cows. These are the lives of the men and women of Adelle."

"Derr, feel free to join in," Tomelai offered.

More interested in observing Loseff's behaviors, Derr passed. "When I have something to offer, I will."

Derr watched Loseff's growing agitation and wondered, *There's more going on inside his head. He's angry with Rotti. There's more behind it. I can't put my finger on it.*

Three times Loseff pounded his fist on the table. "Why won't you share everything with me?"

There it is. Derr reflected, *What haven't we told him, Rotti? What's he digging at?* With a quizzical look over at Tomelai, Derr signaled his friend to burrow for clues.

Tomelai pried, "What do you think I am withholding? As far as I know, I have shared everything with you."

Loseff opened his mouth to speak, then paused as though rolling something around in his brain. The young general's eyes moved back and forth and Derr could see Loseff's agitation growing. The tops of Loseff's ears were now red, and Derr figured something was burning inside his thoughts.

"Say what's on your mind, Loseff," Derr exclaimed.

After a moment of silence, Loseff said matter-of-factly, "Forget about it. Just tell me why you won't invade the UF."

Derr answered for them both, "It's a simple matter, really. You're right, we could invade now, take their lands with the forces we have. Then we'd have to occupy whichever nation we conquer. After that, our forces would be spread over two nations, ours and theirs. Then we'd lose our numeric advantage, not to mention the additional forces we'd need to suppress the uprising in this other country that would invariably follow our occupation. It's a shortsighted approach. Just like the old bull example, there's more to be had once we're better prepared."

Loseff ignored Derr. "Father, in one of the books you asked me to read from the secret library about Second Age military leaders, another young general has inspired me. They called him Alexander the Great. Whatever lands he conquered, he didn't disrupt their culture. He brought the locals into governing because he didn't have the manpower to occupy it. He allowed them to continue their way of life. We can do the same thing. I believe we can take Teth after a few more weeks of drilling the troops. Father, I beg you, let me prove to you I can do this."

Tomelai rested his hand on Loseff's shoulder. "Son, I appreciate your zeal and the fine job you have done preparing farmers and laborers to be soldiers. You may have a point with the approach taken by this Alexander; however, winter is not the time to put it to the test. General Kevine guarantees me that there will be significant supply chain issues should we engage our army in far-off places covered in snow. From what I have read in many of the same books I have given to you, troops win battles, logistics wins wars. Continue to drill your division. You have all my confidence that you will make them the best fighting unit in Adelle's army. You will have Teth... in the spring."

With a shrug, Loseff threw off his father's hand. Standing, General Loseff looked down at his father, the Chancellor, with hatred in his eyes and stormed out.

"He will be alright, Drew. He just needs time to absorb it all. He will calm down."

"I'm not so sure, Rotti. I think he's gonna be a problem."

"Drew, the father in me says you are wrong. The Chancellor in me says nobody can be trusted. And in Tomelai family history, my ancestors have not always waited for nature to take its course... delivering Adelle's next ruler prematurely to power. I can only hope you are wrong. It would break my heart. Just in case you are not, have your people continue to monitor him."

The Apple Orchard

Outpost Apple Orchard: 19th Day of The Harvest Moon

Mithany

With open arms spread wide, the person who appeared to be in charge bellowed, "Welcome to Outpost Apple Orchard."

Mithany looked around at the other seven hundred plus internees as a tall, slender woman with long blond hair, looking to be in her early forties, welcomed the newly arrived residents to their temporary home. That was the promise, anyway, of the compound's commandant, Maverlyn Araukaw—the woman with the long blond hair. As Colonel Ardle previously explained, it would be a brief stay for their own protection, lasting only as long as the coming war necessitated.

"There will soon be five other facilities like this one across Kantos. I hope that you'll find these accommodations acceptable. I know not all the comforts of home could be replicated. You will find me and my staff to be helpful as you settle in, especially during this period of transition."

Araukaw stood on the porch of the administration building set at one end of the compound. Two rows of ten barracks each ran down along each side of the Commandant's private residence that doubled as the central command. A flagpole rose from the ground just outside Araukaw's office, proudly exhibiting Kantos's national flag. It flapped in a gentle breeze as the Commandant prattled on.

"The next several days will keep us all busy. I'm sure you have questions. Be assured my staff looks forward to meeting with you individually in the coming days, where we'll get to know one another. Your questions will be answered then."

With one hand resting on his ever-present cane, Arek turned to Mithany. "You buying any of what she's selling, Sis?"

Slipping her arm under his, Mithany shrugged. "Hard to say. Araukaw is too far away to get a good read on her facial expressions. The tone seems warm enough. Colonel Ardle started out the same way."

"Sis, how're you handling this? From the moment Spetz pointed at you, you haven't fought back. No denials. You just accepted it. It's like you surrendered."

Instead of replying, Mithany pressed her lips together. She wondered the same thing. Why hadn't she protested? Why hadn't she raised an objection? It was like when she was a child, she'd go along hoping to avoid angering her mother; accepting authority without pushing back, with only one goal in mind: to survive the moment without incurring consequences. Arek's question led her to conclude, *Old habits die hard*. She rubbed his arm. "Sometimes it seems Mother sent us down a path neither of us can ever escape from."

"Sis, you're smarter than you look." Arek laughed.

She kicked him in his good leg.

"...there are nineteen lodging units," the Commandant was still talking. She swept her arm across the complex. "These are only temporary. I've not had the chance to prepare more comfortable accommodations, yet in time we will work together to make it feel more suitable for each and every one of you... my honored guests."

"Wow, Sis. That's a pile of hot steaming shit. Wouldn't you agree?"

"Let's give her a chance. Who knows, maybe she means it. Now hush, I want to hear what she has to say."

"... by breaking up into groups of forty for each unit. Couples may remain together and those with children will be given preference. I've been told there are a dozen or so families with young ones, so let's get you situated first. Families will be here in Unit 1, right next to my office. You'll have direct access, day or night."

"See, Arek, she sounds reasonable."

"We'll see how the rest of this goes, Sis... before I give in."

The Commandant offered a pleasant expression to the seven hundred plus who'd been gathered to listen. "Now, for those of you who are not licensed, I'd like you to take up in Unit 11 and in Unit 12, on the other side of my office. There's a big plaque with the unit's number above each door. They're easy to make out," pointing at the plaque to Unit 11 as she spoke.

Arek shook his head. "The two groups that'll cause her the most headaches plopped down right next to her. You know what they say, Sis, keep your enemies close."

"... I would ask that all of you to sort it out amongst yourselves where to live, given only the two provisions concerning Units 1, 11, and 12. Then, when you've settled in, please select one person from each unit as your leader. After you're done, each unit leader will deliver the names of the individuals in their respective housing unit. Once you've provided my staff with the names, your unit is free to get some grub. There's food prepared in the mess hall, at Unit 20. You must be hungry."

Someone shouted, "What if we don't want to stay here?"

Commandant Araukaw again opened her arms wide, "All your questions will be answered when each of you sits down with my staff. We'll get started on that later today." She swiped one hand up as though dismissing everyone. "Now, go explore. Get settled in. We'll talk later."

Anonymous faces yelled out dozens of questions. Commandant Araukaw paid them no heed. She turned, walked through the door to the administrative building, and closed it behind her.

Arek slid his fingers into Mithany's waiting hand. "Sis, watch where Spetz goes, Unit 11 or Unit 12. Wherever he goes, you and me will take the other."

As first impressions go, Mithany thought the food tasted better than she'd expected. Of greater concern, Mithany had her doubts as she sat in a small office waiting for one of the administrative staff to join her for the promised one-on-one meet-and-greet.

The small, windowless room smelled of freshly cut pine. Like most of the camp's construction, everything seemed to have been hastily put together. The squeal of the door opening caught her attention. Not knowing what to expect, her heart raced as the door made its announcement.

In a drab, monotone-green uniform much different from those worn by Colonel Ardle's military unit—a uniform representing governmental authority just the same—a heavyset middle-aged woman stepped through and said, "Well hello, young lady." Sticking out her large, round hand, the woman started off the introduction with a polite tone. Mithany accepted the offer and shook the woman's hand.

"My name is Cwendly. I'll be the chief coordinator for Unit 12, your new home for now. Who might you be?" Pulling out a chair set under the small table, Cwendly sat, oh-faced, and settled her hands on the tabletop.

"Mithany, ma'am."

"And might I ask, Mithany-what?"

"I shouldn't be here, ma'am. I'm supposed to be getting married."

"Oh, that is so nice to hear. Has this interrupted your wedding plans?"

Mithany folded her hands on the table. "Yes, and no."

"What's this young lady's name you're supposed to marry? Did she come with you?"

"No ma'am, *his* name is Reyne. I shouldn't be here. I'm doing what our Covenant asks of me. I'm getting hitched to a man, we plan to make babies, and we hope to live happily ever after. I shouldn't have been part of this Samer roundup."

"Ma'am will not do. Call me Cwendly, everyone else does, darlin'. Now, let's see what we can do about getting you outta here."

With a roll of her head, Mithany welcomed the good news. "Oh, that would be great if you can help."

In a soft, friendly tone, Cwendly said, "Well then, I just have one or two questions and then we'll get you released. Your fiancé, Reyne, is it?"

"Yes, ma'am. I mean, Cwendly."

"Where can I find him, dear? You know, so I can confirm all this?"

"Cwendly," with a flap of her lips, Mithany reluctantly replied, "I don't know."

"Is he in the camp, darlin'? Or somewhere else?"

"He isn't in camp. He left Hensdale because people were trying to kill him. They murdered his brother," Mithany told her inquisitor and hung her head.

"Oh, I'm so sorry, darlin'. You've been through so much and now getting moved to Outpost Apple Orchard." With one hand, she reached across the table to rest it atop Mithany's. "This must be quite a lot for you to handle."

Buoyed by the hopes of leaving, Mithany pressed Cwendly, "What about the other people from Hensdale? You can talk to them. They'll confirm the marriage."

"I'm certain they can, darlin'. Rules require the presence of this fiancé before I can do anything. You understand, whatever the others from Hensdale tell me would just be hearsay. I am so sorry."

Mithany ripped her hands free of Cwendly. "Hearsay? That's why I'm here to begin with. A guy named Spetzer accused me of fornicating with another woman, and because of that one accusation, they swept me into this mess. If hearsay got me here, hearsay can get me out."

With rounded lips forming an almost perfect circle, Cwendly's pudgy nose scrunched—as though she'd just smelled something awful—to join her squinting eyes, "Ooooo... I'm sorry darlin', it doesn't work that way." Sitting back, Cwendly asked, "Tell me about what this guy accused you of. Did you fornicate with this other woman?"

Mithany shrugged. "Well, yes. Please understand, it was only the one time."

Replicating her facial reply, Cwendly again rounded her lips, scrunched her nose, squinted her eyes, and said, "Ooooo... I'm sorry, darlin', that's not going to help you." Nodding her head slowly, Cwendly added, "You don't have The Mark, which means you did have unlicensed sex with another woman. That's a no-no."

Mithany pleaded, "Yeah, but I was thinking about my fiancé Reyne the whole time."

Cwendly looked back quizzically, "How does that work, darlin'? When you're diddling with the other woman's lady bits, they're a lot different from your fiancé's. How does that make you think of him? I don't see it."

The promise of hope fled at that moment, and Mithany's head dropped to her chest. Looking down, Mithany asked, "I'm not getting outta here, am I?"

"Ooooo... I'm so sorry, darlin'. No, you're not."

Dejected, empty, and without hope, Mithany turned her thoughts to Arek. He'd sacrificed his freedom to protect her. It was just as well she wasn't getting out; she couldn't leave Arek alone in this place. Santander didn't really need her to rebuild. And Reyne wasn't back home waiting for her. All things considered, there was nothing in Hensdale to return to.

"Miss Cwendly, what're we really doing here? Am I a prisoner? What would happen if I just walked out the front gate?"

"Ooooo... that's not a good idea, darlin'."

Although Mithany accepted her fate and knew she couldn't leave, she needed to understand the situation better. "I don't see any of you carrying swords like Colonel Ardle's people. What's to stop me?"

"Don't even try, darlin'. I would hate to see anything happen to you."

"I thought this place was meant to protect us from harm. Now you're saying the people here will harm me if I don't behave?"

Changing the subject, Cwendly asked, "Darlin', you never told me your last name. May I have it for my records?"

The duality of her own thoughts concerning her imposed confinement gave Mithany pause to reflect. Angered at being incarcerated, while another part of her broken persona acquiesced to it, she found herself again of two minds. Holding her together as she struggled against her own damaged psyche was her devotion to Arek, and her undying love for Reyne.

"Brenton," she said proudly. "Put me down as Mithany Brenton." She wasn't a Brenton just yet in the eyes of the Temple of Life or the government of Kantos. In her heart, she was. "I answered your question, now it's your turn to answer mine. How many guards are there?"

"Oh, we're not guards, darlin'. We're just people like you."

"Really? All of you dressed in the same ugly green uniforms? Keys hanging from your belt. Keeping us behind locked gates. Not letting us out. You can leave... I can't. If it quacks like a duck."

"I'm sorry you feel that way. I'm only here to protect you. Let's move on, darlin'. We'd like you to look over this document and if you wouldn't mind, please sign it."

Mithany pulled back. "You want me to what?"

"Please, just read it, darlin'." Cwendly opened a pouch, pulled out a single sheet of paper, and slid it across the table.

Skeptical, Mithany slowly reached out, spun the document around, and dragged it across the surface. She looked down and read.

I pledge my unqualified loyalty to the People's Republic of Kantos. I affirm never to take up arms against my country or any of my countrymen and forswear any form of allegiance or obedience to any other foreign government, power, or organization.

Directly below Mithany noticed two blank lines where Cwendly expected her to print and sign her name. Just below the signature line, additional copy read:

Please indicate if you are interested in serving your country as either a soldier, as medical support, a nurse, or in any non-specific capacity deemed appropriate of your skill level in support of defending the People's Republic of Kantos.

Dumbfounded, Mithany's jaw hung open. "You have quite a set of balls, Miss Cwendly... not like the lady bits that troubled you just moments ago... but balls.

You people lock me up as a prisoner of war, in my own country, and then demand I pledge my loyalty to that very same country. What if I don't sign it?"

"Ooooo... that wouldn't be good, darlin'."

Although Cwendly didn't claim to be Mithany's jailer, the circumstances told a different story. Confined in a room, resettled a long way from home, inside a compound with a big fence around it, and asked to sign a loyalty pledge, no other explanation fit. The leaders of Kantos were worried that Samers would depart and support Adelle's cause to break free of the Covenant. Her own government imprisoned them all, its own citizens. Whether she deserved to be, she'd been locked up as one of them, a Samer: not for her own protection... out of bigotry... out of fear. Mithany resented her situation and resented the treatment of all Samers. Notwithstanding, with no way out, she resigned to accept it.

From an outstretched arm resting on the table, Mithany's palm opened facing upward. In unison she wiggled her fingers in a gesture that said, "Give me a pen."

HAPPY TO PAY

YURICH: 19TH DAY OF THE HARVEST MOON

Neladith

The moon, a sight unfamiliar to Neladith on her home world, hung in the Tartican sky, providing more light than Evidar ever extended to any of its inhabitants. Rays from the sun bounced off the satellite's surface to brightly illuminate the massive snowcapped white peaks as seen through Neladith's Evidarian born night-vision. She stopped for a brief moment to admire the grandeur of the mountaintops jutting high across the horizon. Although majestic, the Razors also loomed as an ominous threat to any unfortunate soul forced to attempt its crossing.

Neladith had no such plans.

Not native to Tartica, she hadn't a clue whether a pass over the Razors even existed. Nevertheless, because of the now-dead, former wet-work Evidar operative Dylla Weisner's penchant for details, during the initial briefing on the kill-Reyne-Brenton mission, the dossier briefly touched on a way around the Razors along the southwestern border of Kantos... if the need ever arose for her team to make their way to Teth. The team was gone now, and yet, for Neladith, the need to get around the Razors into Teth was *mission critical*. And Teth was where she expected to find Quith.

Thank you, Dylla. You might've been a cunt, yet I gotta admit, you did prepare me well.

Thinking of Dylla, Neladith recalled the night of her return to Tartica. With vivid details in her mind's eye, Neladith called up the image of Dylla's skull, with flames pouring out its empty orbital cavities, as though furious at being forced to watch Neladith take pleasure in the black ops leader's death. *Ah, happier times*, Neladith thought, with the memory of that evening's sweet carnal release stirred the embers of her ever-present youthful desires.

She lamented there were no campfires to beat back the chill in the air. And while the redness in her eyes from the light sickness all from Evidar experience upon their arrival on Tartica had given way, the cold weather of late autumn was like nothing she ever experienced on the version of Earth from which she hailed.

Although she longed to live out her days in the easy way of life the near-utopia realm of Tartica offered, she wondered if she'd ever adjust to the bitter seasonal climate. Late summer proved amenable enough compared to the ever-present warmth of Evidar. However, the cold not only nipped away at her insatiable craving for the pleasure of satisfying her raging hormones, it had her second guessing her goal to live out her life here.

In awe of the sight before her, she soaked in every detail of the monstrous, snowcapped mountains. She contemplated the symbolism of winter's power over her fragile human body.

She preferred moving through the night cloaked in the comfort of darkness reminiscent of her life on Evidar. Instead, Neladith traveled in daylight for the small measure of warmth it gifted her on her mission to track down Quith. Unfortunately for her hands and feet, day had given way, and any such benefit died with the sun when it dipped below the horizon.

Never on Evidar had she experienced the sensation of frozen feet. She didn't like it much, and her frigid fingers and running nose demanded as much attention as her numb toes. With the Razors imminent ahead, she struggled to bury her body's reaction to the unfamiliar climate and instead focused on the good news the sight of it delivered, Teth couldn't be far off. Setting aside the validity of her assumption that Quith had to show up in Teth at some point, how, or when, she'd find him in a place with so many people was a problem for later.

With all the extensive preparation provided by Dylla, Neladith bemoaned, she was out of matches. While starting a fire the hard way was an option, the hunger niggling at her gut wasn't going to be solved spending another night alone in the woods. Knowing a small village lay somewhere up ahead with the Razors this close presented her with the best option to solve both problems. Armed with desire for salvation from her frozen toes and empty stomach, she continued on for what seemed like forever.

Tired, hungry, and cold, she pushed herself. How long she walked since the sun went down, she couldn't be sure. Hope sparked when her nose picked up on the slight hint of smoke. The sweet aroma of burning wood tickled her nose. It released her inner child. Joyfully, she picked up the pace and set her sights on its source; the small hamlet she'd been made aware of by Dylla's persistent attention to detail in preparing her team.

Not long after encountering the smell, there it was, nestled in a valley between two rounded knolls that framed the foothills to the Razors. Her eyes delighted at seeing the grouping of houses and shoppes lined up on opposite banks of the small river that cut through the village. While the identity of the river escaped her recall, Yurich stuck in her mind as the name of the little hamlet. A warm place to ride out the frosty night was all she desired, and Yurich would fit the bill.

Absent any sign of a welcome, or official boundary, one home apart from all the others became two, then became three. The scene grew into a view of the entire street, with little buildings on both sides opened to her. Racing towards salvation, Neladith studied each of the wooden structures along her side of the river as she ran. Most had smoke flittering into the night air from chimneys poking out the tops. Each represented deliverance. If she couldn't find a public gathering place, she'd have to kill some unfortunate villager for their presumed food-stores and their heat-generating hearth. That option came with risk. The uncertainty of so many unknown variables each homestead presented relegated it to a back-up plan.

Slowing down to walk the well-worn dirt road, a scattering of people passed her before she picked out one young man whom she assessed to be the most likely candidate susceptible to her charms.

"Hi there," she teased. "I'm hoping a good-looking young man such as yourself can help me."

She baited her trap, taking in a deep breath, expanding her chest, and stretching her leather vest's capacity to hold it back. Neladith counted on her display to snare his interest, leading to his cooperation. Being cold and hungry, it was a small price to pay. Light posts lining the street threw off what little each could deliver from their small flames. Yet with enough illumination for the young man to scan her from head to toe... just as she anticipated.

As his eyes settled on her chest, with a grin he replied, "Why, of course. How can I help?"

As expected, Neladith mused, and didn't object to him eye-fucking her. Information was never free, whether back home on Evidar or in the baby-making, procreation-obsessed culture of Tartica. In Neladith's view, people sucked wherever they were from. She expected the worst from everyone. In fact, she counted on it, and took advantage of every weakness human nature afforded. The breast-enamored man standing before her proved no exception.

He was tall, older than her, yet youthful with short black hair neatly combed, and well-built as best she could make out. His coat hid much of what lie beneath, and while certainly not handsome, he was pleasant enough to look at. After a quick assessment, she concluded, *He'll do. Men are so predictable.*

"I'm just passing through and was wondering if there's a tavern where I might warm up a bit and enjoy the company of strangers." Without coin, a hot meal and a few drinks weren't going to be given freely. She fluttered her eyelashes offering him the opportunity to study her face, drawing him into her trap even further. There was always a price to pay. She didn't mind; she was hungry and cold... and hadn't gotten laid in what seemed like forever.

Lifting his gaze, and with a tilt of his head, he paused, then said, "You're in luck. It just so happens I'm heading there myself. Come on, I'll take you there."

Before Neladith could enjoy the success of setting the hook, the man spun around and headed back in the direction whence he came. Neladith jumped in right alongside him. "That's so kind of you. I'm Neladith. You are?" she asked as she slipped her arm under his and mused, *And as I take your arm, I plant in you... a seed of hope.*

He rested his free hand on her entangled arm, accepting the unspoken opportunity to win her affections for the night. "People in these parts just call me Dahsch."

"Well, Dahsch, let's see where this evening takes us." She expected her words would open up his purse strings for a meal, a few drinks, and maybe even a warm bed.

He patted her arm as they walked. In a joyful tone, he said, "Indeed, let's go find out."

She was already starting to warm up. *Nothing like anticipation to get the heat pump working.*

When they pushed through the door of the packed drinking hole, the ruckus she'd heard spilling into the street came to a sudden stop. Every head in the tavern turned toward Neladith. Dahsch leaned in and whispered into Neladith's ear, "We don't get many women in here that look like you. Don't worry, you're with me. Besides, they're harmless... well, most of them."

Neladith offered the onlookers a warm smile and an acknowledging head bob. *I could feast for a month in this place without a single coin in my pocket.*

Someone in the tavern called out, "What are you doing back, Dahsch? Thought you called it a night."

Neladith laughed to herself, *Men from Tartica are just too easy.*

The pair took up their seats at an empty table and ordered a meal. Her presence in the little hamlet's social gathering place elicited a steady flow of curious barflies to her table throughout the meal. Polite and otherwise, they frequently interrupted her. All she wanted was nothing more than to chow down. She feigned interest and excitement through each interruption, recognizing she needed information and couldn't afford to offend a single potential source.

After Neladith filled her belly—at Dahsch's insistence to pay for dinner, no doubt helped along by the teasing flirtations she continued to cast his way—she pushed her empty plate away.

Despite the pretense, she had to admit she was having fun. Even Dahsch provided her a measure of amusement as he attempted to defend his territory, schussing away one would-be suiter after the other, confident the night belonged to him. Through the many interruptions, she downed every drink eagerly paid for by the bevy of well-intentioned table visitors.

The crowd of thirty or so was growing ever more boisterous, and obvious to Neladith, she was the star attraction. In recognition of the conditions on the ground, and determined to seize the opportunity, the time was rife to up her game. "Dahsch, I'll be back in a short while. These folks are just so intriguing. I hope you don't mind if I mingle a bit."

The surprised look on his face told Neladith he did care, or at least worried someone else might steal away his chance. Without a care if he minded or not, she grinned, patted his hand, and said, "Don't fret, I'll be back."

As soon as she rose, the effects of a few too many caught her off guard. She wobbled, taking one step and immediately grabbed hold of a nearby chair rail. Undaunted, she steadied herself, then plunged headlong into the crowd. She engaged them one by one, making her way through the tavern several times, teasing, and taunting each new "friend" she encountered. Even the womenfolk in attendance, the few that there were, seemed to have an interest in her. One female after another eagerly found their way to Neladith, intent on stealing her attention from the men. One woman whispered sweet nothings into Neladith's ear while nibbling at her neck. A particularly cute young lady caught Neladith's eye, but she let it go, having settled on Dahsch as her conquest for the evening. However, before fun and games with Dahsch could begin, she had questions that needed answers.

The lively partiers appeared in good spirits and Neladith figured she had them sufficiently primed for intel gathering. A wee bit drunk herself, and maybe a smidge more than that, didn't hold her back or impact her performance. Just the opposite. Alcohol helped her to create the impression she actually had an interest in what any of them rambled on about, including the occasional proposition.

Following a round of drinks for everyone, paid for by someone in the crowd, a group dance that weaved in and out of the tables passed Neladith from one person to another, and to another, and to another, until she arrived back to her table where Dahsch sat patiently awaiting. She plopped into her chair, leaned in, kissed him on the cheek and said, "Don't pout."

"You're sweating," Dahsch replied, obviously trying to hide his wounded pride.

She brushed aside his feelings. She didn't really care if he was hurt. The people of a town just a stone's throw from Teth provided her the opportunity to gather news of Quith… on the slight chance he passed through here along the way. Intel on Quith was a longshot, yet still more important than some yokel's feelings. Even so, with all she had to drink, her loins stirred and would require attention. She recognized she needed Dahsch for one more thing and needed to reel him in. "Dahsch, I can't thank you enough for bringing me here and for being so kind. I was just having fun. I haven't forgotten you." She looked down at her vest and loosened a few more buttons of her shirt. "Just got one more thing to do and I'm all yours."

With both hands on the table, she steadied herself, pushed off, and came to stand on her chair. Holding out both arms to quiet the room, she readily captured their attention. The ruckus died away, and she said, "I want to thank you all. This has just been a wonderful night." She looked down at Dahsch, "And there's still more to come," she said with a wink. "You've all been so nice. Especially this guy here, Dahsch." And as much as she rarely cared much about others, she had to admit, *These folks are friendly.* "I wish I could stay here forever," she told them. It was partially true. As much as she wanted to remain on Tartica, this place was as good as any. It didn't have Mithany, but she'd burned that bridge when she tried to kill Arek. For a brief moment she lamented, *I wonder what Mithany's doing right now?* before quickly turning her attention back to gathering intel on Quith. "I'm looking for my dad"—she lied—"I was wondering if he's passed through here. You'd know him if you saw him. Middle-aged guy. Lots of muscles. Full head of white hair. He wears a mean scowl all the time." She looked around at their faces hoping to spy any positive recognition.

The dark room was filled with silence as Neladith watched heads turn one way then another while people sought their neighbors for any signs of recognition of Neladith's "father".

One older guy scratched his beard and looked like he was about to speak up, except he didn't.

Disappointed, Neladith prodded, "Anyone?"

The barkeep behind the counter yelled back, "Sorry, Nel, don't look like anyone seen him." He finished by nodding his head at the others. A sea of heads bobbed up and down returning his gesture. An arm shot up and its owner started to chant, "Neladith! Neladith!" and the entire tavern joined in, shouting, "Neladith! Neladith! Neladith!"

Dahsch took hold of Neladith's hand, helping her down off the chair. Once planted in her seat, Neladith's pursed lips signaled to Dasch her disappointment.

He stared back at her with narrow eyes and a strange look on his face. With steepled hands, and index fingers holding up his chin, Dahsch said, "Nel, you've been great. So, I guess I should tell you. They're just too scared to say anything." He leaned in close so as not to be overheard. "Your guy's been through here. For the most part, he kept to himself. Although he did talk to the man behind the bar. The barkeep got the impression your guy's headed to Teth. He told the barkeeper to tell everyone in town that if anyone comes asking after him to reply, "We never saw him." He said if anyone talked, he'd come back here and kill us all. Like anybody could do that."

Neladith knew better. Dahsch should've taken Quith's threat seriously. Quith had done worse. He would come back and kill all these nice people. She didn't care one way or the other if Quith rained death down on the village. She didn't give a shit about any of them. Even so, they'd all be safe because she was going to kill Quith before he ever got the chance to carry out his promise.

Excitement pulsed through her alcohol-soaked veins. *Quith!*

With her own chin resting atop interlinked fingers, intentionally mirroring his body language, she asked, "And when was this?"

"Two nights ago."

Springing out of her chair, Neladith jumped into his lap. She reached out and pinched his cheeks. She gazed into his eyes, pulled his face to hers, and planted her lips on his in a deep, passionate kiss. As she pulled away, biting at his lower lip, a broad grin lit up her face. Excited, she squealed, "You are *definitely* getting lucky tonight!"

She leaped off his lap, snatched his hand, and yanked him out of his chair. "Get us a room," she demanded with a wink. "I'm tired of waiting." As she pulled him close, her free hand shot down to his crotch. Over his pants, with her fingers spread wide, she palmed his privates, took a firm grip, squeezed, and eased her hand up and down several times. "And in between all the fun we're gonna have tonight"—she continued tugging—"you're gonna tell me everything that barkeep told you."

Releasing her grip on what was quickly growing into a semi, she slapped him hard on the ass and giggled, "Giddyup."

It All Fits

Tandure: 20th Day of the Harvest Moon

Loseff

*K**nock... Knock...***

Loseff carefully closed *Dawn of the Third Age,* aggravated at the interruption. The meeting with his father left him few options and drained him of any lingering loyalties to the man. The opportunity Loseff offered his father to share information about the book's contents went unheeded. It fed into Loseff's belief that the Chancellor didn't trust him. Seething anger aimed at his father grew in even greater proportions. The deceit fostered upon Tartican civilization fed into his rejection of the false-utopia paradigm imposed on humanity in the Third Age. It was the final straw. It sparked certainty in his resolve for what had to be done.

Irritation bled out in his reply to the interruption, "Who is it?"

"It's me, Jaynes. Don't be a dick."

The sound of Jaynes's voice dimmed his annoyance. Loseff's dark mood eased slightly, seeing Jaynes's face poke through the tent flaps. Rising from behind his desk, Loseff crossed the length of the enclosure to embrace his childhood friend in a bear hug. "I'm glad to see you."

"Good to see you too, buddy. You know, you should really post a few guards outside your tent. Anyone can just barge in."

"Let them. It's one of the ways I show them I'm not like all the other muckety-mucks."

Jaynes laughed, "You keep telling yourself that. You're a general. You're a muckety-muck by definition."

Loseff turned and headed back to his desk. "It's not that I'm not happy to see you, but why are you here?"

"Can't a guy stop in to see his friend without an ulterior motive?"

"Fair enough." With the sweep of his arm, he added, "Have a seat. I was just reading through one of the last chapters in the book when you so kindly interrupted me."

"I can leave. You're a big important general now."

Loseff slapped both open palms atop his desk. "Don't be a douche. The day I'm too busy for my best friend is the day I join the ranks of all the other assholes in this world."

Jaynes grinned. "Good to hear. As assholes go, you're a general now. The two things go together. It's just the way it is."

"Ouch."

Jaynes flopped into an open chair. He smacked his hands down on the armrests. "I know how you love that book. So tell me what you've been reading about."

"I believe what's written in that book now more than ever."

"I'll bite. Why? What did you come across?"

"Remember how I told you the woman named Beth brought people from the other planet just like ours? Well, it turns out, when they get here, they can't bring anything with them. Including the clothes they wear. Only their bodies cross over."

With an evil smirk, Jaynes rubbed his hands together. "Sounds like a lot of naked. I'm a big fan of naked."

"Who isn't? That's not the point. You know how we do the Feast of Teth every year? Some young woman represents the Goddess Teth incarnate. At the end of the parade, she drops her gown and, without a stitch of clothing, makes her speech welcoming all the children to her. It really happened. It's the Beth chick bringing survivors to our world. The maiden chosen to be our goddess is reenacting the whole thing."

"I never miss that part of the celebration. They pick a nubile young maiden every year to be Teth. It's my favorite holiday. I hooked up with one two years ago. It was like I was fucking the Goddess Teth herself."

"Yes, I know. You've told me that story about a zillion times."

"Well, now it's a zillion and one. Jealous?"

"Listen, you horn dog. The story we base the Feast of Teth on is all over the pages of this book. Not exactly as we celebrate because our version is an allegory. The Beth woman in the book I've been telling you about is Teth! Teth isn't a goddess. She's not the offspring of Mother Earth and Father Sun. She's just some woman who brought all the survivors from her world to ours so they could start over. Their world was almost destroyed. She brought them all here. And there weren't any children. They were all scientists living in outposts doing research. When she brought them here, they became the children of our world, so to speak."

"That's one big leap of faith going from some dame named Beth to a goddess named Teth."

"It's no leap, my friend. It fits perfect. A person injured in the seed vault when the asteroid struck was a good friend of Beth's. He had a head injury that fucked him up pretty bad. After the head injury, he had a hard time saying her name. Like a kid with a speech impediment, he pronounced her name in the only way he could, Teth. Well, he died a few weeks after his injuries. Beth felt so bad that she asked everyone to call her Teth from that point on so no one would ever forget him. Beth is Teth!"

Jaynes leaned back. "Didn't see that one coming."

Loseff did the same and interlaced his fingers behind his head. "It's the final nail in the coffin. I'm absolutely convinced *Dawn of the Third Age* is the real history of Tartica's beginnings."

"Okay, maybe. How did she get elevated to goddess status? Your book tell you that?"

"Oh, ye of little faith. It does."

"Hit me."

"So, this Beth, let's just agree to call her Teth, brought a lot of people here from her world. On her last trip, she's already brought a lot over, and they'd established a settlement she named New Phoenix. She told them she'd be back. But she never returned. After a few years passed without her, they'd decided to honor Teth for saving humanity. Most of them didn't believe in God anyway, and since they needed to create a new religion, they figured, what the fuck, and they based their new religion on her. They knew that if they didn't create a single, harmless religion, the civilization they were building would fall back on all the familiar religions their world constantly fought over. And voila, the Goddess Teth was born."

"That's a bit of a stretch, don't you think?"

"No. I don't. This Mera guy who wrote the book spells it all out. They even changed the name of the settlement from New Phoenix to Teth. This Mera fellow had a real hard-on for her, that's for sure. And what did come as a surprise, this Mera fellow got all the survivors to commit to the Covenant… after he wrote the damn thing himself. Amazing!"

"That, my friend, is one hell of a story."

"That it is, Jaynes… That it is… You can see how it all fits with how we celebrate the Feast of Teth, what's behind the Covenant, and why we follow the Temple of Life faith."

"So, where does it leave us? The last time we talked, you were pretty riled up about your father's part in perpetuating the Big Lie. Anything change? What are you thinking?"

"How many generations of Tomelais knew? Did my grandfather pass the book on to my father? My great grandmother to my grandfather? Is my father going to pass it on to Tane?"

"Could be," Jaynes offered.

"What really pisses me off is that nobody was ever going to tell me. What's changed, you ask? I'm done with all of it. I have my army. I have my own plans. First, I will pay a visit to my dear old dad. This entire Tartican way of life is bullshit. The rules. The laws. They're all meaningless. Time for me to grab the bull by the horns and take a piece for myself. I gave Father a chance to spill it. He didn't. I'm done with him. He's in my way. After I take my slice of the pie, *Dawn of the Third Age* will be copied and shared across Tartica. I'm going to bring it all down."

Loseff read the consternation written across his friend's face. "What's the matter with you? Why are you giving me that look? You're with me? Right?"

Jaynes bit down on his lower lip, saying nothing.

Through squinted eyes, Loseff said, "You're starting to worry me. Say something."

"You trust me, right?" It sounded more like a statement than a question.

Loseff recoiled, "Of course. With my life." After a long pause, he added, "We've been friends since before we could even wipe our own asses. We've told each other everything. Sometimes even a zillion and one times. Don't hold back. What's got you spooked?"

Jaynes let out a huff. "I have to tell you something. It isn't good. And when I do, trust me when I say that I never did what he asked."

Loseff crossed his arms over his chest. "I'm listening."

"Don't give me that face," Jaynes complained. "I said I never betrayed you. You know him even better than I do. It's Derr. He's demanded I spy on you." Holding up both hands as though pleading forgiveness, he added, "I never said anything that would hurt you. You know how Derr can be. By telling you this, I'm royally fucked. You've got to know I would never..." He stopped and hung his head.

"How long?"

Jaynes lifted his gaze to meet Loseff's.

"HOW LONG?!"

Through barely a whisper, Jaynes confessed, "Since you became general."

"What the fuck, Jaynes. You're just telling me this now?"

Holding out both arms as though claiming innocence, Jaynes pleaded, "It never mattered before today."

"And it matters now?"

Sheepishly Jaynes shrugged.

"And I suppose your visit here today had purpose other than a friendly chat?"

"Somehow, Derr knew you found the book, and he's worried how you'd react to it. I fed him nonsense."

"After all we've been through—"

Ignoring Loseff's pained rebuke and his own shame, Jaynes submissively added, "You're thinking of going after your father. Derr will expect me to give him a heads up. You know... to stop you. If you do it, Derr will come after me because I didn't warn him. Like I said, I didn't betray you, and I never will. My silence means it's my life for yours. I'm a dead man walking."

Tipping his head back, Loseff let out a deep breath. "Alright, I get it. It's Derr. And thank you for telling me... Although, a little sooner would have been nice." With an eye roll he added, "Were you ever really interested in hearing about the book or was all this just you digging up information for Derr?"

Jaynes rolled his eyes and pointed a finger back at himself. "Dead man here. I deserve a little credit."

Loseff slammed both hands on his desk and pushed out of his chair. "Stay here. I'm off to find Father. I'll post guards outside my tent with orders that nobody except me is to enter. Not even if this mystical Father Sun magically appears and wants in."

"Derr has people everywhere. I won't be safe here... or anywhere else."

"No one will come looking for you until after the dust settles. When I'm done with Father, all hell's going to break loose. You, me, and the five thousand troops outside my tent are going to hightail it out of here as soon as I get back. We'll be gone from here even before the Community of Soul knows it has a new guest."

I Got You

Outpost Apple Orchard: 19th Day of The Harvest Moon

Mithany

Most of the internees at Outpost Apple Orchard had returned to their respective housing units following dinner service. Inside the nearly empty, rough-cut mess hall, at one of the forty picnic tables lined up in two rows of twenty, Mithany and Arek sat together and continued discussing the day's events long after everyone else departed. The loyalty pledge that prompted harsh reactions and self-reflection consumed Mithany's meal-time discussion with Arek. And, from what Mithany overheard, the pledge appeared to be the hot topic of every discussion throughout the dinner service. Like Mithany and Arek, most signed the troublesome document. Although based on the tension Mithany sensed inside the mess hall, it seemed all who did, did so reluctantly.

Unit 20, the Apple Orchard's designated mess hall, sat at the far end of the *U*-shaped open courtyard, away from the Commandant's office and Unit 12—the barracks the siblings now called home. Arek stood and reached out his hand. "Let's get outta here, Sis." In the lead, Arek stepped through Unit 20's big wooden door with Mithany right behind. Snow flurries drifted across the compound's open courtyard and Mithany reflected on winters at the Brenton Family Alphen Orchard with Reyne. She reflected on the orchard she and Reyne loved so much, and the meaning of the one she found herself confined to.

The sun had dipped below the horizon, and twilight prepared to concede the night. Mithany slipped an arm through her coat sleeve and held out an open palm. Her eyes followed one small flake floating slowly downward until it settled in her hand. She followed the individual journeys of delicate snowflakes as one by one they came to melt upon the warm flesh of her open palm. "Winter will be in full bloom soon. I can't imagine what this place will be like when the temperature really drops. These barracks have thin walls. The least they could've done was used treestone."

With rounded lips, Arek released hot breaths into the chilled air, apparently mesmerized as each puff instantly turned into a wispy gray fog.

Laughing, Mithany asked, "What, are you six years old?"

"It's a prison, Sis. And I'll be right here, freezing my balls off, with you. Locked up together."

"You shouldn't have done it. But I'm glad you're here with me," Mithany conceded, looking out over the dim courtyard. "You'd think they'd put up torches or lume crystals. It's getting dark."

"Guess they don't want us out and about at night, Sis. A subtle way of telling us to stay inside, I suppose."

Arek stuck out his tongue trying to snag snowflakes as they fell.

"How do you do it?" Mithany asked, shaking her head in disbelief. "Stay so positive while we're stuck in here? You were about to join Tetrip to go track down Neladith. You wanted to catch her really bad. Instead, you're trapped in here with me."

"Well, I wanted to be there when we caught up with Nel. In my gut, I knew I would've held Tetrip back. You know, my leg and all. Tetrip's a good man. He'll find her. Either way, I'd rather be here with you," he said, throwing an arm around her shoulder.

Mithany watched her brother turn his attention to playfully chase down the sporadically falling snowflakes with his outstretched tongue.

Jabbing his cane into the hard dirt with each step, he said with a touch of pride, "I'm pretty good at this, Sis. Wouldn't you say?"

With an elbow jabbed into his side, Mithany joked, "I would think so... with all the practice that tongue gets."

"Hah! You never complained, Sis."

Arek continued chasing down the sporadically falling little white flakes. Mithany walked alongside him as they crossed the length of the compound, all the while enjoying his mindless childlike innocence in the face of incarceration. Finally reaching their destination, the pair stood at the bottom of the stairs leading into Unit 12. "Listen, Sis, I gotta stop in the Commandant's office. It'll just take a minute. You go ahead. I'll catch up with you inside the barracks."

"Want me to come with you?"

Waving his hand, Arek replied, "Nah, it won't take long. Just got a quick question. You go ahead and get our bunks set up for the night."

With her back to Unit 12, Mithany didn't move, watching Arek ascend the stairs to the Commandant's office. Thoughts of Arek drifted across her memories and she delighted thinking of the many happy times—and intimate moments—they shared. Without turning around, Arek raised one arm, waved goodbye, and disappeared through the office door.

Stilled in reflection of the special bond she and Arek shared, she suddenly felt cold and alone. She pulled the front panels of her coat tight across her petite frame and turned to go inside.

Turning around, there on the bottom step to Unit 12, blocking her way, stood Spetzer.

Caught off guard, Mithany stumbled back. How he'd snuck up on her without making a sound, puzzled her, but there he was, smiling.

"Spetz, you scared me. What're you doing here?"

Through a creepy grin and squinting eyes, Spetzer jabbed an angry finger at her. "What am I doing here? That's the real question, ain't it? Well, the answer is," he spat, stepping off the bottom rung, "I'm here because of you."

Two young men Mithany didn't recognize emerged from the dark, shadowed space in between Unit 11 and Unit 12.

In a soft voice, Mithany let out, "What do you want, Spetz?" beginning to worry as her eyes followed the pair of strangers getting ever closer.

"I'm here... for you," he said, stepping forward. Poking Mithany in the sternum, anger bled out in his tone. "I'm in this place because of you and your fuckin' brother... Me and my boys will deal with him later."

One foot slid back, then the other, as Mithany backed away. "You're here by your own doing," she told Spetzer in a casual voice, trying to hide her growing fear. "You didn't have to tell Colonel Ardle about Neladith and me. You did this to yourself." Her heart pounded in her chest. The threat lurking behind Spetzer's intention was becoming palpable.

Mithany told herself, *Get out of here, now!* As she spun to make a quick getaway, Spetzer grabbed her from behind. Before she could scream, he slapped one hand over her mouth. His other arm wrapped around her chest. Kicking and struggling against his grip, Spetzer dragged her into the darkness between the barracks.

Fear exploded in her skull.

Her eyes bulged.

STOP IT! LET ME GO! She tried to scream.

Tried to bite his hand.

She failed.

Her legs flailed wildly about.

Spetz lowered her just enough so her heels rode along the hard dirt.

A foot to the balls, not possible.

Spetzer stopped suddenly.

Between the two barracks, they'd arrived.

Dark.

Isolated.

Out of sight.

Hidden.

Pressed against her from behind, Spetzer leaned in close. "Time to pay up, you little cunt. I've waited for this a long time."

The stiff bulge in his crotch jammed into her back.

She knew what came next.

Terror flooded through her. *NOOOOOO!!*

Screams died in her throat failing to escape the hand muzzled across her mouth.

Every muscle in her body struggled to break free. Spetzer was twice her size and had her in a bear hug she couldn't get free of.

"Help me bend her over that bench," Spetzer commanded his two helpers.

As they folded her torso over the top rail, Spetzer pushed her head down and whispered in her ear, "When I'm done with you, those two are each gonna get a turn."

She whipped her head back.

It slammed into Spetzer's chest.

He snapped, "Get her pants down."

NO! NO! she tried to scream.

The words never left her mouth. Spetzer's hand made sure of it.

She wiggled. She squirmed.

She flung her legs backward.

But connected with nothing.

Someone grabbed her ankles.

Squeezed them together.

Someone yanked her pants down around her thighs.

STOP IT! STOOOOOP!

Cold air stung her exposed bum.

"I can't move my hand, or she'll yell for help," Spetzer complained. "One of you get my pants down."

Seconds later, she felt the warm flesh of his hard shaft pressed against the left cheek of her butt.

NOOOOO!

"You two get around front and hold out her arms."

Her heart thundered. *Oh God! No! No! No!*

She couldn't catch her breath.

She gasped for air. *Teth save me!*

Hands gripped her wrists.

The two men pulled her body forward.

Her feet lifted off the ground.

Her butt poked up into the air.

STOP IT! STOP! NO!

Spetzer fumbled at her from behind, trying to find the right angle to stuff it in.

She squirmed and denied him at every attempt.

Fear gripped every cell in her body.

Her heart hammered.

Her mind reeled.

Fear and wrath burned in her gut.

She screamed inside her skull, *NO! STOP!*

She lifted her head. Tears filled her eyes.

Through watery vision, as though in a dream, Arek raced towards her.

Oh God! If you were only real!

She imagined Arek hobbling as he ran.

His cane crashed against the left temple of one of the men holding her wrist.

The man dropped.

He was out.

Onc arm was free.

It's real! Arek's real. Oh God, Arek! HELP ME! HELP ME AREK!

Less than a heartbeat later, Arek smashed the handle end of his cane into the face of the other helper.

Crunch.

The man's head snapped sideways from the blow.

Teeth flew from his mouth.

The man went down.

He didn't move.

Spetzer stumbled back.

His hold on her, gone.

Mithany's feet dropped to the ground.

She spun her body around.

Fury flooded through her.

In an instant, both hands shot behind her, gripping the top rail of the bench.

Her pants still gathered at her thighs, in a heartbeat she lifted her body up. She pulled her feet off the ground. With all the strength her short legs could muster, she bent them back, then whipped her legs with heavy boots at the end, upward, smashing them into his exposed groin.

Instantly, Spetzer doubled over.

He shot both hands over his ruptured scrotum.

Blood leaked out from between his fingers.

Unable to speak, he gurgled in pain.

Arek wound up, swung hard, and crashed the handle end of his cane into Spetzer's skull.

Crack!

Bone shattered.

The sound of it stunned Mithany.

Spetzer's eyes rolled back.

Falling forward, his head plowed into the corner of the bench.

For only a second, it appeared anchored to the spot.

Gravity pulled at the rest of his body.

The impossible angle of his neck shocked Mithany.

His head ripped free an instant later.

Spetzer flopped to the ground.

His legs quivered.

Blood covered his groin.

His entire frame shuddered.

Blood oozed from his head.

His arms jerked twice.

Then... Spetzer stopped moving.

Blood kept flowing.

Half-naked, Spetzer laid there with empty, lifeless eyes staring up into the gently falling snow.

Mithany pulled up her pants. She raced to Arek. Tears flowed down her cheeks.

Trembling, her body slammed into Arek's as she wrapped her arms around him.

With her head buried in his chest, gulping for air, shaking, crying, the caring fingers of Arek's loving hand fanned through her hair. "It's okay now... I got you, Sis."

Several minutes passed.

They didn't speak.

Teth herself couldn't pry Mithany from the embrace.

Mithany kept shaking, shivering uncontrollably.

Through tears of his own, Arek broke the silence. "Sis, forgive me. That should've never happened. I wasn't here for you."

In response, she just squeezed him tighter.

She felt Arek's icy hands on her cheeks. He tipped her head back. Looked into her eyes. "I'm so sorry," he said in a voice ladened with infinite sadness. As his tormented tone reached her ears, it touched her soul and ripped her heart out. His love for her. His pain for her. It was too much for her to handle.

Arek lowered his lips to hers and kissed her. Pulling back, he begged her, "Can you ever forgive me?"

Unable to speak, unable to process thought, a part of her broken mind longed to be with Arek again. He saved her, like he always had when they were children. The ordeal of Spetzer overwhelmed her ability to think. Her mind was shutting down from the trauma. It was as though gears had rusted together somewhere in her brain, and the entire organ seized up.

"Sis, we can't stay here. I know you need time, except we don't have any."

She did the things she knew best; she searched his eyes. *It's always in the eyes.* In them, she glimpsed his pain, his sorrow, his fury at what she'd been forced to endure... it almost matched her own.

"Sis, you need to listen. If we stay here, they'll think you did this. Spetz is the reason you're here. You told that Cwendly lady you don't belong here. When them two jamokes lying on the ground wake up, they aren't going to fess up what they did to you. My guess is that they'll say they saw you or me, or maybe both of us, attack Spetz."

With a crackle in her voice, Mithany looked down at Spetzer's blank stare and asked, "Is Spetz dead?"

Two gentle thumbs from the hands still holding her face gently wiped away the tears in Mithany's eyes. "When I saw what they were doin' to you, my mind exploded. I had to save you. I'm not gonna apologize for what I did. You gotta know, I didn't mean to kill him. I'm sorry I got you in another mess."

A slap that bore little force landed on his chest. "Don't ever say that," Mithany demanded, while swiping snot from her nose with the sleeve of her coat.

"Sis, I won't let them blame you for what I did. Either I confess, or we need to get outta here, now. Even if I tell them why, I don't think it'll make any difference. They'll send us both to a birthing farm. They'll probably send us to different places. For me it'll be pussy galore. For you, it'll be hell."

Mithany forced the words out. "I can't think straight. I'm furious with Spetz. The world should know what kind of person he was... I love you too much to let them separate us."

"It's your call, Sis. I'll do whatever you say."

"We go."

"Alright, Sis. You and me are leaving this place. Together. Right now."

Mithany took a deep breath through mucus-filled nostrils. "Okay." Another swipe of her sleeve cleared her face. Then, with the heels of her palms, she rubbed aside her tears. Determination, rooted in love for her sibling, broke free the seized gears of her mind. She'd grieve through her trauma later. Nothing mattered more to her at that moment than saving Arek. He'd killed Spetz. She wouldn't let them have her brother.

Arek picked up his cane. "They're gonna be doin' roll call in a few minutes. We gotta be gone before then and definitely before anyone finds Spetzer's body. There's a small gap under the right side of the front gates that we came through when we entered this place. I think we can squeeze through it. We gotta go now, Sis."

"There's a guard tower right there at the gate. How?"

Arek grabbed her hand. "Come on. I got an idea."

RUN

Mithany

Mithany tried to push down every bit of the all-consuming fury roiling her gut. Her overwhelming rage proved impossible to control. Yet, saving Arek mattered even more. He protected Mithany her whole life and at this very moment, either she helped him escape the Apple Orchard internment camp, or Arek would be called to account for killing Spetzer.

She bit down on her lower lip as tears filled her eyes. "What's your idea then, Arek?"

"We shimmy under the gate, make for the woods, and then on to Teth," Arek replied, taking hold of her hand and pulling Mithany out of the shadows between the two barracks. "Stay low to the ground. Out of sight. When we get to the stockade, we'll put our backs to it and shimmy along it until we get to the front gate."

Speaking in whispers, Mithany and Arek detailed their escape plans as they slid along the rough-hewn stockade fence posts, staying out of view from the watchful eyes of whomever manned the guard towers. "Sis, if either of us gets separated, the other's got to go on."

"I know you too well. You'd never leave me. What you really mean is if you get separated, I go on without you."

"We have to be realistic, Sis."

"We're in this together. I couldn't go on without you."

"And I without you." He paused. "In case things don't go as planned, promise me."

"No."

"I'm serious, Sis. Promise me."

"No. Now hush, the gate's right up ahead." Her hand slid over the bark covered post reaching for Arek's. Finding her prize, she poured all her love into a gentle squeeze. She was certain he understood.

"Sis, can you see the gap right under the big hinge at the bottom?"

Her words, spoken in volumes barely audible, failed to convey her stunned disbelief. "What? How? It's too narrow."

"Sis, we can make it. Just try. Trust me."

She looked up into his pleading eyes telling her, "You need to go."

It's always in the eyes, she told herself, and she knew he was lying. She always knew when he lied. Not that Arek lied to Mithany, yet he did frequently when their mother caught either of them doing something that set her off—confessing his guilt even when Mithany had been responsible. Experience taught Mithany of Arek's lying tells.

"You gotta go now, Sis."

"I'm not leaving without you."

"Then let's do this together. You go first."

"At the same time or not at all. Not negotiable."

"You win, Sis."

Mithany grabbed hold of Arek's hand to help him to the ground. The gap opened several feet out from the point of the hinge. Yet, the bottom rail of the gate stood barely a foot above the ground.

Her head slipped through the gap easy enough, as did Arek's. The challenge for Mithany proved to be getting her chest through the narrow opening while Arek struggled to wedge his butt through. With their backs on the ground, both grabbed hold of the gate's bottom rail trying to pull themselves through. As Mithany scooched the last of her legs through, Arek remained stuck. Keeping a low profile, she rolled on to her stomach and grabbed both of Arek's arms. She anchored the tips of her boots into the dirt and yanked with all she had. Arek's body didn't move an inch.

But the gate did.

CREAK.

The hinge screamed, breaking through the silence of the evening.

The guard yelled out, "Is someone there?"

Mithany froze.

"Hey, is someone down there?"

"Shit!"

"I see you," the guard shouted. "Stop right there." A second later, a loud horn rang out from the guard tower.

"Go!" Arek demanded.

"No!" Mithany shot back. Instantly, she jumped into a crouch, holding onto Arek's arms. She leaned back with all her weight and pulled on Arek with every bit of anger she held inside her. The all-consuming hatred she harbored for Spetzer gave her strength. Losing Arek wasn't gonna happen. "Agghhh!!" She pulled and kept pulling.

"Hey, I said don't move!" the guard called out over the ongoing horn blasts.

"You're gonna yank my arms off," Arek pleaded.

"I don't care! You're coming with me. Agghhh." And with the last of her energy, straining with all her might, Arek's rump slipped through.

Mithany jumped up. Arek did the same. They started to run.

"Stop you two! This is your last warning. I SAID STOP!"

Ten steps into their getaway, Arek already fell behind. Mithany turned around, snatched Arek's hand, and dragged him limping along.

Thwack.

The sound hit her ears just as Arek's hand slipped through her grasp.

She turned.

Horror washed over her.

An arrow poked through Arek's shoulder.

She looked into his eyes. Confusion. Fear.

He opened his mouth. It hung empty for a second, as though trying to speak. Mithany barely heard what came out. "I love you. Now, run."

Thwack. A second arrow pierced his heart.

Arek looked down in disbelief.

Her eyes bulged. She couldn't believe what she was seeing.

This can be happening!

Her mind reeled.

He looked up at her.

Her heart felt like it exploded.

His legs gave out.

She gasped for air.

She struggled to keep herself upright.

The world was spinning. His body fell in slow motion.

His frame crumbled like a like a rag doll someone let go of.

He landed on his back.

The wooden spikes pushed through his shoulder and chest.

Blood spread out, soaking into his clothes.

Mithany looked down in utter terror.

Arek mouthed one word, "Run," then his lips stopped moving. His eyes went still.

He stared up into the night sky in a gaze as empty as Spetzer's.

Arek was dead.

Mithany screamed. She dropped to her knees. Her face turned to the heavens. Pain bled out of her soul at what Spetz did to her, for Daedyn's murder, for Brenal's death, for Reyne's absence, and an ungodly anguish poured out of her for Arek. It went on for what seemed like forever.

The guard called out. "STOP RIGHT THERE!" The gate creaked. It swung open.

Whoosh. An arrow sped past her cheek. She turned with tears running down her face... and sprinted for the tree line.

One Condition

Black Haven, Concord City

Reyne

While the physical manifestation of the evil presence-induced pain that occurred inside the Void evaporated as soon as Reyne fled the black morass, the intense memory of pure agony pounded against his temples. Gina's voice registered in his mind, yet his thoughts remained locked on the malevolence that scorched his soul only moments ago. Through it all, the beast lurking in his core kept laughing at him. And Gina... seemed like she was a world away.

Moment by moment, her shouting bore into Reyne's awareness. As her words slowly came into focus, he realized she was worried about him. However, her concern, measured against his encounter with the demonic manifestation, meant little to him.

Again and again, she pleaded, "Reyne! What's wrong?! Get up!"

A hand grabbed his shoulder.

The beast kept laughing.

The hand shook him.

Gina kept yelling.

A foot kicked him.

His mind reeled.

The monster inside him roared with laughter.

Anger pooled in his heart.

In that instant, he let the monster out.

Reyne shot up faster than he'd ever moved.

The monster within raced towards the nearest body to vent its fury.

Without thinking, Reyne let the abomination grab Gina by the throat. With one arm, he lifted her off the ground and slammed her into the wall.

The beast sneered into Gina's face and delighted at the fear in her eyes. Her legs kicked wildly about. It paid them no mind.

Buried in the recesses of Reyne's awareness, his balls were on fire. She'd kneed him in the groin. The beast within gave it little notice. It snickered at the woman's feeble efforts. It fed off the misery of Reyne's inflamed sack. And the beast's hold on him grew even stronger.

Just then, a powerful blow struck his right flank.

A direct hit to his liver.

An involuntary reaction overwhelmed his body that even the beast couldn't deny.

Reyne crumbled to the ground.

It broke the spell.

In a fog, Reyne saw Gina standing over him, rubbing her throat. Her screaming cut through his mental haze. "WHAT THE FUCK'S WRONG WITH YOU!"

Through open eyes, unable to control any other part of his body, Reyne looked on as Black Haven Mera pushed Gina aside. He then bent down beside Reyne and put pressure on his shocked liver.

"Breathe slowly," Black Haven's Mera commanded.

With an open palm pressed against Reyne's right side, Black Haven's Mera looked up at Gina. "Miss Gina, I need him. You, I do not need."

As she paced, and still yelling, Gina spat, "You saw what he did. What was I supposed to do, let him choke me to death? Fuck you, . And fuck you too, Reyne!" She stopped, leaned her shoulder blades against the wall, bent one leg at the knee, rested the sole of her foot against the wall, and crossed both arms over her chest. In a huff, she muttered under her breath, "Fuck the both of you."

"Miss Gina, I do not accept such insults lightly. Because Mister Brenton believes he requires your assistance, and your reaction to his assault is not without merit, I will allow it. This time... none other.”

In a pout, Gina relented, “He’ll be fine. I punched him in the liver just hard enough to get him off me. I could’ve hurt him a lot worse. I know what I’m doin’.”

“Apparently, Miss Gina. Few know what a blow to the liver does to a person. You delivered the strike with surgical precision. You have impressed me with your skills. Yet, be warned, do not harm this man again. Whether or not he needs you, it will be your last. If Mister Brenton is to live or die, that is my decision to make, not yours.”

Still pouting, Gina grumbled, “Whatever.”

“Come now, Miss Gina. Do not blemish this moment between us by acting like a petulant child. We have yet to hear from Reyne since his return from the Void. There may still be good news from all this.”

Deep breaths flowed in and out of his lungs as Reyne did as he’d been told. The pressure on his side let up a bit, delivering progressive relief with each heartbeat. While recovering, Reyne remained quiet and listened to every word exchanged between Gina and Black Haven’s Mera.

The beast lurking in his soul had been caged; the malevolence in the Void was gone; the pain at his side was fading. As he prepared to share the information from his connection to Tartica’s Mera in the Void, he knew he couldn’t confess to Gina nor Black Haven’s Mera that he’d unleashed the monster within... intentionally. He did so in a moment of weakness, and Gina would never forgive him.

Black Haven’s Mera rose, held out a hand, and offered Reyne assistance. “You will be fine, young man. Let me help you up.”

Gina looked down at Reyne as he grabbed hold of Mera’s hand. With a hard stare and lording over him, she said, “I taught you everything you know about hand-to-hand combat... not everything *I* know. Keep that in mind if you ever think about going all wacko on me again. And I don’t care if you can’t control it. Next time, I won’t hold back, farm boy.”

“Now that you have said your piece, Miss Gina, Reyne, I am most interested to hear of your venture into the Void. Did you connect with the other Mera?”

As the afternoon rolled on, Reyne detailed his meet up with Tartica's Mera in the Void, including the evil essence and the intense agony it delivered to both himself and Tartica's Mera. In return, as promised, Black Haven's Mera restated what he recalled of Beth Green's process to assist others through the Void.

No longer harboring ill tidings towards Gina for the liver punch, knowing he'd brought it on himself, Reyne said, "Gina, now that we have some idea on getting us both through the Void, I'm not sure it matters anymore. Don't think I can go through that again. Every nerve was on fire. The pain was excruciating." In a peace offering for what they both just done to hurt the other, Reyne joked, "See, excruciating, I know big words too."

"Excruciating? That doesn't count, farm boy. You're out of your league." Reyne took her reply as a sign they could move on.

"Besides," Gina added, "if we don't try, you and I are stuck on this shit hole of a planet forever." She turned to Black Haven's Mera and said, "Yes, this place is a shit hole. Offense intended."

"Miss Gina, you are a handful."

"A handful? ... Are you hitting on me, ?"

"Not what I meant, Miss Gina."

Reyne added, "I know what you meant. And believe me, you don't know the half of it."

"Enough you two," Gina cut them off. "I'm not staying here. Reyne, we gotta do this."

"Mister Brenton, I am inclined to agree with Miss Gina. While I am disappointed to learn this other Mera had no news of Beth, Janek remains a significant problem. His plan threatens your world and puts mine at risk."

Reyne shot back, "Then *you* go. You have a Soul Stone. You battle it out with the Devil's Blacksmith. He can't kill you if you have the Soul Stone. I'll wait here until you get back. You can't comprehend the agony I went through facing that evil in the Void."

"I do, Mister Brenton. I have experienced that very pain. It is why I could not navigate the Void. It drove me back. The other version of me must have experienced that very pain, at the instant I did. As you say, this other version of me is now on Tartica. Although this other Mera is aware of the terrible pain, he made it through one time. I believe it is why he told you he cannot do what he has asked of you: to penetrate the Void, transfigure to Evidar, and eliminate the threat."

Skeptical, Reyne replied, "You do it. Or we get Tartica's Mera to do it."

"Mister Brenton, this other Mera did not expect you to encounter the malevolent entity when you agreed to go. And now, he remains a world away. I am certain he will not connect with you in the Void again. We have no means to offer him your alternate plan. And I cannot, as I have already explained. No, Mister Brenton, you are the only one from your world, or mine, that can be counted on. It must be you."

Reyne drew in a deep breath, tilted his head back, and thought about Mithany. *Every action I take is for Mithany. If I'm gonna get back to her, I gotta face the Void sooner or later. I promised her I'd return, no matter what. Gotta keep my promise. Gotta do this. Buck up.*

Reyne let out a gust, brought his head forward and said, "Alright, I'll do it, and Gina's comin' with me. I got one condition... and it ain't negotiable."

"Your condition, Mister Brenton?"

Reyne held out an open palm.

"Hand over the Soul Stone."

Limits of Endurance

West of Outpost Apple Orchard: 20th Day of the Harvest Moon

Mithany

With Arek's death, Mithany's grip on reality and her desire to go on hung by a thread. One thin, frail fiber of hope remained of the severed, frayed ends of the cord that spanned the gap of Mithany's unraveling life. At one end of the threadbare was a life she shared with Reyne... before Neladith showed up; on the other, all the pain that came after. A single strand of lucidity, the width of a single synapse, held her mind together. A tiny thread, strained to the limits of endurance, was all that kept her soul from being crushed under the weight of unfathomable grief pressing down on her heart.

Denying her the time to understand it all, to grieve, to come to terms with so much pain, guards of the Apple Orchard internment camp were after her. And so she fled. Bitter cold air stole her breath with every step. She struggled to gulp it down through the tears and the misery. She clawed at branches, her hands bleeding, pulling herself through the dense thicket.

Death, murder, betrayal, and love forsaken all came crashing in on her fragile footing on sanity. The Brenton Family Orchard—the home where she and Reyne were to raise a family—burned to the ground. Set ablaze by the very woman who'd seduced her. The woman who'd slain Reyne's brother. The same woman who'd almost killed hers. Betrayal taunted her.

Onward she fled, the distant sounds of yelping hounds tracking her. Scrambling up a bank, her foot slipped. She fell. One knee drove onto the hard forest floor. Agony shot up her leg. She clamped down the torment screaming into her mind to give voice to the pain.

Daedyn, who hid his love for her, year after year. Love she saw in his eyes, but could never return in the way Daedyn longed for. A brother so selfless that he sacrificed his own desires so that she and Reyne could be together. Whose murder impaled spikes into her heart.

A creek! Yes. She broke through the thin layer of ice. Traipsing through the waist-high stream, the shock of the frigid water shrieked into her brain and drilled pain into every pore. And still she trudged through the ice layer, breaking against her thighs with every step, praying she'd defeat the hounds searching for her scent. Reaching the other side, her wet boots and wet pants clung to the flesh of feet and legs she could no longer feel.

Doc Hollid Brenal—the kindly father figure who often healed her physical injuries after she'd endured her mother's rage, and who soothed her emotional wounds so many times—gave his life so that Arek could live. His sacrifice born of a selfless act tortured her soul.

Reyne, her fiancé, the love of her life, ripped from her arms only days before they were to be married. She needed him now more than at any time in her life. Whether he'd ever return to her, she couldn't know. Their forsaken love damned her to face an unknown future alone.

And even more, Arek, her brother, her first love, her protector, her rock... was dead. Neither her petite frame, her pounding heart, nor her riven mind could stand against the unfathomable depth of agony and torment overwhelming her body and her soul.

Plodding aimlessly into the night, ice crystals sank winter's teeth into the fabric of her wet slacks, threatening to steal her resolve. And still, she fled into the darkness of the forest.

Her thoughts were consumed with Arek, paying little attention to anything else as she scampered through whatever brush or tree line that gave her cover. With no memory of how she made it as far as she did, or knowledge of where she was, Mithany came upon a small cabin.

Why she hadn't given up the moment she realized Arek was gone, she didn't know. Arek's plea to her, his dying wish, kept ringing in her head... "Run!" Her heart yearned to stay with him. Yet even with his last breath, he proved to be her protector one last time.

"Run!" She heard his voice in her head, over and over... "Run!"

Not wanting to disappoint Arek in his last moments of life, she did as he demanded, and she ran and kept on running. With every step, her lungs burned with exhaustion. With every labored beat of her heart, her pulse hammered against frozen ears.

A faint light flittered through a gap in the curtains of the unfamiliar little log home. The silent forest off in the distance crept into her awareness. The sound of barking hounds was absent, and she wondered if they'd given up or if she'd evaded her would-be captors. Numb, physically and emotionally, she was shaking. Either the cold, exhaustion, or unbearable grief had taken hold of her body. The thought of its source slipped away quickly as images of Arek, bleeding, dying, flooded in. Only the nagging pain of frozen toes and fingers broke through the fog shrouding her from the present.

Reyne might never return, and Arek's gone. What reason do I have to go on? I could just give up... curl into a ball, right here, and let the cold, dark night take me. What's there to live for?

She bent a knee to the ground. *Nothing matters anymore.* The cold, hard surface sent a jolt into her body and Arek's last words slammed into her mind... "Run!" It cut through the haze of grief and despair clouding her judgement. *He sacrificed himself so I could go on. I can't let him down.*

With the force of a sledgehammer to her chest, a revelation struck her. The horror of it squeezed her heart. Her hand shot over her mouth. She gasped. *The escape he planned was all for me! He knew he wouldn't make it! He gave his life for mine.*

She couldn't breathe. She gulped for air. *Oh, Arek.*

Get up, she demanded of herself. *You have to get up. You have to do it for Arek.*

She rose.

Now, go knock on that door.

With feet that barely felt the hard ground with each step, Mithany climbed the three stairs to stand before the rickety entrance.

The cold biting at her cheeks pushed through her tormented soul to claim awareness in her brain. With fingers as stiff as the wooden door, Mithany gently rapped.

Tap...Tap...Tap...

A woman's apprehensive voice leaked through the door. "Who's there?"

The words Mithany needed to reply refused to escape her lips. Of two minds, part of her pushed down the desire to go on, denying that part of her honoring Arek's sacrifice. She fought back...

Tap...Tap...Tap...

A second later, even more light streamed out the window, grabbing Mithany's attention. She turned towards it. At first, all she saw was a hand pulling back the curtain. Then, slowly, the wrinkled face of an older woman came into view. A nose pressed to the glass. Large tired-looking eyes under disheveled gray hair scanned Mithany up and down.

"What do you want?" the old lady demanded.

The woman's question stung Mithany.

She wanted Arek.

She wanted Daedyn and Hollid.

She wanted Reyne by her side.

The woman in the window could offer none of it.

With hands cupped over her mouth, Mithany blew hot breath into chilled fingers. Her heart thundered in her chest. She paused a moment. Then walked along the front porch into the light. Standing to face the woman, only a thin sheet of glass between them, with tears in her eyes, Mithany forced herself to speak. A hoarse yet faint voice broke free of that part of her trying to give up. Mithany surprised even herself when she gave answer to the woman's question: "I want to live."

A Wish Before Dying

Tandure: 20th Day of the Harvest Moon

Loseff | Derr

Loseff left Jaynes in the command tent and set out to find his father, the Chancellor—to do what had to be done. In Loseff's eyes, he had no other choice: his father would neither release him to attack the enemies of Adelle, nor disclose the truth behind Tartica's founding. The latter proved the more egregious of the two offenses. Loseff couldn't forgive his father's lack of trust in him, the foundation of love between a father and son. Pained to admit it, his father put power over his own son. It stung of betrayal and overwhelmed Loseff's ability to drive the hurt from his heart. His father didn't love him enough to trust him with the lie holding humanity together in the Third Age. Since he read the first words written in *Dawn of the Third Age*, he couldn't shake the pain in his heart his father inflicted.

Having the intention to take deadly action against his father was one thing: actually doing it, another. Entering the small private meeting room his father used to hold intimate discussions, he believed he could do it.

With his hand on the handle, Loseff closed the door behind him. He paused, staring at the back of his hand still on the knob. The same hand he'd use to take his father's life. Turning his gaze to look up into his father's eyes, he felt the blood pulsing against his temples. Buckets of saliva seemed to gather in his throat. The resolve he held to his breast approaching the room threatened to flee him standing face-to-face with his father.

He swallowed hard. "Father." His heart pounded in his chest. The pressure behind his eyes felt like it would push them from their sockets. *Breathe, slow down. You can do this.*

"Son. Please sit. You aren't on my schedule, but I have a few minutes. What brings you here?"

"You do." *Thump... thump... thump...* The sound of his own heartbeat thundered in his ears. He ran his hand down the side of his pants to feel the blade hidden in his pocket.

"Speak quickly, Loseff, Derr is due soon."

It sounded dismissive. With a pang of sorrow at hearing the indifferent tone, Loseff said, "You so easily disregard your only son for a man who is obviously more important to you than I am. That's the way it's been with you my whole life."

"*Tsk...* Son, you have to know that is not true."

"Isn't it?"—he paused—"*Father.*"

Chancellor Tomelai motioned for Loseff to sit.

"I'll stand."

Tomelai folded his hands on the table and sat up straight. "Something is obviously bothering you."

Loseff exploded, unable to control himself. "You! You bother me." Anger gave way to disappointment and, in a soft tone, he added, "I'm your son. How could you pick Derr over me?"

Tomelai slowly lifted his gaze to Loseff. "Son, you, your sister, and your mother always come first. You always have. You always will."

Loseff studied his father's face while the blood coursing through his arteries strained with each beat of his heart, stealing his concentration. "If it were only true," he lamented, sliding his hand over the knife, reassuring his resolve. "Five words...proof of your lies... Dawn of the Third Age."

His father closed his eyes and angled his head back. Loseff's heart felt like it would burst in his chest, waiting to hear his father's explanation. He hoped the words forthcoming from his father would change his mind.

Tomelai brought his head forward. Opening his eyes, he said, "Son. You must understand, that book is only a matter of state. Not an issue of ..."

Loseff exploded, "MY OWN FUCKING FATHER!" Collecting himself, he added, "You left me on the outside, looking in. You never loved me enough..."

Knock... knock...

Loseff's head snapped to face the door. His eyes shot wildly around the room.

The knob squealed.

Loseff's arm swung down. *No time.* He pulled the blade from his pocket and rushed towards his father.

Creak, the sound of hinges screamed a warning to Loseff. *Do it now!*

Tomelai threw his palms against the table, kicking the chair out from under.

Loseff reached his father. They stared into each other's eyes... and Loseff drove his blade into his father's side. His father's eyes went wide. He looked down at Loseff's hand, still on the blade, just before collapsing to the floor.

The door swung open. A familiar head poked through.

Hyperventilating, Loseff backed away against the wall.

Derr. It had to be Derr.

The KCG Captain picked his gaze up from the door handle.

Beyond any measure of surprise, Derr's eyes looked like they would pop out as he screamed, "WHAT HAVE YOU DONE?"

Chancellor Madrotti Tomelai lay dying.

Derr raced to his friend.

He could do nothing.

In all his years of service, Derr protected his chancellor from every conceivable threat without fail. Numerous assassination attempts, all doomed to failure, stopped by Derr's hand. Plots to overthrow the Tomelai dynasty thwarted time after time by the relentless efforts of the KCG to root out conspirators, real or imagined. Insurrectionists and dreamers could not accomplish what the hand of Tomelai's own son achieved.

The cut went too deep. No amount of pressure or life-saving tourniquet could stop his march towards death. Copious amounts of blood had already poured out of Tomelai, and slowing the flow of whatever remained would matter little. His life was forfeit.

Moving to the ground, he lift Tomelai's head between his crossed legs. Seated in a growing puddle of blood, Druin Derr cradled the head of his fallen friend in his lap. Tears dripped down the harsh leathery lines of his cheeks for the first time in decades. Bewilderment plodded across the rest of his face. In that moment, Derr discovered he had a heart only by the fact it was now broken. The only friend he had ever had was close to death.

There would be no saving him—Tomelai nor Derr.

Madrotti Tomelai's breathing grew shallow, his eyes empty, and the leader of Adelle became altogether unresponsive to Derr's every prodding. Derr's pleading eyes stared into the life draining from Tomelai's. The world outside Derr's field of vision ceased to exist. Unsure if Madrotti heard him or even saw him anymore, Druin Derr begged a god he never believed in and never gave a second's consideration—for mercy.

The man he called Rotti spilled blood at an alarming rate. The precise cut along the femoral artery had been delivered with intent by the issue of his loins. Derr broke a second time at the thought of Kaythlin losing her beloved and even more so at the pain it would cause her to find out who had ripped Madrotti from her life—her own son.

With herculean resolve, Derr pulled away from Madrotti's eyes to look up at Loseff standing against the far wall, knife in hand, dripping from it his father's blood. Anger exploded throughout every cell in Derr's body, yet he did not, could not, leave his friend's side. These were Rotti's last moments of life, and Derr would not abandon him. Yet, if untethered from the man he called a brother, Loseff would be dead already.

Clang... Derr looked over to the where the knife landed. His eyes drifted up to Loseff's blood-stained hands. Meeting the wrath Derr intentionally aimed at Loseff, Loseff froze for a second before fleeing from the room. A part of Derr longed to take Loseff's life before he reached the door. He couldn't pull himself from his dying friend. He'd deal with Loseff later.

Neither the offense of regicide nor patricide defined the depth of loss destroying what little remained of Derr's soul. When Madrotti inevitably departed the world, Derr's relationship with Kaythlin would be all that remained to fetter him to humanity. The Kingdom of Adelle didn't matter—it never did. Derr's only earthly bond was to his lifelong companion, not to the country Madrotti held in his grip.

Chancellor Tomelai's eyes had closed, and faint breaths told Derr his time of friendship was slipping away. He bowed his head close to Madrotti's and squeezed his hand. It wouldn't be long now. So when Tomelai's lips moved ever so slightly, Derr flinched. One word formed, hollow of sound, and Derr knew it instantly.

He reeled.

Confusion bloomed.

How could he honor the request?

He couldn't.

He had to.

Derr whispered in Tomelai's ear, "Don't ask of me that."

Facing mortality, the bond they shared for only moments longer drove deep into Derr's soul. Based on his unthinkable request, Madrotti Tomelai understood his childhood mate all too well. Revenge would be at Derr's fingertips the moment death broke their lifelong connection.

But Tomelai did ask.

With Tomelai's life slipping away, a single voiceless word formed on his lips. One final request of his friend, his dying wish: "No."

Never Stood a Chance

Mithany

Shrouded in a blanket draped over her body, Mithany soaked up the heat spilling from the small cast-iron potbelly stove.

"That's some story, young lady," said the woman who took pity on Mithany and opened her small, one-room cabin to her.

Sitting on the floor only a few short feet away from the comforting warmth, Mithany pulled her thighs to her chest, wrapped her arms around her legs, and said, "If it were only just a story..." Then she nestled her head atop her bent knees and glanced over at the pants and socks hanging off the back of a chair drying out, her boots resting just beneath the iron legs of the wood stove.

The woman demanded, "Well, that awful boy who tried to have his way with you got what he deserved."

"Maybe," Mithany lamented. "I hated him at that moment, and still do. He deserved to be punished. I'm just not sure he deserved to die. I don't know... maybe he did. I always thought the Covenant..." She stopped, staring at the flames between the open slats of the small metal door. Without looking up, she continued, "Either way, my brother didn't mean to kill him. He was just trying to save me." Her chin quivered, trying to hold back another eruption of tears.

"I'm so sorry you had to go through all that... and your poor brother."

Unable to break free of the fire's hold on her gaze, as though searching for Arek somewhere in the dancing flames, Mithany didn't reply.

The sparse, one-room cabin held in the heat well enough for Mithany's bones to warm up in quick fashion. With the chill fading, Mithany once again thanked her host. "I don't know how I can ever repay you. I'm not sure how much longer I could have survived out there tonight. Thank you."

"No more of that, young lady. One 'thank you' is enough. Hand me your cup. That tea's gettin' cold."

Handing it over, Mithany looked up and asked, "Do you live here alone? I see two beds."

Narrow eyes glared back at Mithany as the woman's thin, gnarled fingers snatched the cup from Mithany's hand.

"I'm sorry, ma'am. I didn't mean to pry. You've been so kind. Please forgive me."

Humm, the woman released a quick snort through her nose and paused, looking down at Mithany. "Guess I'm still a bit sensitive about that. Nothin' to forgive. Was my daughter's bed."

Not sure how to respond, Mithany took the safest approach and remained quiet. She looked up into the woman's eyes, where she found sorrow hidden in them. *It's always in the eyes*, she reminded herself.

As the woman lifted the kettle off the stovetop, filling the mug with hot tea, and without turning around, she said, "They took her. They took her, just like they took you."

Mithany accepted the return of the mug and snuggled her fingers around it. The warmth soothed her hands, recalling the bitter cold. A nod, offered as a "thank you," intending silence to prod out the rest of the woman's story.

"Don't know why I'm telling you this. Can't say how many times I told my daughter to just get herself a man and fool around with the gals on the side. She wouldn't listen."

Mithany heard anger in her voice.

"She'd tell me every guy she ever tried to have a relationship with either cheated on her or turned out to be a jerk."

Then her tone changed, softened, as sadness replaced anger. "She just gave up on men. Or so she said. She had a taste for women her whole life. Told her it was gonna get her in trouble one day. Told her to play the game; do what the Covenant says... make babies first. The Covenant wants its babies and there ain't no way two ladies squishin' their parts together is gonna get anyone pregnant. She just wouldn't listen."

There were two possibilities as best as Mithany could make out. Either the daughter had been shipped off to a birthing farm or, if it happened more recently, the daughter most likely had been sent to a Samer internment camp—just like the one Mithany escaped from. However, not wanting to cause any offence, Mithany played it safe. "Is she alright? Do you know where they took her?"

"Couple of people showed up in uniforms looking for her. Seems the whole town got called to a meeting. We didn't go. Livin' out here, we didn't even know about it. They said my daughter wasn't licensed. Someone ratted on her. The uniforms took her away last week. I pleaded with them, but there was nothin' she or I could do about it."

Through pursed lips and a swallow, clearly the woman was fighting back tears.

Suddenly, a startling sound bounced about the empty walls.

Thud...

Thud...

Mithany's head spun towards the door. *In the middle of the night!*

"Open this door!" the voice of a man demanded.

Mithany jumped up. It had to be the guards searching for her. She hadn't heard the men or the hounds approach. Frantic, she scanned the room for a hiding place.

The woman grabbed Mithany's shoulder and whispered, "No time." And lifted two floorboards. "Get in and stay quiet."

Wide-eyed and scared, Mithany scurried to comply.

Thud...

Thud...

"Open up or I'll knock it down."

"Who the hell are you?" the woman shouted, then swept Mithany's pants and socks into her arms, throwing the now dry clothing atop Mithany, who huddled in the secret nook.

Mithany pointed. "Boots."

Quietly, the woman dropped them on top of Mithany and lowered the short planks back in place, followed by the sound of a chair sliding overhead. "Not a sound," the woman demanded in hushed tones.

Mithany heard the man call out, "You have three seconds."

"I'm coming. Hold on."

The space beneath the floor was cramped and partially filled with glass jars Mithany guessed held canned provisions. They clanked as she settled in amongst them. Her heart jumped, fearful the sound would give her away, and she instantly stopped moving.

She heard footsteps above her head as the woman made her way to the door.

Creeeeak... It opened. Mithany swallowed hard.

"Why are two people dressed in uniforms pounding on my door at this hour of the night?" The woman spoke loudly, and Mithany suspected it was for her benefit. *Guards in uniforms. They gotta be looking for me.*

Heavy steps reverberated overhead as multiple feet made their way inside.

"What do you want from an old lady?"

A deep, husky voice replied, "We're looking for a woman. Short. Dark hair. Anyone come by here tonight?"

"You scared the bejesus outta me."

She didn't answer, good.

The testosterone-fueled voice replied, "Someone was here, weren't they? Why are there two teacups?"

Shit!

"Like my tea very hot. Once it cools off, I set it on the stove. Pour me another. As if it's any of your business."

A different voice this time said, "Listen, lady, we don't have time for your nonsense. The one we're looking for killed a man. If you seen her, tell us... now. She's dangerous. It's for your own protection."

"My protection?" the old woman spat back. "That's what you people told my daughter when they took her away… it was for her own protection. Didn't believe them then. Don't believe you now. Get out of my house."

"Lady, we ain't goin' nowhere. And as for your daughter, that wasn't us. Sounds like she got swept up in Colonel Ardle's mission."

"What do you know about this Colonel Ardle, and where'd they take my daughter?"

"Alright lady, I'll make a deal with you. Tell me if you seen the one we're looking for, or if you know where she is, and I'll tell you what I know. Does that work for you?"

Nooooo!

The room above Mithany went silent.

"Well, lady? We got a deal?"

A threatening quiet filled the cramped hiding space as Mithany waited on the older woman's reply. A dozen heartbeats later, Mithany's worst fear leaked through the floorboards when the woman said, "Alright. Deal. You spill first."

I'm trapped! She gently reached up to test the plank above her head. It didn't budge. Pulling her arm back, her elbow brushed into one of the canning jars.

Clank…

Her heart jumped. *The jars… Shit!*

"What was that?" One of the men reacted.

No way outta this. I'm as good as dead.

"Sorry, that was me. My foot bumped into a leg of the stove. Door don't fit right. Never did. Now, you were gonna tell me something."

Mithany recalled the iron handle hanging loose on the stove door. Then the man continued, "What I can tell you is that Colonel Ardle's rounding up all the Samers in Kantos, licensed and otherwise… and yes, it's for their own protection, we've been told. Anyway, I'm guessing that since you live so close to the Apple Orchard, your daughter's probably there. The camp ain't more than three miles from here."

"I knew they were building a compound. Heard a lot of commotion. Went to check it out when they first started. Asked about it. They were all hush-hush. Never told me what it was for. Now I know. Maybe you met my daughter. Her name is—"

He cut her off. "Don't bother, names mean nothing to me. I won't recognize any of them. Listen, the camp ain't taking visitors. If you go to the gate, tell them we sent you. The warden can at least tell you if she's in there."

All hope faded from Mithany. Measured against the woman mourning her daughter's apprehension, a stranger's safety didn't measure up. Although she couldn't fault the older woman for making the deal, her heart sank. *I never stood a chance.*

In a sweeter tone than Mithany had heard during her brief visit, the woman replied, "Thank you. That is so kind of you."

"Alright lady, your turn."

"Well, yes, a young woman did show up here tonight. Never met her before. Could be the one you're looking for."

It's all over! She's giving me up.

"Felt sorry for the girl. The story she told me didn't include anyone gettin' killed. Oh my, that's just awful."

A lie... this is good.

"It don't matter what tall tale she spun to you, ma'am. A man's dead. Just tell me what you know."

"Fed her. Let her warm up a bit. Then sent her on her way. Didn't want some stranger sleeping in my home. Not safe. And certainly didn't know she was a killer. Would've turned her away. Just sorry I helped her. Am I in trouble, officer?"

Sent me away...thank you... and thanks be to the Goddess Teth.

"No, ma'am. Not your fault. You didn't know. Did this girl say where she was headed?"

"Let me think... She said there were hounds set on tracking her. Then she said she was from Hensdale. Said something about making it back there after she got the hounds off her tail. I'm guessing she's headed north. Back to Hensdale. Does that help? I hope it does. You have to catch her if she's a killer." She paused.

"Didn't hear no hounds with you, officer."

Curled in a ball under the floorboards, the relentless fear of being discovered gnawed at her as she listened to every deception the old woman spewed. And with each new falsehood misdirecting the guards from their prey, the hope of surviving the night started to take root.

"Well, ma'am, there's more people out there lookin' for her than just us two. The others are following the hounds. Heard they lost the scent. Now that we know where she's headed, we'll get them pointed in the right direction. You've been a big help. By the way, if she returns, keep her here. If we don't find her tonight, I'll send someone back tomorrow to check on you. She's a killer, you know."

The other voice jumped in, "We still have a few more residences to check out. Gotta say, took us some time to find yours all the way out here."

"Like my privacy. No law against it. Now, if you two don't need anything else, I'm goin' back to bed."

Mithany calmed herself. She owed more to the woman than she could ever repay. *That one's a cagey old bird. Those two guards never stood a chance.*

After the men departed, the woman walked back to stand over the spot where Mithany lay underneath and tapped her foot on the floor a few times. "Stay put. They might circle back. I'll get you outta there in a couple of minutes."

"Why did you do that for me?" Mithany asked.

"Didn't do it for you. Did it for me. Found out where they took my daughter. Didn't need to give you up. Would've if I had to. Good thing for you, them two ain't that bright. And besides, didn't trust them. Don't trust nobody. You shouldn't either. Why'da you think I live all the way out here?"

Mithany stared up at the wooden boards between the two of them. "Thank you."

"The border with Teth is just over a mile south of here. When it's safe, I'll let you out. Make your way to Teth. Heard it's in bad shape. Even so, you stay there a while before goin' home. Now, while we wait, tell me about this Outpost Apple Orchard."

Tears from a Stone

Tandure: 20th Day of the Harvest Moon

Derr

Derr's only friend in the world, Chancellor Tomelai, was dead. With his dying breath, Tomelai forced upon Derr an obligation he had no desire to honor; yet, how could he not?

Tears hadn't touched Derr's cheeks in decades. Not when his mother passed away, not when his father took his own life soon thereafter, leaving a nine-year-old Derr to fend for himself. The last time the overwhelming emotion of grief claimed an outlet in water from his eyes, he'd been a mere lad of six. His pet fox, Jinx, had its neck snapped by the neighbor's dog. The beast clamped down on the scruff of Jinx's neck and whipped the tail end of Jinx's body upward with an effortless shake of its jaw. Unfortunately for Jinx, its little neck couldn't bend in a way to accommodate the rest of its body. Not fast enough to reach Jinx when he saw the dog attack, six-year-old Druin Derr blamed himself. The dog didn't live much longer. Little Druin saw to that.

The Chancellor's body lay lifeless in the room where Derr reluctantly left it. With the swipe of his hand against one cheek, then the other, Derr cleared away the telltale signs of tears as he strode through the empty hallway. With each step, Derr was not only further from his dead friend but also further from Tomelai's hold on him to honor the Chancellor's dying command. With each step, his fury at Loseff grew. With each step, the rage consuming him burned hotter. With each step, what little there was left of Derr's humanity—after decades of killing, treachery, torture, and bearing witness to the worst in people—scorched deeper into the dark recesses of his soul.

Arriving at the nearest KCG posted officer, Derr leaned in close to the guard and whispered in her ear, "Come with me."

She looked around at the empty passage and replied aloud, "Yes, Captain Derr. I'll just get one of the others to relieve me."

"That won't be necessary."

"Captain Derr, we have standing orders never to leave this post unguarded."

Anger flared at her for questioning his direct command. His words spit out in a harsh rebuke, "Now, Sergeant. I'll hear of no more objections." He spun, heading back down the hallway with the sound of her footsteps behind him.

They spoke naught as Derr made his way to Tomelai's body with his sergeant in tow.

Facing Kaythlin with the news of her beloved's death and of his own failure to protect him would be the most difficult task he'd ever undertaken in the service of his Chancellor. Yet he considered his obligation to Kaythlin. What did he owe her? While fond of her, and he respected her, his duty had always been exclusively to the Chancellor. He wondered, did that duty obligate him to be the messenger of her husband's death? It was the decent thing to do. What did Derr care about decency? And what of Loseff's role in Tomelai's death, of telling a mother her son killed his father, the only man she ever loved? What would the consequences of such knowledge bring to bear on the First Lady, on the now-Chancellor Tane, and on the future of Adelle?

Would Kaythlin expect him to serve Tane, the soon-to-be installed Chancellor, as he served Tomelai? Derr dedicated his life to protect his boyhood friend who helped him escape the gutter. He did it for the love he held for Rotti, and for no other reason. Derr had no interest in continuing the assignment with Madrotti Tomelai gone. In all his years of service to the Kingdom of Adelle, he had one role that gave meaning to his life: to protect Chancellor Tomelai. In that duty, he failed.

Tomelai's death severed any and all obligations Derr owned to Kaythlin, Tane, or to the Kingdom of Adelle. It all died with Tomelai. He owed nothing to any of them. Besides, he thought, unless he told Kaythlin the truth, she'd see through his deception. She was the most extraordinary woman he'd ever known. Either he told her the truth, or someone else would have to break it to her. So was his choice, and he accepted his fate.

As Derr approached the locked room of his dead friend's body, he owed one last obligation to Tomelai, to protect him one last time. Tomelai's legacy hung in the balance. It depended on Derr, and he wouldn't be denied.

"Sergeant, what I'm to tell you does not leave your lips, save to convey my words to Lieutenant Ferpratt. Should you fail to heed my orders, it will mean death to you, every member of your family, and to every friend you've ever known. Are we clear?"

Her pupils dilated instantly, and Derr sensed fear pouring off the woman. "Are we clear?" he demanded.

"Sir, yes, sir," she replied, and snapped to attention.

Derr held out a key. "This is to open the room behind us. Find Ferpratt immediately and give him this key. No one is to enter save for Ferpratt and Milvoe." Derr looked around, confirming the two of them were alone. "Our Chancellor's been assassinated."

She gasped in shock as her hand shot up to cover her mouth. Shaking, she asked, "How?"

Intent on protecting his friend's legacy, Derr lied. "I don't know. I found him this way and, by the looks of it, it happened recently." Derr feared the knowledge of Loseff as the perpetrator would ripple through Adelle and leave everyone to wonder what Madrotti Tomelai did to his own son to cause such an extreme outcome. He expected many would hate Loseff for his act of regicide, but lingering doubts would always remain about Tomelai the man. Some would elevate the late Chancellor as a hero for his stand against the Covenant. To the contrary, the spectacle of the Tomelai family killing one of their own dragged out in public would cast a dark shadow over Tomelai's tenure as Chancellor. A stain on Tomelai that would continue long into the future. Derr couldn't abide it.

Delivering justice to Loseff would have to be left to him.

Tears dripped down the face of the distraught sergeant.

"Madrotti Tomelai was the finest man I've ever known," Derr began. "We don't want news of this awful event spreading across Adelle. Out of respect for the First Lady and for Tane, who will assume her duties as our new Chancellor, we must keep this under wraps until Tane and Kaythlin can announce his passing properly and with dignity. The citizens of Adelle must not know he died this way."

Sucking in the mucus pooling in her nose as she wiped tears from her eyes, "I understand, Captain." She paused. "Shouldn't you be the one—"

He cut her off. "I am leaving immediately to track down whoever did this before the trail fades and the opportunity to ferret out the truth will be lost forever."

Looking down, she said meekly, "You can count on me, sir."

"Look at me."

She lifted her head.

"Tell Ferpratt of our Chancellor's assassination and that no one is to know of it. Tell him to gather Milvoe, and with your help, secret the Chancellor's body away to his mansion, where Ferpratt will need to notify the First Lady. He's to let the First Lady break it to Tane. He's to tell our First Lady I'm off to find Loseff. Tell the Lieutenant nobody is to know of this."

Derr's message covertly instructed Ferpratt to let Kaythlin and Tane know it was Loseff. The last few choice words directed Ferpratt to dispose of the sergeant to prevent rumors of the Chancellor's death from leaking out. Derr trusted every member of the KCG, but that didn't mean he trusted them absolutely. Human nature being what it is, Derr knew his sergeant would share her story with someone; it was too big not to. Although she'd served the KCG well, with

Tomelai's legacy at stake, the risk was too great to let her live. Derr couldn't take the chance.

"One last thing, Sergeant."

"Yes, sir, what is that?"

"Tell Lieutenant Ferpratt he's to be in charge of the KCG until my return."

Derr had no intentions of ever returning. His service had ended. He owed Kaythlin and Tane nothing. With Tomelai's death, and with plans set in motion to secure his friend's legacy, he just didn't care about anyone or anything, with one exception... Loseff.

Hatred for Loseff seared deep into Derr. Killing Loseff consumed his thought. Yet at the inception of each new idea of how best to torture Tomelai's killer, his friend's dying word, "No," slammed into his brain. Never one to be bound by words, laws, or even the Covenant, Derr had ignored them all in the service of keeping Tomelai safe. Why now should he give credence to a puff of air that carried on it a faint sound? Yet it carried with it the force of a sledgehammer that struck against Derr's craving for retribution. Rotti, his friend, his Chancellor, was gone from the world and would never learn of Loseff's demise at his hand. Nothing could stop Derr from taking revenge; except that one word.

Doubt

Jerithan

Normally a place of worship, the communal temple serving Teth's most notorious slum had been transformed into command central for the defense of Shantytown. Consideration for religious beliefs inscribed in the very document imbedding orthodoxy into every fabric of Tartican civilization, the Covenant of Absolute Universal Obligations took a back seat to preserving their lives and the lives of everyone they loved.

Doubt plagued Jerithan's thoughts. Shantytown put their faith in him to repel a yet-to-be-seen army. While he believed wholeheartedly troops from Adelle had their sights set on Teth, he lacked the experience or the know-how to stop them when they arrived.

The Voice broke through the skepticism rummaging around in Jerithan's head. *"You must not let these people know your mind. Show them your strength, your resolve, not your apprehensions. True leaders are followed because others believe in them. You were that man through all your years as First Lord. Wipe those doubts from showing on your face. Allow these people to see the man you were... the man you are. Give them a reason to believe in you."*

What do I know of war or how to strategize for battle? I want this. Yes, I do. Yet, I am not the least bit a military leader. I am going to get us all killed.

"You are a brilliant tactician. The Prudents you outmaneuvered, the heads of state you manipulated, the flock of the faithful you led so skillfully, all those

experiences have prepared you for this moment. I believe in you. Together, you and I will defeat whatever Adelle's army throws at us. You are so very close to taking your first steps to secure your title, Emperor of Tartica. It all begins here. Seize the opportunity. Take what is yours."

The words sounded good. Jerithan wanted to believe in himself. The lasting effects of Serco's successful coup, however, sent belief in himself deep into the shadows.

The Voice wouldn't relent. *"I can hear your thoughts. You must put Serco aside. He is dead. He has been defeated. You have survived. You have prevailed. You are the victor. Seize your crown. Do not let this opportunity pass. You will not get another."*

Alone in the side room off the open nave of the temple, Jerithan leaned back in his chair and pondered the Voice's advice. He wanted to be the leader the Voice spoke of; he wasn't that man anymore. Derr changed him. Nails changed him. Timble changed him. And the man who'd violated him in the bowels of an Adelleian KCG holding cell changed him forever.

Timble popped his head through the open doorway. The orange-haired man's high-pitch voice broke through Jerithan's introspection. "Hey, Boss. Ya pick a title?"

"What are you talking about?"

"Title? Whatda we call ya?"

"Oh, that. No. It is not important right now. What do you need?"

With both hands resting on the lintel above his head, Timble leaned forward. "Someone's here to see ya. Says it's important. Wouldn't tell me what it's about."

Jerithan motioned his hand and fingers as if to say, "Let him in."

Timble turned, waved an arm, and called out, "Bring her here."

The Voice chided, *"Comport yourself. You are slouching. Show this person and everyone else a strong, confident leader they can follow."*

Jerithan stood, straightened up, and ran his hands over his vestments.

Timble stepped aside, and as the woman entered, two things about her struck Jerithan immediately. She smelled awful. Horse sweat filled the room. And her long cinnamon-colored hair looked more like a bird's nest made of straw.

She bowed.

"That is not necessary," Jerithan told her.

"It's an honor to meetcha, First Lord."

Timble looked like he was about to respond, but Jerithan shook his head at the big man as if to say, "Not important. Let it go."

After eyeing the woman up and down, Jerithan asked, "What brings you here and what is so important?"

"I was workin' in the fields. I lives outside of Merhlich. Don'tcha know, outta nowhere I seen soldiers off in the distance. A lot of 'em. Figure they's headin' towards Teth. Hopped on my horse and hightailed it here. Got family in Shantytown. They says you's the one in charge now. Says I should tell ya what I seen."

Timble asked, "These soldiers see ya?"

She brushed dirt off her sleeve. "Nah."

Jerithan asked, "How long ago did you see them, and can you guess at how many there are?"

With both hands, she tried matting down her hair. "Been riding since late afternoon. Didn't stop. Well, did once. Had to piss."

"Thank you. You have been a big help. Oh, just one more question." Jerithan paused, "What about their numbers? Did they have archers, horses, or anything else you can tell me?"

"I got no idea how many. A shitload, I suppose. More people walkin' in a line than I ever seen. More than a thousand, I reckon. Saw horses. Lots of 'em. Didn't get close enough to see anythin' else."

"Thank you. You must be hungry. Timble, can you have one of your people see to this woman's needs?"

The woman bowed. "Thank you, First Lord."

Hearing others calling him First Lord filled Jerithan with the confidence he thought lost forever. "You may have just saved us all, young lady. I am in your debt."

"Nothin' nobody else wouldn't've done."

Timble called out, "Griz, get yer ass over here. Get this lady somethin' to eat."

Jerithan watched her walk away and mused to the Voice. *I was hoping for more time. We are not ready. We are not done gathering a stockpile of bows, arrows, spears, swords, pitchforks, and the like. These folks aren't soldiers. We have about five hundred volunteers so far. I fear we are doomed.*

"You have time. If these troops stop for the night, they will not arrive until late tomorrow. They will not attack when it is dark. That gives you two days. If they march through the night, they will be here at daybreak. They will be exhausted. That too is advantageous."

Jerithan took in a deep breath and let it out slowly.

"This is your moment. Rally your people. Show them you are their leader. Infuse them with confidence."

Where do I begin?

"Whoever can shoot an arrow, put them atop the parapet of that wall near The Stand. Secure the Anatese, those monkey men living in the treetops of The Stand. They are duty bound to the First Lord, and with Serco gone, that's you. The Anatese will assist in our defense. Ready a small team of your most trusted people. They will need to drop that massive tree trunk across the opening of the entrance into Teth. Do not let it drop until they see the first of Adelle's troops coming through The Stand. By then, it will be too late for them to turn back. Between your archers on the parapet, and the Anatese from above, it will be a bloodbath."

Speaking aloud, Jerithan brooded, "Unless we run out of arrows."

Risk And Reward

Black Haven, Concord City

Reyne | Mera of Black Haven

Frustrated Gina just wasn't getting it, Reyne shrugged. "Don't expect the Void to be easy."

Gina pointed out the obvious. "Nothing worth it ever is, farm boy. Beside who else is gonna do it? Fake Mera can't get through the Void. Says he never could. Our Mera, we can't reach him, and he told you he can't. I certainly don't know how to without piggybacking on your ride through. Nope, no one else, it's gotta be you. And I'm coming with you 'cause you ain't leaving me here."

"Are you sure you're ready? I can't begin to describe how agonizing it'll be. Now that I got the Soul Stone, that thing inside the Void will certainly track us down like it did to me and Mera. There's a good chance you'll experience searing pain... a lot of it."

"Don't be a pussy. We get our asses to Evidar, kill the people we're after, and it's done. What's the alternative if we don't even try? We'll be condemned to spend the rest of our lives on this fuckin' shithole of a planet. Sure, there's risk if we do this. Think of the reward. After we finish our mission, we're goin' home"—she blew mocking air kisses at Reyne—"and you'll get to see your girl."

"Fine. I don't want to hear any complaints from you about how awful it was getting through the Void. That is, *if* we even make it through." From under his lowered brow, he glared at her and waved a finger in her face. "You been warned."

She slapped away the accusing finger. "What's this bullshit about, *if*? Fake

Mera laid out how Beth Green got all those people through the Void. Her process sounded exactly like what we did by accident to get here. Third Eyes connected, touching foreheads, and all that mystical mumbo-jumbo."

"That's just it, Gina. We ended up on Black Haven by accident. I didn't get to Evidar the first time around like I was supposed to, remember? And Beth didn't take the Soul Stone on any of those trips until her last… when she went missing."

"Of course I remember. One second I was on Tartica trying to wake you up to help me save the real Mera, and the next thing I know, I'm buck naked on top of you in this miserable place. Come to think of it though, if we get to Evidar this time, we're gonna do the naked thing together again." Gina paused, closed her eyes, tipped her head back, and she brought it forward again with a broad grin plastered across her face. "Ah, it brings back such happy memories." Teasing, she gave Reyne a wink. "We might as well strip down now and assume the position. I'll get on top, just like the last time we came through the Void together. Mithany will understand… you know, the two of us saving the world and all."

"I thought you were done with that kinda talk?"

"Oh, lighten up, farm boy, I'm only kidding… or am I?"

"Some things never change."

"Well, one thing has changed. You got Fake Mera's Soul Stone. I didn't see that comin'. You came right out and demanded the thing. That's a good boy."

"It just popped into my head like someone whispered into my ear, 'Ask for the Soul Stone,' so I did."

"The look on his face… thought he was gonna kill you right then and there. I gotta admit, you got some set of balls on you. And remember, I've seen them, so I know what I'm talking about. There's hope for you yet, farm boy."

Reyne dropped his head. After a few shakes from side to side and an exasperated huff, "Genius, you missed something. If we succeed on Evidar—you know, kill the Damus and maybe the Devil's Blacksmith too—Fake Mera as you call him, wants his precious Soul Stone back when we're done. It's only a loan. Protection for me if I get injured. That means another trip back here through the Void with that malevolent thing tormenting us every moment we spend in that place. And then, if we survive that, and there ain't no guarantee we will, I gotta get us both through the Void one more time to get back to Tartica. The odds of every trip going as planned, not so good."

"Listen to me, Reyne, it doesn't have to be that way. If it's as painful as you say inside the Void with the evil entity all but certain to attack us, why take the risk? After Evidar, we don't need to return here. Let's just head straight back to Tartica. One less trip. It's not like Fake Mera's gonna come to Hensdale to track you down."

"Can't do it, Gina. Gave the man my word I'd return it. Besides, I don't want to live forever without Mithany. If I had a Soul Stone and Mithany didn't, I'd stay young while Mithany would grow old and die. It would break my heart."

The deep baritone voice of the man Gina called Fake Mera wafted through the ever-present veil of darkness like an unseen foghorn cutting through an impenetrable mist. "Good to hear, Mister Brenton. You just saved both your lives. Now that we have that settled, it is time."

The evil grin sporting Gina's face left Reyne to wonder if she suspected Fake Mera had been spying on them all along, and the double-cross was just a means to draw him out.

Replying to Fake Mera's voice, Reyne asked, "Are you gonna come out where I can see you?"

"No. Just get on with it, Mister Brenton. Evidar awaits you and your duplicitous friend. When your bodies disappear from this world, I will know you have exited the Void and reached Evidar."

Gina chuckled. "We didn't make it to Evidar last time. Let's hope Reyne navigates those troublesome Probability Waves a wee bit better on this trip. You're quite the optimist, Fake Mera."

From the shadows came only Fake Mera's voice. "As it would appear you are as well, Miss Gina."

"I have faith in Reyne. He'll get us there. Ain't that right, farm boy?"
Silence filled the room.

"Ain't that right, Reyne?" Gina asked again, this time more apprehensive.

Again, he offered her no response.

"Reyne?"

An overwhelming sense of foreboding overtook him. The pressure of selecting the exact Probability Wave out of thousands while simultaneously fighting through the unbearable burning sensation from the evil entity, all the while maintaining an unbroken mental connection with Gina's essence as he navigated the Void, was all too much. He answered Gina with the only response the situation demanded of him; he lied. "I'll get us there... somehow."

Black Haven's Mera continued to resonate through the gossamer covering, unseen by either Reyne or Gina. "Good. Enough talk. Get on with it."

With his heart pounding, Reyne lowered his back to the floor, gazing up at the ceiling.

Gina straddled herself over Reyne before positioning one knee on either side of his waist. She leaned down, placing one hand on each side of his head, and pressed her chest into his. Reyne looked into her eyes, only inches from his own, and said, "No... Get off."

As she straightened her back upright, she said, "Only kiddin', farm boy," while lightly rapping her knuckles on his forehead. "We'll do it the way Fake Mera described. The Beth Green method."

Gina didn't move.

Reyne complained, "I'm waiting."

"You sure? I'm quite comfortable where I am."

"Yeah, I'm sure. Get off."

"You make it too easy." Gina laughed, then threw one thigh over his midsection to join her leg on the other side of him. As Gina stood, she quipped, "You're no fun, farm boy."

"How can you be so nonchalant about this? So much can go wrong."

Her smiling face evaporated before Reyne's eyes. In her consummate professional assassin persona, Gina confessed, "I'm fuckin' terrified."

As though from out of nowhere, the words from Black Haven's Mera once again punched through the dark cloak. "Remember your positioning. Feet at opposite ends. Lay on your sides facing each other. Only your foreheads should overlap with each other's bodies. Reyne, your Eye of Heaven needs only to connect with Gina's."

How long Reyne laid there with Gina, in silence—forehead to forehead—he guessed to be an hour or so. Repeatedly, he tried to clear his mind of fear that kept leaking into his thoughts. Memory of the agony delivered by the malevolent entity during his last venture into the Void was like a boot crushing his throat.

For the lack of sleep or lucid dreaming, Reyne remained outside the astral plane, denying him access to the Void. Gina had fallen into a state of slumber. Whether Gina slept or remained awake meant nothing to the process. Gina had been wide-eyed and alert the time he unknowingly pulled her into the Void and brought them both to Black Haven. The only state of consciousness that mattered in the process of transfiguration of enjoined individuals rested on the navigator, Reyne.

Then, unexpectedly, the monster lurking inside his own darkness breached his awareness. It tormented him. It taunted him for being afraid. It spat into his soul for being weak. It haunted his thoughts of Mithany, defiling his memory of her. And it mocked Reyne's reluctance, measured against his promise to do anything to return to her. The monster within told him he was a pitiful excuse of a man. It laughed at him. And the laughter grew louder, ever louder.

Reyne's anger flared. The beast feeding off the hatred in his heart—for Daedyn's killer, for Bade, his baby sister's unthinkable murder, for the assassination of his father, for the cutthroat who took his mother's life—stoked the embers of Reyne's determination.

Perhaps he remained awake, or maybe the threshold of slumber touched his mind. Regardless of how, Reyne's disconnected consciousness hovered above his physical body. He drifted ever farther from it.

As only his mind's essence floated above, Reyne wondered whether his soul had been freed from its corporeal home, or if a soul was even real. He let the query fade from his thoughts as he spotted Black Haven's Mera seated in a corner. Scanning the room, he gazed upon his own form on the floor, while Gina snored softly next to him, forehead to forehead. He laughed, thinking how he'd tell Gina she snored.

This trip through the Void was a necessary step in the journey to return to Mithany. He wondered if the beast would join him as he faced off one more time with the evil entity. Searching his soul, the beast's presence evaded detection, but it didn't matter. He told himself he'd survived contact with the Void's malevolent entity once before, and he'd survive it again. Yet the memory of the searing pain scared him shitless. *For Mithany, I gotta do it. How much pain can I endure for love?* He paused. *No! There is no limit. I WILL NOT FAIL.*

Reyne turned away from the world below and searched for the limits of the astral plane, where the physical realm touched a metaphysical barrier separating his world from the Void.

Time to find out. *Hope Gina's mind is as tough as she is. It's gonna get bumpy.*

Without arms, without legs, without a body, existing only as pure thought, Reyne drove his consciousness to the edge of awareness, where the astral plane ended and the Void began.

The unseeable barrier existed as nothingness, a cloak hiding the Void from the astral plane. Reyne reached out with his mind to touch the barrier. Experience reminded him of how dense it had been.

You did this before. You can do it again. Nothin's gonna stop me.

With only willpower, he drove into the invisible mass blocking his way.

Slowly, ever so slowly, he moved forward. He thought to take one last look back at Gina's body, but recalled how the enveloping barrier no longer permitted him awareness of the physical world. With a burning desire to hold Mithany in his arms driving him, Reyne summoned everything he had to break the metaphysical barrier's hold on him. Yet, something pulled on him from behind, as though unfinished business on Black Haven wouldn't release him.

The harder he pushed himself, the greater the resistance forced itself on him. Determined to break whatever held his consciousness from moving forward, with his love for Mithany in his non-corporeal heart, Reyne struggled against the grip of nothing holding him in place.

With every inch forward he gained, it pulled back.

He thrust his will against it, as though lowering his shoulder to a door.

It repelled him.

Again and again, he thrust his consciousness against the barrier. It denied his every effort.

Then he remembered he had to break the connection of his mind to the material world. Reluctantly leaving thoughts of Mithany behind, Reyne inched forward. Slowly, the barrier gave way. Then, in a flash, his mind broke through the non-existent conundrum of the impossible barrier, and with only the force of willpower, the metaphysical blockade blew apart.

He was free of it.

Reyne crashed through into the Void only to be instantly enveloped by the absence of everything. Emptiness existed in every direction. Not a single photon of light. Infinite nothing, stabbing at him beyond the limits of his thoughts to grasp. The untainted gloom of oblivion encased him. His consciousness was completely, utterly alone in a realm of absolute darkness. How long it took him to break through could have been seconds, minutes, or even years. The answer awaited him once he rejoined his body on Evidar. This was the Void, where time did not exist.

At that instant, Gina's consciousness slammed into his. He sensed the terror in her. Her mind clawed at his as though seeking a safe harbor in an ocean of horrors. Knowing Gina had enjoined her consciousness to his, Reyne turned his attention to finding a path to Evidar: a journey dependent on selecting the correct Probability Wave to get him there. There should have been millions of Probability Waves crashing into his mind. He expected Probability Waves in untold numbers to open into his awareness. None did. *Where were they?* he wondered.

Just then, a third consciousness crashed into his own. A sense of dread pervaded it, and its evil fury attacked him.

The malevolent entity engulfed them both.

An agonizing heat overwhelmed Reyne.

His connection to Gina instantly shattered.

NO! his mind screamed out through the pain. *GINA!*

Before Reyne could do anything to get her back, Gina's essence imploded into a million threads of disconnected energy. With the intensity of a burning sun, the heat-infused pain drilled deep into his own existence. Writhing in agony, Reyne could do nothing, watching as pieces of Gina's consciousness drifted away, evaporating across the emptiness of the Void, into nothing.

Concern for Gina collapsed against the all-consuming seething agony. Reyne screamed, *PAIN! The pain. Agghhhh!*

From his chair, Black Haven's Mera studied the two Tartican bodies on the floor. He'd been observing them, protecting them, from the moment Reyne and Gina took up their respective positions. He'd witnessed Beth transfigure to the other realm hundreds of times as she assisted individuals who otherwise proved incapable of doing it on their own. Her purpose in the hundreds of joint-transfigural ventures was to relocate survivors to a new world, with the promise of a better life. He reflected on memories fifteen centuries old, recalling that each time Beth and the other person enjoined for the journey, they would vanish at the same instant.

Yet only once did Beth attempt a transfiguration with her Soul Stone along for the ride—an attempt from which she never returned. A passage he himself had tried to make with his piece of the Soul Stone embedded in his chest, but had been driven back by the same entity Reyne now faced.

Black Haven's Mera understood the risk of sending Reyne and Gina into the Void. The danger was well worth the reward if they succeeded. He expected the crossing between realms to be difficult.

Stopping his brother Janek, the Devil's Blacksmith, meant everything to him. He'd given up his own Soul Stone to Reyne for that very reason. Bitter memories of when Janek stole Beth's heart from him didn't enter the equation. At least, that's what he told himself.

Without warning, Gina's body arched high off the ground. And just as quickly, it slapped back down against the floorboards. Her legs, arms, and entire frame spasmed wildly. The back of her head smashed against the floor, over and over. Black Haven's Mera instantly recognized it as convulsive shock. Why, he hadn't a clue.

Up from his chair, he kneeled alongside her out-of-control body, placing his palm to her forehead. A quick glance at Reyne, who remained unmoving through it all, eased his concerns.

The involuntary spasmodic movements pulled Gina's forehead from Reyne's, cutting her off from their shared Eye of Heaven's physical connection. While he'd seen harmless disconnects happen during Beth's joint-crossings before, he never witnessed a single violent reaction. He wondered if the malevolent entity was the cause.

Without warning, Gina stopped moving. Her body went limp. Mera took her by the hand. Other than being hot to his touch, he encountered no response. He lightly slapped her cheek. She gave back no physical reaction. He slapped her again with the same result.

"Mahtoney, get in here."

In an instant, Mahtoney popped into the room. "What's wrong, sir?"

Looking up at Mahtoney, he said, "Go for the doctor."

"Yes, sir."

Black Haven's Mera called out, "Miss Gina, wake up."

She didn't respond.

Holding up one finger, he said, "Mahtoney, wait."

With a delicate touch, Black Haven's Mera slipped open Gina's eyelids to discover only an empty gaze. He moved two fingers to her carotid, searching for a pulse.

He turned to Mahtoney. "Forget the doctor."

The man from Black Haven who looked just like Mera of Tarica let go of Gina's hand. It flopped to the floor.

"She's dead."

All Roads Lead to Teth

Teth: 21st Day of the Harvest Moon

Loseff | Derr | Mithany | Quith | Neladith | Mera

The ill-prepared deployment of General Loseff's division from Tandure to Teth was initiated within an hour of Chancellor Tomelai's death at the young general's hand. Five thousand trained, untested troops who'd pledged their fealty to the young general marched all day and through the night to arrive in the shadows of The Stand. The Stand, a narrow strip of giant sequoias stretching from the Bay of Synn to the foothills of the Razors, formed a natural barrier to Teth's southern border. It was all that stood between Loseff and his conquest of the holy city-state.

With his father gone, Teth and all of Tartica were ripe for the taking. The first step to that end awaited him on the other side of The Stand. The holy city of Teth, the center of Tartican civilization, would belong to him before the sun set… of that he was certain.

As the first rays of dawn peeked through the flaps of his hastily erected command tent, Loseff contemplated why Derr didn't try to kill him after he'd stabbed his father. While Loseff failed to comprehend the why of it, it was good enough for him that Derr didn't.

Troops from Adelle's other military units should have come after him by now… but they didn't.

His mother, First Lady Kaythlin, or his sister Tane, the next Chancellor of Adelle, should have demanded answers from him… but they didn't.

Nobody came after him.

Loseff concluded either Derr hadn't said anything... yet, or Tane was being more thorough in her preparation of deployment than he had been in his departure. Either way, Loseff knew that sooner or later, they would come for him. He was determined to be well secured inside Teth, behind The Stand, when Tane eventually arrived. One obstacle remained: the Anatese. He wondered, *Will those monkey men living in the canopy of The Stand try to stop me?*

Derr had risen before dawn and stood alone outside the camp. A pink hue of morning rays broke over the five thousand troops of General Loseff's division. The bitter cold of the late autumn sunrise proved powerless to claim Derr's attention. He'd been unable to sleep. Warring thoughts of his own battled through the night without a victor declared. Opportunity demanded an answer, and Derr was out of time. Soon, rhythmic thumping from the drum corps would pound out the command to assemble.

Dead is dead... ran through Derr's mind over and over. *It's not like Rotti will ever know,* he told himself. While he tried to justify taking revenge on Loseff was the right course of action, as hard as he tried, he couldn't convince himself it wasn't a betrayal. With each new rationalization Derr conceived of, Tomelai's plea not to kill his son kept stomping on the flames of vengeance burning inside him. Nagging him. Telling him to leave Rotti's son alone. That one word was more powerful than all the others he could think of. Derr heard his friend's voice in his head, over and over... *"No."*

Loseff's quick departure from Tandure left Derr little opportunity to resolve his dilemma in the immediate aftermath of Tomelai's murder. Too stunned by Tomelai's dying word for Derr to act in the moment, his hesitation allowed Loseff to escape. Derr considered Loseff's hasty departure well played. However, by surrounding himself with five thousand other faces, Loseff provided Derr a place to hide, where he could track Loseff's every movement while contemplating the young general's fate. To that end, Derr had strategically inserted himself amongst the departing host.

Derr had shaved his head, donned the appropriate leather brigandine, and had embedded himself in Loseff's newest military unit just as the entire division set out for Teth. A unit whose troops kept to themselves. A unit whose makeup didn't include anyone who would know him. The unit called themselves the Brotherhood Company. It was composed exclusively of male Samers. To a man, they were all foreign nationals. All were fervent in their support of Adelle breaking away from the Covenant. A handful of Derr's Grays had been placed amongst the Brotherhood Company prior to Loseff's act of regicide. They owed their loyalties to him, before any loyalty to their fellow Brothers... or to Loseff.

Throughout the march from Tandure to Teth, Derr kept a distant watch over Loseff, all the while struggling to solve the puzzle of his own Gordian Knot. He was careful to stay out of sight of anyone from another unit. Each night in camp, Derr heard and witnessed acts of pleasure between several of the Brothers. He never cared how people got their jollies. If it didn't affect the safety of Chancellor Tomelai, it simply didn't matter. With his friend gone, it mattered even less.

With the night behind him, and the march to Teth completed, morning light streamed through the tight spacing between the giant sequoias of The Stand. Decision day for Derr had arrived. If he was going to kill Loseff, the chaos of battle provided the perfect cover.

Thump... Thump... The drumskins' reverberations struck him like a blow from a hammer to the side of his head. Even though he knew it was coming, it startled him. The sound attacked his ears like a hot poker being driven into his brain; not because of the noise it delivered, for its demand it imposed on him. *Thump... thump... thump...* The division was being called to assemble. A decision had to be made... Time was up.

As the drum corps beat out its command, each thump against the drumheads burrowed into Derr's mind as though Tomelai was screaming out to him from the grave. *Thump, No! ... Thump, No! ... Thump, No! ... Thump, No! ... Thump.*

Derr threw his hands over his ears and called out, "Alright! I won't! Damn it." His words trailed off, "...I won't."

A few of the Brothers nearby turned to Derr. He snapped at them, "Fuck off!"

He had no choice except to give in to his friend's dying wish. Loseff would live. The camp scurried about, preparing to assemble. Derr left the Brotherhood behind and slipped away. Yet, there was blood in the water... Tomelai's blood. Derr had the taste for vengeance, and it demanded action from him. Yet, there was another who started the series of events that ended in Tomelai's downfall. He was in Teth, just on the other side of The Stand... Jerithan Cree.

Through its southern entrance, Derr made his way into Teth, absent any command from Tomelai to hold him back.

Always through its northern entrance, Mithany had been to Teth several times, usually to secure a deal for the raw materials needed to support her leather good shoppe back in Hensdale. On this occasion, necessitated by her need to flee to the safe haven Teth represented, her business partner Arek wasn't at her side.

She'd already shed a flood of tears for her beloved brother. With Arek, Reyne, Daedyn, and Brenal all taken from her, she faced a crossroads: succumb to self-pity or somehow steel her heart against the all-consuming sorrow. The damaged little girl inside her was desperate for the comforts of love to ease her suffering. She'd always unknowingly relented to the demands of her broken mind before.

Arek's death pushed her beyond any ability to cope. With her little girl persona—always lurking in her subconscious, wanting to break free of her control over it—now hovering so very close to claiming its freedom, she struggled to keep it in check. Entangled in every thought of Arek, it threatened to assume control of her riven mental state. A gift her mother's cruelty bestowed upon her from which life had proven, time and time again, she was incapable of overcoming.

Her want for love, her need for love, and her ability to give her love completely to another was both the essential quality of her humanity and her greatest weakness. A weakness born in a child's craving for a mother's love forever denied her.

This time, she'd been pushed too far. Arek's passing broke the scales already weighed down with overwhelming loss, unfathomable pain, and the torment of total abandonment. Absent a single source of love to anchor her, it should have been beyond her abilities to cope. She should have given in to her tormented mind and surrender to her inner child. Instead, from somewhere deep in her core, she somehow found the courage to lock out the ever-present hunger for love.

She caged her heart.

Nothing allowed in.

Nothing allowed out.

She denied her damaged psyche a pathway to gain control over her. Forcing love into the shadows was the only way to survive Arek's death. The only way to endure the agony consuming her soul. Her survival demanded she discard love... without a single thought of the consequences.

As she made her way through the unmanned north portal into Teth, the sight of a city in ruin opened before her eyes. Any compassion for those who'd suffered through it, the Mithany of two days past would have clung to her breast and wept for their loss. In her current frame of mind, it failed to spark the slightest measure of sympathy.

She stopped to take in all the destruction: the burned-out buildings, the broken store fronts, the clutter strewn about the mostly abandoned streets, and pondered the utter chaos that delivered it. Her fingers jingled a few coins in her pocket given her by the old woman who'd hidden her from the Apple Orchard's search party. They wouldn't take her far.

Kantos's guards from the Samer detention center most likely dared not cross the border into Teth, though she couldn't be certain. She needed a place to lie low, and the sanctuary of one of the Temple of Life's communal temples was her best bet.

Spotting a young boy there, only eleven-or-twelve-years old and scavenging through a pile of rubble, she made her way to him. "Hi there, young fellow."

His head snapped around, obviously surprised at her presence. His face was smeared in soot. "Go away. This pile's mine."

"It's all yours. I'm just looking for the nearest communal temple that might still be standing. Can you help me?"

"Sure. Whadda ya got?"

"I don't understand."

He held out his hand. "Nothin's free."

The Mithany of two days past would have felt sympathy for his plight, but she didn't. She experienced annoyance in its place. Reaching into her pocket, she came away with one silver coin and held it out.

He sneered through yellow and black teeth at her offer. "Gonna cost ya two."

She studied his pitiful face, unmoved. "Take the one. I don't have much myself."

"Nope. Two or get lost, lady." He turned his back to her and returned to rummaging.

"Fine." She held out the two silvers. "Now, where is the nearest temple?"

"Coin first. Info after."

She dropped the coins into his filthy, grimy hand.

"Shantytown's about all that's still standin'."

With the sun directly overhead, a sight never seen on Evidar, Quith figured it to be about noon as Tarticans measured time. He'd put the unmanned northern entrance behind him a few days ago after making his way from a small hamlet on the border of Kantos and Teth. Since entering Teth, he'd kept a low profile, not knowing the whereabouts of Evidar agents Kebra and Harvin. Wherever they were, he was certain their quest to find him and kill him remained top of their list.

Betraying the Devil's Blacksmith came with the promise of certain death. The Soul Stone, if he could track down Mera and steal it from him, would solve all his problems. He put aside anger with himself for losing Mera once before and was determined not to let him slip through his grasp again.

First, he had to find him, and Tartica was a big place. He needed help to find the slippery bastard. Dylla's contact in Teth—Nails, who controlled the Thuggery—was his best bet to elicit help in tracking down Mera. Sure, it would cost him a lot of coin, but he'd stolen enough of it along his travels to meet the expected price.

The journey from the hamlet to Teth took less than half a day when he entered the city just as night settled in. Teth was a mess and nothing like the last time he passed through it. It posed a huge problem. With concerns for Kebra's or Harvin's uncertain whereabouts playing on his mind, and now engaged in a field of operation he was wholly unfamiliar with, he remained mostly in the shadows, gathering intel from a myriad of observations, overheard conversations, and from questions asked of select townsfolk he came across.

It had taken a day and a half since entering Teth to compile an adequate lay of the land. He concluded Nails was nowhere to be found, nor were there any reported sightings of the behemoth of a man Harvin, and Thuggery leadership now operated out of a high-class brothel. Confident in his assessment, yet careful, Quith set out to seek help from whomever was in control of the Thuggery. He turned away from the pile of rubble that was once the Temple Palace and headed off to his next stop, the Gift of Flesh Celebratorium.

Midday approached as Neladith looked up ahead to the unmanned northern administrative entrance to Teth. It took her barely half a day since leaving Dasch asleep in the bed they shared the night before... after relieving him of his coin pouch as he slumbered peacefully and contented. She'd gotten little sleep, yet the price was well worth the cost. She and Dasch rolled around on the sheet for hours, engaging in one position after another and taking turns performing pleasure-inducing acts on each other—and with each other—throughout the night. Although Dasch knew little more than what he'd previously provided of the barkeep's conversation with Quith, it was enough to send her into Teth after the rogue Evidar traitor.

Standing before the north portal city entrance, she reflected on her time with Dasch and laughed. Never one to be satisfied with a single orgasm, she played back the evening in her mind and counted eleven. Dasch boasted four for himself, claiming it to be his new personal best. All things considered, she thought four represented a pretty good night for a man. Although she took pity on all men for the recovery time nature imposed on them. She was never happier to be a woman.

She lamented leaving Dasch behind. She had business to attend to. Quith had to die. Death always got her juices flowing, and she planned to circle back to Dasch right after completing her mission.

She'd never been to Teth, and the place looked like shit. Its condition mattered not. If Quith *was* in Teth, he'd certainly seek out contacts familiar to him. Not knowing where to look, or how to get around in this shithole of a city, Neladith recalled her meeting with the Devil's Blacksmith no more than a week ago.

She reflected on his words: "If your efforts take you to Teth, find a man named Jerithan Cree. He is the former First Lord of the Temple of Life. Update him on your progress, and he may have information on Quith."

It's worth a shot.

Midday had come and gone when Mera approached the empty northern checkpoint into Teth. It was on his last visit to the once-beautiful city where he and Reyne learned the identity of the Evidar assassin who killed Reyne's entire biological family—Dylla Weisner. While the awful event happened almost twenty-two years ago, for a man who had existed for over fifteen hundred of them, those twenty-two still seemed like a lifetime ago.

The Soul Stone granted him freedom from death and aging since forcibly acquiring his piece of it from his brother Janek; Mera instinctively understood there were some injuries the Soul Stone couldn't overcome. On alert that Quith wanted to relieve the Soul Stone from him, that problem took a back seat to Mera's purpose in Teth. He had to stop the coming war.

Not much had changed from his last visit, and Mera failed to detect any signs the effort to rebuild had begun. Charred wood framed the few buildings that remained standing. Of those untouched by flame, the damage caused by looters took care of the rest. A boy no older than twelve turned his head from the pile of rubble he was working on. He scanned Mera up and down. Without a word, the dirty-faced lad sneered at Mera as a warning to stay away: the pile belonged to him.

Mera held up both arms with empty palms as if to say, "No problem. It's all yours."

Mera pushed the boy's obvious struggle for survival from his thoughts. He had bigger issues: stopping his brother, The Devil's Blacksmith, and preventing Tartica from jumping into a war that would end civilization's embrace with peace that had gone unchallenged for more than a millennium. If Mera failed, the boy and everyone else on Tartica would pay a deadly price.

"Excuse me, young man," Mera began. "I'm looking for some information. Maybe you can help me."

"Seems there's a bit of that goin' on today." The boy squinted at Mera. He rubbed is hands together, wiping away some of the grime, and held out an open palm. "Gonna cost ya."

"How do I know you'll have the answers I want?"

"Only way to find out, pay the toll."

"As much as I'd like to help you, young man, I'm out of coin."

"Your loss," the boy muttered under his breath, turned from Mera and continued digging through the debris.

Mera considered his options. There would be others he'd come across, yet, he took pity on the boy's plight, even knowing this wasn't anyone to trust. "I tell you what. Looks like you could use a knife as you go poking through that pile. How about we exchange my knife for what you can tell me?"

The boy looked over his shoulder. "Show me the goods."

Reaching into his boot, Mera pulled out a small buck knife he always carried. Holding it out for the boy's inspection, "It's yours. Just answer a few questions for me."

"Knife first. Talk after."

"Let's do it the other way around. Talk first. Knife after."

The boy turned away and returned to rummaging. "Your loss."

Mera considered the boy's situation and concluded the lad needed it more than he did. Besides, he still had the other blade in his other boot. "Alright. We have a deal." As quickly as Mera held it out, the boy snatched it from his hand.

"What's your name, lad?"

"Ain't part of the deal," he answered, while intently inspecting his newly acquired prize.

The two spoke for several minutes, and while the unnamed informant didn't have much to offer, Mera's ears perked up when the lad stated, "That guy Serco who took over, no one's seen him since the Palace burned down. Ma let me watch it go up in flames. Big fire."

"What happened to the guy who used to be the First Lord? His name is Jerithan Cree."

"Ma says he's around. Big shot. Ma says he's takin' over. Says they expect soldiers gonna storm through here any day now. We's got to get ready. That's what I'm doin'. Lookin' for stuff to make weapons. Ma says we gotta be ready. This Jerithan fellow is gonna help us."

Mera knew Jerithan and had interacted with him years ago when Prudent Jerithan had been assigned to Adelle. A stubborn man with a closed mind is how Mera remembered him. "You've been a big help, young man. Where can I find this savior of yours, Jerithan Cree?"

"Ma says he's holed up in Shantytown's communal temple. Makes his headquarters there."

"Thanks, lad," Mera called out as he flipped a coin in the boy's direction. "Look here, I found one," Mera said, smiling at the boy. With a nod of his head, Mera was off to find Jerithan Cree.

WHERE LIES GO TO DIE

TETH: 21ST DAY OF THE HARVEST MOON

Loseff

General Loseff Tomelai looked down at the map of Teth and wondered if the city in its current state resembled anything like the drawing. Joined by the five battalion colonels and ten other military advisors gathered around the table, neither Loseff, nor anyone inside the command tent, had ever planned a military campaign. Peace had reigned over Tartica for more than a millennium. That was about to end.

Loseff's forced hasty departure from Tandure deprived his officers of adequate time to establish a comprehensive strategy to invade the city. Necessity and circumstance had delivered Loseff into the jaws of a difficult situation. He pushed it from his mind. He had to move forward; there was no other choice.

A woman barely into her thirties, who'd been given the rank of colonel because of her leadership skills and for her quick grasp of military strategy gleaned from the books Loseff provided to his officer corps, shook her head. "General Loseff, if I may. It appears we have two immediate issues. First, the choke point funneling us through The Stand." She pointed to the representation on the map of the massive giant sequoia grove that flanked the entire length of Teth's southern border. They went off several miles on either side of its one opening. The otherwise impenetrable densely packed sequoia grove was also a half-mile deep. It had one opening known as The Gate. "We have to move five thousand troops through a dark, dank passage no wider than ten soldiers abreast since it's impossible to squeeze between those trees. We're looking at almost five hundred rows of troops. And that doesn't factor in our cavalry. When we emerge from the other side, our numeric superiority will mean shit." She jabbed her finger at the narrow open space between The Stand and the thirty-foot-tall stone wall guarding Teth's southern entrance. "Coming out ten at a time, we'll be sitting ducks if there's a defensive force stationed atop the parapet. It's a clear shot for archers from the sixty or so feet between The Stand and that fucking wall."

Another officer added, "Even if we make it that far, we're blind as to the theater of engagement we'll be entering once inside Teth."

She nodded, acknowledging the support, and took back control of the discussion. "That's correct. The point is, General, we need intel for what's waiting for us on the other side. I recommend we hold until we get it."

They were both right. Loseff knew it. As much as he imagined himself a well-read military strategist, he put his plans for conquering Tartica at risk with his very first engagement. Despite the killing of his father being something he had to do, it led to his predicament, and now forced his hand. With a high degree of confidence, he expected Tane to have assumed Adelle's chancellorship by now. He was just as certain she'd send the rest of Adelle's military after him for killing their father. That's if Derr told her the truth. He had to assume Derr did at some point. He feared that if he waited to gather intel as advised, he'd be pinned between The Stand blocking his way forward, and Adelle's Second Division screaming for his head. He was trapped. He had to attack Teth before Tane's troops arrived. His only escape was to get inside the city, where his five-thousand-strong division could hold Tane at bay.

An officer who'd once served under Kiple's national police and had been given the rank of Major asked, "Why can't we go around? That'll avoid all these problems."

Loseff rubbed the back of his neck. "I like the way you think. Yet, if it were only possible. I'm guessing you've never been to Teth before. The Stand leads up into the Razors at one end and along the cliffs rising above the Bay of Synn on the other. Neither is an option. However, I thank you for the suggestion. There is a northern entrance into Teth. To take advantage of that approach, we'd need ships to drop us along the shoreline beyond the cliffs… that we don't have."

Just then, Jaynes rushed through the command tent's portal. He hurried to Loseff's side. He leaned in and whispered, "The emissary you sent to meet with the Anatese is back. They refused your request to parlay."

Loseff remained stone-faced for the benefit of the officer corps. *More bad news. This just keeps getting better and better.*

Loseff's heart sank as Jaynes stepped back. They needed clear passage through The Stand. If the Anatese refused to stand down, they were all fucked. The men and women living in the treetops of The Stand would rain down arrows from above—at will.

A lot of his people were going to die.

What choice do I have? I have to assume Chancellor Tane's army is coming for me. Even if I send out scouts to confirm my suspicions, getting them there and back won't leave me enough time to both secure Teth and set up defensive positions to fight her off.

Fifteen sets of eyes looked to their leader, awaiting him to share Jaynes's news. He shook his head up and down as if to say, "Yes." But other words came out. Loseff did what he had to do—choice died with his father—so he lied. "Lieutenant Jaynes informs me Derr has sent one of his Grays to us. He's told the lieutenant that the city is in ruin and mostly defenseless."

"That's extraordinary," the colonel, who'd recommended caution, blurted. "A Gray spoke to someone other than Derr? I never thought I'd see the day."

She squinted at Loseff, and as he scanned the room, hers wasn't the only skeptical face looking back at him.

Through a feigned smile, Loseff replied, "These are extraordinary times, as you say. We owe a great debt to Captain Derr for sharing the men and women reporting to him."

Another of his advisors spoke up. "What of the Anatese?"

Loseff continued stretching the truth. "We simply don't know how they'll react. They certainly know of our presence, and yet haven't taken any discernible defensive measures so far. The city is in ruin. What do they have to defend? I'm taking that as a positive sign."

The same man prodded for more information. "That isn't proof they won't attack us once we're marching through those enormous trees."

A fourth advisor joined in. "We have archers. I'll give the order to shoot flaming arrows into the treetops. It is true, giant sequoias don't burn easily. However, to our benefit, the threat of fire will keep them busy as we march through."

"Does anyone even know how many of them there are?" someone called out.

Turning away from the table, with his back to everyone else, Loseff faced Jaynes. With his brows raised and eyes wide open, as if to say, "Keep the lie going," he asked, "Lieutenant Jaynes?"

"Well… I mean… I think… Derr once said there's no more than two thousand. And half of them are children."

The equivocation in Jaynes's lying reply didn't kill the issue, but it was good enough. Loseff turned back to face his command team. "The Stand is several miles long on either side of our camp. Spread a thousand adults over all that territory with fire reigning down on them, I think we can get past the Anatese in relatively good shape. Just in case, our troops will sprint through The Stand so as not to give the Anatese any opportunity to pile up the casualties."

Loseff anxiously waited, anticipating someone under his command to point out the flaw in his assessment. With five thousand troops threatening to invade Teth, Loseff expected the Anatesse to gather their forces to meet his point of attack. None of the officer corps had experience in war, and to Loseff's relief, no one challenged his intentionally deceitful assumption.

The skeptical colonel pursed her lips and nodded. "It could work."

It could work, Loseff repeated to himself. He wanted to believe it even though it was built on deception necessitated by circumstance. *His* deceptions… and circumstances born out of *his* own actions.

Amused, he considered the irony of relying on lies to achieve his own goal of conquest. He wondered—*Father, do I make you proud using deceit to acquire power?*—just before the reality of what he was about to do sank in.

A lot of people are about to die.

After a short bout of guilt, he accepted the outcome, just as long as he wasn't one of the soon-to-be dead. He'd need a shitload of unlikely events to fall his way to pull it off. Yet, with choice removed from the equation, hoping for good fortune was the only option left to him. He recalled books from the Tomelai Secret Archive he'd read of generals from the Second Age achieving victory in the face of insurmountable odds. He imagined himself just such a general in humanity's first battle of the Third Age.

He told himself, *Lady Luck, I'm counting on you. No, I beg you, please smile on me today. With your help, Teth will be mine before the sun sets over the city.* Although, in his heart, he knew Lady Luck, like the Goddess Teth, was merely the imagining of men.

Putting the best face on a bad situation, Loseff slapped his hands together. "Good. Now, let's lay out our strategy for when we get into the city."

Something Lost

Teth: 21st Day of the Harvest Moon

Quith

A sign hung on the Celebratorium's ornate door: "Closed. So fuck off."

Wood carvings of the pleasures offered inside covered the entry. Quith pounded several times, careful not to strike any sharply sculpted imagery, more concerned about a potential injury to his fists than out of concern for damage to the door. Not getting a response, Quith stepped back and looked over the building's façade. The windows were set high above street level to deter onlookers, he presumed. While the Gift of Flesh was conferred on humanity by Teth herself, the Temple of Life lords–as the premiere purveyors of it to the faithful–weren't so inclined to give away sex shows for free.

After a few failed attempts to leap up and steal a peek inside, Quith went back to pounding on the door. This time, kicking at it incessantly. With his back leaning against it, like an impetuous child denied, Quith watched strangers pass by as the heel of his boot slammed into the door hundreds of times.

Minutes passed.

Clunk...

Clunk...

Clunk...

Over and over and over... *Clunk... Clunk... Clunk...*

Quith could hear it resonating inside the empty foyer. *Clunk... Clunk... Clunk...*

He grinned when he heard an anonymous voice calling out, "Alright! You win! I'm comin', motherfucker. So cut it out."

After a momentary pause, he smirked and kicked it one last time. It sounded like *Clunk...* although Quith knew its true meaning: *Fuck you for making me wait so long.*

The ten-foot-tall doors squealed opened just wide enough for a small woman—missing several teeth—to squeeze her head through. "Whatda ya want?"

"I'm here to see Nails."

"She ain't here. Go away." The woman quickly withdrew her face and stepped back, closing the door.

His foot slipped into the gap between the oak panels. "Then I'll speak with whoever is handling things."

Through the dark shadow of the opening, her head reappeared. "I ain't got time for yer shit. Now fuck off! And stop kickin' the door, asshole."

Quith's foot didn't move. He reached through the opening with a closed fist, then dropped two gold coins to the floor. The sound, *clink... clink...* flittered into the empty chamber.

The woman let go of the door to chase down the coins before they rolled away. Quith pushed through the entryway. Amused, he watched the woman, half bent over, chasing after the coin that was heading into an unreachable corner.

"See, that wasn't so hard."

Light streamed through the windows into the atrium, illuminating the statutes and tapestries depicting every measure of erotica. While it fascinated Quith, since nothing like it existed on Evidar, he had business to attend to.

The woman scooped up the stray coin, straightened up, and offered Quith an eerie gape.

"Who might you be?" Quith asked.

"I might be Chaulky. Then again, might not be."

"Well then, Chaulky, I've a few more coins here that could be yours. All you have to do is lead me to whoever is handling things."

"How much?"

"Two silvers."

"Three!"

"Done."

The pair stood silently staring at each other for several heartbeats before Quith spoke up, "Well then, lead on."

She grinned through black gaps in her mouth where teeth used to be. "Pay up."

He held out a palm with three coins glinting in the light. Her arm shot out to grab the prize. Quith clamped his palm into a fist. "Services first, Chaulky."

Sulking, Chaulky turned from Quith and waved her hand over her head as if to say, "Follow me."

Quith asked, trailing behind the small woman, "Where is everybody? Why are you closed?"

She didn't answer.

"There's another copper in it for you."

She spoke over her shoulder. "Fine. There's talk of an invasion comin'. There's coin to be made in it. Gotta be ready. Got better things to do than just sittin' around here watchin' folks fuckin'."

"Where's Nails?"

"Don't know. Disappeared couple of weeks ago. Ain't seen her since."

"Who's running the show in her absence?"

"Some fancy-pants guy. Chamette. When he ain't here, he sends people to fill in."

"Is Chamette here today?"

"Nope." Chaulky turned and grinned, sticking out an open hand. "We's here. Services done. Pay me."

"We're in a hallway. Where am I going?"

"Yer a dumb shit, ain't ya?" She reached for a doorknob with her other hand.

"Please open the door, Chaulky." Quith jingled the three coins.

Chaulky wiggled her fingers.

"How do I know there's anybody in that room?"

Chaulky threw open the door. "Hey, Boss. Some clown's here to see ya."

Quith dropped the coins into Chaulky's hand, brushed her aside, and stepped into the room. He closed the door behind him.

The man Chaulky called boss was well dressed, large, and had an air of authority about him. He spoke in a husky voice. "Who are you, and what do you want?"

"My name's Quith. I have coin to offer you in exchange for the Thuggery's help."

"What's the job and how much coin you got?"

"First things first. Who am I speaking with?" Quith asked politely.

"Your speakin' with the Thuggery. Who I am doesn't matter."

"It does to me."

"Then we've nothing else to say to each other. Get the fuck out."

"Alright. Have it your way." Quith reached into his vest and dropped three full coin purses onto the desk. "They're all golds. I need the Thuggery to find somebody."

The man opened the pouches and dumped them out. He spread the coins across the desktop and stacked them in sleeves of ten. "Ten piles of ten. One hundred golds. This guy's pretty important. Who do you want us to find?"

Quith reached into his vest a second time and pulled out a drawing. After sliding it forward, Quith said, "He goes by the name of Mera. I'm not sure he's in Teth. If he is, your people will know. Then we'll set him up for an ambush. If he's not in Teth, we'll expand our search."

"I've heard of him. He's been known to pop into the Whispering Eye every now and again. He hooks up with an assassin chick named Gina. I haven't heard anything about either of them since the Whispering Eye burned down."

Quith thought back to his encounter with the unnamed woman who'd killed Dylla... and let him live. "I'm familiar with this Gina person, but it's Mera I'm after."

"I'll get the word out. Where can I find you?"

"I'll be around. Give your folks my description. Have them come find me if anyone spots Mera. If I don't get word from anyone, I'll check back with you in a few days."

The man stood and held out his hand. After the two shook on the deal, the Thuggery associate shrugged. "If we're still here in a few days; word on the street is that an invasion is coming."

"Then it's even more important your people find Mera as soon as possible. I'll double the payment if you find him by the end of the day. How much of it you keep for yourself is your business."

"If he's in Teth, we'll find him."

Something Found

Teth: 21st Day of the Harvest Moon

Quith

Moving through Teth, hiding behind one burnt-out structure after another, Quith followed Mithany from the shadows since chancing upon her earlier in the day. Scurrying from doorway to doorway, concealed behind crowds, practiced stealth easily kept him from Mithany's awareness.

The Thuggery delivered on their end, alerting Quith of Mera's whereabout in the ruined city of Teth. And with Mithany's presence in play, Quith put a plan in place based on conditions on the ground and coordinated its execution with Thuggery support. Attacking Mera directly, a dangerous and difficult foe, proved unnecessary. He'd bait the trap for Mera with Mithany's life as the bargaining chip to achieve his objective. With help from the Thuggery, at the expense of additional coin, funneling Mithany and Mera into Quith's kill box would take time, but Quith was patient.

The disgraced, once lauded Evidar agent trailed his target through the streets of Teth. Mithany moved away from one strategically placed scary-looking Thuggery scoundrel after another until she'd been channeled into the long, narrow, empty alleyway where Mera was located. Turning his back to her as she passed, Quith spun around and sprang from the burned husked remains of the once notorious Whispering Eye. One arm snatched Mithany around her waist. With his free hand, Quith drew a weapon to her exposed gullet, stilling Mithany instantly. Not before she screamed.

With his eyes on Mera, Quith told his captive, "Go ahead, scream."

Off in the distance, Mera's head whipped around. Even at a distance, the surprise Quith read on Mera's face sent a jolt of satisfaction through him.

"Mithany!" Mera raced to fill the space between them, stopping short mere feet from where Quith held Mithany.

With the flat of the knife pressed against Mithany's throat, overconfidence, verging on arrogance, spilled out from Quith. "I've tried to kill you before, Mera. It didn't take. This little lady here, she'll die easy enough."

Tinged with annoyance, Mera replied, "You're not going to kill her. You want me. Not her. She's an innocent."

Quith sneered, "Nobody's innocent."

"If you wanted her dead, she'd be dead already. What do you want, Quith?"

Quith drew his lips up in a smirk. "Funny you should ask. Yet, I got a strong feeling you already know what I want. The night you rose from the burning funeral pyre, it hit me as clear as a sunny day on Tartica... you got the Soul Stone."

Mera took one step toward Quith.

A flash of scintillation jumped off the knife's shiny metal surface when Quith flipped the blade's orientation to deliver its razor-sharp edge against Mithany's exposed neck.

In a polite tone, Quith warned, "Not another step."

Mera stopped. "If you kill her, you won't live a minute longer."

Quith let out a long breath that fluttered between flapping lips. "You may be right about that. But I'll take my chances. The thing is, I don't see you letting this one die. So, do we need this back and forth? Just hand it over."

Mera's foot lifted off the ground.

Quith quickly moved the knife over to where Mithany's carotid artery lay just below the skin. "Eh, eh, eh, don't even try."

Mithany elbowed Quith in the side.

"Be careful, young lady. One slip of my hand and you'll bleed out."

In a calm delivery, Mera offered, "Let her go. We can talk. We'll work something out."

A *tsk* slipped out of Quith before he added, "Now that's disappointing. I thought you held my intelligence in higher esteem. You must think I'm a fuckin' idiot."

Mera pushed up the corners of his mouth.

With a broad, fake grin of his own, Quith responded. "It's a rather simple transaction. No negotiations required. The Soul Stone for her life. I got nothing to lose. The Devil's Blacksmith will hound me until I'm dead. It might take only days or it could take years. They *will* get to me eventually. I'm a dead man walking. With the Soul Stone, I'll survive the inevitable."

"I get your point, Quith. You have quite the conundrum if I don't turn it over."

"Yes, I do. Either they kill me someday, or you give it a try right now. However, you're leaving out something very important... she'll be dead after I slit her throat. Or you can just hand it over and we'll be done with all this."

With his free hand, Quith made circles with his index finger. "I see those wheels turning in your head, Mera. Armies have amassed outside the city. A battle's inevitable. Lots of people are gonna die here today. What's one more? Reyne will never know you let his girlfriend die. Fuck, he's probably dead already. You and I both know he can't survive Evidar. You sent him to his death."

Mithany opened her mouth to speak.

Quith let up on the pressure of the blade against Mithany's throat. "Go ahead, little lady. Speak. I'm guessing you didn't know the danger Mera put your boyfriend in."

"Is all that true, Mera?" Mithany pleaded. "Reyne's not coming back to me?"

"Mithany..." Mera fumbled for words. "I did what I could to prepare him. And he's not alone. He's with a highly skilled assassin. She's my very best. She's already dispatched several of this man's associates."

"Assassin? You mean she's killed people for you? Who are *you*, Mera?"

"I'm sorry, Mithany. I'm the guy trying to head off Tartica's ruination. That's who I am... and Reyne is Tartica's last hope."

Mithany squirmed to break free.

Quith pulled her body in even tighter against his. "I said you can talk, not move."

"Fine," Mithany huffed, and Quith felt her body still before she continued. "Mera, is what this asshole saying true? You sent Reyne to his death?"

"Asshole?" Quith feigned offense.

Ignoring Quith, Mera offered Mithany a breadcrumb. "He's still alive. I've had communications with him. But yes, Evidar is a very dangerous place."

"What happens if you do what this man—this asshole says? If you give him this Soul Stone, whatever that is, what happens to Reyne?"

Mera shrugged. "Direct consequences... if Reyne needs my help, I may not be able to save him."

With raised eyebrows and a quick tilt of his head, Quith, hearing all he cared to, said, "Enough chatter between you two. Time's up, Mera. Hand it over or she dies."

With determination in her voice, Mithany demanded, "Mera, don't do it."

"You're a brave one." Quith's tone changed. In a harsh, threatening voice, he scolded her, "Don't be so quick to die. Unlike Mera over there, you ain't coming back from it."

Mithany squirmed to no effect, failing to break free. The anger in her voice sparked a touch of admiration in Quith when she said, "I don't care. Mera, don't hand it over. Save my Reyne. After I'm gone, when you see him, tell him I'm sorry for not being here when he gets back... and tell him I love him."

Respect for her toughness pushed aside, Quith tightened his arm around her chest and pressed the knife's edge to her skin with his other hand. "Ten...nine... eight..."

Mithany begged Mera, "Save Reyne."

"Five... four... three..."

Mera shouted, "Stop. Alright," as he reached under his shirt.

Softly, Mithany pleaded, "No, Mera... don't."

Quith demanded, "Stop. What're you doing?"

"It's under my—"

Quith cut him off. "Take off the shirt. No funny business."

Slow to comply, Mera removed his top, then rested his palm over his left pectoral muscle. With an open palm and fingers splayed apart, in slow measure, his hand gently pulled away. As the space between Mera's chest and his hand grew by fractions, a red vapor-like object that appeared somewhere between a solid and a gas filled the gap as it rose out of Mera's chest. Once completely removed, Mera held out his upturned hand, and Quith watched in amazement as the cohesive vapor coalesced into a solid crystalline object.

Quith couldn't believe his own eyes. "That's one helluva trick. What do I do? Just hold it over the same spot and let it absorb into my flesh?"

Whether Quith expected Mera to answer really didn't matter. He'd caught the gist of it. "Okay. You're not gonna tell me how it works. I'll figure it out. Seems simple enough."

Excitement tingled down into his fingertips as he held out his hand. As tricky a bastard as any, Quith wasn't going to allow Mera the opportunity for any last-minute heroics. Quith drew just a drop of blood from Mithany's exposed neck, reminding Mera there would be consequences if he tried anything.

Mera dropped the red, semi-transparent, rock-like object into Quith's waiting palm.

Mithany lamented, "Why, Mera?"

"I made a promise to keep you safe."

Stepping back from Mera with Mithany his safety cloak, delight and a childlike giddiness washed over him.

The Soul Stone. It's mine.

Come and get me Harvin... Kebra, I'm ready for you motherfuckers.

With Victory Comes Loss

Teth: 21st Day of the Harvest Moon

Quith

Continuing to backpedal without taking his eyes off Mera, from a safe distance, with the Soul Stone in hand, Quith pushed Mithany from his grasp, slowly moving away from Mithany and Mera.

Mithany rushed to Mera's open arms. "You shouldn't have given it to him."

Mera stroked her long chestnut-brown hair. "It'll be alright. You're safe and that's all that matters. Don't worry, I'll get it back."

With Mera fifty feet away, Quith paused, opened his shirt, and held the mysterious red crystalline rock to his chest. It transformed into a gaseous state before being absorbed into his flesh. Once completed, Quith felt it harden. He rode his hand over the Soul Stone under his skin.

The rush of an otherworldly presence shot through his mind. It flooded his thoughts with images he didn't comprehend. It took all his concentration to push it aside and focus his awareness on Mera.

Mera called out, "You have what you want, Quith."

"That I do, my old nemesis. That I do."

"Enjoy it while you can," Mera shouted. "I *will* find you and get back what is mine."

"Talk like that makes me think I should kill you right now. You're no longer invulnerable."

"You're an idiot, Quith. You have no idea what the Soul Stone can do."

"I know I have it and you don't. Although I suppose there's a slim chance you could get the better of me. I like my odds."

"Let's find out."

With a deep breath and the tilt of head, Quith replied, "Nah, not worth the risk. And besides, I got other plans. Doubt we'll ever see each other again."

Quith bowed, and as he swept his arm across, he kept one eye on Mera. "Well, I'm going to take my leave of you two. And don't worry, Mera, I'm no longer after you... like in the old days. I still don't give a fuck about what the Devil's Blacksmith has up his sleeve for Reyne. He's your problem to deal with. I've got two agents after me to take care of. Boy, are they in for a surprise." Quith smirked at his old nemesis while tapping his knuckles against the imbedded Soul Stone.

Through the deceit of his words and his smirk, he lied. The two agents, Harvin and Kebra, would have to wait. His immediate plans included a quick trip back to Evidar, where he intended to face off with the Devil's Blacksmith. Even if he disposed of the two agents currently after him, until he eliminated the Devil's Blacksmith, the threats on his life would never end. The Devil's Blacksmith would keep sending more and more people after him until he was dead. *But*, Quith thought, *nothing like a little misdirection, don't you think, Mera?*

"Mithany," Mera began, "I can't go after Quith just yet. There's an army threatening Teth. I gotta get to Jerithan Cree. I gotta stop a war. Come with me. It'll give you time to catch me up on why you're in Teth."

Quith barked, "Go stop your war. I don't plan to see you ever again unless you can find me." He laughed, turned, and sped away north, leaving Mera and Mithany behind.

He made his way through Teth, street by street, careful to look over his shoulder from moment to moment for signs of Mera on his tail. He didn't trust Mera and considered his statement to find Jerithan Cree a feint... much like his own heading north out of Teth. From one shadowy place to the next, Quith navigated the ruins of the city until he finally made it back to the Gift of Flesh Celebratorium, where the Thuggery set up shop.

Claims of an army amassed on the other side of The Stand held little interest. He didn't expect to remain in the city much longer. He didn't plan to remain on Tartica either, for that matter. What did he care if the army ripped the city apart?

Once through the doors of the Celebratorium, surprised, Quith locked on to the orgy taking place in the open vestibule. Arms, legs, mouths, breasts, cock, and minge were all intertwined as they writhed up and down across the open space. The distraction of naked men and women, though he focused mainly on the women, all engaged in every sexual act he'd ever imagined, stunned his Evidarian sensibilities. Not that he objected, just stunned. Although one massively oversized erect phallus caught his attention. *That thing's a monster!*

His loins stirred at the scene before his disbelieving eyes. He considered diving into the pile of the twenty or so participants, then thought better of it. Mera had proven himself a wily opponent, and Quith realized he couldn't afford the risk. He called out to no one listening, "I'll be back. But not today."

Tapestries hung on the walls and statues lined the circular room, depicting couples performing the same acts going on in the heap of intermingled bodies. The interior had once been a plush, extravagantly ostentatious center to celebrate the Gift of Flesh. Since the Thuggery took over management of the place following the downfall of the Temple of Life, it had become nothing more than a brothel serving all comers.

Pulling himself from thoughts of pleasure, Quith made his way to the front desk. He dropped a full coin purse on the counter. The young woman was as pretty as she was naked, like all the men and women attending to the clientele. Her attractive face and voluptuous breasts stole his attention. He'd adjusted to Tartica civilization's pervasive nudity over his many transfigurations to the foreign world. Yet, unlike the people of Tartica—forever pursuing their mission of repopulation—on Evidar, for Quith, sex was taken by force more times than it was ever offered to him freely.

Offering Quith a welcoming smile, she asked, "How can I help you today, sir?"

Her tone gently washed over him, soft, feminine, and innocent. "You are quite a gift to the eyes and ears, young lady."

"Thank you, sir. Would you care to share time alone with me?"

Quith considered it, though briefly. "Oh, if I only had the time…Then again, I have an idea." It struck him, time didn't exist in the Void. *Always have an exit plan*, he told himself. *Can't trust the Void. If I'm in it longer than an hour passes on Tartica, fuckin' Mera just might find me asleep in this place. Can't take the chance.* "You keep the coins," he told her. "Set me up in a private room and wait one hour. Then come join me. Can you do that?"

She fluttered her long eyelashes several times and reached out to rest her hand on his. "It will be my pleasure."

As she came around from behind the counter, the full measure of her figure and her beauty almost made Quith forget his concerns for Mera.

With a deep breath he scanned her from head to toe, stopping once or twice along the way. "You are simply stunning," he proclaimed.

"That is so very kind of you, sir. Please follow me. I have just the room for us."

As she stepped gracefully up the wide staircase, Quith couldn't take his eyes off her from behind. A similarly naked young man was making his way down the stairs, holding the hand of a man in a business suit. The young man was well built and well-hung, but Quith paid it no mind. The rhythm of her movements, one rounded cheek rolled up, then down, cheek after cheek, step after step: it had him hypnotized.

She let go of the banister at the top of the landing, walked to a nearby room, and opened a door. "Here we are, sir. Get comfortable, settle in, and as you have requested, I will be back in one hour."

As he looked her over yet again, it took all his inner strength to let her leave. He lamented his loss. He'd never see her again. "Thank you. Remember, one hour. Not a minute sooner. And, this is very important. No one is to disturb me while I await your return."

He watched her close the door and thought, *Fuck you, Mera. This could've been a glorious afternoon.*

Quith settled in on the most comfortable bed he'd ever laid upon. He closed his eyes and, with images of the young woman filling his thoughts, he rubbed one out. The act always put him at ease and greased the wheels of slumber. Satiated, he soon drifted off to the desired unconscious state. As slumber took hold of Quith, it wasn't long before the Void opened to him.

Transfiguration of body and mind back to the dark realm of Evidar awaited him... if everything went as expected.

Into Darkness

Teth: 21st Day of The Harvest Moon

Loseff | Jaynes

Low on the horizon, morning sunlight danced across the canopy of The Stand. Dew clung to the grass, releasing aromatic hints of a typical idyllic autumn morning enjoyed by Tarticans generation after generation—just not this day.

General Loseff Tomelai staked out a position at the front of the column, seated atop his steed. Holding the reins in both hands, he turned to look over his shoulder and called out, "Jaynes, to me."

Adelle's most skilled archers made up the first two rows of troops. Once through The Stand, Loseff wanted his best ready to face the unknown, and he'd be properly protected should the Anatese start shooting at him from above.

Jaynes was positioned in the third row of a formation of eight troops abreast and in a line of soldiers that stretched over four hundred rows deep. Following his prized archers, Jaynes was Loseff's most trusted officer. He wanted Jaynes nearby if all hell broke loose. Rows three through eight were Jaynes's to command.

"Be right there, General. Just helping my good buddy Private Timlin with a few last-minute details."

"He's a grown man and a soldier. Leave him be and get up here."

"May Lady Luck be with you today, Timlin," Jaynes offered with a slap across Timlin's back. "Gotta go."

Lieutenant Jaynes sidled up alongside General Loseff's horse. Looking up, Jaynes offered his childhood friend both a knowing look and a salute. "Sir, yes, sir. Reporting as ordered, sir."

Leaning down, Loseff said, quietly, "This isn't a game," chastising Jaynes. "You might end up dead if you don't stay sharp."

"I know. It's just my way of dealing with it."

Loseff grabbed onto the horn of his saddle, twisted around, and looked back over his shoulder. "It's going to be a bright sunny day. Too bad it won't mean a damn thing inside that dark, dank passageway through The Stand."

"Look on the positive side, Loseff. Tane's army hasn't shown up, and we got the numbers. There's no way the United Front is waiting for us inside Teth. Fingers crossed."

Fingers crossed indeed, Loseff reflected. The scouts he'd sent into The Stand overnight delivered seemingly positive news. They reported the administrative portal at the base of the Wall on Teth's side of The Stand lay open and unmanned. The fact the scouts made it all the way through and back with no sign of the Anatese rallied the morale of his troops, but not his. The scouting party's return meant the Anatese were either unaware of their presence inside The Stand, chose not to tip their hand, or had stayed out of the fight since their benefactor, the Temple of Life, had fallen. He hated the idea of blindly marching his troops into an uncertain theater of battle, notwithstanding his own actions that put him there.

Loseff tugged down on the front panel of his leather armor and sat up straight in his saddle. "I called you over here to tell you to stay sharp. No heroics, just stay alive. When this battle is over, you and I are going to get drunk tonight in my tent." With a salute, General Loseff said, "Good luck, Jaynes." He looked his friend in the eye and said, "Now get back in formation. It's time."

The sun, inching into view, showed itself as a rounded, glowing yellow mass breaching the treetops. General Loseff gave a nod to a young corpsman. A bugle call rang out.

Burump.

Burump.

Burump.

Three ear piercing blasts ordered Adelle's military to attention. Archers, pikeman, foot soldiers all snapped to.

General Loseff rode out, passing along the left side of the column, then the right. He inspected the troops, stopping here and there to offer words of encouragement. He noted each unit's position: where the archers were placed, their weapons, their uniforms, and every detail he could gleam of the troopers' preparedness, including the fear in their eyes.

He wanted to be pleased with himself for whipping inexperienced farmers, merchants, mothers, fathers, and officers into a fighting force. Instead, he scolded himself for putting so many lives at risk.

Loseff called to his Master-of-the-Horse and the two reviewed the strategy for Adelle's calvary. They'd been over it several times in the past day. In a moment of self-realization, Loseff knew he was stalling. He had no way out. He had to move ahead.

He'd witnessed fear in the eyes of many. He didn't count himself amongst them. Hesitant, perhaps because of the uncertainty, but not afraid. He took stock of himself and thought, *I was born for this.*

Loseff rode out to the middle of the long column. He paused, then raised his sword for all to see. "Men and women of Adelle, and to all those from other lands joining us in this struggle. We fight for freedom. We fight for our families. We fight to throw off oppression."

Private Jaynes, with Timlin, his longtime buddy standing to his right, pretended to listen to General Loseff's words, otherwise consumed with death playing on his thoughts. Regardless of the bravado he feigned for Loseff's benefit, he was scared shitless. His heart couldn't beat any harder. His bowels pleaded with him to release their stored accumulation.

He imagined in the melee of soldiers attacking and killing, skill accounted for a lot. He'd trained hard and considered himself a capable soldier. Yet, he reckoned luck the biggest factor separating the survivors from the soon-to-be dead. There were too many ways to die in the confusion of battle to think otherwise.

Jaynes tugged on Timlin's arm. "This is it. It's going to be a glorious fight. Are you ready to kill those fuckers?"

Wild-eyed, Timlin stared back at him and shouted, "Yeah. We're gonna kill those fuckers." And as soon as his words faded away, Jaynes saw the utter terror written on Timlin's face.

Jaynes reassured him, "I got your back, buddy. You got mine."

General Loseff was finishing his call to rouse the troops. "... for love, for god, for country."

Hoots, hollers, shouts, and battle cries all rang out. Jaynes joined in, as he was expected to. He eyed the others to his left and then to his right. *Lady Luck, I'm begging you. Get me through this.* He started to make the sign of the Signum Circulus, but stopped himself.

The one-word command Jaynes feared above all others slammed into his brain. "Onward!"

Jaynes hesitated for a second, as did everyone else, to witness General Loseff signal a unit of archers. In response, a hundred flaming arrows flew overhead, aimed directly at the tops of the giant sequoias. Fire appeared to float in the air as it sailed casually into the morning sky before turning downward. They reloaded, aimed, and released. They repeated it several times, Reload. Aim. Release. After the brief pause, the unit marched on while fire continued flying overhead.

General Loseff cried out, "Into The Stand!"

Jaynes' legs answered the call. He sprinted headlong into The Stand. He wanted to stay behind to see how well the flaming-arrow-ploy worked. It wasn't in the cards for those in the front of the column. As he ran alongside of the others in the third row, he worried that some idiot from behind would trip and impale him before he even reached Teth.

Inside The Stand, the sconces had all been relit at General Loseff's order. The meager flames barely pushed back enough of the ebony veil to matter. Lume hung around his neck on a chain, as it did for many others. The green crystal's soft light helped, yet it swung wildly about as he ran and repeatedly slapped against his face. Disgusted, Jaynes grabbed the crystal and yanked. The chain broke, and he cast it aside.

Jaynes looked up, all the while sprinting. In short bursts, he scanned in search for Anatese above and any sign of the effects from the fire shot into the treetops. The sun remained hidden behind the thick canopy, and the archer's flaming arrows hadn't yet shown themselves from the inside. As Jaynes sped along, taking only quick peeks upward through the darkness, he couldn't make out enough for it to matter.

A man in front and off to the left of him went down. Jaynes's heart felt like it jumped into his throat. And still he kept running, not knowing if the soldier tripped or if the Anatese brought him down. His heart thundered in his chest. He gasped for breath. His eyes shot wildly in every direction. Fear had its claws into Jaynes. A second later, sunlight breached the passage. The end of the tunnel lay just ahead.

Loseff was the first through.

You Never Know Who You're Gonna Meet

Teth: 21st Day of the Harvest Moon

Mithany

"Mithany, I'm so sorry to hear of Arek's passing," Mera remarked as the pair walked the streets of Teth on their way to Shantytown's Communal Temple.

The words hit Mithany like a team of horses slamming into her chest. As determined as she was to lock love out of her heart for her own survival, just hearing Arek's name rattled the cage of her attempt to sequester affections. Arek's death changed her in ways she didn't like. Yet, to go on without him forced her to harden herself against the overwhelming grief threatening to destroy her from the inside out.

"Thank you, Mera," was all she said.

"He was a good man."

Her stomach clenched. "Yes, he was. In more ways than you will ever know." She didn't want to discuss Arek with Mera. Intent on changing the subject, she added, "Before more people suffer my brother's fate, I pray to the Goddess Teth you can stop this war from happening. But I'm worried that you're just one person. What can one man do?"

"I've been around a long time and have witnessed the inevitable not come to pass based on the actions of a single person. My biggest concern is that it's all happening too fast. I may be out of time."

Mera continued talking. Mithany stopped listening. The ruination of the once beautiful city reminded her of her own ravaged mental state eating away at her emotional reserves. She reflected on something she always told herself in difficult times, *The mind and body are one. Where one goes, the other follows.* It had always been a mantra of strength. Now, it was anything but. In mind, body, and soul, Mithany was a husk of the woman Reyne loved.

By the time she refocused on the present, Mera was trailing off. "... temple up ahead."

She pulled herself out from under the self-pity gnawing at her insides to notice the crowd. With the Communal Temple in view, there was an energy on display in the bustle of people coming and going that seemed out of place compared to the rest of Teth. She noticed the noise, the sense of purpose each of them displayed, and more than anything else, she noticed the weapons. People were ferrying bows and arrows, swords, cudgels, and sharp tools of every variety, into and out of the Communal Temple.

Mithany grabbed Mera by the wrist. "That's a place of worship, not an armory. What's going on?"

"Like I told you, there're soldiers from Adelle on the other side of The Stand. All these folks with weapons, it appears they are to be Teth's defenders. Adelle has its sights on Teth. Let's pray we still have time."

"You have to stop them," Mithany pleaded. "These people aren't warriors."

"I know. Come on, let's get inside. Jerithan Cree is supposed to be here. He's the one I need to speak with."

"You go. There's nothing I can do to help. I'll wait right here."

Mera asked, "You sure?"

"Yeah, I'll be fine. You go ahead."

Mera disappeared into a sea of people. She settled on one of the open benches thirty yards from the temple.

Her lips moved as she silently offered a prayer to Teth. Time passed slowly, and she occupied herself remembering happier times with Reyne, Daedyn, and Arek. A half hour passed when a young man stopped right in front of her. "Miss," he began. "There's a lot to do. Each time I cut through here, I noticed you haven't moved. You can't just sit around. We gotta get ready. Jerithan says everybody's got to pitch in. Come on, you can help me." He held out an arm, offering to assist her off the bench.

Looking up at him, she wondered if he would be one of those to die.

"I'm not here to help," she politely told him.

He tilted his head to the side and looked confused. "You have to. We all do."

"I don't believe the Covenant approves of folks killing each other. You do what you feel is best. I'm going to sit here awhile and wait for my friend."

"Jerithan is First Lord again. He says it's okay since we're defending ourselves."

"Killing another human being is never..." She stopped mid-sentence.

Through bulging eyes, a single thought screamed into her brain, *Can't be!*

Ignoring the man and everything else, Mithany jumped out of her seat and bolted. She pushed through anyone in her way. *Can't be* ran through her head over and over. *Can't be. It just can't be.*

Blood pulsed in her veins as she chased down the top of the head she was following, careful not to lose sight of her target. Just as Mithany caught up to the individual she'd been chasing, the person reached for the door to the Communal Temple.

Impossible!

Mithany stopped dead and screamed, "NELADITH?!"

The tall, red-haired youth who tried to kill Arek snapped her head around. The two stared at each other for a brief moment, before Neladith broke the silence. "Mithany?"

Mithany's heart felt like it skipped a beat. Only minutes ago, she scolded a young man, telling him killing was wrong. Coming face-to-face with Neladith, her blood curdled, and she wanted to take back her protestation of murder. She thought of Arek and how Neladith had crippled him. She thought of Daedyn, who Neladith killed. She thought of Reyne, who Neladith tagged for death.

A wide smile swept over Neladith's face. "Imagine meeting you here."

Anger spewed out in Mithany's reply, "Wipe that grin off your face. I never wanted to see you again."

"Aw, come on, don't be that way. I'm happy to see you."

Mithany shouted at her. "You killed Daedyn!"

Neladith shrugged as she started walking towards Mithany. "I didn't mean to. It was Quith's fault. He pointed me at the wrong guy."

"You burned down the orchard!"

Neladith kept moving forward. "Sorry about that."

To Mithany's ears, it sounded more like a question than a statement.

Only two feet away, Neladith stopped.

Profound sadness seeped into Mithany's words. "You're here to take Reyne from me."

Neladith waved both hands in front of her chest. "No. No. No. I'm here to kill Quith," and she opened her arms wide, gesturing for a hug.

Mithany lunged at the woman. She slammed her palms into Neladith's chest, pushing her away.

After stuttering back a few steps, Neladith looked up. Their eyes met. Mithany spied regret on Neladith's face. The red-haired woman couldn't hold Mithany's threatening glare.

It's always in the eyes, Mithany told herself.

When Neladith looked up at Mithany from under her brow, all Mithany could say was, "I hate you."

Someone bumped into Neladith from behind. She spun around. Venom spit out in her words. "Fuck off, asshole!"

When Neladith turned back, she seemed hesitant to glance at Mithany.

Mithany read it as guilt. Guilt for all she had done. Mithany experienced guilt of her own for sleeping with Neladith in a desperate state of longing for Reyne. They briefly shared an intimate connection before Mithany pulled away. The recollection of the two of them writhing naked together drove Mithany's own guilt into her heart, like it had been impaled with red-hot iron spikes.

Mithany yearned for the hatred bottled up inside to propel her into action. To force her to hurt Neladith. To demand she strike at Neladith. She wanted her loathing for Neladith to command her to do as much damage to Neladith as Neladith had done to her.

But instinctively she knew why she couldn't. Another spark of memory shot through her mind. She recalled when Arek told her he walked away from an opportunity to kill Neladith in an act of vengeance. Her own words stung her as she played them in her head. *Arek, it's one of the reasons I love you... you're not the kind of person who can take a life.*

In remembrance of the good man Arek was, she relented. She let go of her desire to see Neladith dead. The burning want for revenge drained from her soul. Her body went slack, as though all her energy had been syphoned off in the revelation. In a tone that announced surrender, Mithany asked in a hushed, somber voice, "Why are you really here, Neladith?"

Stepping closer, Neladith pressed her lips together for a few seconds, then quietly offered, "I'm sorry. I never wanted to hurt you."

"You're a cold-hearted bitch. I doubt you can even feel sorrow."

Neladith took the attack without responding, closing her eyes, tipping her head back, and drawing in a deep breath.

Although Mithany accepted surrender, it didn't mean she forgave Neladith. "It's too late for sorries. Just answer one question: Are you here to find Reyne?"

"No. I told you the truth. I'm here to speak with the First Lord guy, Jerithan. He might know where Quith is." She joked, "I'm hunting Quiths."

Mithany didn't laugh. "Really?"

"Yes, really." Her reply hung between them for what seemed like minutes when Neladith added, "Can we talk?"

Mithany wondered if she had the strength to engage in a conversation with Neladith, whether she could stand to hear her voice, or if she really changed her mind about hurting Neladith. Then it hit her. This was an opportunity to get answers. Answers Mera never provided. She knew people were after Reyne, but Mera never gave her the truth behind it. She decided to endure Neladith's presence, only if Neladith promised to explain why people wanted Reyne dead. Maybe if she knew the truth, she could help save Reyne.

Mithany crossed her arms over her chest. "You know how hard it is for me to be around you?"

"I can't change the past. I only want to talk."

"As if there's any explanation that can justify the things you've done."

With big puppy eyes aimed at Mithany, Neladith raised both hands in prayer mode. "Please?"

"One condition," Mithany demanded.

"Anything," Neladith quickly replied, juddering in place like an excited schoolgirl.

"No lies. Only the truth."

Grinning through her teeth, in a cheery tone, Neladith quipped, "I can do that."

"Alright. Let's go somewhere else. I'm not sure what Mera will do to you if he finds you here with me."

Just then, the Communal Temple bells blared.

Glang...

Glang...

Glang...

Everyone in the courtyard stopped in their tracks. They all looked up at the steeple.

Glang...Glang... It went on and on.

A man burst through the temple doors. "We're under attack!"

Reunion of Sorts

Teth: 21st Day of the Harvest Moon

Jerithan

For almost an hour, Mera pleaded his case to Jerithan, repeatedly calling on Shantytown's de facto leader to lay down his arms. Jerithan was having none of it.

Unexpectedly, the Voice broke into Jerithan's thoughts. *"I am sorry, my friend. I was otherwise occupied. I am here for you now."*

A second later, like a bullhorn into his brain, the Voice erupted, *"MERA! THAT IS MERA! JERITHAN, DO NOT TRUST THIS MAN!"*

The force of it slammed into Jerithan's brain like a sack of rocks had crashed into his skull. He stuttered back several steps.

"Are you alright?" Mera asked, grabbing hold of Jerithan's arm.

With a yank, Jerithan freed himself.

Mera raised both hands over his head. "I'm sorry. I was only trying to help."

"Tell him you do not need his help."

I am confused, Jerithan replied in his mind to the Voice. *He says he is here to help.*

"He is our enemy."

Turning his attention back to Mera, Jerithan replied, "As I have said several times, I have merely organized a defensive force. I do not seek to make war. Your council is noted."

"I can't leave," Mera demanded. "This is how it starts. This is how it always starts."

With his head cocked to the side, Jerithan challenged Mera's observation. "Always? There has never been a war in all our history. Again, I must ask you to leave. Perhaps your efforts would be better spent meeting with the army camped outside our city."

"I will, just as soon as I leave here. Before I do leave, you must stand down. I beg of you to trust me. Give me the chance to stop this madness and I will work to keep anyone from attacking Teth."

"Lies. His words are hollow. I know this man. He cannot be trusted. Do not be taken in by him."

There is obviously a history between you two. Perhaps you care to share?

"Another time."

Heeding the voice in his head's advice, Jerithan deferred. "Mera, I am certain you mean well. You must understand, Teth is a holy city, and I will not abide by anyone defiling her."

Mera's head jerked back. "There is nothing left of Teth that hasn't already been defiled. You're going to get your people killed."

"This is a rare opportunity to be rid of this menace once and for all. Have a dozen or more of your men kill him where he stands. It will take all of them. One blow will not do it."

I cannot order a man murdered inside a holy communal temple. I will lose all credibility. I am the leader of the faith.

"Command your people to do it. Call out to your followers, tell them this man is a spy. Tell them he tried to kill you. Tell them whatever you must. Do not waver. He is very dangerous."

Jerithan raised his arm just as a man burst through the door, shouting, "We're under attack! Where is Jerithan? We're under attack!"

Mera spat, "FUCK!"

The Voice demanded, *"Kill Mera now. Jeri—"* "Mid-word, the Voice's presence disappeared from Jerithan's consciousness as though yanked from his thoughts.

Jerithan searched his mind, only to find the Voice gone. It mattered not. Jerithan brushed it aside. He had bigger problems. Teth was under attack. Blood pulsed inside the veins of his temples. He knew an attack was coming, yet to hear the words declaring it had begun came as a shock.

The packed nave inside the temple erupted in bedlam.

People cried out.

Most ran for weapons.

The terrified stood, immobile, transfixed.

Jerithan's head spun wildly about assessing the situation, only to glimpse Mera fleeing out the door into the street. He spotted a bald man with no eyebrows brush by Mera. Jerithan squinted.

The bald man looked a bit like Derr without hair. *Couldn't be.*

Jerithan turned away. He screamed to be heard over the cacophony of frightened voices. "TIMBLE! Somebody find Timble!"

From out of nowhere, Timble pulled up short. Unaffected to the chaos, by the call to war, Timble answered in his usual jovial manner, "Right here. Whatcha need, Boss?"

"How can you be so... never mind. Are our people on the parapets?"

"Yep. Been up there all night. Stayed outta sight like ya said to."

"Are our best people set to drop the blockade? Those troops cannot get through The Wall."

"Yep. They'll drop it soon as the Anatese spot soldiers in The Stand. Guessin' since someone says we're under attack, might've dropped it by now."

"How many archers volunteered?"

"Three or four hundred I reckon."

"Arrows?"

"Thousands and thousands."

"What if Adelle tries to scale The Wall?"

"Just like you ordered, Anatese will pick 'em off. We're good, Boss. Nobody's gettin' in."

No Time to Mourn

Teth: 21st Day of the Harvest Moon

Jaynes

Metal-tipped death bit into Loseff's troops from every direction.

Jerithan's *Defenders of Teth* rained arrows down on the invaders from atop The Wall's parapet the second Jaynes and the host of Adellean soldiers broke through the exit into the light.

Adelle's elite archer corps never got their chance. Most died the instant they stepped into the gap between the exit of The Stand and the entrance to The Wall.

BOOOM!

A massive sequoia trunk dropped into the opening of The Wall. The sound wave slammed into Jaynes. He recoiled.

It was impenetrable.

No way through.

No way around.

No way above.

No way to advance.

No way into Teth.

Jaynes head spun to see General Loseff jump off his horse. A second later, a dozen wooden bolts drove deep into the beast's flesh.

Within seconds, another front opened. From somewhere behind Jaynes, from somewhere above, Anatese archers in The Stand released a barrage of their own.

Jaynes was trapped.

No place to go.

The Anatese fired arrows from behind him.

The *Defenders of Teth* fired arrows from in front of him.

Jaynes heard Timlin scream.

Three Anatese archers hidden along Adelle's left flank, their bows and arrows popped out from the small space between the colossal trees. Adelleians all around Jaynes dropped in the barrage. Most of his unit was gone.

With bodies squeezed in tight, Jaynes couldn't bring his weapons to bear. No Adelleian could. Soldiers from the rear continued marching forward. Jaynes was being forced back into daylight. Back into the gap between The Stand and The Wall, where terror reigned. Frantic, Jaynes struggled to strong-arm his way back into The Stand's passageway: his only hope to escape certain death. Yet, Adelle's rear, the column of soldiers, pressed forward.

Jaynes shouted, "Fuck me!"

With Timlin at his side, their feet dug into the ground against the force of the advancing column. Four hundred rows deep. His feet didn't stand a chance. Word hadn't reached those in the rear. The column continued to press forward.

Jaynes feet didn't hold.

He was pushed back into the gap.

Cries, screams, and curses flooded the tunnel.

Jaynes had lost sight of Timlin when he heard General Loseff call out, "RE-TREAT! RETREAT!"

Jaynes started shouting, "RETREAT! PASS THE COMMAND DOWN THE LINE! RETREAT!"

Bodies were being forced closer, ever closer.

Soldiers struggled to maneuver.

The calls to retreat echoed inside The Stand.

Adelleian pikemen turned to heed the order. Not all the ten-foot iron-tipped halberds were held high. A halberd swung toward his head. Jaynes saw it in time and jumped back. He tripped and went down. He came face to face with a dead body. Man? Woman? He couldn't tell. He didn't care. He looked up. Arrows flew into the empty space where he'd just been standing. Three wooden bolts buried themselves deep into some poor bastard who'd stepped into his place. *It could've been me. Glad it ain't.*

Feet everywhere threatened to trample him to death. He wouldn't let himself die like that. With elbows, fists, knees, and hips, he opened a gap in the sea of bodies. Jaynes shoved and nudged himself back upright.

He pressed into the soldiers in front. Soldiers from behind jammed into him. He came eyeball-to-eyeball with a woman from his unit. Terror filled her eyes. She wasn't more than seventeen. A second later, a metal tip punched through her throat. Horror flooded Jaynes. She gurgled something unintelligible. A second later, she died where she stood. Lifeless, her arms hung limp. She didn't fall. She couldn't. Her body, pressed between others, carried on.

No time to mourn.

No time to care.

Someone moved. A space opened.

The dead woman dropped.

Jaynes stepped over her body.

Inside the kill box focused his mind. *Survive. Nothing else matters. No one else matters.*

The column moved as one.

He brought his arms to his chest.

Jaynes shoved the person in front.

Slowly they'd effected a retreat.

Jaynes was swept along back into The Stand. It proved no safer. A barrage of arrows from the Anatese in the trees erupted.

Loseff's division was being decimated.

The carnage continued.

I Am Who Is

The Void

Reyne

The Void swallowed Gina.

An instant before Gina's connection was ripped from Reyne's consciousness, awareness of another presence slammed into his thoughts. Its manifestation frayed his nonexistent nerve endings. He feared it to be the malevolent entity.

The moment Gina's connection vanished, Probability Waves in the untold millions slammed into him. The Void's all-consuming ebony gloom engulfed him. Confusion flooded through him like a dam had given way. If it was the evil entity, why wasn't his essence burning? It decimated Gina; why not him? He prayed she somehow survived.

Get to Evidar, he told himself. Yet, his ability to focus on a single destination evaded his every effort, terrified the intense searing sensation would return to consume him. That one thought overwhelmed him. It set him adrift in an endless ocean of untold timelines, thrashing his noncorporeal existence across countless lifespans. Like a drowning man treading water, an unknown presence pulled on him, dragging him under the imagined waterline of the oceanic Probability Wave tsunami he found himself in.

Terrified of drowning.

Terrified of burning.

Terrified the evil entity would envelop him.

He railed against his own fears.

He had to survive.

He had to return to Mithany.

He promised her he would.

Gulping for air that wasn't there, and without lungs to breathe, frantic, Reyne's non-corporeal essence flailed wildly as though he was being plunged beneath some unseen threshold of safety. As though his very being was a spark at the center of a massive explosive energy, everything grabbing, pulling, dragging on his consciousness, shattered.

He was free of it.

The conflagration of Probability Waves vanished.

The all-consuming darkness, gone.

In its place, a single brilliant white light pervaded everywhere into the Void.

Blinding in its presence, the light invading Reyne's consciousness prevented him from sensing anything else. It overwhelmed him. All other thoughts fled him. He became nothing save an empty husk, drained of all thought, consumed by the light.

A statement bellowed across the Void as though it reached into every corner of the universe, "I Am Who Is."

The booming voice was louder than human ears could withstand. Yet, as Reyne existed in the Void as pure thought, energy absent a physical form, the voice entered Reyne's mind directly. It freed him from the disassociation strangling him. He understood it came from somewhere inside the light.

An awareness that he was not alone crept back in. Not just the announcement from whatever entity demanded to be heard, he sensed there were others, like him, in the Void.

Summoning courage, uncertain who or what had spoken to him, Reyne asked, "Who are you?"

"I Am Who Is. I will have silence!" The voice modulated between male and female.

The force of it rippled across Reyne's consciousness, threatening to disassemble his energy into a wisp along a breeze, dissipating his existence into the Void.

Somehow, Reyne maintained cohesion, and in accepting the command, Reyne remained silent.

"I will have what is mine," the entity demanded. "You are all here to return what should never have been lost." The modulation intensified with every word.

A woman spoke. "I don't understand."

Reyne knew it to be another like him, not the malevolence of before, and his thoughts immediately jumped to Gina. His nonphysical heart grasped at hope. "Gina?"

Much softer this time, the entity replied, "I am sorry, Reyne Brenton. She is forever gone from your ability to comprehend."

Sadness gripped Reyne. He didn't understand what I Am Who Is meant, but he knew he'd never see Gina again. He tried to plea for a clearer explaination, but the being continued speaking, modulating from male to female, from young to old. The words meant nothing to Reyne at the moment. Gina was gone forever. His heart sank.

The strange woman spoke again. "I don't understand."

This time, Reyne realized she had given sound to her words in a sweet, feminine voice. Hers were spoken words... sounds. And unlike Reyne existing in the Void as only thought separated from his body, the unknown female before him appeared fully formed and naked. She appeared as though the process of transfiguration had delivered her to her final destination, not to Tartica or Evidar but here, inside the Void. Reyne couldn't grasp how or why this woman's physical embodiment existed inside the Void, while he remained as noncorporeal energy. Even more disturbing, she looked familiar. He'd seen her before. Recognition, like a bolt of lightning, shot through him. This woman, with him inside the impossibility of the Void, was the spitting image of the statue adorning the entrance to Teth. The statue of her stood alongside her brothers, along with Mother Earth and Father Sun.

A man's voice, directed at the woman, startled Reyne.

The unfamiliar man asked, "Beth? Is that you? Could it really be you?"

"Janek?" replied the woman who looked exactly like the Goddess Teth.

Reyne's mind shuttered in the realization that one of the other entities he sensed in the Void with him looked like the living embodiment of Teth herself, and the other, a man who the woman called Janek... was the proper name of none other than the Devil's Blacksmith.

Before he could gather his thoughts, the Devil's Blacksmith spoke. "Beth, where have you been these fifteen hundred years? How are you here? You have not aged a day. I missed you so."

"Janek? It is you. Fifteen hundred years? What are you talking about? We spoke two days ago. You were there when I entered the Void. We said we'd make one last try to help you transfigure into the new world I'd discovered. I was coming back from there... for you. I only left the new world moments ago."

"Like you, I do not understand. Just moments ago, my consciousness in the Void was connected with someone on Tartica. A Tartica fifteen hundred years from when you left it."

The purest white light Reyne had ever experienced blazed as it spoke into his mind, in constantly shifting personas. It drowned out the discussion between the Devil's Blacksmith and a woman who looked like Teth incarnate. "All will be explained. First, you must all release what you have called the Soul Stone from your possession."

A fourth consciousness spat out, "No fuckin' way."

The Devil's Blacksmith snapped, "Quith! You traitorous bastard."

Quith quickly added, "Like the rest of you, I just entered the Void after a most pleasant experience on Tartica. And yeah, Mister Devil's Blacksmith, I was coming for you."

The white light roared, "Enough!" and an intense heat burst out in every direction. It swept through Reyne with tremendous force. He didn't know how, but Reyne sensed the universe rumble in its wake.

Reyne cowered against the blast. It tore through him, threatening to scatter his current state of existence into nothingness. The edge of his consciousness was being pulled away from its core as though the decaying leaves of late autumn were being ripped from their branches by a powerful wind.

As the voice died away, Reyne recovered and wondered why he was there. The voice spoke of the Soul Stone. He recalled who possessed each of the four pieces of the Soul Stone. Reyne accepted the Devil's Blacksmith and a woman he called Beth each held fragments. Including the piece Reyne held made three. Mera from Tartica should have been the fourth. Somehow, a man the Devil's Blacksmith called Quith had Mera's Soul Stone. Reyne had connected with Tartica's version of Mera in the Void just days earlier. So how did Quith end up with it? Was Mera, like Gina, gone? How else could Quith have acquired it, he wondered. An intense sense of loss settled in his soul at the thought of never seeing Gina or Mera again.

Time did not exist in the Void if what Mera told him was accurate, yet Mera said nothing about a blazing white-light entity. Reyne had experienced an unknown presence in the Void. The first encounter with the malevolence left Reyne curled in a ball, recovering from the intense burning sensation after he fled. This new entity seemed different.

I Am Who Is turned down the intensity when it next addressed the four Soul Stone holders. "Know this, I have shielded you all from the radiation herein. It has the power to scatter your existence, molecule by molecule, electron by electron, in a drawn-out and rather painful process. I do not seek your demise. I seek only what is mine. It is true, you must break the bond of the Soul Stone's hold on you. I cannot extract it from each of you without causing it damage: damage that would reverberate into your world. I ask only for the return of what is mine, not for you to experience the Heat of Creation."

Quith shot back, "If this Soul Stone is all it's cracked up to be, I'll take my chances."

"Know this, Selundra Quith. The timeline you have embarked on does not deliver Janek Meraturoc's death as you have hoped. There were other Probability Waves of your life force that could have brought you to that end. Those are lost to you. What remains is a host of Probability Waves that all deliver certain death for you in the realm of what you call Evidar. Keep the Soul Stone and you will die on that world."

The Devil's Blacksmith sneered. "You are a traitor, Quith. You thought to kill me!"

Quith ignored the Devil's Blacksmith and mocked I Am Who Is. "Mister I Am What I Am, sounds like bullshit to me. You could be anybody making your way through the Void when you came upon us. You want the Soul Stone for yourself. So big deal, you know a few tricks. You can make big bright lights... oooh, you're so scary. I ain't buying it. I'm keeping my piece of the rock. Do your worst, Mister, I Is What I Is."

"You misunderstand, Selundra Quith. It is as though I am a man asking an ant to give up the crumb it holds in its mandibles. The ant cannot fathom the meaning of the man's words nor fully appreciate the man's true power over it. It is not the fault of the ant that it does not understand, and so I will proceed with benevolence in place of force. Return what is not yours."

"No."

"Know this, Selundra Quith. You and the others are no longer in the place you called the Void. The explosive force you, Reyne Brenton, and Janek Meraturoc experienced occurred when I removed you from it and moved you into the inner sanctum of my domain, a place beyond time and space. This is where all the Probability Waves of all the possible futures of everything in existence—yours and every atom in the universe—transition into the past. Three of you, your physical bodies, are still in the realms from which you initiated your journey into the place you call the Void."

A compelling awareness of Beth's physical presence as the living embodiment of Teth sparked Reyne's curiosity as to why I Am Who Is left her out of his account. "What of the woman? She got her body. Me and the others don't."

"Know this, Beth Green," I Am Who Is demanded. "Your presence is born of a different circumstance. You have been here from the point you attempted your last transfiguration. Janek Meraturoc believes that occurred fifteen hundred years ago, as he reckons time. When you left the Void to begin the final phase of your transfiguration to Evidar, you passed from that part of my domain you call the Void into my inner sanctum. That is when your body reconnected with its consciousness. As time does not exist in my domain, you perceive that you have only just arrived. As for the others, I require your physical bodies to relieve you of what is not yours."

In an instant, Reyne experienced a jolt as though struck by lightning. His mind and physical form were again one, floating in a haze of brilliant white light streaming off the entity. In less time than Reyne proved capable of perceiving, the three consciousnesses within the domain of I Am Who Is, transformed. As a physical being once again, Reyne needed his ears to hear and his eyes to see. The ever-present awareness of all things around him was cut off. Also shut out were the thoughts of the entity flowing directly into his mind.

With solid eyes and a body sans clothing, the light radiating in all directions blinded him momentarily before his pupils adjusted. As his sight settled in, a warm, comforting embrace flowed over his naked body.

Reyne quietly stated, "I don't understand what's happening."

"Nor could you, Reyne Brenton."

Reyne ran his eyes over its flesh, trying to determine if his body had actually joined him in the domain of I Am Who Is. When he looked around, as he hung motionless, he laughed to himself. It struck him as amusing that, naked like him, the Devil's Blacksmith, the powerful man from Evidar threatening all of Tartica, was hung like a squirrel.

Although Reyne did not give voice to his thoughts, I Am Who Is knew Reyne's mind and answered. "Yes, Reyne Brenton, your body is back with your consciousness. You are whole. And Janek Meratoruc's physicality amuses you."

The entity's words hit his ears like a gentle summer breeze: peaceful, comforting, patronly, in continually shifting vocalizations.

I Am Who Is explained, "Imagine the tiniest sliver of time that separates the past from the future. Try to conceive of the exact instance an event moves from what you perceive as the present into the past. That is where you are. You exist with me, here, beyond space, beyond time, along the edge of Reality's Event Horizon."

Reyne shrugged. "I don't get it. It sounds like you said we're in the present. Where are we?"

"The present is an illusion. It does not exist. The concept of 'the present' has a place in your thoughts to help you understand the world around you. In actuality, everything you experience has already taken place. Some you experienced long ago, others in the very recent past. Yet the past just the same. In your world, the light you see while looking at your hands travels in very small measures of time to reach your eyes. Yet, it consumes time. Your thoughts travel along pathways in your brain. Though lightning fast, they consume time. Your mind is constantly collecting information from what has already occurred—sights, smells, sounds, touch, thoughts, tastes, events—and builds a construct you call the present. The present is a mere illusion of perception. In truth, you, and all Reality, exists in the past. In my domain, I transition all that the future holds across the threshold of the Event Horizon of Reality to become *what is*."

Reyne asked, "Am I all here?" He spread his fingers wide and cupped the entirety of his manhood with one hand, testing the reality of the situation. "Doesn't seem like any part of me is still on Black Haven."

"You are all here, Reyne Brenton. Now, you and the others will release your bonds with what you call the Soul Stone, and I will send you on your way."

As the first to act, Beth placed her palm to her breast. She slowly pulled her hand away. The Soul Stone started to rise out of her flesh, following her hand's movement.

With one hand of his own held out, as if to say, "stop," Reyne pleaded, "I don't know you, Beth, but can you just wait before you turn your Soul Stone over to him, or her, or whatever that thing is?"

She stopped, and the Soul Stone, which no longer appeared solid, looked more like a cohesive vapor reabsorbed into her skin.

Reyne started to say, "I Am Who Is, before we do this—"

Quith cut him off. "It's a con. Don't be stupid. None of us should turn over anything to I Be Who I Be." Quith's smirk told Reyne the fourth Soul Stone bearer enjoyed his incessant mockery of the entity.

The Devil's Blacksmith gave a response that stunned Reyne when he said, "My world, Evidar, what's to become of it if I turn this over to you? And I have been trying to move my body to join Beth. I cannot seem to move."

The Devil's Blacksmith disappeared.

And just as quickly reappeared alongside Beth. The Devil's Blacksmith beamed, held Beth's face in his palms, and gently pressed his lips to hers. There was a tenderness to the Devil's Blacksmith that Reyne never expected.

Reyne figured that for the Devil's Blacksmith it had been fifteen hundred years since the two had been apart. For Beth, two days at best. Reyne had only known the stories of the man he'd called the Devil's Blacksmith. Mera spoke of a reputation known for cruelty, without concern for anyone save himself or his plans. As a witness to the Devil's Blacksmith's tenderness towards Beth, it confused Reyne. However, it didn't dissuade him from fearing the threat the man posed to Tartica, and even more importantly, to Mithany.

The inconsistency of the Devil's Blacksmith's known character, measured against his demonstrated kindness towards the woman, held Reyne's thoughts before he shook it off. "Mister or Missus I Am Who Is, I gotta know what comes next. That guy over there threatens everyone in my realm, and I can't just hand over the Soul Stone knowing he's still a threat. So, I gotta have reassurances. I gotta know who I'm trusting."

The Devil's Blacksmith, Janek, appeared to ignore Reyne's plea to I Am Who Is, lost in love, gazing into Beth's eyes.

With a voice somewhere between masculine and feminine, I Am Who Is gave Reyne little in the way of reassurances in a reply, "I have been called many names by the inhabitants of billions of worlds across the universe. I have witnessed the dawn of time because I have created it. I exist as I always have at the Event Horizon of Reality. I see all that may come to pass and stand outside of time and space, ensuring that it does. The object you call the Soul Stone is a small fragment of energy from the Event Horizon of Reality. Its displacement coalesced from a form of energy you could not possibly understand, into a solid state of matter beyond anything you can comprehend. As solidified energy, it arrived on your planet in your reckoning of time in the Earth year of 2089. Its subsequent fragmentation into four separate pieces triggered multiple versions of Earth that now exist in separate dimensions."

Janek looked up from staring longingly into Beth's face. "That little piece of space rock caused Evidar to exist as it does?"

"That, and so much more. Know this, Janek Meraturoc. The woman you call a Damus, Sonja Emosh, is a talented interpreter of what the Void holds, yet her assessment of the forces that she speculated would pull the different dimensions of Earth into one could never have come to pass. It is only with the Soul Stone's reunification, returned to its place within the Event Horizon of Reality, will Earth be returned to its singular state."

With his hand over his eyes as though on lookout, Quith spun around three hundred sixty degrees. "I don't see any Event Horizon. More lies, no doubt."

"Know this, Selundra Quith. The threshold of the Event Horizon of Reality pervades every centimeter of the universe, and that tiny fragment's displacement from it has led to all this. I must return it to its correct state and reabsorb its energy into the fabric of Reality's Event Horizon. Only then will Earth, in all its forms, be set right."

Janek, having lived in the Second Age, before the Great Destruction, tilted his head. "Is that the Dark Energy that puzzled..."

A gentle laugh rolled across the white expanse. Or at least, that's how Reyne heard it. Reyne knew nothing of Dark Energy and had a more important question on his mind. "Are you God?"

"I Am Who Is... who always was... and who will always be."

Humbled beyond any measure of a man, Reyne believed he'd been granted the impossible—an audience before God. And yet, he still worried for Tartica... for Mithany. "What do you mean by set Earth right?"

"Know this, Reyne Brenton. From the moment of displacement of a sliver of the Event Horizon of Reality, when soon thereafter Beth Green picked up what she believed to be a simple meteorite, there have been so many timelines that I have examined, it is beyond the human brain's capacity to comprehend."

Beth asked, "Did I cause all this?"

"No. Beth Green, you were but the first vessel. The fault is not yours."

"Oh, thank God. Oh, I'm sorry... I didn't mean anything by..." Beth stopped mid-sentence.

"Know this, Beth Green. From the time of your fortuitous discovery, I have sifted through trillions of timelines from each of the thousands of lives, their possible futures, and events that have nudged, weaved, and intersected into this singular pattern that has forged you four together in a seemingly improbable series of circumstances to bring you four Soul Stone bearers into the Void at the same instance. As each of you releases the Soul Stone's hold, I will join the fragments together, return its energy to Reality's Event Horizon in the exact location Earth experienced in space and time from which it departed, and set Earth along the momentum of its past—where it always should have been. Where it belonged."

Quith jumped in. "Why go through all this? Just wave your hand and do all that mumbo-jumbo bullshit any god should be able to do. That is, if you're really God. I'm bettin' you ain't."

"I Am Who Is is the only name I claim. And the consequences of what you suggest are beyond your capacity to understand. However, this will help you grasp my meaning."

At that instant, an equation appeared as solid black objects hanging in place across the whiteness. The objects appeared as tens of thousands of letters, numbers, mathematical symbols, and functions all strung into a single incomprehensible mathematical formula.

"Know this. What you see before you is the delicate balance of Reality, as I have set in motion, to be governed without my constant input by putting forth one unified law of physics, including all aspects known to your kind and those beyond all understanding. Given the interconnected relationship of all things in the universe expressed in the mathematics that you see before you, Selundra Quith, tell me which of the variables might I tinker with by the waving of my hand? And based on the impact of that change to the unified law of physics, please point out to me how you might control the cascade effect such an adjustment would cause throughout the entirety of Reality."

And just as quickly as the equation appeared, it was gone. "Know this, Selundra Quith. Yes, I could tinker. Yet, the change needed would deliver consequences that would ripple across the universe. For that reason, I prefer the simpler and less destructive approach: the four of you simply return the Soul Stone as I have requested."

Quith faced the others. "See what I mean. He gives answers in riddles that no one can understand. I bet those numbers and symbols don't amount to dick," he said, palming his crotch while yanking the covering hand up and down twice for emphasis. "It's all a bunch of shit. He just wants the Soul Stone so he can live forever. If he's a god, he'd just take it. Sorry if it upsets any of you, but I ain't giving mine up to this fraud."

"Mister Quith," Beth began, "are you sure you want to take the chance you are not in the presence of God? You might at least cover your bases with a bit more respect."

"He ain't fuckin' God," Quith sneered.

Reyne considered Quith's argument that it could all be a ruse. However, the statement by I Am Who Is of setting Earth right held greater consequences for Mithany than any impact he could foresee if Quith's reading of the unknown entity proved accurate. He didn't believe Quith had the right assessment of the entity, yet it had to be considered. Beth's point was well taken, at least by Reyne.

Before Reyne could give voice to his thoughts, the Devil's Blacksmith looked away from Beth and said to I Am Who Is, "Your words hold promise for Evidar. If I accept who you say you are, please explain to me the exact nature of the outcome you intend for my world."

"Fuck that," Quith blurted out. "There's nothing to explain. If Mister I Yam What I Yam needs all our fragments, then Earth ain't going nowhere, cause what's mine is mine. It ain't ever going to be his. You three can do whatever you want. I heard enough. I'm outta here."

TANE'S REVENGE

TETH: 21ST DAY OF THE HARVEST MOON

Jaynes

A semicircle of infantry personnel armed with pikes, arrows, and swords stretched from either side of the only way in or out of The Stand. The host met Jaynes and the survivors of Loseff's retreating forces as they raced into daylight. They'd escaped from the kill box of death inside the dark tunnel of The Stand only to face a new threat. Those who'd survived, anyway.

Thousands of Chancellor Tane's military awaited their arrival. How Tane knew it was Loseff who killed their father, Jaynes hadn't a clue. *It had to be Derr or one of his minions.* It didn't matter, Tane was here, and his chance of surviving just went to shit.

Jaynes turned to see flames dancing across the treetops. His heart sank. It hadn't been enough to distract the Anatese. Jaynes and all of what remained of Loseff's forces were cut off from behind. They couldn't go back. They couldn't go forward.

Everyone, including Jaynes, who'd made it out alive, were trapped.

Tane Tomelai, sitting atop the very steed that once belonged to her now dead father, held up one arm. Within the span of a few heartbeats, silence settled over the battlefield. "There need not be any further death this day. I'm only here for the traitor, Loseff Tomelai."

Jaynes had lost track of Loseff and wasn't even sure if Loseff was still alive.

Jaynes's heart soared when he heard the voice of his friend Loseff call out,

"Hello dear sister." Only to sink into despair when Loseff addressed his troops before Tane could reply. "Listen to me, all of you. This woman is a usurper. She killed our Chancellor." And without giving his troops any time to sort it out, Loseff shouted, "CHARGE! CHARGE!"

In unison, Loseff's remaining troops sped towards Tane's forces. A handful dropped their weapons where they stood.

Jaynes's pulse hammered in his chest, as though frantically pumping fuel into his depleted muscles.

The men and women in front of Jaynes drove headlong into Tane's center line. Many went down. Pikemen on both sides rammed their killing points into their fellow Adelleians. From the rear, Jaynes could see Tane's center give way, only to be struck with fear as both flanks of the semicircle closed in.

Jayne drew his sword.

Mayhem followed. Metal against metal rang out.

Clang. Clang. Clang. The sound went on incessantly. It filled his eardrums.

Bodies were crashing into their line from the flank.

There was nowhere to turn.

No space to maneuver.

Jaynes wanted to flee. Wanted to escape. But there was no escape. To give up was to die.

A woman charged at him.

Her sword held high overhead.

Jaynes pushed someone to the ground and stepped aside as her sword came down hard.

She missed.

Jaynes swept his at her, hoping to lop off her outstretched hands.

He missed her hands. *Clang.* He struck her weapon.

Metal vibrations reverberated through her hand. It dropped from her grasp.

Her head snapped around to face Jaynes. Pure terror was written across her face. A body crashed into Jaynes from behind. It propelled him forward. Beyond his own doing, his sword drove into the young woman's chest. Surprise stunned them both. Her more than him.

Jaynes tracked her eyes. She looked down at his half-buried blade.... down at her own death. He withdrew his weapon dripping in blood. The girl crumbled to the ground. Out of the corner of his eye, he saw a killing strike headed for his neck.

This is where I die!

From out of nowhere, Timlin's sword swung upward. It threw back the death-blow aimed at Jaynes. Jaynes turned. Intent on a quick thank you. Only to witness steel poke through Timlin's chest. Timlin's eyes went wide. He died before Jaynes could thank him.

Jaynes screamed.

He wanted to mourn.

He wanted to flee the battle.

He wanted to thank Lady Luck.

He wanted to live.

Loseff's troops were being corralled. Tane's advancing forces left little room to maneuver. Jaynes was being pushed, shoved, compelled away from his friend's lifeless body. Loseff's forces were being pressed in tight yet again.

Jaynes struggled to bring his weapon to bear. Telling himself it was the man who killed Timlin, he pushed the point of his sword into an enemy's side.

Loseff's calvary broke through Tane's line and swept along the left flank. Jaynes could only guess they intended to come around the enemy from behind. Archers Tane held out of the melee seconds later released a barrage of projectiles in the calvary's direction. Every one of Loseff's calvary, riddled with arrows, fell from their mounts.

The smell of piss, shit, and blood threatened to overwhelm Jaynes's senses.

Blood from the dead and dying.

Piss and shit from the living and the dead.

Jaynes gagged at the stench.

The cacophony of battle went on relentlessly. At what point fear faded and survival instincts took control, Jaynes did not know. He killed anyone in Tane's colors—mostly from behind. He killed women in blue. He killed men in blue. He killed anything before it killed him. Each engagement with an enemy combatant lasted mere seconds. Thrust... parry... jab... Next... thrust... parry... stab. Next... dodge... swing... slice.

Clang. Clang. Slash.

No time to think.

Clang. Clang. Stab.

Jaynes was never great with a sword. His opponents proved worse.

Clang. Clang. Thrust.

It went on and on. His luck couldn't hold out. His arms were spent. His lungs screamed for relief. Jaynes struggled against fatigue. So many others weren't so lucky to be only dog-tired. Exhaustion threatened to take him. He fought it. *You're still alive, suck it up.*

Soldiers dressed like him were dead and dying all around him. Even more of Tane's troops lay motionless. Most were once simple farmers, enjoined to the defense of Adelle. Adelleian fought against Adelleian.

Space started to open as more and more joined the afterlife in the Community of Souls.

Someone slammed into Jaynes, knocking him to the ground. Looking up, it was one of his own fleeing the battlefield. Jaynes wanted to join her.

Everything inside him told him to run. He resisted the call, if only for his unyielding commitment to Loseff.

An arrow flew into the space where he'd just been standing. It struck the fleeing woman in the back. She tumbled forward and didn't move. Without concern for his dead compatriot, Jaynes offered the Signum Circulus. *Thank you, Teth.*

A hand shot down. It was General Loseff's. He was without his mount. "Get up, soldier," he ordered. "Now!"

After pulling Jaynes to his feet, General Loseff spun away, yelling as he ran, "Glad you're still alive, Jaynes."

Loseff didn't get far. Two of Tane's troops attacked the general. Relentless in their attack, they swung blow after blow at the young leader. Loseff held his own.

Jaynes charged into the fight. He plunged his sword into the back of one man. General Loseff gave him a knowing wink, and together they attacked the other.

A man charged at General Loseff. Jaynes raced to cut him off. Just as he approached, the man swept his weapon just inches from Loseff's neck. Jaynes dropped, skimming his knees along the ground, avoiding the sword whipping through the air. Momentum carried him forward along the blood-soaked ground. With his pommel in both hands, his sword sliced into the man's leg just below the knee. The enemy sank to the ground, screaming in pain. Flesh hung from his exposed bone. Blood gushed from the cut. Jaynes sprang up. He stood over the man. A heartbeat later, he ran his sword through the man's heart.

General Loseff charged into the ongoing battle, leaving Jaynes on his own. Jaynes put it out of his mind. Staying alive took all his attention.

Dead bodies lay in every direction.

His arms screamed for relief.

His lungs begged for respite. But he was still better off than Timlin.

The injured, maimed, and those who had not yet given way to death continued to cry out. They littered the arena. None of the living gave them any mind.

Blood oozed from somewhere on his face. He tasted its coppery offense.

Huurrong. Huurrong. The sound of bugle calls cut through the din of battle.

The order to regroup was music to Jaynes's ears. Faintly he could hear Loseff shouting, "TO ME! TO ME!"

Jaynes immediately raced towards the safety of Loseff's regrouping troops. As he bolted from the skirmish, several running alongside him didn't make it. Tane's archers released a barrage upon those in retreat.

Lady Luck allowed Jaynes his escape. He figured he should've been dead, at least four times over.

The few archers under Loseff's command that were still alive kept Tane's foot soldiers from pursuit.

Jaynes sprinted faster than he had ever done in his life.

He pulled up, dropping his sword at his feet. Doubled over to catch his breath, he gave no mind to anything around him.

While sucking wind from out of the corner of his eye, Jaynes glimpsed General Loseff mounting a riderless steed.

Loseff quickly signaled. In response, three blasts rang out.

Burump...

Burump...

Burump.

Loseff yelled out, "Form up!"

"Fuck me!" Jaynes shouted, but he did as ordered.

Loseff rode up and down the troops. "I know you're tired. So am I. But we have them. We've whittled them down. We've got them now. Their flanks are gone. Ram straight into the center mass. Nothing fancy. We can finish this today!"

Jaynes didn't believe a word of it. Loseff's forces were less than half of what they were. Tane's archers would cut them down before they ever reached the center mass. Loseff was more than his friend and his commander. Jaynes loved Loseff with all his heart.

Loseff never knew. Could never know.

It was his secret. The source of Derr's blackmail.

Loseff shouted, "CHARGE!"

Jaynes didn't have a choice. He couldn't let Loseff down; not now, not ever.

He readied to charge.

... and prepared himself to die for the love of a man who never knew.

General Loseff grabbed hold of the reins with one hand. Thrust his sword high in the air and drove his spurs into the flanks of his horse... just as an arrow pierced Loseff's chest.

THE DOOR

THE VOID

Reyne

Reyne wasn't sure what Quith expected in declaring, "I'm outta here".

Not a thing changed for Quith, or anyone else, in the place I Am Who Is asserted existed beyond space and time. Reyne wondered if Tartica continued to roll forward in time while he remained within the sanctum of I Am Who Is, or if time had come to a standstill outside its boundaries. And if time did continue moving in the world of Tartica without him, at what rate? Was it progressing slowly, or was Mithany's life speeding through the years without him?

Quith looked around and demanded, "Where's the fuckin' door?"

I Am Who Is was slow to reply. "Know this, Selundra Quith, the exit you seek requires your access to what you call a Probability Wave: the representation of the infinite possible futures the course of your life flows from moment to moment. In this sanctum sanctorum, you will not find one. All the possible futures of everything across the universe exist in what you call the Void. You are not in the Void. You are at Reality's Event Horizon. Not before it, where the future lies. Not behind it, where the past exists. You are at the very instant the future becomes the past. Your departure will come when I deposit you to one side of it, or the other."

Beth asked, "Mister Quith, maybe you want to rethink the whole 'this is a con' angle?"

"Fuck off," Quith shot back.

With a voice that continued modulating between old, young, male, female, kindly, and firm, I Am Who Is stated, "The door you seek, Selundra Quith, requires a key. That key is the return of the Soul Stone. Release it and you are free to go. Choose not to, and know this, eternity along the very edge of Reality's Event Horizon awaits you."

"That don't seem so bad. Live forever in here. Yeah, sure, why not?"

"To what end, Selundra Quith? While I have freed Beth Green from her stasis, absent all awareness, you will receive no such benefit. You will experience no interactions. You will be unable to move. You will remain here, without a future and without access to the past, waiting for the moment to slip across the Event Horizon of Reality."

"I don't see the problem. You do it. And Beth over there has been here while the world crept along for fifteen hundred years. She did just fine."

"Know this, Selundra Quith, you have been granted cognitive thought as my guests. That gift will not be afforded you beyond this discussion." I Am Who Is turned his focus to Beth. "For Selundra Quith's benefit, Beth Green, please share your experience within Reality's Event Horizon as the world outside consumed fifteen hundred years."

Beth didn't hesitate. "I don't have any experience with any of it. As far as I am aware, I just departed one world, hoping to return to another for Janek. That happened only moments ago in my mind and now you tell me it's been over fifteen centuries since I departed that world."

"Quith, don't be an idiot," Reyne demanded. "That Beth chick existed for all that time, sure, except she didn't experience any of it. What good is living forever if you aren't aware of a single second of it?"

"Mister Quith," Beth added, "aside from Janek, everyone I ever knew, ever loved, is gone. I enjoyed nothing, experienced nothing in all the time I've been here. My life... what life, I didn't have one. I would trade it all back to live out my days with Janek, without the Soul Stone, for whatever time nature afforded us. I gained nothing being here. It was as though I didn't exist."

Pushing back, Quith queried, "Why now? Why didn't you just take back the Soul Stone from Beth Green from the start? Before it got broken up."

"Know this, all of you. What you name as the Soul Stone fragmented before Beth Green ever entered the Void with it in her possession. When she did enter with the Soul Stone intact, it had already been riven. Before that, there existed not a single timeline that enabled an expedited return of the damaged part of Reality's Event Horizon. This gathering here, now, is the first and only timeline wherein the entirety of the Soul Stone pieces have—or ever would—come together inside the Void."

Beth added her recollections. "I remember the first time I tried to hold on to the Soul Stone in my hand during a transfiguration between realms. Like everything external to my body, like clothes, it didn't make it through. I wasn't ever able to take the Soul Stone with me except on my last trip. That's when I realized I needed to embed it under my skin if I was ever going to get it through the Void."

Janek added, "And before that, Beth broke a piece off as a gift to me. Then Mera and I fought over the piece of Soul Stone Beth gave me. It fragmented again during that struggle. I had never been able to enter the Void, even with Beth's help, up to that point. On the day Mera stole the smaller fragment just before he escaped to Tartica, it was the last time I ever saw him."

The voice emanating from the white cloud of energy calling itself I Am Who Is continued transforming personas from word to word. "Fragmentation continued when Albert Meratoruc entered the Void with it under his skin. On that day his reality was split in two. He exists in two worlds. One version of Albert Meratoruc was driven back; the other pushed through, neither to ever enter the Void again."

"It seems like it happened only yesterday," Beth lamented.

"Beth Green's life would have ended within mere seconds upon her ill-fated effort to rejoin Janek Meratoruc," I Am Who Is continued. "Her fragment of the Reality's Event Horizon would never enter the Void again. All access to her piece of the Soul Stone would have vanished. Before Beth Green could forever be lost to me, I held her here, awaiting the arrival of all the fragments."

Caught up in the experience of the Void, losing Gina, and coming face-to-face with a being that just might be God, recognition of Quith eluded Reyne. A jolt of awareness struck at Reyne's heart. "YOU!" Reyne screamed at Quith. "You were there! You and the woman with the red eyes killed my brother."

In that instant, Reyne let the monster lurking in his soul, feeding off his anger—out. It yearned for vengeance. It howled in his thoughts. But the beast unleashed couldn't move. The monster inside him screamed in pain, unable to satiate its hunger for death—Quith's death.

At that instant, I Am Who Is reached into his soul and quelled the beast. Reyne didn't want his fury caged. He was powerless to stop I Am Who Is. An inner peace spread through Reyne. The entity spoke into his thoughts. In Daedyn's voice, I Am Who Is said, "I know your torment, your hatred for Selundra Quith. And I know the love you carry for Daedyn. Only you can change the momentum of your life's path. Along every possible future in which you pursue the vengeance you crave through this other persona you have created to seek it out, will lead to your undoing."

With Reyne's inner beast settled at the doing of I Am Who Is, he asked aloud, "So, what's good for me ain't good for you? When I was in the Void, Gina and I experienced a malevolent entity attack our consciousnesses and struck at us both with a burning sensation of unbelievable intensity. If I am to release what's inside me, what gives you the right to hold on to yours?"

"Know this, Reyne Brenton, what you encountered was not of my doing," I Am Who Is replied. "There are other forces within the Void that seek their own purpose. The one you speak of does not desire to see Reality's Event Horizon restored. It sought to turn you away. To prevent you from returning the Soul Stone to its proper place. As it did to Albert Meratoruc. Keeping the Soul Stone from me, separated by multiple dimensions of Earth. Its purpose was to diverge too many timelines, making recovering the fragments improbable. The other Soul Stone holders did not experience similar pain in the Void as you and the one you name Mera. Their separate paths drove convergence into exceedingly more permutations. Yet, timelines and life-paths weaved together; some ended before their time, others extended beyond their natural limits, all influenced by my followers existing in the Void, in order to gather you, the holders of these precious fragments, together at this convergence."

"What, there's more like you?" Quith interrupted.

"No, Selundra Quith. Not like me. Yet the Void is a place wherein lesser entities exist. Some attempt to influence the momentum of lives such as yours to their own end. Other forces in the Void strive to keep those like you from straying. Know this: I accept only the deserving into my sanctum to experience eternity in peace and grace. All must earn it by means of free will. The forces nudging those like you only open your thoughts to possibilities. The choices you make are your own as you cross over Reality's Event Horizon from moment to moment."

Reyne's thoughts drifted to his family. "What of my brother, Daedyn? My parents? What of my baby sister, Bade? Are they here with you?"

"Reyne Brenton, that is not for you to know until your physical existence comes to an end."

Janek interrupted Reyne's query, apparently uninterested and wanting to return to the topic of the Void. "To what other purpose do these entities exert influence?"

"Know this, Janek Meraturoc, the nature of Reality is beyond your comprehension. The entity Reyne Brenton encountered is a powerful force working towards a universe unlike any you would recognize or desire. It is through this entity's efforts a piece of Reality's Event Horizon you call the Soul Stone was torn from its moorings. In so doing, it created havoc on the worlds all you come from and many others. It must be restored."

"Why do you allow entities like that to exist?" Beth asked.

"Know this, Beth Green. It is a consequence of free will. To receive others into my sanctum, they must meet my terms for acceptance. If I programmed all to act only in ways that earned them a place, it would be hollow. There can be no differentiation between the deserving and all others without the freedom to choose for oneself."

"Alright," Janek began, "I'll give you my Soul Stone because it will save my world from the darkness imposed upon it."

"Know this, Janek Meratoruc. The worlds you name Evidar, Tartica, and Black Haven are of one Earth. All will be returned to one Earth, as it should have always been before the breaking."

Reyne asked, "What does that mean, 'returned to one Earth'? I'm not doing this without seeing Mithany again."

"And you shall," I Am Who Is stated in a comforting tone. "Return your Soul Stone, and with my gratitude, you will both be together as you desire."

Reyne didn't fully understand everything or what had been promised, yet he believed in his heart he'd be reunited with Mithany; nothing else mattered. With a hand over his breast, Reyne slowly pulled it away. What had been a solid red crystalline rock transformed into a cohesive vapor holding its shape as it rose out of his chest. As he tried to clasp his fingers around it, the vapor filtered through them and flittered away.

Janek and Beth did the same as Quith stood silent, looking on.

Quith looked down, shaking his head. "I don't have much of a choice, do I?"

I Am Who Is replied, "Know this, Selundra Quith. The reality you create is forged by the choices you make. You have knowledge of the consequences of the decision you now face. Your own free will dictates your future. I will not compel you."

With both hands steepled over his mouth, Quith pulled them apart and said, "Just one thing. When you return us, I need assurance Janek over there won't try to kill me."

I Am Who Is did not answer. Janek did. "If you release your Soul Stone to help save our planet, you will have my gratitude, not my vengeance."

"Ah, fuck it," Quith lamented as he placed his hand over his chest. As the Soul Stone rose out of his flesh, transforming into a plasma-like energy mass, Quith said, "Who wants to live forever, anyway? Here, take it. It's yours."

The solidity of Quith's physical body started to dissipate as soon as his piece of Soul Stone—a fragment of Reality's Event Horizon—had been delivered to I Am Who Is.

And just as quickly, Quith was gone.

Before Reyne's eyes, Janek, the man he knew as the Devil's Blacksmith, along with the woman named Beth Green, also disappeared. Lifting his hand to his face with increasingly translucent fingers, his time in the sanctum of I Am Who Is, a being who just might be God, was coming to an end. The only thoughts rolling around in his mind were of reuniting with the woman he loved. With his body almost completely dematerialized, he called out, "Wherever Mithany is, send me there."

"Know this, Reyne Brenton. I do not change what is. Your future is what you have made of it. Yet, there is one Probability Wave to take you where this is possible."

"If you sent me down that Probability Wave, you'd have my gratitude."

"As you have mine, Reyne Brenton. This moment, the return of Reality to what should have been, to set all things right, turned on you. In all the infinite permutations of countless lives, the choices you made as your life flowed across the Event Horizon of Reality from moment to moment, and the other lives your decisions have impacted; yours was the singular path to retrieve the Soul Stone from the man you name Mera on the world you name Black Haven. And the man you name Mera from the world you name Tartica would never again enter the Void. Nor would he have delivered Selundra Quith his Soul Stone but for the promise you demanded of him: to preserve the life of the woman you so love. Because of you, he relinquished it to Selundra Quith, who carried it into the Void.

"You were the key to restoring Reality along its intended path. You have my gratitude. When all is set right, I will do for you what I have done for no other, and grant you what you have earned, and what your heart so desires: a new life with Mithany."

"New? Wait, what does that..."

Convergence Wakes

Teth: 21st Day of the Harvest Moon

Neladith | Derr | Quith | Mera | | Janek | Reyne

Neladith snatched Mithany's hand and dragged her from the chaos erupting in front of the Communal Temple. As they sped away, Neladith complained, "Stop fighting me. You won't be safe around here. Someone's gonna stick a weapon in your hand and tell you, you gotta fight."

Neladith felt Mithany let up on the resistance and figured while she had Mithany's partial acceptance, there was no better time to get the conversation started. As they ran, Neladith said, "What did you want to ask me?"

In between breaths, Mithany got right to it. "Tell me everything."

"I was sent here to do a job. Never thought I'd connect with someone like you. I told you once that there was another just like you where I come from. I loved her. She's dead. You look just like her. You reopened my black heart from the moment I saw you. I could've loved you. It wasn't meant to be. That's on me. I could've found peace on Tartica. I'll never be free of the Devil's Blacksmith. Even though I have to do what he asks of me, because of what I did do to Arek, I suppose I owe you that much."

By the time the pair reached the burned-out Temple Palace in the center of Teth, Neladith had explained everything: two Earths; transfiguration; Quith's order that killed Daedyn; all she knew about Mera; her fondness for Arek; Evidar's version of Mithany; the Devil's Blacksmith. Nothing was left out, including the secret Arek shared of forbidden sibling lovers.

Both women pulled up to a stop. They bent over with hands on knees to rest.

"Two versions of Earth. I find that hard to believe," Mithany said, huffing.

"All true. Your boy, Reyne, was the last one from Tartica who could do it. My boss wanted him eliminated."

Both rose at the same time. Mithany stared into Neladith's eyes as though searching for something.

"Look, Mithany, I'm not gonna lie and say I'm sorry. I did what was asked of me for the good of my people."

"Wait, you already told me you were sorry back at the Communal Temple."

"I'm sorry I hurt you. That's all I meant. Not for what I had to do. Like I said, I thought there could've been something between us."

Mithany snipped, "That's never gonna happen. My life will never be the same because of you. You took so much from me. You caused it all. Daedyn's death. That sweet old man, Doc Hollid, died trying to save Arek's life from what you did to him. And then me and Arek were sent to that concentration camp because you seduced me." She was shouting now. "I came damn close to being raped in there!" Mithany hung her head and continued in a soft voice, as though she'd given up, "You forced Reyne from my life. You crippled my brother, and now Arek's dead. All of it because of you. No one else... just you."

Neladith didn't know anything about concentration camps or of the trauma Mithany endured while there. Now wasn't the time to dig deeper. Neladith simply accepted responsibility for fucking up Mithany's life and said, "I know..."

"My faith tells me to forgive you... I can't."

Neladith froze. Off in the distance, a small pocket of air, no more than ten feet around, began to shimmer and vibrate. It stole her attention from Mithany. Light all around it appeared to flow around the anomaly, being denied access. Translucent colors shifted and rumbled as though bubbles of reality rose from the ground beneath the strange irregularity. The world around the abnormality stood still: all the while, the sight of the event flowed into Neladith's brain in real time. Like sand poured into a clear glass, a foot, then a leg followed by a torso took shape inside the coalescing bubble of reality. When the head inside the air-pocket-oddity took form, Neladith gasped. Naked, Reyne appeared out of thin air. Neladith knew in an instant he must have transfigured from somewhere. It didn't make sense how he'd transfigured into the middle of a crowded city, awake. But there he stood.

Before Neladith could react, Reyne instantly grasped awareness of her presence. Pointing, he screamed, "YOU! I'LL KILL YOU!"

With Mithany's back to Reyne, her head whipped around.

"Reyne! Reyne! It's really you." She took off after him.

Neladith saw the anger in his eyes and the hatred written across his face. Snorting and grunting, he charged at her like a wild beast.

Mithany must have seen it too; she screamed at the top of her lungs, "REYNE! STOP!"

To Neladith's surprise, the voice wasn't that of the diminutive woman she'd known. It had power. Resonance. And it halted Reyne in his tracks fifteen yards away from Mithany, who herself had stopped midway between them.

He looked confused. His face contorted and shifted back and forth several times, as though battling some unimaginable internal struggle. It seemed obvious to Neladith Reyne was trying to break free of Mithany's hold over him, to squeeze the life out of Neladith herself.

Mithany turned to Neladith. "Go. Get out of here. I didn't tell you that I saw Quith. He told me he was heading north. If you're really not here to kill Reyne, go... or I'll release him."

The Devil's Blacksmith had tasked her to hunt down Quith. And, if she came across Reyne, she had orders to kill him too. For Mithany's sake, she'd pretend she never saw Reyne.

A pang of sadness washed over Neladith. She wanted more time with Mithany. She nodded and waved to Mithany, did an about face—and headed for the north gate out of Teth.

Neladith turned back only once, just as Mithany jumped into Reyne's arms.

She longed to put herself in Reyne's place, watching the two lovers share a passionate embrace. The life she wanted, with the woman she so desired—that could never be—tugged at her heart.

Neladith looked away, unable to bear it. She fucked it all up herself because of the choices she made. She knew there was no one else to blame.

She started running. She ran from a life on Tartica she could never have. Or maybe she was running towrds her destiny: to kill a man because she'd been told to by the Devil's Blacksmith. Either way, she fled, leaving Mithany behind. The faster and faster she raced from the woman she could have loved, an overwhelming sense of loss had a hold on her... and she lamented at what might have been.

Derr moved through the chaos of Shantytown's Communal Temple. Although the nave was spacious, there were a lot of people crowded inside. There weren't enough people in all of Teth to stop Derr from taking down the man who set off the series of event that culminated in Tomelai's death.

Derr studied Jerithan's eyes as they tracked his every movement. Derr was always watching.

Drawing closer to his target, he could hear Jerithan plead for Timble's help.

Timble moved quickly to put himself between Jerithan and Derr, now only a few feet apart.

With a blade in his hand, Derr pointed it at Jerithan. "You're a coward, Cree. Face me like a man."

Jerithan confessed, "You may be right about that, Captain Derr."

"If not for you, Chancellor Tomelai would still be alive."

Shaking his head, Jerithan objected, "You are mistaken. I didn't even know the man is dead."

"But you did try to kill him. And everything that followed flowed from the dominos you set in motion. For that, you will die."

Anger spewed out of Jerithan. "I am not the cause of all this chaos. I didn't destroy the Covenant. You did that. Tomelai did that. You brought all this on yourselves."

"Maybe," Derr confided, "but none of it would have happened if you hadn't sent Nails into The Stand to assassinate Tomelai. Every action Tomelai took in the aftermath was in response to your failed attempt to kill him. The breaking from the Covenant. Teth, Kantos, Greenlin, all declared war against Tomelai because of what you started. And all the chaos that followed... it led to his murder. No, Cree, you are the spark that set fire to this conflagration. I should have killed you when I had you in custody. That was my mistake. I won't make another."

"Timble, this man speaks the truth. I did try to have Tomelai killed. All the rest after that was this man's own doing. I failed, and Tomelai lived through it. I wash my hands of Tomelai's death."

Derr demanded, "Step aside, Timble."

"Can't letcha do that, Cap."

"You're a good man, Timble. A good man who's done a lot of bad things to survive. I don't want to hurt you. So, step out of my way."

Timble shrugged. "Can't."

Derr offered, "Last chance."

Timble shook his head. "Big mistake, Cap. I will kill ya if I got to."

Derr snickered. "I doubt that very much."

Timble crossed his arms. "Ball's in your court. I ain't movin'."

"So be it."

Derr sprung forward like a jack-in-the-box had popped.

Timble coiled his fists, ready to strike.

At the very last instant, before reaching Timble, Derr dropped to his knees.

He slid past Timble. As he passed, he sliced a blade across the back of Timble's ankle, severing his Achilles tendon.

Blood gushed from the wound.

Derr's momentum carried him beyond the big man's reach.

Timble grunted in pain. He turned, stepped to grab Derr, but crumbled to the ground.

Derr spang up. He raced to Jerithan.

Jerithan screamed and brought both arms up to cover his face.

Derr thrust his knife downward.

The blade never made it.

Derr's essence, Jerithan's essence, and everything in Derr's line of sight began to transform. What was once solid flittered away like dust particles being sucked into a vacuum from above. Derr's blade dissipated into thin air as what remained of his arm passed through Jerithan's translucent form. Seconds later, the entire communal temple, including Derr and everyone in it, dematerialized.

Quith woke and eased his eyes open. He looked around.

Back where I started, inside the Gift of Flesh Celebratorium. Hum... Tartica... I guess that's where I Am Who Is sent me. Hum... wonder if the Devil's Blacksmith is as good as his word.

He also wondered how long the Void and I Am Who Is kept him: seconds, minutes, hours, days? He ran his hands down the sides of his exposed flesh, lying atop the clothing he left behind when his body entered I Am Who Is's inner sanctum.

Giving up the Soul Stone to I Am Who Is was a bitter pill to swallow. However, he was alive, and that was better than the alternatives he'd been offered. And the Devil's Blacksmith gave his word he no longer wanted Quith dead after Quith gave up his piece of Soul Stone.

He stared at the erotic fresco lining the walls of the room.

I'm here now. Might as well make the best of it.

The expertly detailed mural sparked his desire to connect with the woman he first met standing behind the Celebratorium of Flesh's counter. He wondered if the young woman with the voluptuous breasts had already come and gone, or if she would be joining him soon. He considered slipping back into his clothes, but decided against it, hoping the young woman would be joining soon enough. If she didn't show up shortly, he'd go and get her. Sans clothing, he was ready for her either way.

Crash.

Quith's head snapped to the sound.

The door flung open.

A giant of a man stood in the doorway.

Quith's worst fear grinned at him. Harvin.

Behind Harvin he saw the diminutive and deadly Kebra.

In a deep, testosterone-infused voice Harvin said, "Time to die, Quith."

Quith's arm lunged for his knife on the nightstand.

Harvin moved fast. He brought his fist crashing down on Quith's outstretched arm. Quith heard it snap. It hurt like a motherfucker. The blade dropped from his hand.

Quith drove the pain from his mind. He swung his leg upward. His heel slammed into Harvin.

Harvin laughed, then clamped one enormous hand on Quith's ankle. He yanked Quith off the bed.

Quith hit the ground hard. He sprung up at Harvin like a coiled snake. He drove his shoulder into Harvin's gut.

Harvin didn't move. Quith looked up. Harvin grinned, as though amused at Quith's feeble efforts. Before Quith could back away, Harvin wrapped his humongous arms around him. With his back pressed against Harvin and his arms pinned, Quith squirmed violently.

He threw his head back. It smashed into Harvin's face.

Quith sneered at Kebra looking on.

Harvin whispered into Quith's ear, "Is that all you got?"

Kebra stepped forward. With one hand, she cupped his exposed manhood and gave it a gentle squeeze. "I'm going to miss these. We were always so good together in bed." With a scowl, her other hand drove a knife deep into Quith's chest. "Sorry, lover. Orders are orders. You fucked up. Reyne's supposed to be dead. Your mistake let him live. All this never should've happened."

Quith grimaced, then went limp.

As she pulled her blade out, blood flowed from the wound.

A labored heartbeat later, everything in the room started to fade.

Harvin tossed Quith's body to the floor like it was nothing more than a rag doll. Standing there, looking confused, Harvin grew more transparent by the second. The big man turned to Kebra as though she might know the answer to what was happening. She gasped, looking down at her own fading limbs. She looked like a ghost dissipating before Quith's dying eyes.

Quith blinked, only to see Harvin's entire body as nothing more than a vapor of smoke drifting away. Quith didn't know what was happening, but it didn't matter. He knew he wouldn't live through whatever it was. Kebra had made sure of that.

Quith looked down at the blood leaking from his own evaporating flesh... and died.

Mera raced up the stone stairway of The Wall, frantic to witness the attack in progress. Atop the parapet, he looked down at the sixty feet separating The Wall from The Stand. Dead and dying soldiers littered the expanse.

He was alone. A hundred or more men, women, and teenagers, all with bows in their hand, were celebrating. A raggedy-dressed woman thrust her bow high and proudly proclaimed to Mera, "For simple folks, we showed 'em who's boss."

The other *Defenders of Teth*, Jerithan supporters, all shouted in unison, "Hoorah! Hoorah!"

In a hurried voice, Mera demanded, "Where's the rest of the invaders?"

She beamed in a toothless grin. "Turned tail and ran. We was too much for 'em."

Mera asked, "Where's the drop-release?"

She pointed with the tip of her bow.

A heartbeat later, Mera grabbed hold of a thick cable that was part of the blockade release mechanism used to drop several tons of a single giant sequoia tree trunk across the administrative portal of The Wall. The invading force had been cut off from a way into Teth and entered a kill box framed by Shantytown archers on The Wall and Anatase bowmen in the trees.

He cut a length of cord from the spent apparatus and wrapped it around a crenelation. He threw the rest to dangle over the side and shimmied down.

Speeding through the dark passage, Mera tripped over dead bodies several times. All the flames of the sconces lining the tunnel-like enclosure had been doused by the Anatase. Mera imagined the panic and chaos Adelle's military must have experienced with the Anatase firing arrows from above as thousands of tightly packed Adelleian warriors fumbled in the dark to escape death.

How many times he fell, Mera lost count, before finding a discarded piece of the light-giving lume crystal. As he neared the end, light filtered in through the opening, as did the sounds of metal on metal and the din of battle.

Confusion raced through his mind. *Who could they be fighting? Fuck! Fuck! Fuck! I'm too late.*

As he emerged, it hit him. Off in the distance, Mera spotted Tane Tomelai commanding an army. He frantically scanned the battle in progress. To his horror, he witnessed Loseff fall from his saddle with an arrow piercing through his back. *It's a civil war!*

A heartbeat later, the entire combat zone and countryside surrounding it broke apart into tiny little pieces, like someone had torn a painting of a battle scene into a million fragments. Swords, pikes, and all weaponry either scattered into fine particles or sliced into ghostly, fading bodies where solid men and women once stood. Slowly at first, piece by piece, shreds of reality were carried off on a gentle breeze. Mera turned around, terrified at the sight of The Stand breaking apart into minute wooden shards floating upward into an undulating blue sky.

Ripples rolled through the clouds and the heavens overhead like a stone dropped into a pool of water.

Mera tore his eyes away from the heavens only to watch helplessly as Tane's army and Loseff's forces were all blown away like sand flowing off the top of a dune.

Anger exploded inside Mera. *Convergence... It has to be Janek. He's succeeded. FUCK!... I failed! We're all doomed!*

Panicked that Janek, his brother the Devil's Blacksmith, had won, Mera looked down at his open palms only to see his hands become dust... and inch by inch, pieces of himself drifted away on the wind. There was no pain, only confusion. His arms and the rest of his body followed, his hands flittering away into nothing. Before his brain ever realized it, Mera and everything was gone.

From deep in his underground compound, in a room where he'd been sequestered for his every venture into the Void, Janek, a man known to others as the Devil's Blacksmith, opened his eyes. Each time he entered the Void, Janek was never able to complete the transfiguration process into Tartica. He settled for a connection to Jerithan Cree's thoughts, as he did over the lifetimes of so many others during the long years since the Great Destruction condemned him to Evidar. So, when he woke, absent clothing, he immediately understood his time inside the sanctum of I Am Who Is was real. It gave him hope for Evidar's future.

Yet, even more importantly, he realized he wasn't alone. Lying next to him, Beth stirred. She looked back at him with loving eyes. An emotion he hadn't experienced in a millennium filled his heart with joy.

"Janek, where are we?" Beth asked as she curled up next to him. She nestled her head on his chest, and he felt her flesh press against his. He ran his fingers through her hair.

The hands that were responsible for the death of thousands over a period of fifteen hundred years gently and lovingly stroked her arm. "A lot has changed since you have been gone, my dear." With Beth in his arms, his world had been transformed. "I profoundly missed you, my love." He confessed. "Everything I did was for this moment. To have you back."

"Well," she giggled, "in the two days I've been gone, I missed you too."

He gazed into her eyes and wanted to lose himself in them for all eternity. "In all this time, I only ever wanted you."

Beth rolled on top, sat up, straddled her knees on either side of his waist, leaned forward, and gently pressed her lips to his.

Passion for the woman he'd lost to the Void so long ago unlocked his otherwise stone-cold heart. A desire he hadn't experienced in what seemed like forever coursed through him. The man he became to deliver Evidar's salvation from its imposed desolation was still in there. Yet, being reunited with Beth, he wanted to be the man she remembered.

He flipped her over on her back, and it wasn't long before they were making love. He almost exploded the instant he entered her. Yet, her gentle moans soothed him in ways he hadn't felt since she'd been gone. She always made him a better man.

As he thrust in slow, gentle, rhythmic movements, he never wanted it to end. When he looked up from the intense gaze both were locked into, he realized the room was filling with light. Light Evidar hadn't seen since the Great Destruction. The ceiling overhead, and all the ground above it, was drifting upward in tiny fragments. The ever-present ashen-gray atmosphere was both peeling away and undulating in waves rippling across the sky.

He gently eased himself into Beth ever deeper. Holding her face in his hands, and with all the stored-up passion he'd buried away over the centuries, he kissed her one last time just as he released his seed. He understood the meaning of the light.

He leaned in, nibbling at her ear, and whispered, "The vow of I Am Who Is begins."

While still inside her, united as one, Janek's and Beth's bodies, entangled in each other's arms, were whisked away like hundreds of delicate flower petals released from their stems by a summer breeze.

The beast lurking inside Reyne howled in anger at the sight of Neladith. The words of I Am Who Is warning Reyne of it being his undoing failed to deny the beast its escape. It stole all control from Reyne and raced towards the woman who'd killed his brother. Like a raging bull, he stormed through the open street, unaware of anything, or anyone, except for Neladith.

Faintly, Mithany's voice broke through the monster-within's defenses. Her voice—"REYNE! STOP!"—hit him like a hammer crashed against his skull.

He froze.

The beast shrieked at the intrusion. It would not be denied vengeance. Peering out from eyes Reyne did not control, Reyne spied Mithany standing between the beast consuming his soul and Neladith.

Reyne struggled to regain control over his own malevolence. Nothing mattered more than his return to Mithany. The forces of hatred feeding off his craving for revenge would have none of it.

He hungered for Mithany.

He lusted for revenge.

Back and forth, the internal conflict raged. It was tearing him apart. His face contorted from moment to moment between venomous contempt and pure joy. His eyes shifted wildly between Neladith and Mithany.

As Neladith turned and fled, the beast roared, demanding Reyne release it to give chase. It took every ounce of willpower for Reyne to hold it back. But neither would the monster-within capitulate to Reyne's burning desire to hold Mithany in his arms.

Mithany's body slammed into his. She jumped onto him. She wrapped her arms around him. The monster-within shrieked as though it had been attacked. Mithany grabbed hold of his cheeks, driving her lips hard into his.

Her touch, the love she poured into her kiss, delivered victory to Reyne over the malignancy consuming him. The spell of the monster lurking in his soul was broken by love infused into his heart through that one kiss. Mithany's love spread into his soul like an army conquering land it had previously lost a hostile invader.

Mithany's love defeated what he could not.

The beast was gone.

Through eyes he now controlled, he gazed lovingly into hers. He threw his arms around her and returned every bit of love she gave to him. He smiled, thinking of something she tried to teach him: *It's in the eyes. It's always in the eyes.* He finally understood.

Tears of joy dripped down his cheeks as they did hers. Words proved inadequate to express the depth of emotions overwhelming him. Their embrace spoke to Reyne's soul in ways words never could... and it seemed to go on, endless in time.

With Mithany's legs wrapped around his waist, Reyne held her off the ground as she planted her lips, peck by peck, over every inch of his face. The last, a fiery kiss that burned deep into his core, stirred the passion in Reyne's loins. She gently pulled her lips from his, looked down, and stared into his eyes. "I'm so happy. You've come back to me."

With a grin that stretched from ear to ear, Reyne studied her face like he never wanted to forget it. "I missed you so much."

She lovingly tapped his chest. "I was so worried. You could have told me what you were up to. And why are you naked?"

Reyne looked up. Terror clutched his chest: he couldn't lose her again.

The scene behind Mithany was coming apart. The sky above was swelling, rolling in wave after wave. The burned-out buildings were drifting upward in fragmented pieces before turning transparent and evaporating into nothing as they rose.

Mithany shrieked, "Reyne! What's happening?"

Reyne squeezed Mithany even tighter. Her hair began to rise like static electricity had taken hold. Her body started fading. She screamed, "Reyne, your... your... I can see through you."

His heart thundered, fearful of losing her. Then he remembered, "I think I met God. He?—She?—promised me that you and I will be..."

Before he could finish, Mithany... Tartica... and everything else in the world... was gone.

Déjà Vu

Antarctica: April 2, 2089

Beth

Beth Green and seven hundred ninety-three researchers, scientists, and military personnel from McMurdo Station squeezed into every available snow-worthy transport vehicle. The cross-continent trek to Concordia Station high on the southeastern Antarctic Plateau was their best bet to survive Asteroid TQ-680's promised planet-wide annihilation.

Most considered the likelihood of escaping TQ-680's wrath folly. Humanity was doomed, and there would be no reprieve. Beth didn't agree. She believed in hope. Sitting and waiting for death seemed even less rational. With the odds stacked against her, it was still better than doing nothing.

Snow-Cats, Sherps, Hägglunds and every available snow-terrain-worthy vehicle had been commandeered for the high-risk journey. Rolling across the Antarctic plateau for four days in tight quarters and no showers, the insides of Unit 37 smelled a bit ripe. Tempers were short, and the trip was long. Beth considered it a small sacrifice to endure should the convoy make it to Concordia Station.

It was warm inside the three-year-old Snow-Cat Trooper designated as Unit 37—the last in the caravan. The Trooper model was built to accommodate sixteen passengers. Beth, along with twenty-eight others, crammed into the vehicle. Beth sat back and listened to the weather report squealing through the shortwave radio. Colonel Jase Breslin from Unit 1 reported that high winds and lower temperatures would be upon them soon. He commanded the thirty-seven-vehicle-long convoy to a halt. Everyone was ordered outside to stretch their legs. The coming weather was expected to confine them inside the tightly packed snow crawlers for the next twenty-four hours.

At 2:36 PM local time, they still had three hours and sixteen minutes of daylight based on Colonel Breslin's best calculation of their location. Outside, the temperature of minus six degrees Fahrenheit was expected to drop quickly as soon as night fell over the barren landscape.

Beth stepped out of the Snow-Cat. She looked up at the larger numerals on the side. *Wait, 37, that's not right. I could've sworn I was in Unit 36. My mind's playing tricks on me again.* Beth noticed several other instances where things seemed different than she remembered. Even a few of the folks from McMurdo Station, now part of the caravan, she'd never seen before today, but somehow she knew them. She shook it off, figuring the thin air atop Antarctica's Eastern Plateau had given her a touch of hypoxia.

She looked down at her boots and wondered if anything alive had ever stepped foot on that very spot. It seemed an odd thought to have, inasmuch as she sensed she'd been there before. She laughed to herself, thinking just about every scene atop the plateau looked just like any other. *It's got to be the thin air*, she told herself. *I'll grab some oxygen once we get rolling again.*

The sunlight reflecting off the open endless expanse of white was blinding, even with the polarized mountain glasses she sported. Like her fellow travelers who'd been ordered out of their snow crawlers, she shook out her legs, stretched her arms wide, twisted her back at the waist, and even jogged in place. The prospect of being confined inside a cramped space with smelly, irritable people for a whole day didn't play well. The respite, even at six degrees below zero, proved a welcome diversion.

As Beth stared out at the unbroken veil of whiteness, a sense of déjà vu wouldn't release its hold on her.

Impossible, I've never been here before... Nobody's ever been here.

Yet a faint memory told her she had. She distinctly remembered the same series of events unfolding in vivid detail: *The Colonel called the convoy to a stop; I stepped out; I stretched, but something's missing. Yes, the rock. I found a little red meteorite. I was here before.* She scanned the horizon for the meteorite but came away empty. *Hmmm, nothing. Strange. I could have sworn...*

Before Beth could sort it out, she heard the crackle of the shortwave radio emanating from inside Unit 37. Turning her head to listen, her heart soared when the caller's familiar voice announced, "Snow Queen. Come in, Snow Queen."

She knew his cadence, his tone, his pitch, even through the electronic hum. She hadn't heard from Janek in days. Excited, she pushed aside two people unintentionally blocking the Snow-Cat's door.

"Snow Queen, this is Iceberg. Come in, Snow Queen."

Beth stumbled on the steps. She got up quickly. She yanked off her glove. Her hand was shaking as she pressed the mic call-button to speak. "Janek! Oh, thank God. Where are you?"

"Never mind that, Beth," Janek began, but immediately switched to shouting. Beth swore she heard, "IT'S GOING TO MISS US!" Janek's shouting stretched the limits of the radio's ability to reproduce his words. Stunned, Beth demanded, "Say again. Repeat, Iceberg. You're breaking up."

In a soft voice he repeated, "TQ-680 is going to miss Earth."

"Oh my god! Oh my god!" Beth screamed. Then she turned from the radio and yelled out the door of the snow crawler for anyone to hear. "IT'S OVER. EARTH IS SAFE! Spread the news."

Others just outside Unit 37 waved frantically as they jumped up and down, drawing attention for everyone to join them.

Janek explained, "Beth, I just got off the shortwave with a buddy of mine. They're going to announce it at any moment. They plan to spread it to all the ham radio operators across the globe. The best hope is that there are enough good people out there to quickly put governments back together. Asteroid TQ-680 is slowing down. It's going to miss Earth. IT'S GOING TO MISS US!"

From Beth's perspective, the open door of Unit 37 looked like a Picasso. The mixture of heads, hair, and ears intermingled and pressed together filled the open space like some surreal painting. A few seconds passed. The ears and heads pulled back. They collectively looked at each other, wondering if they'd heard Iceberg correctly. Then, suddenly, everyone erupted in a loud cheer.

People raced wildly about, sharing the joyous news. Beth briefly watched in amusement before huddling over the shortwave with her back to the door, trying to steal a moment of intimacy with Janek. "Honey, what happened? How is this possible?"

"All my contact told me was that the asteroid is now clocking in at 49,500 miles per hour. It's a one percent drop in speed. They don't know how it's possible. TQ-680 is currently twenty million miles from us. Earth will pass through its orbit where NASA originally thought TQ-680 would hit. Now, they figure TQ-680 will arrive at that same spot some hours after Earth has already come and gone. It's going to be close, less than 270,000 miles."

Another voice broke into the call, "Hey, Snow Queen, remember me? Thor's Hammer here. That's great news. I'll get it out ASAP to my contacts. Thanks, Iceberg. I just hope there's enough of civilization left to be saved."

With tears in her eyes, Beth whispered into the mic, "I love you, Janek. When will I see you again?"

"Soon. There's a lot to do. The second I heard the news, I wanted to share it with you… I love you so much and can't wait to see you… Beth, as much as I want to keep talking, I've got to go. I'll touch base with you later today. Is that okay?"

"Yes, it is, my love."

"Until then. Iceberg out."

Earth had been saved.

The laws of physics couldn't explain it.

Beth didn't care; she believed science and God were not mutually exclusive. She had her faith, and that combined with the compelling sense of déjà vu gnawing at her. In her heart of hearts, Beth knew the hand of God accounted for TQ-680's sudden change in speed.

Epilogue

Antarctica, April 2, 2089

Reyne

A young researcher—a twenty-two-year-old agricultural specialist—grabbed hold of the doorframe and popped his head into Unit 37. "Beth, you sure this isn't all just bullshit?"

The joy of Janek's voice and the news TQ-680 would miss Earth had Beth in a great mood. "Listen, Ryan, I know it sounds crazy, the asteroid just slowing down and all that. Janek would never lie to me. I trust him. Earth is saved."

Ryan spread his arm open as though to give praise. "Then it's a miracle."

"Science can't explain it, Ryan. It *is* a miracle."

"I guess all us non-believing scientists have God to thank." Ryan turned his head around to his fiancée and continued, "Isn't that right, Mithany?"

The youthful, petite, chestnut-brown-haired woman punched Ryan in the arm. "Who's Mithany?"

"I'm sorry, did I say Mithany?"

"Yeah, you did."

Beth laughed at the young couple. "I remember when I was your age."

"I'm sorry, Melanie." Ryan began his apology. "It's the weirdest thing. When I looked at you, the name Mithany just popped into my head. You were her. You know there's no one else."

"If we hadn't been stuck together at McMurdo this past year, you'd be in trouble, mister."

Beth interrupted the young lovers, "Ryan, Melanie, can you two do me a favor?"

Melanie answered for them both. "Sure, what do you need?"

"Can you find Father Jerry? I think we owe our thanks to God. There's no other way to explain it. TQ-680 was dead set in Earth's path. Now it's not. Ask Father Jerry to offer a benediction, or at the very least a prayer expressing our thanks. Who knows, maybe he'll gain a few converts." Beth wondered, *Father Jerry, that's a new name... but I know him. I've got to hit the oxygen... hypoxia, it's got to be.*

Ryan grabbed hold of Melanie's hand. They walked off to find the middle-aged, overweight, balding, gray-haired McMurdo Station chaplin. "Converts from this crowd. Not gonna happen."

The word spread fast, as though quantum entanglement shared the news with every brain cell of those in the caravan the instant Janek spoke the words, "It's going to miss us."

People were scattered over the length of the convoy celebrating. Yet, Ryan didn't see Father Jerry anywhere.

Ryan pulled up next to one of the Colonel's men. "Excuse me, Captain Derrmont. Have you seen Father Jerry?" The steel-blue-eyed man with sandy-colored hair and the reputation for being direct just shook his head as he continued stoically watching others celebrate. Ryan thought Derrmont a strange man, always watching what others were doing. It gave him the creeps.

Lieutenant McFurpet slapped Captain Derrmont across the back. "Lighten up, Derr. The world ain't gonna end. We've been saved. You can remove that stick from your ass, if only for one day."

The captain, unaffected by the slight, replied, "It's Captain Derrmont to you. We're still in uniform. And yes, Lieutenant, it looks like Earth will survive. All's the more reason to maintain military decorum. Now, fuck off."

Melanie pulled Ryan away. "Let those two deal with their issues. Come on, there's Unit 32. Maybe Father Jerry's in there."

As they made their way to Unit 32, Melanie asked Ryan, "Have you seen your brother Jayden? We should be celebrating with him."

"Haven't seen him since we got out to stretch. Besides, he'll use this news to weasel his way into some woman's pants. I love my brother, but some things never change."

Melanie pointed, "There's 32. Father Jerry is assigned to 32... I think."

The door to the cab was closed. Ryan put his face to the glass. Steamed over, Ryan was unable to peer through the gray sheen.

"There's people inside, I can hear them."

Melanie suggested, "Pound on the door."

Ryan rapped the side of his hand on the door several times. "Open up." Getting no response, he kept pounding.

A minute later the door flung open. A young, wiry, buxom redhead sat in the driver's seat with her legs crossed and her boots resting on the steering column. She was securing the last few buttons of her shirt. "Ah, it's you, Melanie. Come on in."

Ryan complained, "What? Am I chopped liver? And what took you so long?"

With a huge, guilty smirk written across her face, Nelly shrugged and buttoned her pants.

Ryan took a shot at Nelly for making him wait. "Don't know why you're still here, anyway. All the other interns got shipped out before winter set in."

Nelly smiled at Melanie, ignoring Ryan's presence. And without looking at him, she replied, "Janek hired me to stay on just before he left Antarctica. I work for him now, and I get college credit too." She turned and grinned at Ryan. "It gives me more time to steal Melanie from you."

Ryan rolled his eyes. "Like Melanie would ever be with a woman, let alone you."

"Enough, you two," Melanie interrupted. "Nelly, have you seen Father Jerry?"

Winking at Melanie, Nelly replied, "Nope." And then called out, "Erik, say hello to your sister."

An arm rose over the top of a seat three rows back. Without getting up, Erik waved and muttered, "Hi, Sis."

Nelly snickered. "I must've worn him out. You know, Melanie, your brother can charm the pants off of anybody."

Laughing, Melanie turned to Ryan and joked, "...and he often does. That's my brother."

Ryan started to say, "When...how did...never mind. Come on, Melanie, let's leave these two alone."

Once back outside the cab, it was one giant party. No one seemed affected by the sub-zero temperatures. Earth had escaped a great destructive event that threatened all of humanity. A little cold wasn't going to put a damper on the party.

Melanie positioned her hand over her brow and squinted. "Ryan, you see that?" She grabbed Ryan's arm and pointed. "Can you see it? Over there, sitting on top of the snow. The way the light catches it just right. It's red. It's little... but something's out there."

APPENDIX 1: THE COVENANT OF ABSOLUTE UNIVERSAL OBLIGATIONS

In the course of history, when profound circumstances threaten the very existence of every man, woman, and child, we, the one thousand seven hundred forty-two souls that remain of Humanity must rise up and endeavor to take extraordinary and necessary actions to secure the survival of humankind. Foremost amongst these actions is to unequivocally set forth this Declaration of a Covenant, establishing the Absolute Universal nature of certain Obligations that each person owes to all others, without exception and in perpetuity, until such time the long-term survival of humankind is, without question, able to secure itself a future without concern for extinction as a species. We, therefore, set forth this Declaration, a Covenant of Absolute Universal Obligations, to be unencumbered by any law; be it Man's or God's in any form, by any government or by any religious authority, made by any man or any woman or on behalf of any community, until such time as a prognosis of the unconditional survival of our kind is secured.

First and principally among these is the Universal Obligation to Procreation; to spread the seed and nurture in the womb the future generations of humankind. It shall be the Absolute Universal Obligation, above all other laws, for all men and women between the ages of sixteen years and forty-five years to bring forward into this world at least three children attaining the age of fifteen years. Without exception, we recognize this Absolute Universal Obligation upon all but for those medically determined infertile by way of natural cause; for those that surpass the age of forty-five; and without regard for any individual's carnal desire to know another of one's own gender, each must endeavor to Procreate for the General Welfare inherent in the perforce propagation of our species. Recognizing the sacrifices that may be visited upon loving and caring souls, a general waiver may be granted to allow for the individual pursuit of same gender couplings, upon recognition in law of one's fulfillment of the Absolute Universal Obligation to Procreations having been attained. This waiver cannot be denied for any reason to any individual having fulfilled their Obligation of Procreation.

Second and as well Absolute, we recognize the Universal Obligation to Preserve Human Life; to do no harm nor to place any human life at risk; to take no human life either by direct action or indirect action or by inaction, by any man, by any woman, by any child or by any community or governing body at any level; to require intervention on behalf of any person having knowledge of another being at risk of imminent death, and to do so without regard for one's own safety, save death itself.

Third and as well Absolute, we recognize the Universal Obligation to Promote the General Welfare. Incumbent upon all to effort a positive contribution to the wellbeing of the community of humanity through actions that may be recognized in a myriad of diverse services, products, or other unconventional efforts that Promote the General Welfare. Promotion of the General Welfare being Universal upon all humankind may take sway in and be all-consuming at all times in some, while limited in others but rare moments in life yet Absolute and Universal, nonetheless is the Obligation to Promote the General Welfare. Reward nor recognition is the desired payment for the fulfillment of the Universal Obligation to Promotion of the General Welfare yet may be so without encumbrance by the will of man, woman or by the force of community as expressed in laws or religious strictures.

Fourth, and as well Absolute, we recognize the Universal Obligation to the Natural Path. The Obligation to pursue life by way of the natural gifts of Earth's offerings to the exclusion of all else that is not firmly rooted in the natural world. We recognize the purported circumstances contributing to the Great Destruction and seek to begin a new path for humanity that enjoins us all towards a different, more enlightened course rooted in the Gifts of Nature.

These Declared and Absolute Universal Obligations are demanding of action by each and every person for each and every Obligation. We recognize that we cannot leave Humanity's future to the fortuitous whims of events or the inevitable consequences of humankind's collective or individual actions and therefore establish the Council of D'CAUO to speak as one voice for all humankind concerning the interpretation and implementation of this Declaration of the Absolute Covenant of Universal Obligations. In so agreeing, we bind us all; we remaining few souls, now and forever, along with all future progeny, including any and all future governing bodies, persons, leaders, or religions, until such time as the future of the human race is secure and as such is so recognized by the Council or D'CAUO. So say we all declared this first day of the Summer Moon in the year eighty-six of the Third Age.

APPENDIX 2: GLOSSARY

Acolyte: Initiate in the Temple of Life religious order.

Adelle, Kingdom of: (Ah-deel) One of four independent nations on the Tartic continent. Its head of state is Chancellor Madrotti Tomelai. A council representing the citizens of Adelle exists in an advisory capacity absent any real authority. Adelle is an administrative dictatorship with a vast bureaucracy.

Aderlee: (Ah-der-lee) A version of Aderlee exists on both Evidar and Black Haven. On Black Haven he serves the Devil's Hammer.

Alphen: (Owl-fin) A hearty nut growing along a narrow band on the continent of Tartica in the nation of Kantos. It is said one medium size nut provides the same energy to the body as a full meal. Governments prize them as a means to economically feed the poor.

Anatese: (Ann-a-tess-ee) People-like inhabitants of The Stand's canopy. Human-like, deformed and enhanced by natural selection over the unknown length of time their kind have lived atop the giant sequoias of The Stand.

Araukaw, Maverlyn: (Ah-roo-kaw) The commandant of the Samer internment camp, Outpost Apple Orchard.

Arek: (Air-ek) Brother of Mithany. A tall, once-charming co-owner of a leather goods shoppe in Hensdale. After being tortured and nearly killed by Nelaith, he survived a changed man. Twenty-three years of age and dedicated to protecting Mithany throughout his life.

Beth Green: A woman from the Second Age who found the Soul Stone. She is the love interest of Janek, and the one who'd discovered other dimensions of Earth existed following the Great Destruction.

Black Haven: Alternate version of Earth existing in another dimension opposite in many ways from Tartica's version of Earth, yet identical to Evidar.

Brenal, Hollid: (Breen-ul) He was the village doctor serving in Hensdale before giving his life to save Arek.

Breslin, Jase: (Bres-lyn) A man of the Second Age. He is a US Air Force Colonel and commander of McMurdo Air Force Base on Antarctica.

Celebratoria: An elaborate cathedral of worship. Each is dedicated to one of the Six Gifts.

Chamette, Ja'Rou: An elite, wealthy older man living in Tandure. An owner of banks and several legitimate businesses. He is a powerful mover and shaker inside the circles of the Hidden Hand as well as influential in coordinating Thuggery ventures in Adelle for a price.

Communion of the Circle: Also known as **Communal Celebration,** which is guided by a Communal Leader and enjoins the Temple of Life faithful in religious services each week.

Covenant of Absolute Universal Obligations: Agreement amongst the last remaining people of earth. It set forth rules and obligations every person by necessity must adhere to. The purpose was to create the best conditions for humanity to survive. It placed forced obligations on every living person; to procreate, to help others, to harm no one, and to live a lifestyle respectful of Nature's offerings. It bound humanity in perpetuity until such time as the future of humanity was secured.

Cwendly: (sah-wend-lee) Female guard at Outpost Apple Orchard.

Daedyn: (Day-din) Reyne's brother murdered in 1542 of the Third Age by Evidar assassins. Almost twenty-two years old when he died. He lived with his brother Reyne before his death. He and Reyne worked the alphen groves together as partners after their parents died when they were both fourteen years old.

Damus: Title afforded to an individual capable of extremely complicate mathematical calculations interpreting Probability Waves experienced while inside the

Void in order to predict the future of events and of individuals.

Dasch: (Dah-sh) A young man living in the Tartican hamlet of Yurich who is befriended by Neladith.

Devil's Blacksmith: Moniker given to the one man whose singular focus is to reunite Evidar and Tartica's versions of Earth. Others use his name, but never in his presence. The descriptive grew out of his relentless actions to forge a future for his dark world, with nothing but his iron will, under wildly impossible circumstances, and with total disregard for the suffering it would inflict on the entire population of Tartica. See Janek.

Devil's Hammer: Moniker given to Mera of Black Haven by the people Black Haven.

Dimenk: (Dem-ink) President of Greenlin. She is thirty-five years old. An astute politician of considerable respect. No children and was elected by its citizens to a life term as president. She has large appetites for everything. One of the three leaders of the United Front.

Druin Derr: (Drew-in Dur) Leader of the KCG. The second most powerful person in Adelle. Childhood friend and trusted confidant of Chancellor Madrotti Tomelai.

Dylla Weisner: (Die-la Why-s-ner) Black Ops Team Leader from Evidar overseeing all operations to eliminate Tweeners on Tartica before being killed by Gina.

Emosh, Sanja: (Ee-moe-sh, San-jah) A young woman from Evidar currently holding the title as that realm's only Damus.

Evidar: (Ev-eh-dar) Alternate version of Earth existing in another dimension opposite in many ways from Tartica's version of earth.

Ferpratt, Wilem: (Will-um Fur-prat) A top Lieutenant in the KCG. Trusted ally of Druin Derr.

First Lord: Highest-ranking Prudent and leader of the Temple of Life faith.

Gifts, The Six: Gifted by the Goddess Teth to humanity: the Gift of Love, the Gift of Knowledge, the Gift of Life, the Gift of Renewal, the Gift of Flesh, and the Gift of Nature.

Gina: She is a skilled assassin from Tartica who trained Reyne for his mission to Evidar. During Reyne's transfiguration from Tartica to Evidar, she was swept into the process and unwittingly ended up with Reyne on Black Haven.

Goddess Teth: Patron goddess of the children of Earth, daughter of Sun and Earth born just before the Great Destruction and savior of the world. She gathered up and lead the survivors of the Great Destruction in the Second Age to Tartica, where she enabled humanity to grow and survive. A religion grew up around her legend.

Grafph: (Graff) Evidar agent capable of moving between both earth realities, Evidar and Tartica. A security specialist and an assassin. Murdered by Quith.

Great Yetgnal: (Yet-nul) A monstrous creature standing over nine feet tall. Hair covers their entire humanoid shape. They roam the continent in Tartica's forests and have no known predators. The race is at the top of the food chain. Rarely seen by people as its kind chooses to stay clear of man but holds no fear of humans or any other living lifeform.

Greenlin: One of four independent nations on the Tartican continent lead by President Dimenk.

Guildin: (Gild-en) One monetary unit of currency used throughout Tartica and minted in silver or gold. The amount of metal in each coin determined it monetary value as stamped on its face. The back side of each coin varies to reflect the national treasury from which it was minted. The guildin coin denominations in circulation are 1, 5, 10, 20, 50 and 100. Guilin paper notes are also in circulation in denominations from 100 up to 10,000; however Guilin Notes are used mostly between governments, businesses, and amongst financial institutions.

Harvin: (Har-vin) Male agent of Evidar, sent to Tartica to hunt down Reyne after Quith's team failed to kill him. Also assigned to terminate the traitor Quith.

Hensdale: Home of Reyne. A small village in the nation of Kantos. A farming community with sundry merchants and services supporting an agriculturally based lifestyle.

Hermens, Minkin; (Her-mens) Prime Minister of Kantos. She is one of the three leaders of the United Front.

Hidden Hand: Loose association of wealthy elites in Tandure who operate in the shadows to manipulate the governmental bureaucracies, press, and businesses—legitimate and otherwise—to both influence the implementation of government policies to suit their needs and to ensure they amass as much money as possible for themselves.

Janek: Leader of the Evidarian effort to merge the multiple dimensions of Earth into one. He prefers the title of Architect but is dis-affectionately and fearfully referred to as the Devil's Blacksmith.

Jaynes, Verek: (Janes) Close friend and ally of Loseff Tomelai and appointed as General Loseff Tomelai's adjutant.

Jerithan Cree: (Jer-eh-than) Prudent of the Temple of Life. He listens to the Voice in his thoughts, who also provides insights to help Jerithan. Once dreamed of consolidating all secular and religious power under his rule. He recently served as its First Lord before being stripped of that position in a vote of revocation orchestrated by Prudent Serco.

Judjurex: (Jud-jir-ex) A position of authority in many smaller villages in the nation of Kanton. Charge with enforcing local laws and customs with the authority to investigate, determine innocence or guilt, and the sole authority to carry out whatever punishment he or she deems appropriate.

Kaythlin Tomelai: (Kay-th-lin) First Lady of Tandure and wife of Madrotti Tomelai. She is loved by the citizens of Adelle and is very smart, charming, attractive, and deadly.

Kebra: (Keh-bra) Female agent of Evidar sent to Tartica to hunt down Reyne after Quith's team failed. Also assigned to terminate the traitor Quith. She partners up with Harvin to fulfill their assignement.

Kevine: (Kah-veen) The thirty-five-year-old manager of one of Adelle busiest ports, pulled from civilian life to be its chief supply officer as General of Logistics.

Kingdom's Chancellor's Guard, KCG: Adelle's security apparatchik comprising loyal men and women tasked with maintaining Madrotti Tomelai in power. An arm of Adelle's government with license to do whatever, to whomever, in the name of the good of the country inside the Kingdom of Adelle and, surreptitiously, outside its borders.

Kiple: General of the Kingdom of Adelle's national civil police promoted to the rank of Adelle military as its chief of staff, Commander General.

Loseff Tomelai: (Low-sef) Son of Tomelai and Kaythlin, age nineteen. Given the rank of general by his father, the Chancellor of Adelle.

Madrotti Tomelai: (Ma-drot-tee Tom-eh-lay) Chancellor for life of the Kingdom of Adelle. Middle aged, dark hair with graying temples. Physically fit and dedicated to power. Married to Kaythlin and together they have two adult children, Tane, a daughter, and Loseff, a son.

Mahtoney: (Ma-toe-knee) A young man from Black Haven who serves Black Haven's version of Mera.

"Mera" Meratoruc: (Meh-ra) He is Reyne's mysterious protector from Tartica. Little is known of his background.

Mera of Black Haven: (Meh-ra) He is an alternate version of Mera from Tarica existing in the dimension of Earth known as Black Haven. He is called Fake Mera by both Gina and Reyne.

Mithany: (Myth-ah-nee) She is Reyne's fiancée. She grew up in Hensdale. She is petite, has brown hair, feminine, and competitive. She has developed the ability to read people's facial expressions, a skill forced upon her in childhood as she sought to protect herself from her mother's anger. She is everything to Reyne. Twenty-one years old and sister to an older brother, Arek.

Nails: The head of the loose-knit organization called the Thuggery, whose purpose is to control the crime in Teth. Taken prisoner by Derr and put to death by Kaythlin Tomelai.

Neladith: (Nel-eh-deth) Young female assassin from Evidar, initially tasked by the Devil's Blacksmith of Evidar to kill Reyne. Assigned the code name Agent Arrow. An identical version of Neladith exists in the alternate dimension of Earth known as Black Haven. Neladith of Black Haven is given the nickname of Red by Gina.

Outpost Apple Orchard: An internment camp for Samers.

Prudent: Highest rank in the Temple of Life's religious hierarchy. Thirty-two sit on the Council of Prudents. The Council elects its First Lord, who is answerable to them.

Quith, Selundra: (Sa-lun-dra Kw-ith) Reported to Dylla before her death and was the on-site field leader of the Evidar ops team tasked with eliminating Reyne. He is middle-aged, well-built, and has a full head of white hair. After he botched Reyne's assassination, with all Evidar agents turning on him, Quith became a traitor to Evidar.

Razors, The: A mountain range that cuts the continent of Tartica almost in half. High peaks cut across Tartica. The northwestern part of the range is virtually impassable.

Red: The nickname given to Neladith of Black Haven by Gina to differentiate Red from the version of Neladith from Evidar.

Revocation: The official process whereby the Council of Prudents can vote to remove a sitting First Lord.

Reyne Brenton: (Rain) A young man, almost twenty-two years old, and the owner, along with his brother, of an alphen nut orchard on the outskirts of Hensdale. Inherited after the death of their parents. He is above average height, with green eyes and black hair. He is polite and well like by his community. He is engaged to be married to his childhood sweetheart, Mithany. He is one of only a handful of Tweeners when his adventure begins.

Samer: A person who prefers sexual relations with another of the same gender. Licensed Samers are given a registration tattoo, called The Mark, permitting them to legally engage with another of the same sex after meeting the Covenant's child-bearing requirements. Unlicensed Samers also exist in large numbers in violation of Covenant strictures because they do not meet licensing requirements or refuse to take The Mark.

Santander: (San-tan-dur) General Manger of the Brenton Family Orchard and friend to Mithany and Arek.

S'Leen: (Sah-leen) A Prudent serving on the Council of Prudents and long-time ally of Jerithan. She is elevated to the rank of Second Lord under First Lord Serco.

Second Lord: Second highest-ranking Prudent. Much of the apparatus of the Temple of Life reports to the Second Lord.

Serco, Garragent: (Sir-coe, Gar-a-jent) Prudent initially assigned to the Kingdom of Adelle. On the Council of Prudents and leader of the opposition to Prudent Jerithan Cree. He rises to the rank of First Lord. One of the three leaders of the United Front.

Signum Circulus: Religious sign. Starting at the breastplate, the thumb circles the heart, and with an open palm, concludes with a hand coming to rest over the heart.

Spetzer Bilseck: (Spit-z-her) A young man who lives in Hensdale and is about the same age as Reyne. He drinks a lot and has pursued Mithany as his would-be-girlfriend since early in his teenage years, to no avail. Also called Spetz.

Stand, The: A natural structure of giant sequoia trees that form a barrier along the southern border of Teth.

Tandure: (Tan-d-your) Capital of the Kingdom of Adelle. The epicenter of wealthy elites in Adelle.

Tane Tomelai: Daughter of Tomelai and Kaythlin. As the oldest child, age twenty-three, she is the heir apparent chancellor to the Kingdom of Adelle.

Tartica: (Tar-teh-ka) The last remaining place on Earth where human life is known to exist in the year 1543 of the Third Age. A civilization dedicated to "natural living" and intent on avoiding their Second Age ancestors' mistakes. Although what is truly known of the Great Destruction can only be loosely claimed by what little remained of historical records, or as to the causes of the Second Age of Man's downfall. When exactly the Second Age ended, and how long after that the Third Age of Man began, has been lost to time. Yet, with the establishment of The Covenant of Absolute Universal Obligations, came the de facto demarcation of human history as the beginning of the Third Age.

Temple of Life: Religion built on a reverence for Nature, and on the life of Teth. Dominant religion almost to the exclusion of all others. It preaches a way of life devoted to the Obligations of the Covenant and to the Six Gifts.

Teth: City and nation-state. Seat of Temple of Life religion, and the cultural and economic center of Tartica. Teth is also the name of the goddess on which the Temple of Life faith is founded.

Tetrip: (Tet-trip) Judjurex of Hensdale. He is older and well respected in his role.

The Mark: A registration tattoo permitting an individual to legally engage in same-sex couplings.

Thuggery: Loose association of criminals in Teth. Organized to maintain peace amongst criminal gangs and competing interests.

Timble: A citizen of Teth, living in amongst its poorest inhabitants in Shantytown, and an associate of the Thuggery. He briefly served as bodyguard to Jerithan.

Timlin: Private in the Adelle army and close friend of Jaynes.

Transfiguration: The process of moving between dimensions. Very few exist in any of the known dimensions of Earth (Tartica, Black Haven, or Evidar) who are capable of entering the Void to complete the transfiguration process.

Tweener: A person with the ability to transfigure between the worlds of Evidar, Black Haven, and Earth.

United Front: A treaty signed by the nations of Kantos, Greenlin, and Teth, with the stated purpose of mutual defense against the Kingdom of Adelle and with the stated goal of militarily forcing Adelle back into the Covenant.

Voice, The: The progenitor of thoughts reaching into Jerithan Cree's mind. Unknown to Jerithan, it is the voice of Janek, the Devil's Blacksmith.

Void, The: A place that exists beyond space and time through which all possible futures flow. Anyone capable of transfiguration must access The Void to navigate to their intended destination in an alternate dimension.

BOOKS BY R.C. VIELEE

The Utopia Falling Saga:

Utopia Falling: A Darkness Rises
Chaos Ascending: A Feast of Betrayal
Salvation Bleeding: Forge of the Soul Stone

To explore more, visit https://www.RCVielee.com

About the Author

Robert Vielee

Robert grew up in a small town in northern New Jersey.
He is married with four children and now lives
with his family in Pennsylvania. Before turning his
attention to writing, Robert's creative drive took him across
North America as a freelance nature photographer—while
holding down a day job. He loves nature, reading epic
fantasy, and most of all, his family.
Connect online with Robert on his author website
RCVielee.com

Acknowledgments

I would like to thank the many people I've encountered on this adventure who have been mentors, educators, and supporters. To the readers of the early draft, whose input helped improve the story, including Roger, Mark, and The Gathering Place Writers Group, thank you. To the editors Ciara, Lucija, and Kim whose expertise contributed immensely—I could not have gotten this far without you. My heartfelt thanks to all.

To my loving wife Louise, thank you for your understanding and patience. To my wonderful children, whose creativity knowingly and unknowingly contributed here and there.

Connect With The Author

Thank you for reading *Salvation Bleeding: Forge of the Soul Stone*. Building a relationship with readers is very important to me. Please let me know what you think of the book by leaving a review on the retailer's website where you purchased your copy or another you prefer. It would mean a lot to me and is easy to do.

Join my newsletter to receive advance notices on upcoming books, as well as progress reports, blog posts, and the occasional "extra" for those in my reader's group.

https://www.rcvielee.com/newsletter

You can also follow me on social media.

https://www.instagram.com/rcvielee
https://www.facebook.com/bob.vielee
https://www.twitter.com/rcvielee
https://www.goodreads.com